CASSIE EDWARDS

THE SAVAGE SERIES

**Winner of the *Romantic Times*
Lifetime Achievement Award
for Best Indian Series!**

LOVE SLAVE

"You know of this chief's innocence, do you not?" Cloud Eagle asked.

Alicia closed her eyes, held her head back so that her red hair streamed down her perfect back, and trembled with ecstasy. "Yes, I am sure you are innocent of *one* crime," she said in a husky whisper. "But not of another."

"There was more than one crime that you accused me of?" he said, yanking her close so that their bodies molded together.

"My heart," she said, giggling. "You are guilty of having stolen my heart."

SAVAGE
SPIRIT

CASSIE EDWARDS

LEISURE BOOKS NEW YORK CITY

Diane DuSchene, this one is for you!
—Cassie

A LEISURE BOOK®

August 1994

Published by

Dorchester Publishing Co., Inc.
276 Fifth Avenue
New York, NY 10001

Cover Art by John Ennis

Printed in the United States of America.

Listen to the spirits in the mist,
they call into our Apache hearts.

They give us courage and strength
when we are in doubt.

When our children cry out in hunger,
they call out, *"Nu´uka Biza´a´yo´n´
ouudaah´ndida nzhu´."* Come, little
one, don't say anything. It is good.

When our warriors go into battle,
they give them knowledge of what
is to come.

When our bodies grow weak with age,
they tell us we are young in spirit.

They release our souls to the great
world beyond, when it is time to
go to the great counsel fire in the sky.

Listen to the spirits in the mist,
they call into our Apache hearts.

—Stephanie Jimenez,
Apache

SAVAGE SPIRIT

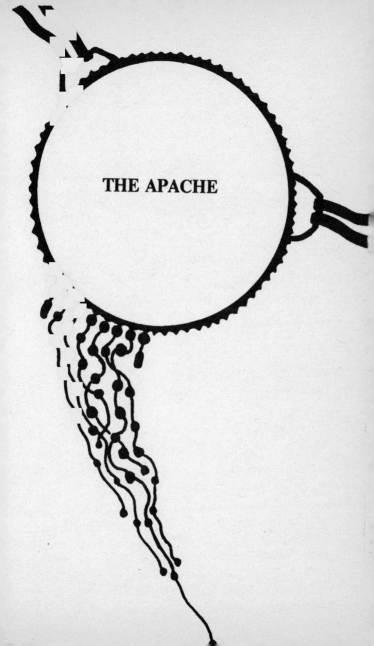

THE APACHE

Chapter One

We met as strangers from two walks of life.
We became friends to learn each other's cultures,
as if born into it.
We endured the challenges of life that drew us
together to become lovers.
We will never be apart from each other's embrace,
Not even when we are called to walk hand-
in-hand,
In the hereafter land.

—YVONNE G. SANTOMAURO

The Arizona Territory—1859

A cloud of dust surrounded the Apache warriors.
The sun spread a red haze over the riders and
into the canyon in the distance. As the sun gradually lowered in the sky, the redness deepened,
highlighting the cottonwoods a short distance
away, where Chief Cloud Eagle suddenly spied

11

the campsite of a wagon train that had stopped for the night. The camp beside the Gila River was not far downriver from Chief Cloud Eagle's stronghold.

He tightened his reins only slightly to slow the speed of his stocky roan. His gaze locked on the group seated beside the campfire, then shifted and focused on a man who sat somewhat away from the others on a small stool, at an easel. Cloud Eagle surmised that this man was painting the brilliant sunset which he faced. The artist gazed at length at the view before returning his brush to the canvas.

Red Crow, Cloud Eagle's best friend and confidante, sidled his horse up next to his chief's, his breechclout fluttering against his muscled thighs in the evening breeze. "Do we stop or pass them by?" he said in the Apache language to Cloud Eagle. "Will they not want us to share our bounty with them?"

Similarly dressed in a breechclout and moccasins, his long, flowing, coal-black hair held in place with a band of flannel cloth tightly bound about his head, Cloud Eagle glanced over his shoulder at the warriors who rode behind him and Red Crow, and then at the travois fastened to several of the Apache horses. They bore the rewards of their hard labor these past several days. The Great Spirit had blessed their hunt with many bundles of fox and beaver pelts, as well as much fresh meat.

Then Cloud Eagle looked over at Red Crow. "The white man hunts for his own supper," he said. "We hunt for ours. What we have remains ours."

Cloud Eagle's lips lifted into a slow smile.

"Unless they have something of value that they might want to *trade* for what we carry with us today," he said. "Some white travelers have strange but sometimes useful tools never before known to the Apache."

Red Crow smiled and nodded at his friend's suggestion.

"The white travelers are surely aware of our presence by now. Let us go and greet them," Cloud Eagle said, nudging his horse forward with his knees. He yelled over his shoulder for his men to hang back and wait as he and Red Crow went into the white man's camp.

His warriors gave dutiful nods of acquiescence.

Looking to see that his two pet coyotes were keeping up with him, Cloud Eagle slapped his thigh to call them nearer. He laughed when Gray and Snow came bounding up beside his horse. Their fur was thick. Their eyes were bright and alert, their legs long and lean.

"Now if the Apache do not put fear into the heart of those white men," Cloud Eagle said to his coyotes, "the sight of you two might. My pets, behave yourselves."

They responded with sharp, confident barks. Their bushy tails wagged as they leapt and bounced beside Cloud Eagle's stocky roan.

Cloud Eagle focused his attention on the wagon train again. There were only three wagons and very few travelers. But even though the number was small, he was always curious when white-skinned Americans came near his stronghold. Miners were flooding into the hills and canyons, taking metal from the ground. Many settlers were raising homes in every direction.

13

The Apache were at peace with the United States Army. The California Road had been opened and wagon trains and troops were seen daily on it. They had not been molested by Cloud Eagle's Coyotero band of Apache. He and his people had given their word of peace. It had been kept.

Cloud Eagle had resented the intrusion upon his land in the beginning. In time, knowing that war gained his people nothing, he had signed a peace pact with the United States Government.

But there were others who put fear and dread into the hearts of all travelers—Indian renegades and white outlaws.

Cloud Eagle had stood back and watched the huge wagons which came to supply the growing mining industry of the Arizona Territory.

He had also made an agreement with the United States Government permitting the mail stagecoaches to operate through his territory. He had seen no threat in allowing the mail route across his land.

But he always worried about those who came in the covered wagons. How could he trust them?

Cloud Eagle and Red Crow approached the wagons in a peaceful manner. Cloud Eagle returned the white men's stares, then held his palm in the air. "Peace," he said, looking slowly from man to man. He slipped from his saddle to the ground.

Red Crow stayed on his horse a moment longer. His eyes alert, his hand resting on the butt of his rifle where it was slung in its gunboot at the side of his horse, he watched the white men. When he saw that the men posed no threat to his chief, he dismounted and walked stealthily behind Cloud Eagle, his hand resting on his sheathed knife at his right hip.

The coyotes followed proudly and confidently on either side of Cloud Eagle. He walked square-shouldered and tall toward the white men who stood stiffly around the fire, watching him, with the exception of the man who still sat at his easel.

Cloud Eagle's eyes searched the faces of the men and looked deeply into their eyes. In them he saw a guarded fear, and he understood why. There were only about twelve of them compared to his band of thirty-five Apache warriors. If there was even a hint that their chief was stepping into a trap, his warriors would not hesitate to turn their weapons against the travelers.

Cloud Eagle stepped up to the circle of men. Red Crow sidled up beside him, while the coyotes sniffed and explored the camp.

"I am Chief Cloud Eagle of the El Pinal Coyotero Apache," Cloud Eagle said. "The peace word has been given by this Apache chief. We do not attack blue coat soldiers or settlers. And you? Why do you come to my country?"

Cloud Eagle quickly noticed how the men's eyes shifted to the man who was now standing at his easel.

This indicated to Cloud Eagle that this man was their leader. He sauntered over to him and extended a hand of friendship toward him. He gazed in fascination at the lanky man's bright red hair and full beard. Then he studied his dark eyes. They spoke of a man of gentle ways, one who might be kind and warm of heart.

"You are the leader?" Cloud Eagle said, glad

15

when the man did not hesitate to accept his gesture of friendship.

Charlie Cline, who dreaded all Apache, forced a smile at the tall Indian. He was relieved to find that the Indian was cordial and friendly and spoke English well enough to be understood.

This made Charlie more hopeful that he would find his sister safe and unharmed. He had worried about her ever since he had learned that she was all alone in the Arizona Territory.

From his studies before he started this journey, Charlie had discovered that in all of the Coyotero Apaches' dealings with travelers and traders, they were the most reliable and friendly of the Apache bands. There had been no documented robberies or slaughters committed by them.

He also knew that the El Pinal Coyotero took their names from Pinal Mountain. They were known to live in and around the base of this mountain. Their country was rich in timber, with many beautiful mountain streams and fertile valleys for cultivating their crops. The Coyotero Apache were known to raise wheat, corn, beans, and pumpkins in abundance.

In this particular, they were far in advance of all of the other Apache. Charlie hoped that meant that they were also far advanced in how to treat white people humanely.

"Am I the leader of this wagon train?" Charlie said, finding the Apache's grip firm and confident. "You might say that. I'm Charlie Cline. These men are accompanying me from Saint Louis."

"And why did you leave the city that I know well?" Cloud Eagle said, dropping his hand to his side.

"You know of Saint Louis?" Charlie said, lifting an eyebrow. He eyed the coyotes uneasily as they sniffed at his feet. Then when they wandered away, he looked squarely into Cloud Eagle's eyes again.

"You have been there?" he said, trying to evade talk of his own reason for being so far from home. He didn't want to speak his sister's name to this Apache, even though this chief seemed trustworthy enough.

He most certainly did not want this Apache's offer to help in the search. Alicia was too beautiful to place before the eyes of any man who might have need of a wife out in this god-forsaken land. Charlie wanted to make sure she returned to Saint Louis where everything was civil and where the right men could come courting her.

"No, Cloud Eagle has not been there. Some winters ago, this Apache had the privilege of knowing a man from Saint Louis," Cloud Eagle said, his eyes filled with a sudden haunting sadness. "Good Heart. A man who came to our people injured. He was made well and treated as a brother among my people. He did not leave for two winters. He became as one with us. He taught my band of Apache the language of his people. We taught him many things of our culture. He was an explorer whose restlessness took him away from us again. We have not seen him since." He looked into the distance. "Perhaps he is in Saint Louis again?"

"I know of no one called Good Heart," Charlie said, absently pulling on his red beard. "But of course, I would not know him by that name. It was one given to him by you, was it not?"

"Yes, that is so," Cloud Eagle said, nodding.

"The name given to him at birth was, I believe, Alex Burton."

"I do not know any Alex Burton," Charlie said, turning slowly when Cloud Eagle's interest was drawn away from him to his paintings. He followed Cloud Eagle to his easel.

Cloud Eagle leaned over and studied the painting of the sunset, appreciating its mystery and beauty. He reached a hand to the painting and touched oils that were not yet dry, then drew his hand back and studied the red tip of his fingers. The smell of the oil in the paints drew his fingers to his nose. He sniffed the scent, then looked quizzically at Charlie.

"Your paints differ from the Apache's," he said, sniffing his fingers again. "You do not make your paints from that which grows from the earth, or the earth itself?"

"No," Charlie said. "They are made from . . ."

Charlie got no further with his explanation. He stiffened when Cloud Eagle ventured over to his wagon and, reaching inside the back flap, brought out several of his framed paintings.

Charlie glanced over at the other men. They were close friends who had been kind enough to accompany him on this journey of the heart. He could tell that they were nervous at the chief's actions.

But they knew, as did Charlie, that with so many Apache warriors near, it was foolish to consider stopping him.

Charlie turned his worried gaze back to Cloud Eagle, watching guardedly as the Apache chief chose one painting, in particular to admire and study. It was a painting of Charlie's sister Alicia just before she had left Saint Louis with her father

18

and mother two years ago, when his father had become involved in the newly established Overland Mail stagecoach line. Charlie had stayed behind. He was the curator of the art museum in Saint Louis and had not wanted to give up his position to go to the wild west.

A wire from his sister stating that their mother and father had been killed in cross fire during a fight between renegade Indians and the United States Army, and that she was going to stay in Arizona to continue working on the stagecoach line, had changed everything for Charlie. He feared that Alicia was daring enough even to be a stagecoach driver, and that thought had struck fear into his heart.

After he had made the necessary arrangements for his departure, he had come for her. He had stopped only long enough each evening to make camp and to paint just before sunset.

He cringed even now when he remembered the many times that he had watched his father teaching his sister daring tricks on horses and the art of firing all sorts of firearms. She had developed into a fiery, adventurous young lady of eighteen, and he feared for her life.

Cloud Eagle placed the painting of Alicia before his eyes. He positioned it so that the remaining light of the evening played on it, enabling him to see it better.

Taken by the loveliness of the woman in the painting, Cloud Eagle sucked in a wild breath. This mystically beautiful woman with the pale skin of snow held the color of the skies in her eyes and the flame of the sun in her hair. Her smile was like a thousand suns!

Never had he seen anything like this painting,

or the woman who was captured on it. Her beauty made his heart clap like thunder inside his chest.

He turned to Charlie. "Chief Cloud Eagle wishes to have this painting," he said abruptly. "You will be paid well for it." He gestured with his free hand toward the fresh kill—the juicy meat on the travois and the many valuable pelts. "You can choose from the meat or the pelts. Whichever you prefer." He paused as he studied the painting even more closely. "This woman. Her name. Tell me her name. Tell me where I can find her."

Charlie's insides grew cold. He saw the danger in telling this Indian that this was his sister. He was definitely not going to tell him that Alicia was in the Arizona Territory!

And he *wouldn't* part with the painting. It might be the only way to find Alicia in this damnable wild country, where faces might be remembered far longer than a name.

Yet Charlie could not help but hungrily eye the meat. Neither he nor his friends were crack shots when it came to hunting for game. They were all hungry.

But his sister's safety came first.

His friends knew this and did not interfere when he spoke aloud his decision to this Apache chief.

"Sorry," Charlie said determinedly, nervously shuffling his feet. "I can't part with the painting."

"Trade," Cloud Eagle said, once again gesturing toward the fresh kill. "A fair trade. Your painting for meat."

"I'm not going to part with the painting," Charlie said, his voice firm. "Its value cannot be matched by meat, or anything else. Please give it to me."

Cloud Eagle hesitated, his jaw tight, his heart thundering within his chest. He wanted this painting. Yet he would not take it by force. He did not want to disturb the peace pact that had been signed with the white leaders and blue-coated soldiers at Fort Thomas.

Charlie saw Cloud Eagle's hesitation. Fearing the Indian's anger, he scarcely breathed. It was evident in the Apache's midnight-dark eyes. Charlie expected him to take the painting anyway, and was surprised when he didn't.

Charlie's hands shook when Cloud Eagle thrust the painting into them.

"Her name?" Cloud Eagle said, his tone cold. "Where can I find her?"

When Charlie did not offer a response, Cloud Eagle glared down at the shorter man, who seemed frozen by fear. It seemed to have stolen his ability to speak.

Cloud Eagle looked slowly at the other men as they came and stood in a cluster around the bearded man who held the precious painting.

Cloud Eagle then slapped his thigh, a command for his coyote pets to follow him. He turned and walked stiffly back to his horse and swung himself into his saddle. Red Crow quickly mounted his own steed.

Holding his hand in the air, Cloud Eagle gave the command to leave. He whirled his horse around and rode away in a canter. But he could not deny that the painting had disturbed him. His thoughts were pinned to the woman in the portrait like a deerskin to a tree.

Suddenly he was not himself.

* * *

Alicia Cline was ready to lock up the stagecoach mail station for the night but stopped when she saw a mail sack in a corner of the room. She placed her hands on her hips and flashed her eyes angrily at Milton Powers. He was slumped in a chair tipping a bottle of whiskey to his lips, his boots propped on her desk.

"Milton, damn it, you forgot to place the second mail sack on the stagecoach," Alicia said, staring at him as he gulped down big swallows of whiskey.

When he didn't respond, she stamped over to him and slapped his feet off her desk. "*And, Milton, how many times have I told you to keep your damn feet off my desk?*" she said, her voice stiff with anger.

Milton looked up at her with bloodshot eyes and laughed sarcastically. "What makes you think I'm gonna take orders from a woman?" he said, pushing himself clumsily up from the chair. He staggered drunkenly over to Alicia and gazed down at her from his lanky, six-foot-four height. "Notice I didn't refer to you as a 'lady.' I ain't never seen you dressed in nothin' but men's clothes." He slapped at the heavy pistol holstered at her waist. "You even wear a gun. I'd say that's anything but ladylike."

His insults made Alicia's eyes waver. She gazed down at her attire. Since she had left Saint Louis, and especially since her parents' deaths, she had almost forgotten what it was like to wear a dress. It was imperative to protect herself from women-hungry men who often had not seen a lady since they left their civilized lives behind. In this land, men outnumbered women almost one hundred to one. The only way to remain safe was to look and behave like a man.

And she could confess to having learned this art of disguise very well since her parents' untimely deaths. She had grown quite accustomed to wearing men's breeches and shirts, although she had chosen to wear soft, fringed buckskins instead of the stiff, dark clothes that most men wore.

She had even gotten used to tucking her brilliant red hair beneath a wide-brimmed sombrero. And she wouldn't part with her pistol. Not even when, after a long, weary day, it sometimes felt as if it weighed as much as she did.

She stared at her leather cowboy boots. When they had been new, she had kept them spanking clean and free of dust. But now that the newness had worn off and she'd learned that they rubbed blisters on her toes more often than not, she scarcely ran a rag over them or gave them a layer of polish to protect the leather.

Shrugging, she looked up at Milton again. "How could you have been so lax in your job that you let the stagecoach get away from here without all of the mail sacks?" she said, again placing her hands on her hips. "You're nothing but a dimwit, Milton. When you're drinking, you scarcely know your head from your toes."

"Aw, quit your jawin'," Milton grumbled. With a callused finger, he lifted her chin and smiled down at her. "You know you love me."

She shuddered and slapped his hand away. "Keep your hands off me. You have to know that I'm going to report you to the superintendent in charge," she spat. "I don't know why anyone hired you in the first place. You are nothing but a lazy, no good, drunken bum. . . ."

Then she paled and placed her hands to her cheeks. "No," she gasped. She looked over at the mail sack. She just realized that it might be the one in which she had placed the letter to her brother Charlie, telling him that she had been relocated to a new stage station. The last station where she'd been assigned had burned to the ground. If Charlie decided to come for her, to encourage her to return to Saint Louis with him, as he had threatened in his last letter to her, he wouldn't know how to find her.

She was also afraid that her brother might get lost in the Arizona Territory while looking for her. She had no intention of going back to Saint Louis with him, but Charlie would take more convincing than mere words. He might even try to drag her back to Saint Louis, to a life *he* wanted for her, no matter what she wanted herself.

She scrambled over to the mail sack, opened it, and dumped its contents on the floor. She sat down on the floor, and as she sorted the mail out, she tossed letters aside. When she didn't find the one she was after, she sighed with relief. The letter was in the other bag. And that was good. This was the last mailing that would go out for weeks.

When she began shoveling the mail back inside the bag, her eyes suddenly narrowed on one that showed her handwriting. Her heart sank. In her hasty search, she had not seen it.

"Damn it," she said, giving Milton a harried, frustrated look. She held the letter up. "Do you see this? It's the letter to my brother Charlie. Because of your negligence, he isn't going to know that I've relocated."

"So what?" Milton said casually. He took another long swallow of whiskey, then glared down at Alicia. "He's probably not comin' anyhow. He's probably feelin' lucky to be rid of you. I know that I'd feel damn lucky if I never saw or heard from you again. You ain't nothin' but trouble. Do you hear? Trouble."

He staggered from the stage station, leaving Alicia with her frustrations. She stared down at the mail. "There's only one thing left to do," she said. "I've got to catch up with the stagecoach. I sure as hell don't want to have to ride clear to Fort Thomas."

Slinging the heavy bag over her left shoulder, she left the stage station in a half run. She cringed at the thought of what her mother would say if she could see her today in the filthy buckskins, or could hear her swearing. She had tried her hardest to raise Alicia as a lady, as sweet and delicate as herself.

But Alicia had followed her father's teachings. Although she sometimes wished that she could dress up in something pretty, the way she had dressed while she was a part of Saint Louis's most affluent circle of society, she could not deny that she was quite content living the free life that she had found in the Arizona Territory.

A man was all that was missing in her life. Recently, she had begun to wonder what it would be like to be kissed and held by a man.

Milton interrupted her train of thought. "Where the hell do you think you're goin'?" he demanded as he walked clumsily toward Alicia as she slung the heavy mail sack onto her horse, behind her saddle.

"I'm taking care of business since you chose not to," Alicia said, giving Milton a stern look.

Now there was a man that she could never have feelings for.

He was worthless. She even suspected that, during one of his drunken sprees, Milton had accidentally started the fire that destroyed the last stage station.

Milton staggered over to her horse and stared drunkenly at the mail sack, then up at Alicia as she swung herself into her saddle. "You ain't goin' anywhere," he said, reaching for the bag.

"Stand away from me and my horse, Milton, or I swear, I'll run right over you," Alicia said, picking up her reins.

"You're takin' off this time of evenin' to catch up with the stagecoach?" he said, his voice rising in pitch.

"I don't see *you* making any effort to correct your mistake," Alicia said, frowning down at him. "So, yes. I'm going to try my damnedest to get the mail where it belongs."

"You're a fool for sure," Milton said, stepping away from her horse.

"I'd rather be accused of being a fool than a drunken bum," Alicia said, snapping her reins. She rode off in a hard gallop, into the sunset.

"Go ahead. Go and get yourself killed," Milton shouted after her. "Who cares anyhow? I know I don't. You don't have the makin's of ever bein' a lady, so what man would care about the likes of you?"

He staggered toward the log cabin, shrugging. "Aw, let her go," he argued with himself when he had one moment of regret, thinking that he ought to go after her. "If the damn Injuns catch up with her, then she won't be around to tattle about my negligence."

He turned and shielded his face from the sunset with one hand. In the distance he could see her riding like a bolt of lightning across the land. "You wench," he said thickly. "You stupid, stubborn, dumb wench."

Chapter Two

Riding along the dusty California Road, Alicia kept glancing toward the sky. Soon it would be dark, and she hadn't seen hide nor hair of the stagecoach. The only alternatives were for her to either turn back or seek shelter for the night. It was obvious that she was not going to catch up with the stagecoach tonight.

She glanced guardedly from side to side. Every time she rode alone at night, she chanced being accosted by renegades or outlaws. Tonight she had to risk it. It was absolutely imperative that Charlie receive her letter.

But what if Charlie had already left Saint Louis for the Arizona Territory? she worried to herself. She realized that he might never find her.

"Big brother, why can't you just leave well enough alone?" she whispered to herself. "You have your life. I have mine."

The road wound into a canyon. She stiffened.

The crooks and crannies of the canyon could conceal thieves.

Alicia sank her heels into the flanks of her horse and rode into the canyon, the horse's hooves echoing back at her like claps of thunder. She frowned up at the small sliver of sky that was revealed overhead. Only a faint trace of daylight remained. She must ride free of the canyon before total blackness flooded the area. She would be in a better position to defend herself against a sudden ambush.

Her heart pounding, she rode onward.

When she finally rode out into open country again, she sighed heavily and lifted her eyes to the sky. "Thank you, Lord," she whispered. "I guess my speaking a few curse words now and then hasn't made you turn your eyes away from me after all."

But she knew that she wasn't safe just yet. She slapped her reins and rode onward.

Night suddenly enfolded her like a dark shroud. Clouds slid over the moon, then sailed away again. Every so often, she heard the haunting sound of a wolf baying at the moon. An owl screeched in the trees at her right side.

Then the thing that Alicia feared most happened. She heard a single *pn-n-ng*, then a crash of rifle fire from behind her, which rocked her in her saddle.

She took a quick glance over her shoulder and drew in a ragged, frightened breath when she discovered horsemen rapidly coming up behind her. Her heart sank when she made out many renegade Indians and white outlaws. She knew that she didn't have a chance in hell of defending herself.

She bent lower over her saddle and sent her horse into a neck-breaking gallop, as though hellfire was raging around her. She rode through a hail of bullets down a steep incline.

Suddenly she felt the sting of a bullet as it entered her left thigh. The pain was intense, as if a burning brand were being pressed into her flesh.

Instinct led her to grab her leg. She cringed when she discovered blood seeping through her buckskin trousers, spreading like ink on a blotter across the soft material.

Then an Indian rode up beside her and with one yank took the mail sack from her horse.

As she grabbed for the sack, cursing the Indian, she lost her balance.

Screaming, she tumbled from her horse. Her head hit the dirt-packed road with a sudden impact. For a moment she was surrounded by a spinning blackness, then she lay quietly unconscious.

A short distance away, Cloud Eagle's ears picked up the sound of gunfire. He wheeled his horse to a quick stop and turned his ear into the wind, listening. When he heard nothing more, he started to ride onward, then stopped again.

Red Crow sidled his horse up beside Cloud Eagle's. "I heard it also," he said, always able to read his friend's thoughts. "Should we go and see the cause of the gunfire?"

Knowing the many innocent people who were being accosted almost nightly along the busy California Road, and knowing that they were white people, intruders on Cloud Eagle's land, he did not respond to Red Crow right away. A part of him wished that no more white people would come to the Arizona Territory. He felt that those who were stopped by renegades or outlaws deserved what they got for interfering in the lives of the Apache.

Yet he had signed a pact of peace with the white people's government. He had even found many white people with whom he had made a close alliance. Those who were fired upon tonight might be the same sort of person as Good Heart, or others whom Cloud Eagle had grown to admire in the white community.

"The firing is over," Cloud Eagle finally said. "But that does not mean that the person or persons fired upon are not still alive, and in mortal danger." He paused. "Yes, we will go and see what we can do."

He turned to his warriors and told them to stay behind, except for Red Crow.

Then he and Red Crow rode hard across the shadowed land, the coyotes bounding along behind them.

The moon spilled a path along the road, lighting up the countryside for a far distance ahead of them. Cloud Eagle and Red Crow exchanged quick glances when a horse came thundering toward them, the reins blowing in the wind, the saddle empty.

Then their attention was drawn elsewhere.

"Up ahead!" Cloud Eagle shouted at Red Crow. "Many riders! They are riding away from us."

"What they left behind is what I fear," Red Crow said. He squinted his eyes in an effort to focus on an object lying in the road ahead.

"I see it also," Cloud Eagle said, before Red

31

Crow got the words from his mouth. "More than likely the man is dead."

"Shall we pursue those who are responsible for the ambush?" Red Crow shouted back.

"Did you see their number?" Cloud Eagle said, frowning.

Red Crow nodded.

"Then you know that we are outnumbered and should not risk our lives foolishly," Cloud Eagle said.

"*In-gew*. All right," Red Crow said, again nodding.

They rode in a harder gallop until they came to the figure lying lifelessly in the road.

Red Crow stayed in his saddle with his rifle drawn, while Cloud Eagle quickly dismounted and knelt down beside the one who had been attacked.

The coyote pets held back, then inched closer. Cloud Eagle's eyes widened in disbelief when he discovered that this person was most certainly not a man. The fall had knocked the hat from her head, and her brilliant red hair spilled across her shoulders.

"This is not a man," he said up to Red Crow. He was puzzled by her attire. "See the hair? White men do not wear hair as long as the Apache. Only their women wear hair this long."

"But she is dressed as a boy," Red Crow, puzzled, responded. "How can that be? Why would she wear clothes that hide the curves of a woman beneath them?"

"She is white. Who can say why white women do anything?" Cloud Eagle said, shrugging. "Are they not a mystery to the Apache?"

"Yes, that is so," Red Crow said, nodding. "Is she dead or alive?"

"She breathes," Cloud Eagle responded, leaning closer to take a better look at the fallen one.

He looked in undisguised wonderment at her face. He had already seen this face today. It was the woman in the painting that belonged to the white man!

Stunned by this discovery, his gaze swept over her. He allowed himself a more leisurely look at her. Her lips were full and perfectly shaped. Her lashes were thick, like dark crescents across her pale cheeks.

His fingers touched her hair and felt its softness, and he was again taken by the color as he had been when he had seen her likeness in the painting. It was the color of tongues of flame!

He stared at the soiled buckskin breeches and shirt, then at the curves that their tightness defined.

She was so very *much* a woman, with well-rounded breasts, a tiny waist, and slim hips.

His musings at having found the woman of the painting were interrupted when he discovered the wound on the thigh of her left leg. Blood was seeping from it and spreading through the material of her breeches, pooling on the ground like a miniature sun.

He knew that he did not want this woman to die from loss of blood. Acting quickly, he swept his knife from its sheath at his right side. The blade gleamed in the moonlight like a blade of ice. With precise movements, he cut the leg of the woman's breeches open.

He sighed with relief. She had only a flesh wound. He would not have to scar her body by digging into her lovely flesh to get the bullet out.

Yet even though this was only a flesh wound, it was bad enough for her to be losing too much blood.

Quickly he removed his headband and tied a tourniquet around her leg. Soon the flow of the blood stopped.

"And how is the fallen one?" Red Crow asked, having silently watched as Cloud Eagle ministered to the woman.

"She will live," Cloud Eagle said, flashing a wide smile over his shoulder at Red Crow. "And do you know who this woman is? Red Crow, it is the woman in the painting today, the painting that the white man would not part with."

"How can that be?" Red Crow said, dismounting to take a look at Alicia. He was taken aback by the resemblance, and by her loveliness. If he was not happy with his two wives, he could very easily take a liking to this woman. Even if she did wear the clothes of a man.

"You see, my friend?" Cloud Eagle crowed. "It *is* the woman."

"And what will you do with her now that you have seen to her wound?" Red Crow asked, raising an eyebrow at Cloud Eagle.

"I know not where she belongs, so she will go with you and me," Cloud Eagle said, his heart pounding at the thought of having this woman in his possession, even for a short while. It would give him time to search his soul as to why he was so intrigued with her.

He flinched and his spine stiffened when the woman uttered a soft moan and he saw that her eyelashes were fluttering. He recalled the color of her eyes in the painting. They had been so blue, it was as though they had captured the sky in them.

Alicia slowly opened her eyes. She became quickly aware of the pounding of her head and the pain in her left leg.

She groaned as she tried to move. Then, when she felt a presence there, with her, her eyes flew wide open.

A scream froze in her throat when she saw an Indian leaning over her, staring at her. Believing this was one of the renegades who had ambushed her, she was gripped by fear.

Her gaze was drawn to the two coyotes who stood near the Indian. They bared their sharp fangs at her and growled.

Instinct caused her to reach for the pistol holstered at her waist.

Cloud Eagle moved just as quickly, grabbing the pistol from her and thrusting the firearm into the waist of his breechclout.

"You damn lowdown, thieving Injun," Alicia hissed out as she glared up at Cloud Eagle.

Cloud Eagle's midnight-dark eyes filled with an angry fire. "You should be careful whom you call ugly, wrongful names," he said, his voice tight.

Alicia cowered beneath his steady stare, awaiting his next move. It suddenly dawned on her that this man had it in his power to decide whether she was going to live or die.

Chapter Three

Alicia's eyes shifted to the two coyotes. She squirmed uneasily as they paced before her, their steel-gray eyes studying her. "Can't you do something about those damn animals?" she said, giving Cloud Eagle a quick, angry glance, though she was no longer as afraid of the animals as before. It was obvious they were the Indian's pets.

Cloud Eagle bent over and patted Snow and Gray. He then stood tall and square-shouldered, revealing his corded muscles. "Go. Go to Red Crow," he said, pointing to him.

After the coyotes bounded away from him, Cloud Eagle turned his eyes to Red Crow. "My friend, go and find this woman's horse," he said, his raven-black hair rippling in the breeze. "Take my pets with you. The woman finds them troublesome."

Red Crow questioned Cloud Eagle for a

moment with his dark eyes. His hesitation was not so much because of his friend's command. It was because of Cloud Eagle's attentiveness to the white woman.

Red Crow saw danger in his best friend's interest in the female. As he saw it, there was no place in either of their lives for a white woman. If he had his way, he would leave her stranded and let the animals of the night have their way with her.

But it was evident that Cloud Eagle had other plans for her, and it was up to Red Crow to accept his friend's decisions. Cloud Eagle was not only his best friend, but his chief. Never had Red Crow openly questioned anything that Cloud Eagle commanded.

Nor would he reveal to Cloud Eagle that he was questioning his reasons for his actions tonight.

Red Crow nodded to Cloud Eagle. He whistled to Snow and Gray, then rode off at a brisk gallop, the coyotes trailing behind him.

Cloud Eagle turned his attention back to Alicia.

Scarcely breathing, she stared up at him.

"And so you have sent your coyotes away," she said. "What does that prove? That you are my friend?" She laughed sarcastically. "I think not. I can see right through this ploy meant to make me trust you."

She paused and grabbed at her throbbing leg when a pain shot through it, then stared once again defiantly up at Cloud Eagle. "I never trust thieving Injuns," she hissed out. She winced again as the pain worsened. "Especially one who has shot me."

Her reference to Cloud Eagle as a "thieving Injun" and her assumption that he had shot her sent ripples of anger through Cloud Eagle. But he held his feelings deeply within him, practicing the restraint that he had learned as a child. He would find ways to change the woman's mind.

It puzzled him that she did not recognize him as a friendly Apache. Yet perhaps she saw no difference between one tribe of Indians and another.

He had to correct this misconception immediately. Her friendship was of the utmost importance to him. He was mystified by her and her strange ways. Her behavior was different from that of any woman he had ever known.

"You have nothing to fear," he said. He held his hands out and spread his fingers. "The Apache are like the fingers—separate. We live in small bands. If one band is destroyed by enemies, all others may live."

He placed a hand over his heart. "My name is Cloud Eagle," he said, pride showing in the depths of his midnight-dark eyes. "I am of the El Pinal Coyotero Apache. I have made peace with people of your skin coloring. My people are well known for their peaceful ways. You are of this region? You should know of the Coyotero Apache's peaceful ways and realize that I mean you no harm. I have come to your rescue. I wish to help you with your wound. You should allow it."

She had not yet learned to trust Indians since she had arrived in the Arizona Territory, but Alicia listened guardedly to what Cloud Eagle said. She did know that the Coyotero Apache were peace-loving Indians.

Even still, she was afraid to trust him. Of late there had been many raids and abductions along the California Road.

Although she had been told that Indian renegades and outlaws were responsible, she could not allow herself to let her guard down and trust anyone completely. Especially an Indian.

Knowing that a show of courage was essential under these circumstances, she tried to hide the fear and apprehension that she could not shake. And although her leg and her head were throbbing fiercely, she scooted to a sitting position and sent Cloud Eagle a defiant stare.

She found that this tactic unnerved her more than him. His handsomeness was uniquely disarming. She had seen many Indians in this area, but never had she seen this man, nor anyone as handsome. He was over six feet tall, sinewy and muscular. His hair was long and flowing and black. His cheekbones were high, his features sternly chiseled, firm but not hard.

He was scarcely dressed, his breechclout covering his loins, but nothing more. His only other attire was moccasins.

Cloud Eagle was puzzled by her lingering silence. He bent to one knee before her. "Do I not speak your language well enough?" he said, his eyes devouring the loveliness of her face and the red brilliance of her hair. "Is this why you do not answer Cloud Eagle?"

"Surprisingly, you do speak English well enough to be understood," Alicia said, blowing a strand of hair out of her eyes. "So you should understand me when I tell you that I want my mail sack returned. Give it to me this instant. Do you hear?"

"I know of no mail sack," Cloud Eagle said, raising an eyebrow.

"You expect me to believe that?" Alicia asked,

her voice shrill. "The last thing I remember before being shot were renegade Indians on all sides of me." She swallowed hard. "I am foolish for trying to reason with you. You are probably the one who shot me."

"You do not listen to what I have said," Cloud Eagle growled, impatience showing in the stiffness of his words. "I have said that I am not the enemy. I did not take anything from you. I did not shoot you. My arrival frightened off those who are truly responsible."

"You are quite skilled at lying, aren't you?" Alicia said, glaring at him. "Or should I say quite *practiced*."

This sent a flood of rage throughout Cloud Eagle. His jaw clenched. Yet he kept his anger at bay. "Cloud Eagle never speaks anything but the truth," he said tightly. "The Apache hold it a high virtue always to speak the truth. The Apache adheres more strictly to his social code than the white man does to his. The Apache code of morals is deep-rooted and binding."

Knowing that she had angered, even insulted Cloud Eagle, Alicia's eyes wavered. She felt fear worming its way inside her heart again. She must find a way to escape the wrath of this Indian.

She searched with her eyes for her horse. It was nowhere to be seen. It had more than likely run off during the ambush. Then she recalled Cloud Eagle commanding his companion to go and search for it.

"Come," Cloud Eagle said, placing a gentle hand on Alicia's elbow. "I will take you to my stronghold. Your wound will be seen to."

Alicia jerked her elbow away. "I'm not going anywhere with you," she said, although she was quite aware of Cloud Eagle's gentleness toward her, and puzzled by it. She tried to rise to her feet, to search for her horse. "And I most certainly don't need your help."

Cloud Eagle stepped away from her and gave her the chance to do as she pleased. He knew that she would not get far. He smiled wryly when her legs buckled beneath her and she was once again on the ground.

Disgruntled and in pain, Alicia turned slow eyes up to Cloud Eagle. She became angry all over again when she saw the smug look on his face. "All right," she snapped at him. "I'm *not* able to help myself. You don't have to enjoy my misery so much."

Cloud Eagle bent to one knee again. He placed a gentle hand on her cheek. "This Apache does not enjoy your misery," he said. "But it is good to know that you have no choice but to accept my offer of help."

Alicia slapped his hand away, but not before she realized that his mere touch made her heart thud strangely. She had never experienced such feelings with a man. And fearing these feelings, as well as the man, she reached for her pistol.

Cloud Eagle covered her firearm with his massive hand much more quickly than Alicia could blink her eyes.

She guardedly watched him as he gave her a heated glance, looked down at her pistol, and looked at her again.

"You do not need a man's weapon," he said. "I am a man. I will protect you."

"And who is going to protect me from *you?*" Alicia hissed out. She eyed the pistol, though she knew that she could not reach it. "If you hadn't

41

stopped me, I would have—"

"And could you have really shot me?" he said, interrupting her. He leaned closer. "If I gave it back to you, would you shoot me?"

With his face so close that she could feel the warmth of his breath on her lips, Alicia felt herself weaken with a desire she had never known before. Here she was, face to face with the man who might have shot her, and she felt like an awkward schoolgirl dreamily awaiting her first kiss.

"To gain my freedom?" she stammered. "Yes, I would shoot you if I had the chance. I would shoot anyone who was a threat to me. That's why I carry a weapon."

"It did not protect you when you were ambushed," Cloud Eagle said, slowly running his forefinger across the angle of her cheek and down and around her chin.

Finding it hard to battle the feelings that he was arousing in her, Alicia closed her eyes and swallowed hard. There was only one way to stop this. And she must, or perhaps lose her reason, which was already slipping away under the attention of this handsome Apache warrior.

"Get your rotten, filthy hands off me," she blurted out, flinging her head up to watch his reaction.

Cloud Eagle flinched as though someone had thrown cold water on his face. Yet he did not allow his feelings to show beyond that.

He eased away from Alicia, his gaze holding hers steadily. "Your insults are not from the heart," he said, placing one of his hands over his own heart. "It is in your voice. It is in the way your eyes waver when you look into mine. Your insults are all pretense."

"That isn't so," Alicia said, her voice weakening beneath his steady stare.

"My little *ish-kay-nay* says what she does not mean in order to look courageous and brave in this Apache's eyes," Cloud Eagle said, smiling at her. "And it is understood why you feel as though you must do this. I am but a stranger to you now. But tomorrow? You will then know me well enough to realize that I am a valuable friend."

"*Ish-kay-nay?*" Alicia said guardedly. "What does that mean?"

"The Apache word means 'boy,'" Cloud Eagle said, his lips drawing into a slow smile. "You have earned this nickname because you dress as a boy and behave as a boy and can probably do most things boys do."

Alicia lifted her chin defiantly. "You are wrong," she defended. "I am dressed as a *man,* not a boy. I need to disguise myself against men such as you who take advantage of women."

She paused.

When she noticed that nothing she said seemed to affect him, she went further to prove to him that she was not just any female who was at the mercy of a man.

"I am proud of my ability to shoot, ride, and rope as well as any man," she bragged. "And don't you forget it."

She paused again, then said, "*And* I don't appreciate your Apache nickname. My name is Alicia. Alicia Cline."

Her breath was taken away when Cloud Eagle swept her into his arms and carried her toward his horse. She wanted to struggle when he placed her on his strawberry roan, on a splendid leopard-skin saddle, but the renewed pain in her leg momentarily stole her resistance away.

Just as Cloud Eagle swung himself into the saddle behind Alicia, Red Crow rode up with her horse trailing from a rope behind him.

Seeing her horse reawakened the fight in Alicia. She shoved at Cloud Eagle's chest and tried to pry his arm from around her waist.

She fought against her captivity, and also the melting sensation caused by the closeness of Cloud Eagle's body. These strange feelings were new to her, and most frightening.

"Let me down," she cried. "At least allow me to travel on my own horse."

"You will be more comfortable on my steed," Cloud Eagle said, his arm tightening around her waist. "Your leg will pain you less if you are not in charge of a horse."

"My leg would not pain me at all if you had not shot me," Alicia shouted back.

"I have said that I am not responsible for your injury, and I will say it no more," Cloud Eagle said flatly. He sank his heels into the flanks of his horse and snapped the reins. His roan rode off at a soft trot, Red Crow following him.

"I am responsible for stopping the blood flow from your wound," he said to Alicia. "Had I not, you would not be lucid enough to spar with this Apache chief."

Alicia glanced down at the cloth that was tied around her leg as a tourniquet. Her heart skipped a beat when she recognized that it was an Indian headband. While she had argued with Cloud Eagle, she had not noticed.

Then something else came to her that he had just said. She turned and eyed him with wonder.

"Chief?" she said softly. "You are a chief?"

He nodded. "Chief Cloud Eagle," he said, giving her another smile that disarmed her.

Alicia felt herself falling more and more under the charm of this man and was well aware of the dangers. "That does not impress me at all," she said. "And as for your having placed your headband on my leg to stop the blood flow, I am sure it was done only for your own selfish purposes. Does it make you feel powerful to be in full control of my destiny?"

When he did not answer her, but gazed on past her as he pressed his roan into a harder gallop toward the distant mountains, she wondered just what sort of destiny he might have charted out for her.

She looked over her shoulder at her horse. If she could just find a way to escape! Thank God, her horse was there if she was given the chance.

When another pain shot through her leg, she closed her eyes and gritted her teeth. Even if she did manage to get on her horse, it would be almost unbearable to ride it while her leg was in this shape. She had to bide her time until she was better.

Then she would show this Apache chief a thing or two—that nothing or no one could keep her down for long.

Not even him, or his ability to make her mind-less by his mere presence!

Cloud Eagle relaxed his arm and held her softly against him. "Rest," he whispered in her ear. "Sleep and rest."

So bone-tired and weary, Alicia could not help but close her eyes.

As she snuggled against Cloud Eagle's broad

chest, she was very aware of the thumping of his heart. It matched the thunderous beating of her own.

He was the cause of her anxious heartbeats. She wondered if she was the cause of *his?* She sighed and allowed herself to enjoy these strange, wondrous feelings, at least for now.

Once she escaped, she would forget that Chief Cloud Eagle had for a while made her feel like a woman.

Chapter Four

Alicia slept sporadically. When she was awake, she was always aware of Cloud Eagle's arm around her waist. She was getting used to the pain in her leg, but not to Cloud Eagle's presence. She knew that she should hate him, yet she found something about the way he held her comforting. She snuggled against his bare chest. She inhaled and enjoyed his manly scent.

She was jolted completely awake when Cloud Eagle drew his steed to a sudden halt. When she opened her eyes, her insides froze. She was no longer in the company of only two Apache warriors, but several. She looked guardedly from man to man, looking for one who might be familiar to her from the ambush.

And where were the white outlaws? Had they ridden on ahead with her mail sack? Was Cloud Eagle not in charge, after all?

Her gaze went to the many travois and she

raised an eyebrow. The Indians with the travois attached to their horses could definitely not have taken part in the ambush. The travois would have held them back. Perhaps those men with the travois had surely stayed behind while the others participated in the ambush.

Alicia stiffened as Cloud Eagle instructed the warriors to go on without him. Red Crow was included in that command, leaving Alicia and Cloud Eagle alone, except for the two pet coyotes.

Alicia panicked inside when her horse was taken from her sight by Red Crow. There went her only means of escape. Now what? she silently despaired.

Alicia turned angry, accusing eyes to Cloud Eagle. "Why did you send them away? Is my mail sack hidden among the pelts on one of those travois? Is that why? Or is the mail sack with the outlaws who rode with you during the ambush?" she demanded.

He looked past her. He nudged the flanks of his horse with his heels and sent it into a soft lope again across the moon-splashed land, his coyotes dutifully following.

"And why couldn't I have kept my horse with me?" Alicia continued relentlessly.

For the most part, Cloud Eagle ignored her references to her mail sack and also her lengthy, foolish questions. He realized that he was in the company of one stubborn woman.

"My warriors will return to the stronghold," he said blandly. "We will follow, but at a slower pace. It is best for you that you are not forced to be on a horse for much longer. We will make camp. There you will rest. There I will treat your wound."

He frowned at her. "And you have no need for your horse while you are with Cloud Eagle," he said. Alicia felt threatened more by the way his dark eyes mesmerized her than by the fact that she no longer had her horse nearby.

She turned her eyes quickly away, swallowed hard, and grew quiet.

They rode for a while longer, then stopped in a secluded place by a quiet, serene stream, where they were shielded by towering cliffs.

This caused a wave of renewed apprehension to spread through Alicia. In such a secluded place, Cloud Eagle could have his way with her.

Her heart pounded out her fear as Cloud Eagle drew tight rein, dismounted, and lifted her from the saddle. She hoped that she was wrong to be afraid of him. She fervently wished that his intentions toward her were pure, and that all he wanted was to truly help her.

Alicia clung around Cloud Eagle's neck as he carried her to a wall of rock. He set her down with the wall at her back. It still held the heat of the sun which had beaten there all day.

She leaned away from it and surveyed her surroundings. The stream widened into a basin ten yards across, where very large cottonwood trees spread their limbs overhead. All was still except for an occasional baying wolf that sent its eerie call into the night.

"It's so quiet here," Alicia said as Cloud Eagle spread a blanket beside her. "The distant wolves and the trickling water are the only sounds that I hear."

"It is the tribal doctrine to avoid noisy water, which keeps one from hearing other sounds," Cloud Eagle said, now bringing willows and alders and quickly weaving a shelter. He nodded toward the blanket. "Take the blanket inside the shelter. I must see to my horse. Then I will return and see to your wound and share my food with you."

Alicia nodded. Feeling more certain as each moment passed that he meant her no harm, she did as he asked. She settled down on the blanket and held her throbbing head between her hands as she watched Cloud Eagle care for his roan. She noticed his gentleness toward the animal. He meticulously plucked burrs from the matted tail, one by one. When that was finished, he led his horse to the water, where he patiently gave it a long drink before hobbling the roan in a grassy draw.

Cloud Eagle wandered away and Alicia lost sight of him momentarily. She had a fleeting thought of seizing the moment to escape.

Then another pain rippled up and down her leg, reminding her of just how helpless she was. She moaned and rocked back and forth as she held her leg between her hands, then stiffened and scarcely breathed when the pet coyotes came and sniffed at her. She sighed heavily when they sauntered away and stretched out beside the stream.

Cloud Eagle soon returned. He came into the small shelter and sat down beside her.

Puzzled by what he was now doing, Alicia closely watched him crush some strange sort of roots between two rocks.

Cloud Eagle sensed Alicia's puzzlement. "I searched until I found the herb I need to doctor your wound," he explained, his eyes still on what he was doing. "I am making a powder from the root of the *ocotillo*. It will help your wound heal quickly."

Alicia moved farther away from him. "I don't want any powder from any root placed on my wound," she argued. "I prefer allowing it to heal on its own."

She paused when he cast her an angry stare, then continued. "A doctor lives not far from my stage station. Take me there. He will see to my wound, thank you."

"You are closer to my stronghold than any stage station that I am aware of," Cloud Eagle argued. He took a handful of the *ocotillo* powder to Alicia. He brushed it from the palm of his hand onto the blanket, then took Alicia by the wrist and urged her next to him. "Sit still. This will not take long."

"No, don't!" Alicia cried. She tried to slide away from him again, but the pain in her leg stopped her.

Panting, she fell onto her back. "It looks as though I don't have any choice, doesn't it?" she said exhaustedly. "You apparently aren't aware of my stage station. It has been in service for only a few days. It is much closer than you realize. But even if you knew that my stage station was not far away, you still would not take me there, would you?"

"You may behave and dress as a man, but you do not have the sense of distance or direction that a man has, especially an Apache," Cloud Eagle said. He ignored the way she flinched when he drew a knife from its sheath at his right side and placed it where her buckskin breeches had already been ripped open.

He could tell that she was holding her breath

as he ripped the breeches leg open more widely with the knife. "I do know of this newest stage station," he said dryly. "I know where it is located. It is a day's ride away." He paused and gave her a lingering stare. "Were you going or coming from the stage station?"

"That is none of your business," Alicia said stubbornly. "But you made it your business, didn't you? You waited until I got far enough from the stage station to ambush me. You took my mail sack. Why? There wasn't anything of importance in it except—except the letter to my brother. Now you may be the cause of his getting lost in this godforsaken land."

"Your brother?" Cloud Eagle said, raising an eyebrow. "What about your brother?"

Alicia grew pale, thinking that she might have said too much. If this Apache chief sent his warriors to look for her brother, there was no telling what would happen to her sweet Charlie.

"Nothing," she said, looking away from him.

"When one speaks of blood kin, it is usually not done without good reason," Cloud Eagle said, laying his knife aside. "Especially if there is concern about the relative." He briefly thought about the man with the portrait, but that thought was driven out of his mind when his fingers touched Alicia's wound, and she cried out with pain.

Quickly he placed a hand over her mouth. "Silence," he said angrily. "Do you wish to draw those responsible for the ambush to us? You would soon realize that I have told the truth."

Alicia's eyes were wide above his clasped hand. Her pulse raced at the very thought that he might be truly a friend, for she would die a slow death inside should he prove to be her arch enemy.

Although she was fighting her feelings for him with every fiber of her being, the more she was with him, the more she realized that she could care for this handsome Apache.

Perhaps she already did, she thought.

She grabbed his hand from her mouth. "You are a good actor," she scoffed. "You are going to have to do more than act as though you are wary of someone finding us here to convince me that you are not the very one you are warning me against."

Cloud Eagle gave her a frustrated look, then removed the headband from her leg. He took it to the stream and gave it a good dunking, washing the blood from it as well as he could. He went to his horse, took a large buckskin pouch from his saddle, and carried it to the river.

Taking a cloth from inside the pouch, he leaned it into the water and gave it a good soaking, then came back to Alicia.

"What I am going to do will hurt, but it is best so that the wound will have a better chance to heal," Cloud Eagle said.

He gently laid the damp cloth on Alicia's wound and bathed it as she held her breath and watched.

Too taken by his gentle ways and his attentiveness to her, Alicia ignored the pain. Again his handsomeness was unnerving her. In the light of the moon, she could see how his body rippled with power. She studied his square-jawed face that was framed by black hair. His eyes were black and burning.

She was indeed touched by his tender, caring ways, yet she still could not allow herself to trust him.

"You continue with your ploy that is meant to make me trust you," Alicia said, sighing heavily. "Yet you are surely the man responsible for my present dilemma. Heed my warning, Cloud Eagle. When I am missed, someone will come looking for me. Milton Powers works with me at the stage station, and although at times he acts as though he despises the very ground I walk on, he won't allow Indians to get away with stealing the mail sack and abducting me."

Instantly jealous to hear her speak another man's name, Cloud Eagle stared down at her. "Who is this man with the strange name?" he demanded. "This Milton. Is he your special man?"

Enjoying his piqued interest, and feeling as though she had a slight edge over him at least for the moment, Alicia smiled and offered him no more information. Although he was seeing to her wound, she would not be fooled that easily by him.

Realizing that he was not going to get any more answers from her about this white man, Cloud Eagle proceeded to doctor her wound. He would get answers from her later. She would give them to him willingly.

Alicia looked down at her wound. It was cleansed thoroughly. She winced when Cloud Eagle sprinkled the powdered *ocotillo* on it, then closed the torn buckskin back over it and secured the headband just above this, to hold the buckskin fabric in place.

"That will do until we reach my stronghold," Cloud Eagle said, slipping his knife back inside its sheath. "If it is not healed by then, a shaman will be called to make you well."

A tremor of apprehension swept through Alicia. "I want no shaman near me," she said, catching his angry look at the sarcastic sound of her voice. "Anyhow, I'm sure one won't be required. I heal quickly. I will be as good as new in a couple of days."

Cloud Eagle left long enough to get his sack of food. When he returned, Alicia watched hungrily as he removed some jerked meat from the buckskin pouch. He held out a piece of the jerky toward Alicia. "Cloud Eagle is always ready to share what he has with his fellows and deeming you as one of them, eat what I offer you."

Alicia did not have to be asked twice. She tore into the meat with her teeth, jerking a good portion free. She began chewing it ravenously.

Cloud Eagle left again and returned a short while later to offer her fruit from the giant cactus, the yucca.

She accepted this and ate it, not only to quell her hunger, but to quench her thirst. She enjoyed the taste, which was something like the taste of the figs and bananas she had once sampled in Saint Louis.

The air was damp, crisp, and bone-cutting in the soft and moon-filled dark of night. Thickets of piñon scattered the starlight, making silvery slashes on the ground.

Alicia shivered and hugged herself. "Aren't you going to build a fire?" she asked, her stomach now pleasantly full. Sleep was the next best thing, perhaps only second to being held again by Cloud Eagle. She fought this want with all of her being, for she did not want to allow herself to feel anything for Cloud Eagle but loathing.

"The same as noise, fire must be avoided

tonight at all costs," Cloud Eagle explained. He left the shelter, went to his horse, and untied a Mexican serape which was lashed to the back of his saddle.

He brought it to Alicia. He doubled it and gently passed it over her shoulders and tied it under her chin by a stout buckskin thong.

"That should keep you comfortable enough until the sun comes into the sky with its warmth tomorrow," Cloud Eagle said.

Alicia clung to the serape, drawing it more tightly against her, yet still she shivered.

Cloud Eagle went to his horse again and removed a buckskin blanket from another leather pouch that hung from his horse's side, behind his saddle.

He took this back to Alicia. "Lie down," he said, giving her a soft look. "I shall spread this over you."

"I don't think anything can give me enough warmth," Alicia said, yet did as he instructed. "I've never been so cold."

She trembled beneath the buckskin blanket.

Cloud Eagle knelt over her, wishing there were more that he could do to ensure her warmth for the night. He knew that she would not accept his body warmth.

He glanced down at Gray as his coyote meandered into the shelter and stretched out at Cloud Eagle's feet. An idea came to Cloud Eagle's mind that made him smile.

"Go, Gray," he said, pointing to Alicia. "Down. Lie down with the woman. Share your body warmth with her."

Gray cocked his head and gave Cloud Eagle a puzzled look. When the command was repeated, the coyote crawled on all fours to Alicia, then snuggled close beside her.

The coyote so close to Alicia made fear rise inside her, so much that an uncontrollable shudder of dread rushed through her.

"Send him away," she said in a weak voice as she pleaded up at Cloud Eagle with her eyes. "Please? I'll be warm enough without the coyote."

"Gray is gentler than most white men's pet dogs," Cloud Eagle said, settling down on a blanket a short distance from Alicia. He snapped his fingers and Snow came bounding toward him. "Snow will warm me for the night. Gray will warm you."

Alicia watched Snow settle in beside Cloud Eagle. When she saw the devotion between master and coyote, she looked down at Gray and saw that he was just as obedient toward her.

Slowly her fear subsided. She scooted closer to Gray and draped an arm over him. Smiling, she closed her eyes when she felt the warmth of his body enter hers. She felt as though she had found a friend.

Friends.

Oh, Lord, she despaired. She needed friends at this time in her life when everything was so foreign from anything she had ever known.

She flinched and her eyes opened widely when a night hawk whistled an alarm from somewhere close by. Far off, the scream of a cougar echoed, hollow and alone.

Alicia noticed that a coyote's sharp, sudden bark caused Snow's ears to lift and her eyes to become hauntingly anxious.

Alicia also noticed how Cloud Eagle ran a

calming hand over his pet. It was as though he understood the cries of the heart that disturbed someone when hunger for a mate needed to be fed.

Cloud Eagle stared over at Alicia. The moonlight was wafting through the open shelter, playing on the soft, beautiful features of her face. His insides grew warm at the sight and nearness of her. He recalled how she had looked in the portrait. She had been totally feminine in appearance in a lovely, low-swept dress, her hair lying in soft curls across her pale shoulders. He vowed to himself that he would soon discard her ugly clothes that were meant only for a man, and turn her into a woman—in every respect.

Alicia stared back at him, her insides swimming with a lazy warmth. She could see something new in his eyes and realized that it was a look of hungry need.

Her heart skipped a beat.

Was he like his pet coyote?

If so, who would stroke his flesh and calm him into forgetting such needs?

Oh, dear Lord, she thought. She wished to be the one. Just the thought of touching his body intimately set small fires alight within her.

And fearing these new feelings, she turned her back to him. She inhaled a shaky, nervous breath and closed her eyes.

But sleep would not come to her.

She kept seeing, feeling, and wanting him.

Chapter Five

While the gray before dawn still ghosted the land, distorting shapes of cactus and bush, Cloud Eagle awakened Alicia.

She blinked her eyes open with a start, momentarily disoriented. And then, as she gazed up into midnight-dark eyes and a smile that warmed her through and through, she remembered where she was.

"It is time to move onward," Cloud Eagle said. He awakened Snow, drew the coyote into his arms, and gave her a bear hug, then shoved her away. Snow meandered off and joined Gray down by the stream to take her morning drink of water.

Alicia yawned, stretched her arms above her head, then sat up. She groaned when pain shot through her wound as she moved her leg too much in one direction.

Yet she realized that the pain was not half as

bad as yesterday. She had to admit that Cloud Eagle's medicinal herb had helped her.

"The pain will be almost totally gone by tomorrow," Cloud Eagle said. When he saw that she was trying to get up, he stopped her by placing his hands gently on her shoulders. "Stay. I will bring water and food to you."

"I imagine I should say thank you," Alicia said, combing her hair back from her eyes with her fingers. "But I would not even be here if not for you and your renegades, so I won't waste my breath."

Cloud Eagle gave her a hard, perturbed stare, then went to his horse and took several things from his buckskin pouch.

Alicia watched him carry a small wooden dish to the river and fill it with water. She watched him place a cloth in the dish and bring it back to her.

"Bathe as best you can today with this, and tomorrow, when your leg is better and we are at my stronghold, I will carry you into the river for a true bath," Cloud Eagle said, placing the dish of water next to her.

Cloud Eagle left her to her privacy in the small shelter. She continued to watch him as he walked toward the stream.

Then, embarrassed, she gasped when he dropped his breechclout to the ground and stepped out of his moccasins, leaving him stark naked.

Her heart pounded at the sight of his nude body. She had never seen a man undressed before, especially a man who already disturbed her heart in too many strange ways.

Realizing just how well-built he was in places that she had never seen before, she inhaled a quavering breath and covered her mouth with one hand.

"Good Lord, are all men as well-proportioned as that?" she whispered, her face hot with a blush.

She watched him wade into the stream. He then sat down in the water and splashed it over his muscular shoulders and chest.

Mesmerized, Alicia continued watching, forgetting that she had her own bath to attend to. This handsome Apache had not only stolen her breath away this morning, but most certainly had taken her heart as well. Not until now did she realize that wanting a man could be so exciting. The proof of that was in how her pulse raced and her heart pounded.

"Alicia Cline, shame on you for such sultry thoughts," she whispered to herself.

When he rose to his full height, the water rippling along his copper flesh, she was in awe of him all over again.

He turned suddenly toward her.

Their eyes met and held.

Alicia was afraid that he could read her thoughts by the expression on her face and by the blush on her cheeks. Embarrassed anew, she turned her eyes quickly away.

But shutting him out of her sight did not erase him from her memory. As she began to scrub her face with the soft cloth, she fought longings that she had never felt before.

And she hated it that Cloud Eagle had caught her staring at him. If he did lust after her, she might have just encouraged him to try his hand at kissing her. If so, what then might he try with her?

61

Her heart skipped a beat when she focused her thoughts once again on that part of his anatomy that stirred her imagination to thoughts that she had always been taught were sinful.

"Mama," she whispered, as though her mother were there to listen. "Surely you enjoyed sinning with father. You always went to bed with him so eagerly and willingly."

She nodded, as though her mother were there, responding. "Yes, Mama, I know that you had a wedding band on your finger when you bedded with Papa," Alicia whispered. She rolled her sleeves up to wash her arms. "But Mama, surely you felt the same as I before those vows. It is such a delicious feeling, Mama, when I think of being held within Cloud Eagle's arms. And when I think of touching him where he is so different from me, a strange, wondrous thrill overwhelms me."

Cloud Eagle left the water. He drew on his breechclout and stepped into his moccasins. He straightened his hair over his shoulders as he walked toward Alicia.

When he got close enough to hear her, he cocked an eyebrow, wondering who she was talking to. Perhaps one of her Gods that he did not know about?

He shrugged and sat down with her inside the shelter.

"We must be on our way soon," he said, interrupting Alicia's pretended conversation with her mother. "The heat will be with us most of the day. Do you think you can withstand such heat?"

"If you can, so can I," Alicia said, shoving the basin of water toward him. "I would think you would know by now that I am not a fragile flower that wilts in the sun."

Cloud Eagle chuckled.

He gave Alicia a piece of jerky from his small bag. He watched her tear a piece of it away with her teeth. He was amazed at how eagerly she ate. She ate ravenously and as much as he did.

Yet she was so tiny. He knew that if he placed his hands around her waist, surely his fingertips would meet.

Alicia ate hungrily and smiled awkwardly at Cloud Eagle when she caught him watching her. The memory of how he had looked without his breechclout seemed stuck in her thoughts. Surely he was recalling her staring at him, or why else would he be gazing at her in such a way?

When he returned her smile, she looked away from him. Suddenly her appetite was gone. What she truly wanted was to experience how it would feel to be kissed by him. She knew that she was wrong to allow her thoughts to wander so when she still suspected that he might be one of the renegades who had ambushed her.

Yet moment by moment she was coming to doubt that he was capable of such a horrendous act as that. Or else why would he continue to treat her as though she were a princess? If he had wanted her only to take advantage of her body, he would have not waited this long. He would have forced himself on her the moment they were left alone. He may have even left her to die after he had fed his manly hungers.

But he was still behaving like a gentleman. Except for disrobing in front of her. Had that been to titillate her thoughts in order to draw her into seduction? she wondered.

Or was it a natural thing for Indians to undress in front of one another?

She was grateful for one thing—that he had not asked her to get undressed for her bath. Yet he *had* said that he was going to carry her into the river for a bath later.

Certainly he would not do it while she was fully clothed!

Snow and Gray came and sat down between Cloud Eagle and Alicia. Cloud Eagle gave them some jerked meat, then gave each of them a pat as they began chewing their morning meal.

Having eaten all that she wanted, Alicia reached a hand to Gray and stroked his thick gray fur.

She smiled down at the coyote when he offered her a grateful look. If coyotes could smile, Alicia thought, this animal with friendly eyes would be smiling. It was obvious that Cloud Eagle spoiled both pets rotten. And they returned the favor by being devoted to him and those whom he befriended.

"You are no longer frightened of my coyotes?" Cloud Eagle asked, reaching to pat Gray himself.

"I especially like Gray," Alicia said, her heart lurching when her hand accidentally grazed Cloud Eagle's as he continued gently patting Gray's head. She could feel her face become hot with a blush when her eyes met and held Cloud Eagle's. Her heart beat thunderously within her chest when Cloud Eagle reached his hand over Gray and twined his fingers through Alicia's hair and drew her lips close to his.

When their lips met in a sweet and tender kiss, Alicia felt as though she were soaring. She closed her eyes and did not draw away when he held her closer, his lips now pressed hard into hers, his tongue darting.

Weakness consumed Alicia. Her thoughts were clouded, making her aware of nothing more than the bliss of his kiss.

Then, remembering her fears of where this might lead, and thinking that this might have been a ploy of his to pull her into wanting to share intimate moments with him, Alicia came to her senses. She wrenched herself away from him.

A wounded look came into Cloud Eagle's eyes as she stared defiantly at him.

"Don't do that again," she said, her voice breaking with emotion. Her heart pounded so hard she felt dizzy. "I'm not something to be used. Surely there are many women at your stronghold who can feed your hungers of the flesh. Just remember that once we arrive there, I am not one of them."

Confused by how she could change from one moment to another, Cloud Eagle took her by the wrists and drew her lips close again. "There are two wives awaiting my arrival," he said, his breath hot on her lips. "Can you say that truly pleases you to know that I have two wives who are very willing to feed my hungers? Or do I see jealousy flash in your eyes at the mention of wives?"

Alicia's mouth dropped open in surprise. She was stunned numb by his confession. "You are married?" she murmured, before she could stop the words from flowing across her lips. "You have two wives?" She could not help but admit to feeling the pangs of jealousy. It was cutting clean into her heart.

"I am an Apache chief," Cloud Eagle said, his eyes dancing. "An Apache chief can take as many wives as he wishes. Perhaps I will make you my third."

Alicia gasped and paled. "Never!" she said in a hiss. "I would share a man with no one."

"Especially Cloud Eagle?" he teased back.

When Alicia did not reply and only sat there, breathless over his nearness, Cloud Eagle once again twined his fingers through her hair and brought her lips to his. He kissed her passionately, then released her.

"Your kiss speaks a different meaning than your words to Cloud Eagle," he said.

He smiled knowingly at her again, then left the small shelter.

Certain now that she was in love for the first time in her life, yet feeling as though it were a wasted love, Alicia watched Cloud Eagle prepare to leave. He took the blanket that he had slept on, shook it free of dust, and slapped it across his horse's broad back. With one hand, he swung the saddle up, buckled the cinches, and tested and dropped the stirrups.

Without any words spoken between them, Cloud Eagle went for Alicia and carried her to the panther-skin saddle. Soon they were traveling again, the coyotes following and playing with one another behind them.

The slow-rising sun was flinging crimson banners across the sky, but the valley was still in chilly shadow. But it did not take long for the sun to become glaring and hot over the eastern rim of the desert.

Alicia was amazed at what the brighter light of day revealed. There were canyons to enter by and canyons to leave by, but she and Cloud Eagle were still surrounded by a high wall. Shadows deepened as they rode into the foothills of the mountain. The flow of a ravine gave off the warm smell of sweet grass as water splashed from the rocks. They rode past a desert hackberry that was in full foliage, a deer bird picking the yellow berries.

After several more hours of travel, they rode into another narrow canyon. In its depths were lush grass greened by the river's moisture, piñon trees, mesquite, live oak, and wild bursts of flowers carrying a warmth to the cooling air of the higher elevations.

Deep springs were cradled in the canyon. Westward, the horizon swallowed the sun, belching red skyward and turning the desert purple.

Fear grabbed at Alicia's insides when she saw something else. Small fires flared before many Apache lodges in the distance.

Alicia was almost used to being with Cloud Eagle, no longer feeling threatened by him, but now that the stronghold was so close, where so many Apache were housed, apprehension crept into her heart again.

There were at least two hundred tepees. They were made from buffalo skins, tanned white, fired by the sun, and swept by the wind. They sat in an uneven line on the bare banks of the Gila River. The Gila was revered by the Apache as the river that flowed into the sunset without end.

Alicia was aware of, and welcomed, Cloud Eagle's comforting arm around her waist as she sat before him in the saddle. But the closer they came to the stronghold, the more her heart pounded with fear of what lay ahead of her, of how she would be received among Cloud Eagle's people.

To put that worry from her mind for now, she looked past the stronghold. In the valley were vast fields. Indian women were busy working there amidst a bountiful crop of corn, squash, and pumpkins.

Alicia then looked again toward the dwellings in the village. Stunted cottonwoods sat among the tepees, their leaves rustling in the wind with the sound of rain. Several women had stepped to the entranceways of their tepees and had lifted the buckskin flaps, watching their chief bring a stranger into their midst. The children stopped playing long enough to stare. Several dogs met Snow and Gray's approach, barking and bouncing playfully around them.

Spring Dawn and Lost Wind, Cloud Eagle's wives, huddled together at the entranceway of their tepee, slyly watching the white woman.

"Lost Wind, do you see how our husband holds the white woman so possessively?" Spring Dawn said in a harsh whisper. "Red Crow warned us that she was being brought to our stronghold and that Cloud Eagle was looking after her. But he did not warn us about her loveliness, nor about Cloud Eagle's possessiveness of her. What are we to think? What are we to do?"

"It is not easy to see our husband with another woman, especially one whose skin is white," Lost Wind said, fidgeting with the end of one of her braids. She twisted and untwisted it around her finger. "We have neither one given our husband a child which he desires so badly. What if we are abandoned by him? What if he chooses the white woman over us?"

"Do not think such a thing," Spring Dawn scolded. "Though barren, we are bound to him with vows of marriage."

"The bond can easily be broken if he chooses," Lost Wind said. She gasped with horror when Cloud Eagle reined in his horse close to the lodge and very delicately and devotedly lifted the white woman from his saddle. Lost Wind chewed her lower lip in frustration as Cloud Eagle carried the white woman toward the tepee.

"Do you not see how he treats her?" Spring Dawn whispered to Lost Wind. "It is as though she is everything to him. Surely he has brought her to our village to be his third wife."

"What if he replaces us with her?" Lost Wind whined pitifully. "I do not want to lose him. I so admire his large and powerful frame. His daring exploits, his wise teachings in council, have surrounded him with a large and influential band. This has given him prestige and sway among the various branches of our people and carries his influence far and wide. This has given you and me much prestige by being married to him. We do not want to lose all of this to this white woman!"

"Never," Spring Dawn hissed. She shied away from Cloud Eagle as he brushed past her and Lost Wind. Her eyes only momentarily met and held the white woman's. Her insides recoiled when she noticed how the venom in Spring Dawn and Lost Wind's eyes caused the white woman to cling more tightly around Cloud Eagle's neck, as though she expected him to protect her.

Spring Dawn grabbed Lost Wind's hand, and together they entered the tepee and stood in the shadows, watching.

Cloud Eagle placed Alicia on a pallet of furs beside a slow-burning fire. She continued to be aware of the two sets of eyes on her. She was

69

overwhelmed with jealousy to know that these two women were Cloud Eagle's wives and that they had shared more with him than she could even imagine.

Alicia could tell by their behavior and by the way they were staring at her, eyeing her like panthers from the shadows, that they were extremely jealous of her. She suddenly felt trapped and tried to ignore them as Cloud Eagle worked at making things more comfortable for her.

Cloud Eagle turned to his wives. "Bring this woman food," he flatly ordered.

Disgruntled, Lost Wind left the lodge. She returned a short time later with a platter of mesquite beans and cakes made of *pitahaya*, and a mug of cool water to drink.

Cloud Eagle sat down beside Alicia to wait for her to finish eating and drinking. Then he would see that she got a proper rest. Much lay ahead of her that would require all her strength.

Alicia would have rather refused the food, but she was too weak from hunger to be so stubborn. All the while she ate, she watched the two women for any sudden movements they might make. They both had knives in sheaths at their waists. One lunge at her with the knife, so quickly that Cloud Eagle could not stop them, and Alicia could be dead.

She was relieved when they made no moves toward her. She still watched them until her platter was empty and she had drunk every last drop of the cool, refreshing water.

When Cloud Eagle saw that Alicia's platter was empty, he took it and handed it over his shoulder to Lost Wind. "The ride has been long," he said softly to Alicia. He placed his hands at her shoulders and eased her down onto the furs. "Sleep. Rest."

Worn out and aching from the long journey, and now comfortably full from the food, Alicia nodded and snuggled into the furs. She closed her eyes in an effort to forget the staring, jealous women.

But nothing she did made her forget that she was being closely scrutinized.

Lost Wind scooted closer to Spring Dawn. "I would not object to a woman of our own coloring being brought into this lodge for such tender care from our husband," she whispered. "But not this white woman. Cloud Eagle is surely going to take her as his wife."

When Cloud Eagle lay down beside Alicia, and Alicia allowed it, Spring Dawn and Lost Wind emitted low gasps and fled into the dark shadows of the night outside the lodge.

"My heart is hurt," Lost Wind said, sobbing. "It has been a long time since Cloud Eagle has slept with us. And now he sleeps with a white woman? I am humiliated. I am filled with rage."

Spring Dawn nodded as tears sprang from her eyes. "If Cloud Eagle's mother and father were alive, they would stop his nonsensical ways," she murmured. "But alas, they were killed in wars past with renegade Comanche. Cloud Eagle is not only our chief now, he obeys no rule but his own."

In the lodge, Cloud Eagle could not rest. He rose and sat by the fire. His eyes never left Alicia. She was sleeping peacefully, her breathing low and even and sweet.

Grumbling to himself, Cloud Eagle left the tepee and ran to the river. Without removing his clothes, he dove in headfirst, hoping to cool his thoughts and his hungers.

Alicia trembled as she dreamed of being held within Cloud Eagle's arms, his lips pressed hard against hers. His hands were awakening her to new desires as they caressed her breasts.

She awakened with a start, her pulse racing. She leaned up on one elbow and realized that she had only been dreaming, yet she wished that the dream were real.

She jumped with a start when Spring Dawn and Lost Wind entered the tepee and stared at her, then left again.

She feared them now, more than she could have ever feared Cloud Eagle in the beginning when they had first met. She had conquered her fear of him. Now she had the jealousy and fear of his wives to overcome.

Chapter Six

The next morning when Alicia awakened, she remembered where she was the instant she saw the peaked roof of the tepee, where showers of morning light were spraying through the smoke hole.

She lowered her eyes, then tightened inside when she found Cloud Eagle sitting on the far side of the lodge, watching her. Had he sat there all night? The last thing that she recalled from the previous evening was allowing him to lie down beside her because she had been too tired to care where he slept.

She also recalled him leaving her side just as quickly, to sit away from her. As she had drifted to sleep, she had felt his eyes on her.

Just as they were now.

Alicia smiled awkwardly at him, then swept her eyes over him. She realized now that he had not watched her the long night, after all. He had changed his clothes. Today he wore beaded leggings, a red undershirt with a deerskin cover shirt, and a headband of red cotton.

It was less unnerving for her to see him more fully clothed. Wearing only the breechclout, with his muscled body so blatantly revealed to her, it had been hard not to remember how he had looked with nothing at all on.

When Cloud Eagle did not return the smile, Alicia felt seized with apprehension and fear all over again. He seemed lost in thought. Was he trying to decide what he was going to do with her now that he had brought her to his village? Had his wives complained to him about the presence of a white woman in their lodge?

She glanced around the tepee. His wives were not there. Had he sent them away? Or had they left on their own? Would they return soon and cause her more awkwardness?

The worries came to her, tumbling around in her brain like sagebrush blowing absently along in the sand.

She was glad when Gray came to her and snuggled next to her as she awaited Cloud Eagle's next moves. This was a new day. Oh, Lord, she despaired. What was it going to bring?

She eased her hand to her sore leg and felt around the festered area of the wound. She flinched. It still pained her.

Yet she was aware that it was much better. If she felt a worse threat than she already faced, she might even be able to get to her horse and escape.

She glanced toward the closed flaps at the entranceway, wondering where her horse was.

And her pistol? Where was *it*?

She stroked Gray's fur and frowned at Cloud Eagle, confused by his continued silence. Never, since she had met him, had he been this distant, this aloof. She feared the cause.

Cloud Eagle was aware of confusing Alicia by his silence. But he was not ready to speak to her just yet this morning. His troubled thoughts had kept him from sleeping all night. Today he had to make decisions and be on about his usual business.

Yet his thoughts were not clear and manageable as they were before he had met the white woman. He was nettled with many complications now—two wives, and yet no children, and a white woman he desired to have as a wife.

These were seeds for deeper pondering, for where man's cunning ended, woman's cunning began. A man who wished to master a woman must first master himself!

He was in no mood at this time for clear thinking and making logical decisions. There was no solid ground for his thoughts to stand upon. The only thing that mattered now was that the white woman was in his dwelling where the scent of dried grass blended with the smell of her.

He smiled to himself, thinking that, yes, she was there, and she would not soon be going anywhere.

Neither her wound nor he would allow it.

Cloud Eagle went to the fire and shoved more wood into the flames.

Alicia silently watched him, then tried her luck at breaking the silence between them.

"Your wives," she said, moving into a sitting position. "Where are they?"

She savored the warmth of the fire, which was

chasing the moist chill from the air this early morning.

Cloud Eagle turned his eyes to her. "Do not concern yourself about my wives," he said in an indifferent tone. "They are useless, troublesome women."

Cloud Eagle found it easy to condemn his wives for his lodge being without the laughter of children, when deep inside his heart there was the nagging fear that *he* was the cause.

Two wives? Both barren? No. That did not seem logical.

But until proven otherwise, he would cast the blame on them to save face for himself. It would be deplorable to think that a powerful Apache chief was not virile enough to send fertile seeds into the wombs of his wives.

No. He would not allow himself to believe that, or else all was lost to him. He would lose face among his people. He would be a child again in their eyes, instead of a man!

He turned back to his task of placing more wood on the fire. Alicia watched him, stunned by his attitude about his wives, wary of it. She also recalled how they had treated her so coldly, their every movement, their every angry stare, filled with jealousy.

Alicia studied Cloud Eagle's handsome features, understanding why his wives saw her as a threat. No woman would want to gain, then lose, the love of this powerfully handsome Apache chief. Perhaps not even herself.

When he suddenly left and she was alone with her thoughts and fears of what might become of her today, she felt Cloud Eagle's absence like a heavy weight around her shoulders. She tried to rise, but the pain was still too severe to put her full weight on the leg.

Unhappily, she watched the entrance flap, waiting for it to rise again. She wondered who would enter next—Cloud Eagle, his wives, or those she had not yet become acquainted with?

She fought back the hungry ache at the pit of her stomach. Food should be her last concern. Survival was her prime concern. Although Cloud Eagle had treated her as though she were something special, his attitude today had changed.

He was no longer as friendly. He did not seem as kind. Perhaps he had thought over her presence more carefully and realized that she did not belong in his stronghold.

How he was going to be rid of her was anyone's guess.

Just as Alicia had decided to lie back down, she jerked herself to a sitting position again when Cloud Eagle came back into the tepee. Her eyes widened when he brought her a basin of water, in which floated a bar of soap and a cloth with which to bathe herself.

She then gazed at the dress that was draped over one of his arms, and the moccasins that were peeking out from beneath the dress, folded into the skirt.

"Bathe and dress," he said, handing the dress and moccasins to her after he placed the basin of water on the floor beside her. "No longer will you look like an *ish-kay-nay*. You will be a woman."

He smiled slowly down at her. "But I would still rather address you with an Indian name than a white. *Ish-kay-nay* has worked thus far. So shall it remain, evermore. It will remind us both of how you were before you became transformed into a true woman."

Alicia knew that arguing with him about anything, especially a foolish Indian name, was a waste of time.

She hesitated, then took the clothes. She would be glad to get out of her stinking, blood-ravaged breeches and sweaty shirt. Even the moccasins looked inviting. It was a good excuse to throw the damnable boots into the fire.

"Call me what you must," she said sourly. "I won't be here long enough for it to matter."

"No thank-you again for my gift of clothes that I give you?" Cloud Eagle said, then shrugged and rose to leave. As he walked away, he spoke to her over his shoulder. "You will bathe in privacy. I meet in council with my warriors. My wives are busy with morning chores in the garden."

Alicia stared at him. She so badly wanted to thank him for being so generous with her after she had doubted him.

But the words just would not come. He still had not proven to her that he was not involved in the ambush. Until she knew absolutely that he was not, she would not let her guard down.

Then she recalled and blushed over those times when she had allowed herself to forget that he was possibly her enemy.

When he had kissed her.

Oh, Lord, it had been so hard to think that he could shoot her, then be so sweet to her.

She pursed her lips as he left the tepee, thinking that perhaps guilt was his reason for treating her so grandly—guilt for having taken advantage of a woman, when he thought he had ambushed and shot a man!

"A noble warrior and chief," she whispered sarcastically to herself as she plucked the soap from the water. "Hah. Scoundrel is more like it."

She placed the soap to her nose and sniffed. Lilacs. It smelled like lilacs. She would never have thought that Indians would own bars of soap.

Unless they had been taken forcefully from innocent travelers.

"Or traded for at a trading post?" she hoped aloud.

As quickly as she could, to avoid anyone who might decide to come into the tepee too soon, she stripped off her clothes. She laid them aside and momentarily covered her breasts with her folded arms.

Voices. She heard voices that were too close for comfort. If Cloud Eagle had told her to change clothes purposely to get her fully undressed, he could come at any moment.

Her heart pounded. She glued her eyes to the entrance flap.

When the voices passed on by outside and faded into the breeze, she sighed heavily and proceeded to take her sponge bath.

She wished for a regular bath, where she could immerse herself fully in the water. But as she became sparkling clean, smelling like the flowers of the forests that she had explored near Saint Louis, she again recalled Cloud Eagle telling her that he would take her into the river for a bath.

"When?" she whispered, once again staring at the entrance flap.

Her shoulders slouched with relief, realizing that it would surely not be today. He would not have brought her bath water if he had planned to give her a dunking in the river.

After she was finished with her bath, she slipped the dress over her head. It was made of deerskin and extended to the knees with a fringe. It was ornamented with bits of bright, tiny pieces of glass.

She then slipped her feet into the moccasins. They came only a little above the ankles, with button-like projections at the toes.

The dress felt cottony soft against her flesh, but she felt something hard in the pocket that distracted her. She slipped her hand inside the pocket and withdrew a strange-looking gadget. She eyed it curiously. It looked as though it had been made from stiff porcupine quills.

"Is this meant to be used as a comb or hairbrush?" she whispered, arching an eyebrow.

She smiled as she recalled how Cloud Eagle had admired her hair shortly after he had discovered that she was a woman instead of a man. He apparently still found her hair fascinating. The comb could be his way of telling her to make her hair more presentable and lovely for him.

"For meanness I shouldn't," she said as she ran her fingers over the quills.

Yet she knew that *she* would feel much better if she rid her hair of its witch's knots and tangles.

Stretching her sore leg out on the pallet of furs, she proceeded to comb her hair. In only moments she had it lying across her shoulders in a coppery sheen. She ran her fingers through it, enjoying its clean, slick feel. She had managed to give it a slight washing in the basin so that even it now smelled like flowers.

She lay the comb aside and shoved the basin away from her. Her stomach ached and growled. There was no way to forget how hungry she was.

And just as she was allowing herself to recall the wonders of a bacon-and-egg breakfast with flapjacks piled a mile high, dripping in butter and sorghum, Cloud Eagle entered, carrying a tray of food.

As he placed the tray before Alicia, she eyed it hungrily, then slipped her eyes upward and gazed at Cloud Eagle. She was very aware of how he was staring at her. It made her pulse race. The strange feelings that were now troubling the pit of her stomach were not only hunger pangs, but something else too. She had experienced this feeling before with Cloud Eagle. It was sweet and sensual.

And she knew the dangers in that. They were alone. Their feelings for one another lay heavy in the air. She wanted him, surely as a woman wanted a man.

And she could not allow him to know this. Not until she totally trusted him. She did not want to be put off guard by any more of his kisses.

To try and forget his presence, Alicia dove into the food and began eating with her fingers. There were all sorts of vegetables and meats, and the fruit of the yucca. As she ate, she could still feel his eyes on her, even when she realized that he had gone to sit on the other side of the fire from her.

Cloud Eagle could not help but stare at Alicia. He had seen how beautiful she was in the painting. Today, she was just as breathtaking. Her long hair fell beautifully over her shoulders, its brilliant red color more pronounced against the white doeskin dress. She was alluring, slender, and dainty. The clean fragrance of her skin wafted across the fire. He inhaled and closed his eyes, wanting her so badly at this moment that it hurt.

He knew that her want was just as fierce. He had felt it in the way she responded to his kisses. He had seen it in her eyes.

Even when she had been defiant and spiteful to him, he had seen that she could not hide her feelings beneath such a false exterior.

Comfortably full, Alicia pushed the half-emptied platter aside. She drew a blanket around her shoulders as Cloud Eagle rose from the floor and approached her. When he got too close, she inched her way back on the pallet of furs.

"Stay away from me," she warned. "You are a thief. You are an abductor. Once I am well enough, I will escape from your clutches. Just you wait and see. I know the art of moving through the dark without being detected as well as any Apache."

Tired of the accusations and her false front of pretending to hate him, Cloud Eagle stopped and glared down at her, then left the tepee without a word.

When he returned with Red Crow at his side, Alicia grew quiet and tense. She looked guardedly from one to the other, waiting to see what Cloud Eagle's next tactic might be.

What truly concerned her was that she now had two Apaches facing her with disgruntled looks on their faces.

And she had no idea what sort of man Red Crow was, or what his status in life might be— whether or not he already had a wife, or many. If Cloud Eagle was tired of bantering with her, he might just have decided to give her to another Apache warrior for his pleasure.

"Red Crow, I have brought you here to stand in front of the white woman so that she can hear me give you the command to take your choice of warriors to Sandy Whiskers' outpost," Cloud Eagle said, his eyes never leaving Alicia. "I am almost certain that the sandy-haired, bearded Englishman is responsible for this woman's ambush. Go to him. Demand the return of this woman's mail sack. Then bring it to me to prove the innocence of our band of Apache. It is the only way this woman will know that none of our Apache took part in the ambush."

Red Crow stared angrily down at Alicia. He saw her as an interference in the lives of the Apache. But he had received the direct order from his chief. He nodded and left.

Alicia was silent for a moment. She and Cloud Eagle exchanged unwavering gazes, then she laughed sarcastically. "Sandy Whiskers is a peaceful man," she said, giving Cloud Eagle her most defiant look. "All he is guilty of is trading furs. The United States Army ignores Sandy Whiskers' activities. They see his presence in the area as unimportant. He has built a wall around his outpost only because he does not feel safe from renegade Indians like you."

Cloud Eagle returned the sarcasm. "The stocky Englishman has the white-eyed pony soldiers at Fort Thomas fooled. But not Cloud Eagle," he said, his eyes narrowing. "This Apache knows that the Englishman trapper has outlaws and Indian renegades under his command who occasionally raid stagecoaches and attack white settlers. I have not pointed these indiscretions out to the United States Government because I use the Englishman for my own purposes. For my silence, the Englishman pays the Apache quite well—with farming implements, clothing, and firearms. It is the Apache's way to blackmail the evil Englishman."

"If what you say is true, then you are no better than Sandy Whiskers if you allow him to wreak havoc on the countryside," she accused him.

"What this Apache chief does, he does for the survival of his people," he said, placing a hand over his heart. "Much has been taken from the Apache. Cloud Eagle is taking back what he can, one item at a time."

Fueled by anger and what she felt was deceit, Alicia tried to stand in an effort to leave. She fell back down onto the pallet of furs. Wincing with pain, she felt tears flooding her eyes. She grabbed her leg.

"You are still in pain?" Cloud Eagle said. Seeing her discomfort erased from his mind all of the anger and frustration that he had felt moments ago. "The herbal mixture did not altogether work. I will go for Moon Shadow, the stronghold's shaman. Besides the chief, he is the most powerful and most influential member of our tribe."

"No!" Alicia screamed at him. "I don't want any shaman near me. A shaman is good for nothing but to feed on your people's fear of witchcraft."

Cloud Eagle took a shaky step away from her, his eyes filled with horror. "Do not say such things," he said, his voice wary. "Yes, our shaman has an ever-present consciousness of the supernatural. But it is because the Apache have a dread of witches—those malevolent beings that work their evil spells through certain animals and natural forces. The bear, the owl, the snake. The shaman protects us from these things we fear. He does not play *upon* those fears, as you suggest."

"I don't care what you say, or what *you* think about this shaman. I do not wish to be in his company," Alicia said stiffly.

"I go for Moon Shadow now, and not only for his healing powers over wounds, but over souls that need mending," Cloud Eagle said, then left her alone with her dread.

"I've got to get out of here," Alicia whispered.

Sweat pearled her brow as she again tried to stand on the leg. She struggled and groaned, then fell again to the pallet of furs.

Breathing hard, Alicia felt helpless. She watched the entrance flap, waiting for it to rise.

She then looked desperately around her. She needed something to throw at the shaman as soon as he entered the tepee. That would certainly discourage him from practicing his voodoo over her.

The platter of half-eaten food caught her eye. Smiling devilishly, she lifted it into her hand and watched again, and waited.

Chapter Seven

When Cloud Eagle still did not return with the shaman, Alicia set the platter of food aside.

Moments later, strange chanting and praying from somewhere outside the tepee caused her spine to stiffen. She swallowed hard. Moon Shadow had surely arrived.

The shaman's chants became higher in pitch, mystical and frightening. Alicia had not told Cloud Eagle that she was also superstitious, perhaps as much as the Apache.

And she had heard people talk about *hoddentin*—a powder made from the tule plant—which a shaman sometimes used while performing his duties. She hoped that Moon Shadow would not use it around her. Although for the most part people saw it as harmless, because of her superstitions, she feared it.

She recalled having read about *hoddentin*. The Apache sprinkled it on the body of the dead, and anything pertaining to death was morbid to Alicia. She had not yet totally gotten over the death of her parents.

The entrance flap was quickly drawn aside and Cloud Eagle entered, then moved to one side to allow Moon Shadow's entrance.

Alicia stared at the medicine man. She had never seen anyone quite like him before. His hair was as white as snow and so long that it dragged on the floor as he slowly entered the tepee.

He wore an ornamented buckskin medicine shirt. The decorations were symbolic of the sun, moon, stars, rain, lightning, rainbow, and clouds. Also she could make out other designs of snakes, centipedes, and tarantulas.

Her eyes narrowed as she stared at one of the most mysterious accessories of the shaman—the medicine cord. There were four cords, beautifully decorated. She had heard rumors that the cords were so sacred that strangers were not allowed to look upon or talk about them. They were known to be in evidence on the person of the medicine man only on the most important occasions, as they were believed to possess the very greatest efficacy. Only the leading shaman could make them.

For Cloud Eagle to have allowed Alicia to look upon the shaman's medicine cords made her realize just how important she was to him.

Yet that did not make the shaman's practices any more acceptable to her.

She gave Cloud Eagle a pleading look when he gave her a quick glance. Still he did not take the shaman away. He allowed Moon Shadow to approach her, his monotonous chants unnerving her.

Cassie Edwards

Moon Shadow stopped and stood over Alicia.
When he reached for a small pouch tied at his
waist, fear gripped her heart. *Hoddentin*. He was
surely going to sprinkle her with *hoddentin*. The
memory of her parents in their coffins suddenly
burned a path through her mind!

In her mind's eye she could remember the waxy
appearances of their faces.

In her mind's eye she could see the wounds on
their brows that no amount of makeup could
hide—the result of an outlaw's bullets.

Panic seized her when Moon Shadow sprinkled
some of the powdery substance into the palm of
his hand. She grabbed a piece of firewood and
threw it at him. "Get out!" she screamed. "I have
no use for you. Don't come near me. I don't want
you to perform your hocus-pocus on me. I will
get well in good time, on my own. I already feel
stronger."

She sucked in a wild breath when she saw the
complete look of horror in Moon Shadow's dark
eyes as he stopped dead in his tracks after the
piece of wood struck him on the leg.

Cloud Eagle's eyes widened and his insides
froze when he saw Alicia's blatant disrespect
toward his shaman. Of course, she had warned
him not to bring the shaman to her. He had even
seen her initial fear of the shaman when he had
entered.

Yet he had never expected her to react in such
a violent way.

His mouth opened to shout at her, to tell her
not to throw anything else at Moon Shadow, but
he was too late. Alicia had already thrown the
platter of food at his people's spiritual leader.

Cloud Eagle sighed with relief when the plate

fell short and the food did not splash all over Moon Shadow's medicine shirt. That would be sacrilegious, a sin punishable by death.

And Cloud Eagle wanted nothing to happen to Alicia.

That was the main reason he had brought the shaman to her. To heal her.

Cloud Eagle waited with bated breath to see Moon Shadow's reaction. He was not at all surprised when the shaman turned on a heel and left without saying a word, nor did he cast Cloud Eagle even the slightest glance.

Cloud Eagle expected that this incident would never be spoken about between them. Moon Shadow knew Cloud Eagle's special feelings for the white woman. Cloud Eagle had revealed them to the shaman when he had asked him to come and heal her.

Moon Shadow had honored his chief's wishes by coming. So would he honor his chief's feelings about the white woman by not doing anything to jeopardize her safety in the stronghold of the Coyotero Apache.

Moon Shadow's exit left a strained silence behind him. Cloud Eagle's and Alicia's eyes locked. Nothing was said between them for a moment longer.

Then Cloud Eagle tightened his jaw. His eyes were filled with fire. It was like the last nine miles to water when one was thirsty, those few steps it took before his hands closed upon Alicia's wrists. Glaring at her, he pushed her down onto the pallet.

"You know that what you did was wrong," he said between clenched teeth. "And you know that you should be punished for such disrespect."

"Go ahead," Alicia demanded. She was angry, yet at the same time breathless as he leaned down over her, his powerful body so close. "Punish me. What do I care? And do not expect me to apologize for what I did. I told you not to bring the shaman into your tepee while I am here. My beliefs do not include a medicine man."

"Knowing that you are different from most women, and that you stand up and defend what you feel is right, is why I will not punish you," Cloud Eagle said, his lips drawing closer to hers. "Do you not know how you fire this chief's insides?"

Before she could talk back to him, Cloud Eagle grabbed her by the hair and yanked her face close to his. Holding her there, he burned a kiss onto her lips.

Alicia gasped, then melted into his embrace.

She was left shaken when he jerked himself free of her and left the tepee.

Stunned, she reached her fingers to her lips. They were still pulsing from the hard, passionate kiss. She realized that she was caught in his spell and felt helpless and torn because of it. If moments ago, when she reacted to the shaman in such a violent way, was an example of how she might feel about other Apache beliefs and customs, there would surely be no place for her in the life of an Apache chief.

But on the other hand, she found that more and more, as time wore on, her thoughts drifted to Cloud Eagle and how it might feel to spend forever with him.

Then she just as quickly reminded herself that even though he had over and over again confessed to being innocent of the crime that she was accusing him of, she did not have absolute proof. Until she did, she would have to continue putting on a protective front. The kiss that they had shared only a few heart-beats ago was a mistake and must not be repeated.

Spring Dawn and Lost Wind entered the lodge. Glaring at Alicia, they sat down beside the fire.

She looked guardedly from one to the other. They both looked bone-weary and sweaty, which had to mean that they had already labored hard this morning. The day had just begun and yet they had returned to their lodge. She wondered if she was the cause for their return to the tepee instead of continuing their work outside.

Had Cloud Eagle sent them there to guard her so that she would not escape in his absence?

She cast that conclusion aside. It was obvious that if she tried to escape, those two women would be more than eager to assist her and Cloud Eagle was intelligent enough to know that. He surely knew jealousy when he saw it.

Cloud Eagle ran to the river and sat down beneath a cottonwood tree. Troubled, he stared into the water. The image of Alicia was everlasting in his head, the fiery taste of her still in his mouth. Until he met her, he had given his undivided attention to his future, as the master of tribal affairs. He had taken two wives to guard himself well from the clutches of only one particular woman. To be chief of a household was one thing and chief of a tribe quite another. Now he felt like a wall of black cloud with a fork of lightning in the center!

He shifted his weight, then rose slowly to his feet and began pacing beside the river. He knew that there were two ways to break this spell that he was suddenly caught up in.

He could take Alicia as his wife.

Or he could turn his back on her and return her to her people.

After much more pacing and much more thinking, he knew what the choice must be. Alicia was a part of him now, almost as much as the air that he breathed.

Alicia stared at the entrance flap, wishing that Cloud Eagle would return. She didn't feel safe alone with the two jealous wives.

Yet she didn't feel all that safe while with him. His most recent kiss surely preceded even more intimate moments with him. What she feared most was that she might yield to him, whereas until she met Cloud Eagle, no other man had ever so much as dared come near her.

She feared that beautifully delicious feeling that Cloud Eagle had aroused in her which made her aware of her femininity.

Alicia breathed shallowly when Lost Wind left, then returned with a platter of food and sat it before Alicia.

The growling of Alicia's stomach made her know that more time than she realized had passed. She looked up at the smoke hole. The sun was at its center point in the sky. It was noon, when she usually ate her second meal of the day.

Alicia eyed Cloud Eagle's two wives suspiciously when she noticed that they were not eating, but were watching her with amusement in their eyes.

Then she studied the food laid out before her. Could she safely eat something that the jealous wives gave her? Yet the food looked innocent enough—like some sort of meat. And its smell was tantalizing.

Wanting to busy her fingers while awaiting Cloud Eagle's return, and wanting to fill the hunger that was gnawing at the pit of her stomach, Alicia picked up one piece of the meat and placed it delicately into her mouth. She chewed it slowly, trying to guess what it might be. Though the taste was somewhat peculiar, it was good.

Curiosity got the best of her.

"What have I been served?" she asked as she picked up another piece of the meat.

Lost Wind and Spring Dawn gave each other mischievous smiles, then gazed at Alicia and giggled.

"We have prepared lizard for the white woman," Lost Wind said, once again giggling as she watched for Alicia's reaction.

Alicia gagged and threw the remainder of the meat into the fire. Swallowing hard, she desperately wiped at her mouth with her hands. "You spiteful wenches," she hissed.

Chapter Eight

Stony silence fell inside the tepee when Cloud Eagle entered. His jaw was set. His eyes were on Alicia.

Seeing something different about his attitude, Alicia followed his movements as he walked past her and grabbed his bow and slipped it over his shoulders, then fastened a quiver made of a wildcat's pelt with the tail hanging down at his back.

When he went to Alicia and swept her into his arms and carried her toward the entranceway, she was so stunned by the suddenness of his action that she did not have the chance to lodge a complaint.

They were so quickly gone from the tepee, and she was so quickly placed on the saddle of panther skin on his horse, that she was left breathless.

"*Ish-kay-nay*, say nothing spiteful about what I do," Cloud Eagle said as he swung himself into the saddle behind her. "I am going to take you to a special place."

Alicia looked over her shoulder at him. Their eyes momentarily locked. "Where? Where are you taking me?" she asked guardedly.

"You did not allow my shaman to perform his magic over you to help heal your leg," Cloud Eagle said, lifting the reins. "You will surely not object to a thing of nature that can work healing powers on one's wounds."

"Nature?" Alicia said, grabbing at her sore leg when the horse jolted into a soft trot through the stronghold. "Cloud Eagle, please don't tell me that you are going to place more herbal medications on my leg. What you used before did seem to help. But how can you be sure that any other herbs might work as well?"

He clung around her waist and held her close to him as he left the stronghold and sent his roan into a gallop. "No more herbs," he said flatly. "Water. Water will show you its healing powers."

"You are going farther upstream, away from the stronghold, so that we can have privacy in a river?" she asked warily.

"No," he said, his mood lightening. His eyes danced into hers. "No river."

"Then where?" Alicia asked impatiently.

"Cloud Eagle takes you where hot springs flow freely from the ground," he said, glad that she was not sparring with him angrily. He knew that she had a soft, vulnerable side. Slowly it was being revealed to him. "This water has healing powers."

"Of course you will insist on going into the water with me," she said, forcing sarcasm into her voice. She turned her eyes from him and envisioned him as she had seen him nude that one time. The remembrance sent waves of sensual pleasure through her.

"And you would object?" Cloud Eagle said, recalling how he had caught her staring at him the one time she had seen him naked.

He smiled. More than once he had seen the hunger of a woman for a man in her eyes. He had tasted it on her lips as he had kissed her.

And no matter how spiteful she pretended to be, she was nothing at all like Lost Wind, who knew the art of being spiteful so well.

Lost Wind's ugly disposition was her true personality.

Alicia's was all pretense.

Soon that would change, he convinced himself. Patience. He just had to practice being patient until she revealed her true self to him, and her true feelings for him.

His question drew Alicia's eyes back to him. "What did you say?" she gasped.

"I asked you if you would object if I joined you in the water," he repeated, his eyes dancing into hers.

"You think that I would not?" she asked, her voice quavering.

"I think not," Cloud Eagle said. His lips tugged into a slow, teasing smile.

Alicia's lips parted, then she failed to come up with a reply that could sting the confidence from his voice.

She turned her eyes away again, her pulse racing. And to try and forget what might happen these next few hours, she concentrated on everything but Cloud Eagle and her tumultuous feelings about him.

They rode past fruit-bearing plants at the foot of the mountain, then past piñon nuts growing in cool groves. Bees were humming around various blossoms.

They rode onward until the sun began its descent in the sky and frogs sang along the riverbank.

Still they rode onward until the evening took on the soft glow of twilight.

Alicia wondered if they would ever come to their destination. She was sore and aching all over. The wound on her leg throbbed.

"The older people of the Apache tribe think highly of going to the hot springs, to boil themselves after the chill leaves the air," Cloud Eagle said, suddenly breaking the silence between himself and Alicia. "It is also a place of conference, where headmen and medicine men sit for hours while waiting for those thoughts which come best when the sweat is flowing free."

"How can such a place be so popular with your people when it is so far away from your stronghold?" Alicia asked wearily. "We've been traveling for hours. Lord, Cloud Eagle, are we about there?"

"Yes, soon," Cloud Eagle said, nodding. "And the distance ensures privacy."

"Privacy?" Alicia said sarcastically. "When so many have access to it?"

"Cloud Eagle knows when it is being used, and by whom," he said. "Tonight it is solely ours."

The thought of being alone with him, away from everyone else, caused another sensual thrill

97

to soar through Alicia, one that she did not wish to feel.

Yet she could not deny that she was being caught up more and more in a web of desire for him. She could not deny the thunderous beating of her heart when she recalled his fiery kisses and the passion they had aroused in her.

She was fighting these feelings, as well as Cloud Eagle, but losing the battle. Her heart, her need for Cloud Eagle, was becoming the victor.

Oh, but if she could just be certain that he was not capable of crimes against the white community. It would make it much simpler to love him.

"There is a waterfall close to the spring," Cloud Eagle said, guessing the cause for her silence. He knew that she wanted him. He knew that she was fighting this want with every fiber of her being.

He also knew that she was losing the battle and that her heart would be the victor.

"The uppermost cup of the falls that tumble into the spring is a huge, smooth basin where one can sit on a hot day in the spray until chilled to the bone and then step out onto a dry cleft and know what it means to be brought back to life by the sun on the rocks," he continued saying.

"You speak as though you have been there often," Alicia said, turning to gaze up at him. "Have you taken many—many women there?"

"Cloud Eagle has taken no woman to the hot springs, until now," he said thickly.

His dark eyes, and the meaning behind his words, caused Alicia's insides to melt.

She turned away from him again. Night came quickly. She was almost swallowed whole by her wildly beating heart when she saw the waterfall up ahead in the moonlight, and then the misty haze that spiraled up from the stream at the foot of the falls.

Her knees weakened, for she knew that she had arrived at the place where she might lose all of her reason, and even all her inhibitions. She wanted Cloud Eagle that much. Her every nerve ending seemed to cry out to be caressed by his masterful hands.

Cloud Eagle drew a tight rein and stopped his horse close beside the hot springs. He dismounted and spread a blanket on the ground. He then helped Alicia down from the saddle and carried her to the blanket.

Breathless, her eyes wide, Alicia watched Cloud Eagle unsaddle his horse, then stake it to a strong picket pin in the tall grass. She gasped when she recognized a small pouch that he took from his saddle. It looked similar to the one used by the shaman. And she knew that she was right when Cloud Eagle opened the pouch and sprinkled some of the *hoddentin* powder into the palm of his hand.

He took a pinch of the *hoddentin* and blew it toward the dark east. Another pinch he blew west.

She breathed much more easily when he placed the pouch back inside his saddlebag. She could not get over her dread of the powder. It reminded her again of the differences in her own culture and the Apache. It made her realize the foolishness of allowing herself to feel anything but a loathing for this Apache.

But when he came to her, all muscle and so handsome, and sat down beside her, again revealing his gentle ways to her, she knew that she could never loathe this man.

When he removed the quiver of arrows from his back, slipped the bow from across his shoulder, and laid them beside the blanket, Alicia imagined that this was the moment when he would ask her to disrobe, and when he would also remove his clothes, so that they could enter the water together.

The prospect unnerved her because she knew that he would have to carry her. Her leg was too sore to attempt entering the water alone.

"The *hoddentin* powder has been offered to the spirits so that goodness will attend your thoughts," Cloud Eagle said, looking past her at the hazy steam that was rising from the water. "These springs flow from the spirit hills in which the sun dies each evening. It smiles upon my people with its bounty."

Alicia badly wanted to point out the error of these things that he said, but she could not find it within herself this time to tell him that these things that he did and said were foolish.

This time something held back such spiteful words and she knew that it was his mysterious allure that was drawing her into caring for him. He was such a gentle man. He was so thoughtful. Not once had he given her a true reason to fear him. From the beginning he had treated her with a respect and gentleness that she had never gotten from any other man—except her father.

She had avoided all other men like poison. That was the only way she could survive in a land where she had been left alone, without family.

Fleetingly she remembered Charlie and wondered where he might be.

The letter.

If she could have only gotten the letter to him.

Suddenly all her concerns for her brother, and her special feelings for Cloud Eagle, fled from Alicia's mind when a low growl rolled through the air.

Cloud Eagle sprang to his feet, took an arrow from his quiver, and notched the arrow to his bow. He searched with his eyes for the beast that filled the night with its threatening sounds. He looked overhead. Creeping along a limb was the most dreaded of the night creatures—the mountain panther.

Cloud Eagle stumbled backwards and dropped his bow and arrow as the panther leapt upon him and tore at the flesh of one of his arms with its jagged teeth. Cloud Eagle struggled with the panther and was finally able to grab the beast by the throat and hold it at bay.

Her father having taught her the skills of archery, Alicia moved quickly. Everything within her knew that she wanted no further harm to come to Cloud Eagle. She loved him. With all of her heart and soul, she adored him. She pulled the bowstring taut and released an arrow.

The arrow flew through the air and struck the panther in a hind leg. A terrible scream of pain followed. Cloud Eagle then knocked the animal away.

The panther staggered and stumbled. The chill moonlight held the cat in its glow. Its terrible green eyes were still fixed on Cloud Eagle. The panther growled deeply. There was hunger and pain in its face.

Trembling, knowing that she must kill the panther to save Cloud Eagle, Alicia scrambled for another arrow and sent it into the panther's side, stopping the animal just as it was preparing to leap again.

When the animal fell over dead, Cloud Eagle rose to his feet. He was stunned by it all, especially by Alicia's showing that she cared enough to save his life. It proved that he might be able to pull her into totally loving him.

Horrified by the sight of the wound on Cloud Eagle's arm, Alicia dropped the bow and arrow to the ground. She took his hand and led him to the stream.

Cupping water into her hands, she slowly drizzled it over Cloud Eagle's wound; all the while, Cloud Eagle gazed at her with dark, wondering eyes.

Forgetting the pain of his wound, Cloud Eagle suddenly pulled Alicia into his arms and kissed her passionately.

She twined her arms around his neck and returned the kiss, body and soul lost to this gorgeous man.

She no longer resented being with him. She wanted to be there, to be loved by him.

Cloud Eagle picked Alicia up and carried her far from the death scene. He laid her beneath a cottonwood tree and began to slowly undress her. He was not surprised when she allowed it. He could read the passion in her eyes. He had felt it in her kiss.

"Your arm," Alicia questioned softly. "Surely it pains you too much to . . ."

He placed a soft hand over her mouth, stopping her words. "I feel nothing at this moment but my need for you," he said huskily. "Do you want me as well? You proved your love by saving my life."

Totally undressed, and not ashamed of it as

she would have expected, Alicia reached her arms around Cloud Eagle's neck and drew his mouth to her lips. This action gave him her permission to teach her the meaning of being a true woman.

As they kissed, Cloud Eagle disrobed. Shadows seemed to dance across the water as Alicia drifted toward him and started to yield to his lovemaking, then pulled away from him.

"Your wives?" she said faintly, questioning him with her eyes.

"They share my lodge, but not my heart, or my bed," he said huskily. "For so long I have not seen them as wives. They have been useless to me. From this night forth, Cloud Eagle will never again refer to them as wives."

Alicia heard in his voice the sincerity of his words, and although she did not understand his feelings for the women he had married, she felt the freedom to love him as she so very much desired.

And how he loved her.

It was with an exquisite tenderness.

As his fingers ran down her body, caressing her, she shivered. Then his fingers surrounded her slim, white thighs and lifted her to him as he moved over her.

She held her breath when he parted her legs and she felt the hardness of his manhood resting against her flesh. Her pulse raced when he probed softly at the center of her desire. In her mind's eye, she was recalling how large he was.

Her heart fluttered wildly with the thought of him filling her so magnificently. And when he reached her shield of womanhood, tenderly breaking it, the pain was brief.

She relaxed and savored how it felt to have a

man enter her for the first time. She became dizzy with pleasure when he began taking delicate, leisurely thrusts within her.

She clung around his neck.

She kissed him with a fierce abandon.

As though practiced, she lifted her hips to make herself more accessible and open for him. The sensations he was arousing within her as he buried himself more deeply inside her were searing. She was no longer even aware of the pain in her leg. His loving her was erasing everything from her consciousness but sheer blissful pleasure.

One kiss blended into another. Cloud Eagle tried to keep his weight off her sore leg. He tried to protect his wounded arm by holding it away from her.

But it was hard to concentrate on anything but loving her. He was filled with a drugged passion that he had never experienced before.

He cupped her breasts, the soft touch of them causing his senses to reel in drunken pleasure.

His hands on her breasts caused a searing, scorching flame to shoot through Alicia. She roamed her hands over his muscled shoulders, sleek back, and hard buttocks with wildness and desperation.

Feelings that she never knew before were being awakened within her. She felt as though she were floating, flying, soaring with joy. She was wild and weak with sexual excitement.

Then she felt the ultimate pleasure sweep through her. She shuddered, arched, and cried out, just as Cloud Eagle's body shook and quavered into hers, his groans filling the night air.

With a sob, Alicia clung to him.

He leaned away from her and looked down into

her eyes. "Why do you cry?" he asked, brushing a damp strand of her hair from her eyes. "Did I hurt you?"

"I'm not sure why I'm crying," Alicia said, wiping tears from her cheeks. She smiled awkwardly up at him. "I rarely cry. But Cloud Eagle, I couldn't help it. You brought feelings out in me that were so deliciously sweet. Did I do the same for you?"

"I could never describe the extent of my feelings for you," Cloud Eagle said, brushing a kiss across her lips. He caressed her breasts, causing Alicia to close her eyes and moan with pleasure.

She trembled with ecstasy when he placed his mouth over a nipple and lapped it with his tongue. She sighed heavily when he rose away from her. She looked up at him, her eyes roaming slowly over his nakedness, seeing him as nothing less than beautiful.

Her eyes locked on that part of him that had sent her into another world. She leaned up on her knees and touched him there. She circled him with her fingers and looked smilingly up at him.

He placed a hand over hers and guided her hand into caressing him. He closed his eyes and stiffened when he felt the pleasure mounting again.

Alicia could sense the thrill that she was causing Cloud Eagle and continued moving her hand even when he removed his from over hers. She watched in total surprise when something soon spilled forth from his manhood just as he gave off another groan of pleasure.

He stepped away from her and gave her no explanation. Instead, he grabbed her up into his arms and carried her into the steaming water.

Giggling and laughing, they bathed each other with the warm water, stopping only long enough to kiss and to touch each other's bodies.

Soon Cloud Eagle carried her to dry land. "Did you feel the healing power of the water?" he asked, slowly dressing her.

"How could I be aware of anything other than you?" Alicia asked, amazed at how free she felt now to speak peacefully and lovingly with him. "Cloud Eagle, I'm not even sure yet that you are not the renegade who caused my misery, and I gave my all to you. Wouldn't you call that foolish?"

"You are foolish to continue clouding your thoughts with doubts," he scolded. He cupped her chin with a hand. "Could I have just loved you so tenderly if I did not do it from the heart?"

"You could have had a change of heart since the ambush," Alicia murmured, then wished she hadn't when she saw the hurt in his eyes.

"I do not wish to discuss it anymore," Cloud Eagle said, searching her face. "As I look at you, I see the light of the stars in your eyes. When you laugh, it is like the morning sun. You would warm the soul of any man."

His words were hypnotizing Alicia. She was speechless. She trembled when he drew her into his arms. "You are no longer an *ish-kay-nay*. You are a woman."

They kissed and clung to one another.

Then Cloud Eagle left her and dressed, his eyes on the panther in the distance. "My heart is mourning for the beast that was killed tonight," he said sadly. "It was a creature that had the same needs as humans. Tonight its hunger led it into a reckless action."

Fully clothed, Cloud Eagle lifted Alicia into his arms and carried her to the blanket that he had earlier spread for her. "Rest while I remove the animal's pelt," he said, jerking his knife from its sheath at his side. "It is yours. You killed the animal. It will be with us always, the proof of your love for this Apache chief."

Alicia reached a hand to his arm that had been injured. She ran her fingers just beneath the raw wound. "This should be bandaged," she murmured.

"The wound is nothing to worry about," Cloud Eagle said. "The water has sent its healing powers into it. The scars left by the panther's attack will be there, always, to remind me of this night and what turned your mood around in favor of this Apache chief. If not for the panther's attack, you might have never proven your love for me."

She leaned up on her knees and gently kissed his arm just beneath the wound, then placed her hands on his cheeks. "Cloud Eagle, I couldn't have held back my feelings for you much longer," she said softly. "They are so intense. They are so real."

She drew his lips to hers and kissed him, then eased away from him and sat down on the blanket. She watched Cloud Eagle and the mastery of each of his movements as he removed the pelt from the panther. She would not let any doubts ruin these precious moments with him. Her heart soared with love for this Apache chief.

Chapter Nine

The next day everything seemed different for Alicia in the way she felt about being in Cloud Eagle's stronghold. As she ate her morning meal, she watched Cloud Eagle as he peered into a fragment of glass, meticulously plucking hairs from his face. She smiled softly at him and at his way of shaving. She didn't find it crude, but innocent as were so many of the Indians' customs.

She blushed like a young schoolgirl when her thoughts drifted to the previous evening and to the way she had given herself so openly and fully to Cloud Eagle. Deep within herself she knew that she no longer doubted his honesty. It did not take Red Crow's arrival with the mail sack to prove that Cloud Eagle had not ambushed her. No man as gentle and caring as Cloud Eagle was toward her could be a marauding, murdering thief. Cloud Eagle seemed bathed in goodness, clear to the core of himself.

"You are quiet this morning," Cloud Eagle said as he slipped his mirror and tweezers into a buckskin pouch. He laid this among his personal belongings, then went to Alicia and took her empty platter and set it aside. He drew her into his arms.

"You regret having given yourself to me with such fervor?" he said huskily. "Would you rather I not hold you even now? I do need to kiss you, you know."

Her head spinning with rapture, Alicia twined her arms around Cloud Eagle's neck. "I regret nothing except not knowing you sooner," she murmured. "Cloud Eagle, I have never known such a sweet and loving man. You have changed my feelings about men. Except for my father, all the men I knew before you were brash, selfish boors."

"Boors?" Cloud Eagle questioned, raising an eyebrow. "This word boor. I do not understand its use."

Alicia laughed softly. "No, you wouldn't," she said in a low, sultry tone. "That just proves again the goodness that I have found in you."

She urged his lips to hers. Leaning closer to him, she drowned in ecstasy as they kissed and moaned against his lips when he slipped his hands down to caress her breasts through the smooth buckskin material of her dress. She flicked her tongue through his lips, amazed at herself for knowing, somehow, that this could be an even more exciting way to kiss.

Their moment of passion was interrupted when Gray came into the tepee from his early morning stroll, growling. He pushed himself between them, nudging them apart.

Sensing that something was wrong by Gray's odd behavior, Cloud Eagle knelt and stroked his coyote's fur comfortingly. "What is it?" he asked. "What troubles you?"

Gray whined pitifully and gave the entranceway a quick glance. He ran there and yelped several times, then bounced back to Cloud Eagle.

Alicia watched, then realized that Snow had not come into the tepee with Gray. "Snow," she said. "Could Gray be telling you that something has happened to Snow? Don't she and Gray usually stay together?"

Cloud Eagle sighed heavily. "Snow has done this before," he said, turning his dark eyes to Alicia. "One other time the call of the wild recaptured my she-coyote's heart. She left to mate with one of her own kind. She returned later with two pups."

Alicia glanced down at Gray, then up at Cloud Eagle. "But I thought that Gray and Snow were mates," she said, eyes wide.

"Gray is one of Snow's pups," he said, smiling when he saw the surprise in Alicia's expression. "The other pup wandered off to answer its own call of the wild."

"Then that's why Gray shows such devotion to Snow and is so upset over her absence," Alicia said, bending to give Gray an affectionate hug.

"Yes, that is the reason," Cloud Eagle said. He moved to the back of the tepee where his weapons were stored. He grabbed his bow and positioned his quiver of arrows on his back. "I will go and search for Snow just to make sure nothing has happened to her."

"I want to go also."

"I will go alone. Gray will stay and keep you company."

"If you think that is best," Alicia murmured, finding it surprisingly easy to agree with him. But since last night, when they had made love, she had felt different in every way. She doubted that she would ever argue with him again, about anything.

Cloud Eagle knelt before Gray and stroked the coyote's back. "You stay with Alicia," he commanded. "Stay. Do not follow."

Gray looked dutifully up at Cloud Eagle as though he understood English as well as a human, then barked softly.

When Cloud Eagle rose again and gave Alicia a lingering look, she moved to Gray and knelt down beside him and hugged him. "Go on," she murmured. "Gray and I will do just fine while you are gone."

She did not tell him that she was uneasy about his leaving the stronghold, especially when she knew two women who must hate her with a vengeance. Until last night, before she knew that Cloud Eagle no longer slept with or loved the women he had chosen as his wives, she had understood why they would despise the very ground that she walked on and felt some sympathy toward them.

But now, when she knew that trouble had been brewing between Cloud Eagle and his wives long before she had entered their lives, she could not condone their behavior toward her. They had to know that they had already lost his love.

No man as sweet and gentle as Cloud Eagle

would treat his wives the way he did unless he had a good reason.

She hoped to discover what the reason was soon.

"I love you, Cloud Eagle," she blurted out just as Cloud Eagle nudged the entrance flap aside with his elbow.

Cloud Eagle stopped. He looked down at Alicia and smiled warmly, his heart soaring over the confession of her love for him. "My love for you is everlasting," he said, then turned and left.

Had he told the two other women the same thing? Alicia fretted to herself. Had he told them that his love for them was everlasting?

Alicia had to find out, somehow, why he no longer loved them or claimed them as his wives. But knowing that she could not be the cause was enough for now.

Restless, she looked around the tepee for something to do. She could take the dishes to the river and wash them. That would also give her just the right amount of exercise to get the strength back in her wounded leg.

Gathering up the dishes and whistling for Gray, she left the tepee. The day was brilliant and bright; the sun was spiraling through the cottonwood trees as she hobbled beneath them.

When a fresh pain stabbed through her leg, she tried to ignore it. She walked onward, ignoring the stares from the Apache women, children, and men. She was glad when she reached the edge of the stronghold and was alone as she headed for the river, Gray devotedly beside her.

"You're my pal, aren't you, Gray?" Alicia asked, smiling down at him. Then she laughed softly. "I never thought that I would become friends with a coyote. But you're more dog than coyote, aren't you, Gray?"

Her smile faded when she thought of Snow. "I hope Snow is all right," she said beneath her breath.

She stopped with alarm when Lost Wind and Spring Dawn stepped from behind a heavy stand of bushes and blocked her way. Gray snarled and showed his fangs as he edged protectively closer to Alicia.

"Down, Gray," Alicia said, patting his head. "I'm sure they don't mean me any harm."

"White woman go away," Lost Wind said in a low hiss. "Leave. Now. You not wanted in Apache stronghold."

Spring Dawn took a bold step closer. "Your hair would look pretty on a scalp pole," she threatened, smiling devilishly at Alicia. "You go or I take scalp."

Alicia's color paled and her heart skipped a beat. She had no idea the women hated her this much.

Faced with such threats, and not sure if the women were actually capable of carrying them out, Alicia realized that she must look brave in their eyes or lose everything. Now that she had found a man who made her heart sing, she was not about to allow anyone to force her to give him up. Cloud Eagle had told her that he no longer looked to these women as his wives. She would take him at his word and fight for her right to have him for herself. Divorce was practiced in her world, and there was no shame in being in love with a divorced man, or one who would soon be divorced. She had to believe that the custom was the same in the Apache world.

"Step aside," Alicia said, lifting her chin stubbornly. "Go about your business. I shall tend to my own."

"You are our business," Spring Dawn said, stepping to Lost Wind's side. "Leave or we will force you to."

"And what would you tell Cloud Eagle about my absence?" Alicia asked, looking steadily from one to the other. "And don't you know that he would come for me if I did leave?"

"Out of sight, out of heart," Lost Wind said, laughing. "You are just a thing that has intrigued him for a short while. He would thank us if we rid his life of you."

Before Alicia could respond, Spring Dawn and Lost Wind ran up to her and spat on her face.

Enraged and gagging in horror, Alicia dropped the wooden platters to the ground. "How dare you," she cried, wiping the spit from her face.

Spring Dawn and Lost Wind moved to each side of Alicia and began kicking her.

"Stop!" Alicia screamed, pushing and shoving at the women. "You're crazy!"

Under any other circumstances, Alicia would not have stood and taken any abuse from anyone, especially these women. But she was afraid to fight back, unsure of what the people of the village might do to her, especially in Cloud Eagle's absence.

Stars seemed to explode in her head when Lost Wind hit the wound on her leg with her fist. The pain was excruciating.

Without further thought of what anybody might do if she fought the Apache women, Alicia tore into them. Her pride, and her sore leg, had taken all they could.

Gray barked and snarled as the three women tangled and rolled across the ground. Alicia ignored the pain that stabbed through her wounded leg. All that she could think about was defending herself and putting enough fear into the hearts of these women that they would never try anything with her again.

She scratched. She pulled hair. She slapped. She pummeled one and then the other with her fists until suddenly Spring Dawn and Lost Wind ran away from her, squealing.

Breathless, her whole body throbbing with pain, Alicia sat down on the ground and held her leg between her hands. Moaning, she slowly rocked back and forth.

Whining, as though he sympathized with her, Gray nudged up against Alicia and looked at her with his large gray eyes.

"I shouldn't have done that, Gray," Alicia said, sobbing when the pain became almost too much to bear. "But I couldn't allow them to humiliate me in such a way. And when Lost Wind hit my sore leg, there was no holding me back."

Through a blur of tears, she looked toward the stronghold. "I hope Cloud Eagle returns soon," she murmured. "Before Spring Dawn and Lost Wind spread rumors that might endanger me."

She placed her arms around Gray's neck and hugged him tightly. "Gray, oh, Gray, what am I to do?" she whispered. "Should I just disappear from Cloud Eagle's life? Would it be simpler for everyone concerned?"

She closed her eyes and recalled his gentleness and his ways of loving her. "No," she whispered. "I can't go. I don't want to leave Cloud Eagle ever. I love him so, Gray. Oh, how I do love him."

She sat there for a while longer, then slowly pushed herself up from the ground. She looked down at herself, groaning. The dress was stained with grass and mud. She was filthy from her head to her toes. She could even smell perspiration that had been brought forth from the strain of the fight.

She knew that she must bathe herself and wash her dress before she could return to the stronghold. And when she did return, she would go there with a lifted chin.

She prayed that Cloud Eagle would have returned by then. For the first time in her life, she felt the need for a man at her side.

Cloud Eagle pushed his way through the tangled brush of the mountainside. His eyes were alert for all movements. Thus far all he had seen were fox, squirrels, chipmunks, and deer.

When a covey of partridges suddenly shot into the air a few feet away from him, Cloud Eagle jumped with alarm, an arrow quickly notched onto his bow. But as his eyes followed the flight of the birds, he lowered the bow, removed the arrow, and slipped it back inside its quiver.

He then continued his search for Snow. It gave him a lonesome, empty feeling to think that Snow had decided to seek out a mate. He knew now that it could be several months before he saw his pet again. By then, would Snow be as tame as before?

The other time, she had returned as tame and affectionate as she had been before she left. It would depend on the coyote she mated with. If her mate taught her not to trust humans, then Snow would be lost to Cloud Eagle forever.

Shrugging, knowing that destiny would have its way with Snow regardless of anyone's feelings, Cloud Eagle chose to give up the search.

Just as he turned to return to his stronghold, he found himself face to face with Ten Bears, Lost Wind's brother. Knowing that the warrior had to be stalking him for Cloud Eagle not to have heard his approach, Cloud Eagle stood his ground, his jaw tight. He presumed Ten Bears' reason for being there was to find out why Alicia was in his lodge.

"And so you have joined the search for my pet she-coyote?" Cloud Eagle said, although he knew that was not the reason for Ten Bears' presence. He hoped to find a way to stop an altercation before it began.

"Your pet is no concern of mine," Ten Bears said stiffly. He placed a hand on the knife sheathed at his right side. "My sister is my sole purpose for following you. We now have privacy while we discuss my sister."

"So speak," Cloud Eagle said flatly. "But guard your words well. This is no ordinary man you are speaking with. This is your chief."

"I know well that you are my chief," Ten Bears said, sarcasm thick in his words. "But that was not of Ten Bears' choice."

Cloud Eagle clenched his fingers around his bow so hard that his knuckles grew white.

But he said nothing. He waited for Ten Bears to condemn himself. Lack of respect for an Apache chief was not tolerated.

"My sister came to me red-faced with humiliation and crying," Ten Bears said, his eyes flashing. "Her hair was dirty and her dress was ripped. She says the white woman is responsible."

117

Cloud Eagle's eyebrows arched.

Still he said nothing.

"She said the white woman attacked her down by the river," Ten Bears continued. "Also Spring Dawn. I found them both hiding behind your tepee afterwards. They are scared of your woman. They said she fights and has claws like a panther."

Cloud Eagle was taken aback by this. He realized that Alicia had the spunk and fire of ten women. But he could not envision her fighting two women at a time without first having been provoked—especially not Apache women. Alicia would not want to cause hard feelings among his people.

And he knew that she would not have started a fight while her leg still pained her.

He hated to think of what Spring Dawn and Lost Wind had in mind when they decided to take Alicia on in a fight. And he was certain that was what had happened.

"I demand to know what your true intentions are for this crazed white woman," Ten Bears spat out venomously. "Do you make her your wife to the exclusion of your Apache wives?"

Anger flooded Cloud Eagle's insides. This warrior was making demands of him? And this warrior called Alicia a crazed woman?

Ten Bears had stepped across the line of what was wrong and right while addressing his chief. His error brought a quick response from Cloud Eagle.

"What I have planned for the white woman is not your affair," Cloud Eagle hissed between clenched teeth. "Cloud Eagle is your chief. My affairs are my own."

"The white woman and this singular favoritism toward her breeds trouble in our stronghold," Ten Bears spat back.

"The Apache are slow to quarrel within the tribe, so why do you?" Cloud Eagle asked heatedly. "What sets you apart from the others and makes your tongue become loose with your chief?"

With a sneering smile, Ten Bears conveyed his answer. "My sister," he stated. "I demand that you do not replace my sister in your lodge with a red-headed white woman!"

"Who are you to make demands of your chief?" Cloud Eagle fired back. "You speak out of turn and disrespectfully to your chief one time too often. Because of this, I have no choice but to challenge you to a fight. The fight will be witnessed by all of our people. If you are the victor, I shall give up my title of chief and hand it over to you. If you are the loser, you shall be banished from our stronghold forever."

Cloud Eagle paused, then said something more which caused Ten Bears to teeter with the shock of it. "When you leave, you must take your sister with you," Cloud Eagle said, his voice void of emotion. "She is an embarrassment to me. She is of no use to me anymore. She is childless. To have a wife who is childless for as long as your sister has been unable to bear me a child takes away my virility in the eyes of my people."

Ten Bears stared blankly at Cloud Eagle, then turned and ran away from him.

Cloud Eagle followed behind him slowly, his thoughts troubled. He understood how it must look to his people to have taken a white woman into his lodge.

Yet before her arrival, his people had witnessed him sleeping outside his lodge for many sunrises and had to understand that for some time now the marriage was all but over between their chief and his barren wives. Alicia had nothing to do with it. It had been only a matter of time before he would have rid himself of those wives to take another.

He must have a child.

If not, his world would not be complete.

His jaw went slack and his eyes grew heavy with further thoughts about his virility. If a third wife bore him no child, he would then know, as would his people, that he was the cause, not the women he had taken to bed with him.

The thought of such a discovery caused an acute emptiness to overwhelm him.

Chapter Ten

Alicia was glad to return to the safe haven of Cloud Eagle's lodge. While she was safe inside it, she doubted there would be any repercussions over what had transpired with Spring Dawn and Lost Wind.

She even doubted the two women would enter the tepee alone with her. Though she hated doing it, she seemed to have struck fear into the hearts of Spring Dawn and Lost Wind.

It was never her intention to interrupt a family's harmony. And she knew that she hadn't. Nothing was at all normal between Cloud Eagle and his wives.

Leaning closer to the fire in the firepit, Alicia rubbed her wet hair briskly with her fingers in an effort to dry it. If nothing else had gone off as it should since Cloud Eagle's departure to look for Snow, at least her bath in the river had felt wonderfully invigorating.

She laughed and glanced over at Gray. He had even leapt into the water with her and had swum masterfully at her side. She watched him lick one paw and then another, his way of drying himself.

Moment by moment she found herself becoming more attached to Gray. Snow had always kept distant from her, but she no less wanted to see Snow returned to the safety of Cloud Eagle's protection.

"Don't fret, Gray," she said, reaching out to stroke his damp fur. "Snow will return to you. I'm not sure just when, but I'm certain she will return to you and Cloud Eagle."

As though Gray understood her, he whimpered and nudged his nose into the palm of her hand. "You are so gentle," Alicia murmured. "But of course you would be. The one who taught you how to trust men is gentle."

She looked with longing toward the entrance flap, then through the smoke hole overhead.

The sky was darkening. Cloud Eagle had been gone for far too long.

She watched the fire-thrown shadows dance across the walls of the lodge. Then she stared into the flames.

She found herself missing Cloud Eagle more than she would ever have thought possible. Because of him, her life had suddenly turned around into something sweet.

And she doubted that she would ever wear man's clothes again. How could she? She felt feminine through and through.

Because of Cloud Eagle, she felt like a woman.

Her head jerked around when Cloud Eagle entered the tepee. At first glance, she could tell that something was terribly wrong with him. She had never seen him frown so hard. She had never seen him in such an ugly mood.

She said nothing as he slammed his bow and quiver of arrows down at the back of the tepee with the rest of his weapons. She feared hearing the answer if she asked if he had found Snow. His frown had to mean that the news would not be good.

Cold and withdrawn, Cloud Eagle moved to his haunches on the far side of the fire, far from Alicia. He said nothing, just stared at the dancing flames.

Even when Gray went to him and nudged his side with his nose, Cloud Eagle was not responsive.

Alicia moved shakily to her feet. She flinched when pressing her full weight on her leg caused it to pulse even more painfully as a result of the pounding that Lost Wind had given it.

Limping, she went to Cloud Eagle. Easing down beside him, opposite where Gray had stretched out, Alicia placed a gentle hand on Cloud Eagle's arm.

"Surely the news you've brought back about Snow isn't good," she murmured. "I'm sorry, Cloud Eagle. I know what she meant to you."

Cloud Eagle mumbled something beneath his breath, then turned his midnight-dark eyes to Alicia. "My search was in vain," he said sadly. "Snow has eluded me again. I am certain now that she has gone away to mate with one of her kind."

Alicia forked an eyebrow. "But, Cloud Eagle, I thought perhaps your ugly mood was because you had found Snow and that she was . . . was . . ."

123

"My mood has nothing to do with Snow," Cloud Eagle said, anger flaming in his eyes again at the thought that Ten Bears had given him no choice but to challenge him in a fight. "It is something else."

Again he turned his eyes to the fire, his jaws and lips tight.

"Cloud Eagle, don't go silent on me again," Alicia murmured, placing a gentle hand to his sleek copper cheek. "Tell me what has upset you. Sometimes it helps to talk about it."

"Ten Bears," Cloud Eagle ground out between clenched teeth. "He is the cause."

"Ten Bears?" Alicia said, puzzled. "Who is Ten Bears? What did he do?"

"Ten Bears is Lost Wind's brother," Cloud Eagle said, looking slowly over at Alicia, his eyes locking with hers. "His disrespect for me as chief caused me to challenge him to a fight. It is not a good thing to fight one's own warrior."

He paused and ran his fingers through his long black hair. "It must be done or others might feel free to show disrespect also," he mumbled.

Alicia grew cold inside. "In truth, the fight is over me, isn't it?" she dared to say, not wanting it to be true. "He came to you over my presence here, didn't he?"

"Had I not brought you to my lodge, Ten Bears would have found other reasons to face his chief with insults," Cloud Eagle said solemnly. "Ten Bears is a troubled man who seeks trouble from others so that they can join his misery."

"Cloud Eagle, no matter what you say, I feel responsible for what has transpired between you and Ten Bears," she said softly. "Even between Spring Dawn and Lost Wind." She lowered her head and swallowed hard. "I will leave. All trouble will leave with me. Things can return to the way they were. Your two wives can surely make you happy again."

"Have I not told you that in my eyes and deep inside my heart, they are no longer my wives?" Cloud Eagle said, turning to Alicia. He took her wrists and slowly lowered her to the pelts that were spread on the floor. He leaned over her, his breath warm on her lips. "They have not made this chief happy for many moons now. This man who no longer felt as though he was a husband has slept outside at night while Spring Dawn and Lost Wind slept inside. Do you not see? I was going to send them away anyhow. They are both barren. Unable to bear children. I want, I hunger for, children."

"That is the reason they have lost favor in your eyes?" Alicia said softly. "Because they cannot give you children?"

"That and other reasons," Cloud Eagle said. "Lost Wind has a loose, spiteful tongue. Spring Dawn is learning this from Lost Wind. They do not fit into this chief's life any longer."

"I see," Alicia said, paling when she recalled her own spiteful tongue those first days with Cloud Eagle. He seemed to have overlooked it. Or possibly he had known that it had all been pretense on her part.

"But still," she quickly added. "I feel as though I have interfered."

Her heart pounded as he gripped her shoulders and his mouth brushed her cheeks and ears. She shivered with ecstasy when he tenderly kissed her eyelids.

"It would be best that I were not here at all,"

she managed to get out between gasps of building passion when his hand left her shoulder and slid beneath the skirt of her dress.

"Do you truly wish to leave?" Cloud Eagle said, gazing at her with passion-heavy eyes. He placed his hand over the frond of hair at the juncture of her thighs and began stroking her.

Alicia tried to control her ragged breathing. She clung around his neck. "Never," she moaned, his burning lips brushing hers with feathery kisses. "Oh, Lord, Cloud Eagle. I love you. I never want to leave you."

He pressed his lips into hers.

Alicia's gasping breath was like sudden lightning flashes in the dark. Frenzied with desire, she opened her legs to his caresses.

When he drew away from her, she reached out for him.

But when she saw why he had stopped his lovemaking, she smiled and joined him as she removed her clothes as he tossed his own away.

When she was fully disrobed, his eyes widened. Tenderly he touched the bruises she had gotten during her fight with Spring Dawn and Lost Wind. She looked down at them and shuddered. The bruises were dark purple already, turning into yellowish-gray.

Then Cloud Eagle reached for her leg and lifted it closer to get a better look. The wound was red and raw-looking there and contusions surrounded it.

He gazed up at Alicia and questioned her with his eyes.

"This happened while you were gone," she confessed.

"Ten Bears said that you attacked his sister and

Spring Dawn," he said. "I knew that could not be so. They ambushed you, did they not?"

"Yes," Alicia said, trembling when he leaned a kiss to the throbbing wound on her leg. "I was going to the river to wash the breakfast dishes. Suddenly they were there."

She paused as he lowered her to the pallet of furs, then straddled her. His hands were moving over her in a soft caress as she continued talking, yet finding it hard to speak as her mind was slowly clouded with a dizzying rapture.

"I didn't want to fight them," she said, sighing deeply when his hands moved over her breasts and he began kneading them. "They gave me no choice. After they spat on my face . . ."

A quick anger entered Cloud Eagle's eyes. He reached his hands to her face and framed it. "They spat on you?" he said, his voice filled with emotion.

"They hate me so, Cloud Eagle," Alicia said, her voice breaking. "They hold me responsible for all their disappointments, I am sure."

"Only because they do not want to accept their own shortcomings," Cloud Eagle said. Once again he softly kneaded her breasts, his thumbs grazing the nipples. "It is easy to cast blame elsewhere."

Guilt surged through him at the thought of casting blame. Was he not, in fact, also responsible for such blame-casting? If he ever discovered that he had wrongly criticized his wives for being childless when it was himself who was at fault, he would hang his head in shame.

"I'm sorry if my presence caused your decision to send them away from your lodge to come perhaps sooner than it would had I not been around to complicate things," Alicia murmured, moaning when his mouth moved over one of her nipples.

"Do you forget that I brought you here?" Cloud Eagle said, casting the thoughts of his possible shortcomings from his mind. "That you did not come here of your own free will?"

Knowing that what he said was true, Alicia said nothing more. And it was hard to think rationally while he was teasing her breast with one hand, and stroking her pulsing cleft with the other. She whimpered tiny cries as pleasure began to rise like hot flashes within her.

But somewhere, where she was lucid and still had some control of her consciousness, she felt sorry for the women who had lost the love of this wonderful man.

But she understood Cloud Eagle's reasoning.

He was a virile man. He needed a woman to match his virility.

He was a gentle, caring man. He needed a woman who appreciated this side of his nature.

Hopefully she could fill both needs.

She wished never to be banished from him. She would be happy to spend an eternity with him in his stronghold.

She had adapted to life without a mother and father in the wilds of the Arizona Territory. She would adapt as well to the ways of the Apache!

His mouth sought hers, and his burning hot lips closed over hers in a quavering kiss. She was aware of him nudging her legs apart, then knew why.

She shuddered with desire when she felt the strength of his manhood enter her, filling her so magnificently. She lifted her legs around his hips, forgetting the pain in her wound, the bliss taking over when the pain began.

As he moved rhythmically within her, she felt the curling heat of pleasure spreading within her.

His hands cupped her swelling breasts. His mouth moved from one breast to the other, his tongue lapping, his teeth nipping, leaving Alicia breathless and shaking.

Cloud Eagle felt a tremor from deep within, the silver flames of desire leaping through him like flashes of lightning.

He emitted a husky groan as Alicia's hips strained even more tightly against his, drawing him more deeply within her, the walls of her womanhood tight against his throbbing hardness.

He thrust within her with maddening force, his perspiration-dampened hair thrashing and flailing like a whip around his shoulders.

Again he took her mouth by storm, his hands gripping her breasts.

His body tightened and grew still, then he plunged into her again, the hard nipples of her breasts stark against the palms of his hands.

Alicia felt the passion peaking.

She felt as though she were drowning in pleasure.

She was shaking all over when the climax caught her, sudden as a whip's crack.

Cloud Eagle's own passion peaked. He wrapped his arms around Alicia and held her tightly as he drove into her, spasmodic gasps erupting from deep within him when the pleasure overwhelmed him.

Their bodies quavered together, then grew still.

Alicia stroked his hard, manly buttocks, then reached around and cupped him as he slid from within her.

He gasped as she softly stroked him, giving his throbbing member life enough to maintain its fullness for a moment longer.

Then he eased her hand away and held it to his chest as their eyes met.

"Will you stay?" he asked, stroking the tender flesh between her thighs with his free hand.

"Yes—oh, Lord, yes," she murmured.

He rolled over and pressed his body against hers and gave her a heated kiss.

She flung her arms around him and spread her legs apart when she felt him hardening against her thigh again.

When he entered her, she cried out against his lips.

This time their climax came quickly and fulfillingly, leaving them both exhausted.

Cloud Eagle rolled away from her and lay on his back, as though deep in thought. "I want to tell you about myself, my people, and anything else you might want to know that will familiarize you with the way the Apache live," he said, turning to face her.

She turned on her side and smiled at him. "Tell me everything," she murmured. "I so badly want to know."

"Long ago, when I was only a seed of thought somewhere in the heavens, my ancestors first saw the white men," he began. "The Apache went down on the plains to meet the white men and gave them venison and meal. The white men gave the Apache shirts and money. They shook hands and promised to be brothers. Those white men left. Others came later who wore blue coats and carried guns. Although I always felt that there was an eventual end to everything, there was no end to the bluecoats. When the Apache sought to visit them, some of our people were killed. My people fled back into the mountains."

His eyes became haunted. "Trust had to be gained again by the white pony soldiers," he said in a low voice. "And for the most part, for *our* band of Apache, a truce has held between us. But there are others who speak even now of warring with the soldiers. There is one who calls himself Geronimo whose economy is an economy of war. War is his trade. He says it is the way of the Apache! I see a time when he will go against the white pony soldiers and learn for himself that because of the harm this warring will bring to his Chiricahua band of Apache, peace is a better way for them."

"I have heard of Geronimo," Alicia said, leaning on an elbow. "Most fear him."

"It is this fear that will cause his end to come to him," Cloud Eagle said, rising to a sitting position. He reached for Alicia and drew her up next to him. "He who will run into the face of danger is considered little better than a fool."

He continued telling her about the ways of his people, Gray asleep beside them.

Then Cloud Eagle lowered her to the pallet of furs again. "Enough talk of serious things," he said, laughing lightly.

He leaned over her.

His mouth browsed over her at leisure, teaching her ways of loving that if she were not with him, she would think forbidden. But under his patient, unhurried mouth, Alicia's resistance melted, and

131

she banished all doubts from her mind. She became caught up once again in a frenzied desire. Her stomach churned wildly when he parted the soft hair at the juncture of her thighs and placed his lips to her throbbing center.

Her whole body tingled with aliveness when his tongue began a slow, wondrous caress. There was a stirring fire within her, soon fanned to roaring flames.

She had never felt so alive. She closed her eyes and enjoyed the incredible sweetness that swept through her.

When her body soon and unexpectedly exploded in spasms of desire, her eyes flew open, silently questioning Cloud Eagle about this strange way of finding total pleasure without him participating in the usual way.

"There are many ways of making love," Cloud Eagle said. He drew her into his embrace. "Stay with this Apache chief. He will teach you the ways."

Alicia twined her arms around his neck and drew his lips to hers. "Teach me, teach me," she whispered against his lips.

He smiled.

Chapter Eleven

Still trembling from Cloud Eagle's passionate lovemaking, Alicia slipped back into her dress. She glanced upward and stiffened when, through the smoke hole, she could see that it was totally dark outside.

She smoothed the dress down her thighs, then turned to Cloud Eagle, who was tying a bright scarf around his head. His body was already sheathed in fringed buckskin.

"Lost Wind and Spring Dawn," she said. "Where are they? By now they are usually back inside your lodge."

"You have the answer," he said. "Why ask the question?"

"I don't know what you mean," Alicia said, stiffening.

"They no longer share this lodge, or anything, with Cloud Eagle," he said matter-of-factly. He placed his fingers to Alicia's shoulders and drew her close. "They are no longer a part of my life."

"You divorced them this quickly?" Alicia asked, her eyes wide. "This easily?"

"If a white man and woman are not happy with one another, is a divorce not done as quickly?" Cloud Eagle said, questioning her with his dark eyes.

"Divorces take much time, and usually many arguments, before they are granted in the white community," Alicia said softly. "The wives take much when they leave. Is it the same for the Apache women who are divorced by their husbands?"

"The Apache women take with them what they brought into the marriage," Cloud Eagle said, bending to slide a log into the flames of the fire. "Themselves."

"Where will they spend the night?"

"They have made themselves a lodge on the far side of the stronghold away from mine."

Alicia gasped. "When were they instructed to do this?" she asked, recalling their attack on her. Had they known then that they were no longer Cloud Eagle's wives? Was the attack meant to frighten her into leaving so that Cloud Eagle might reconsider and take them back?

"After Ten Bears came to me and told me about your misfortune today with Spring Dawn and Lost Wind, it was then that I returned to the stronghold and told them that it was time for them to find a new direction in life, to find a life with another man," Cloud Eagle said. "I scolded them for not giving this chief offspring. I also warned them to be decent to you."

"And?" Alicia said, leaning nearer to him. "What did they say?"

Cloud Eagle placed a gentle hand to her cheek. "I am their chief," he said, smiling slowly. "What can they say?"

"You were their chief and they still attacked me."

"That is over and done with," he said firmly. "They are no longer my wives. They no longer have cause to annoy you. But if they do, they know they will have me, their chief, to answer to."

His smile faded. "And should Ten Bears lose the duel with me, his sister, Lost Wind, will leave the stronghold with him," he said solemnly.

"What?" Alicia gasped.

"That is part of the bargain between Ten Bears and Cloud Eagle," he said, then looked toward the closed entrance flap when a horse stopped just outside his lodge. "Someone has come. Perhaps it is Red Crow. He will have the mail sack to prove our total innocence in your eyes."

He swept her into his arms and leaned down into her face. He brushed a kiss across her lips, kissed the tip of her nose, and then her eyelids. "Proof is no longer needed, is it?" he said huskily. "You know of this chief's innocence, do you not?"

She closed her eyes, held her head back so that her red hair streamed down her perfect back, and trembled with ecstasy. "Yes, I am sure you are innocent of *one* crime," she said in a husky whisper. "But not of another."

"There was more than one crime that you accuse me of?" he said, yanking her close so that their bodies molded together.

"My heart," she said, smiling. "You are guilty of having stolen my heart."

He almost swallowed her whole with a passionate kiss, then drew quickly away when Red Crow spoke up from outside the entrance flap, calling Cloud Eagle's name.

"Enter," Cloud Eagle said. He took a step toward the entranceway to welcome Red Crow into the lodge.

When Red Crow entered, Alicia's gaze fell on the mail sack. She was not as relieved to see it as she had expected to be. She knew of Cloud Eagle's innocence without it. And now, under these newest circumstances, the letter to her brother was meaningless. She never planned to return to the drudgery of working at any stage station again. At long last, she had found her rightful home with Cloud Eagle, where she wished to stay, forever and ever.

She would rewrite the letter and place it in the mail sack and hope that Cloud Eagle could find a way to get it to Fort Thomas for the next stagecoach to Saint Louis.

But she understood that she might already be too late. If her brother was already on his way to the Arizona Territory, all of her efforts to get a letter to him, *any* letter, were in vain.

It made chills ride her spine to think that she might never see Charlie again. If he became a target for the renegades and outlaws, he might not have someone like Cloud Eagle to come to his rescue.

"My friend, you have done well," Cloud Eagle said, taking the mail sack from Red Crow.

Red Crow's interest did not seem to be on the mail sack. He looked past Cloud Eagle and gazed with narrowed eyes at Alicia.

Then he took a step away from Cloud Eagle,

making Cloud Eagle's hand drop to his side, and gazed with an intense frown at his chief. "I saw your wives cooking outside a newly erected lodge on the far side of the stronghold," he said solemnly. "Why is that, Cloud Eagle? Do they not reside in your lodge any longer? Have you sent them away?"

Cloud Eagle did not respond immediately. He took the mail sack to Alicia and gave it to her and smiled as she clutched it to her chest with total trust in her eyes as she gazed lovingly up at him.

It was good, he thought, that the question of guilt about the mail sack was resolved.

But to his close friend, and perhaps his people as a whole, there was one major question that would need to be answered.

His choice of women—rather, his choice of *wives*, for he did plan to take Alicia as his wife soon. She had said that she wanted to stay with him forever. He would make her prove that statement by taking him as a husband. She would have to know that marriage to an Apache would differ greatly from marriage to a white man. The Apache did not have as many worldly goods to offer a woman.

He had to hope that their shared love would be enough for now. This woman made his insides turn warm just to be near her.

He went back to Red Crow. "Would you sit and have a smoke?" he asked, nodding toward a colorful pipe that rested on a flat stone beside the lodge fire.

"Another time," Red Crow said, again glancing at Alicia. "It is best to be with wives this time of evening." He turned quizzical eyes back to Cloud

Eagle. He stepped closer and spoke beneath his breath, only loud enough for Cloud Eagle's ears. "You take this woman as your wife soon?"

"Yes, soon," Cloud Eagle said back, as quietly. This was a private thing, not yet spoken of between himself and Alicia. He did not wish for her to hear his intentions in words spoken between friends instead of between her and Cloud Eagle.

"And what if Spring Dawn and Lost Wind make life miserable for this white woman? When you are away, they might tease and torture her," Red Crow whispered back, his concern sincere for how it would look for Cloud Eagle, not so much for Alicia.

"They know not to," Cloud Eagle hissed back in a harsh whisper. "But if they do these things to my woman, they in turn will be teased and tortured."

"It is rumored that your white woman was accosted by Spring Dawn and Lost Wind earlier in the day," Red Crow said, having heard this as he was met by warriors upon his return to the stronghold. "Does that not forewarn you of worse problems now that you have banished them from your lodge and your life?"

"This altercation that you speak of took place before they were told they were divorced from me," Cloud Eagle said. "Now that they know their standing with me, there will be no more trouble."

"Gossip also spread to me of a duel that has been arranged between you and Ten Bears," Red Crow added. "Is that wise? He is known for his skill at fighting."

"You belittle me by doubting your chief's ability

to defend himself," Cloud Eagle scolded heatedly as he leaned into Red Crow's face. "Perhaps it is *you* who should be challenged."

"No disrespect was meant," Red Crow said, then clasped his hands onto Cloud Eagle's shoulders. "You know that my concerns for you are because of our bond of friendship and brotherhood. It is not because I doubt you."

"That is good," Cloud Eagle said, nodding. "Now say no more about it, nor about my choice of women. My mind is made up. I want only one woman. Alicia feeds my every need, my every hunger."

"My chief's heart has spoken," Red Crow said, nodding. "This friend will say no more about it."

"Your wives await you, my friend," Cloud Eagle said, gesturing with a hand toward the entrance flap. "Go to them. They deserve your devotion. Have they not each given you offspring to carry your name on even after you are walking the road to the hereafter?"

"It is true that they have filled my lodge with the laughter of children," Red Crow said. He looked over at Alicia. "Perhaps soon children will brighten your life and your lodge."

Cloud Eagle looked at Alicia. It was true that children were important to him, so important that he had sent two barren wives away.

But as for this woman who would soon be his wife—would she bear him children?

If she disappointed him also, how could he send her away? He wanted her with every fiber of his being. This was a sort of want he had never felt before, one that would not easily be cast aside.

Again, doubts of his own virility momentarily flooded his senses, but he quickly brushed them away. Deep down inside himself, he knew that he could not live with such doubts for much longer. He must have a son to prove his virility!

"Perhaps," he murmured. "Perhaps soon. Perhaps *many*."

Red Crow and Cloud Eagle embraced, then Red Crow left.

Cloud Eagle went to Alicia. He lifted the mail sack from her arms. "You have it—now what will you do with it?" he said, laying it aside.

"It would please me so much if it could be taken to Fort Thomas," Alicia said softly. "Of course I know the risks. Whoever is seen with the mail sack could be accused of having stolen it. But perhaps it could be done at night. Perhaps it could be left in front of the station so that it could be found the next day?"

"It is that important to you?" he said, framing her face between his hands.

"There is a letter in the mail sack that is important to me," she murmured. "It must be rewritten, then the mail sack must be taken to Fort Thomas, or the nearest stage station, as soon as possible."

She rubbed her sore leg. "I would go myself, but I doubt that I could travel that far on horseback quite yet," she said.

"After you rewrite the letter, I will see that the mail sack is delivered for you to Fort Thomas," Cloud Eagle said and drew her into his embrace. He stroked her back through the soft buckskin of her dress. "And so you now have absolute proof of this Apache's innocence?"

"Damn Sandy Whiskers," Alicia said, snuggling closer to Cloud Eagle. "How could I have been so blind not to realize that he was mixed up in underhanded schemes? One look into his empty gray eyes turns one's insides cold. I've never trusted him. Yet I never thought that he could be responsible for anything as horrible as being the leader of a gang that ambushes innocent travelers."

She leaned away from Cloud Eagle and searched his eyes. "Something must be done about him," she said softly. "He must be reported. He must be *stopped.*"

"In due time," Cloud Eagle said. He wove his fingers through her lustrously long hair and led her lips close to his. "Remember, *Ish-kay-nay,* Sandy Whiskers' supplies make winters less perilous for my people. When Sandy Whiskers fails to be of use to the Apache, then his activities will be revealed."

"But Cloud Eagle, the innocent people that he has harmed," Alicia pleaded, ignoring his continued use of *Ish-kay-nay* as his nickname for her. She knew that he no longer saw her as a boy!

"For you, to *please* you, I will send patrols out to watch for those who might plan to ambush and kill. They will be stopped," he promised. "Will that make you happy?"

"I will sleep much better knowing that someone out there cares about what happens to those who come to this land seeking fortune and opportunity," Alicia murmured. "The soldiers' hands seem tied at times."

"There will never be enough soldiers or Apaches to stop the evil that floods our land," Cloud Eagle said. He took her by the hand and pulled her down on the pallet of furs beside him.

"I know, and that is frightening," Alicia said,

inhaling a shaky breath when Cloud Eagle swept a hand up the skirt of her dress and began caressing her. "I fear so for my . . ."

She did not get the word 'brother' out before Cloud Eagle silenced her with a heated kiss. She strained her body up against his and moaned with rapture when he thrust a finger deeply within her. He knew ways of stopping her from worrying. Her head was already spinning as a delicious languor stole over her.

Chapter Twelve

The next morning, when the birds were in the sky before the sun, Cloud Eagle awakened Alicia.

"Is something wrong?" she asked, yawning and wiping her eyes as she turned to him. Gray came to her and playfully nudged her with his nose.

"Sleep eluded me last night," Cloud Eagle said somberly.

"Why?" Alicia asked, leaning up on one elbow. Fear gripped her heart when a thought came to her. Was he feeling guilty for having discarded his two wives? Had he discovered, in their absence, that he cared deeply for them after all? Had he decided to send *her* away?

"I have been thinking about the upcoming duel with Ten Bears," he said quietly. He left their pallet of furs and slipped into his clothes. "To clear my mind before the duel, I am going hunting."

Afraid to be left alone, a keen apprehension

rose within Alicia. Although Cloud Eagle had assured her that she had nothing to fear from Spring Dawn and Lost Wind, she was not totally convinced of it.

Also, she now had someone else to be wary of. Ten Bears. If he was angry enough to challenge his chief to a duel, could he not at this moment feel that he had nothing to lose if he killed the white woman, the one he held responsible for his sister's being sent from Cloud Eagle's lodge?

Alicia pushed herself slowly to her feet. She expected her leg to throb from the pressure that she was putting on it. Instead the pain was all but gone.

"Let me go with you," she said, scurrying into her clothes. "Please?"

"No. That is not wise," Cloud Eagle said as he tied a headband around his head. "Women are taboo on the hunt. They bring bad luck."

"Do you truly believe that?" Alicia said, slipping her soft moccasins on.

Cloud Eagle ignored her skepticism about this custom. He secured his quiver of arrows on his back, and grabbed his powerful bow and a lance.

"Stay," he said, giving Alicia a firm stare. He gave Gray the same stare and order.

Obeying, Gray stretched out beside the fire.

Knowing that she had no choice but to obey when she saw that Cloud Eagle's mind was made up, Alicia nodded and sat down beside the glowing embers of the fire beside Gray.

When Cloud Eagle left without another word, Alicia began placing wood in the fire pit. Leaning over, she blew at the embers, causing sparks to fly. Soon the blaze took hold and flames began caressing the wood in streamers of fire.

Grateful to at least have Gray there to relieve her loneliness, Alicia cuddled him closer and stared into the flames. She prayed that this day would go by in a flash and bring Cloud Eagle back to her.

How strange it was, she thought to herself, that she now depended so much on someone besides herself for her existence. Since her parents' deaths, she had become solely responsible for her well being.

"Charlie," she whispered to herself. "I do miss *you*, Charlie."

But she had not wanted to live her brother's sort of life for some time now. It had been boring. When she awakened every morning in Saint Louis, it had always been the same, with the same dull routine stretched out before her.

Out in the Arizona Territory, no one knew from moment to moment what was around the corner, or who. That was the excitement of it all.

But now she wanted the security of knowing that nothing would come between her and her beloved Apache chief.

She glanced over at the closed entrance flap. Anyone could come at any time to spoil her future with Cloud Eagle. There were no locks to stop them.

Cloud Eagle stepped outside and froze in his steps when he found Ten Bears standing in the shadows of the lodge next to Cloud Eagle's. He wondered how long Ten Bears had been standing there. Perhaps all night? That might have been why Cloud Eagle could not sleep. He might have sensed Ten Bears's presence all along.

Cloud Eagle gripped his lance tightly and

glanced over his shoulder at his own lodge. Alicia was alone, trustingly alone. If Ten Bears wanted to avenge his sister's expulsion from Cloud Eagle's lodge before the duel, he might act out his revenge in Cloud Eagle's absence by taking his anger out on Alicia.

This thought sent Cloud Eagle back inside his tepee. He laid his bow and his lance down. He went to Alicia and took her gently by the wrist. "Come," he said in a low growl. "You will come with me on the hunt after all."

Stunned by Cloud Eagle's change of mind, Alicia was at a loss for words. She stumbled to her feet. "Why do you want me to come now, when only moments ago you would not allow it?" she asked, her eyes searching his. "Do you no longer see my presence on the hunt as taboo?"

"My feeling about that has not changed, but there is more danger of bringing bad luck into my life in leaving you here than taking you with me," Cloud Eagle said. He nodded toward her moccasins. "Take off your moccasins."

Alicia was becoming more confused by the minute. "If I am going with you, why would I remove my moccasins?" she asked, looking blankly up at him. "Why would you want me to go in my bare feet?"

She watched him go to a small chest. She slipped her moccasins off as he bent over the chest and raised the lid.

"You will not go in your bare feet," Cloud Eagle said, taking a pair of moccasins from the chest. "You will wear my mother's moccasins. They are special."

When Cloud Eagle took the moccasins to Alicia, she looked at them, noting how different they were from those that she had been wearing.

She slipped one on. It reached halfway up her thigh and had tough soles that were curved up at the toe, which ended in a sort of button the size of a dollar coin. The tops pushed down below the knees into a fold.

"These high moccasins will protect your feet and legs from venomous reptiles and thorny desert plants," Cloud Eagle explained. "We will do much walking today. You will need this protection."

Alicia placed the other moccasin on her foot. They were not as comfortable as those that she had been wearing since her arrival at the Apache stronghold, but they were still much more comfortable than the boots she had normally worn before.

"Come," Cloud Eagle said, again picking up his bow and lance.

With Gray dutifully following behind them, Alicia followed Cloud Eagle outside. She immediately saw why he had changed his mind about her accompanying him on the hunt. Ten Bears was lurking in the shadows, leering at her.

Chills rode Alicia's spine. Never had she seen such hate in a man's eyes. She knew that if Cloud Eagle lost the duel, her days were numbered.

She rushed away beside Cloud Eagle toward the corral. As he saddled his horse and secured his lance and bow at one side, Alicia saddled her own mount with the pelt from the leopard she had killed.

He went back to Alicia. "Your leg," he said, placing his arms at her waist to draw her against him. "Does it allow you to ride? It will be for only a short distance. Then we will walk as we

147

hunt. Does your leg allow such varied activity this morning?"

"It feels much better," she murmured, smiling up at him. "But still not well enough to ride clear to Fort Thomas or a stage station. Thank you for sending a warrior to deliver the mail sack. It's so important to me that it is finally in the right hands."

"Had you been well enough to make the delivery yourself, would you have delivered the mail sack there, then returned to Cloud Eagle?"

"Need you ask? Don't you truly know?"

"In my heart, yes."

"And you are right. Your heart and mine are now as one, Cloud Eagle."

He gave her a soft kiss, then lifted her into her saddle.

"Darling, your arm," Alicia said, gazing at the healed scratches left from the panther's attack. "It is a miracle how it healed so quickly."

"That is because shortly after the attack we made love and then entered the water that heals."

"Making love has healing powers?" Alicia teased back.

"When it is with you, yes."

Filled with love and adoration, Alicia watched him mount his roan. Each of his movements was filled with strength and exactness. She felt honored to be loved by such a man. In his presence, she felt as though she should be somebody else. It was just too unreal that such a man as he should care for her this much.

Before she met him, she had begun to think that there was no special man in the Arizona Territory with whom she could share anything, much less a future. Then Cloud Eagle came along—a *very* special man. Things had not been the same since.

They rode off at a soft lope into the lightening sky of morning, Gray bouncing along behind them.

It felt good to Alicia to be riding a horse again, in control of the reins herself. Her leg ached, but not so badly that she was disturbed by it. It was too wonderful to be alone with Cloud Eagle and to be a part of his hunting adventure.

She held her chin high, even ignoring the hunger pangs that were gnawing at her. Hunger seemed of no importance while riding free as the wind beside her beloved Apache chief.

She inhaled the sweet fragrance of the morning air.

She marveled at the sky and how beautifully it was streaked with shades of crimson, pink, and turquoise. It was enchanting.

Alicia's attention was drawn elsewhere when a cliff hawk sailed smoothly down from the sky and soared between canyon walls to search out snakes and rodents.

They rode a while longer, then dismounted and led the horses instead of riding them.

Alicia walked proudly beside Cloud Eagle as they made their way in and out of thickets. Their movements caused small, vulnerable animals to run for cover, Gray sometimes taking off after them, yelping.

There was hardly any conversation between Cloud Eagle and Alicia except that he had told her that they were hunting for deer, gophers, and—to her horror—lizards! He had explained that the Apache did not eat bear meat, turkey, or fish, though they hunted turkey, hawks, and eagles for their feathers and mink, beaver, and muskrat for their pelts.

Carrying his lance, with his bow slung over his shoulder, Cloud Eagle held out an arm to stop Alicia. She stopped immediately and stood stone-still beside him.

Her eyes followed Cloud Eagle's. They had come upon a circle of feeding deer. They were well hidden behind bushes, but yet so close that she could see all the details of their faces—the long, thick eyelashes; the shiny, black noses; their beautiful dark eyes.

A deer suddenly sensed alarm and hopped out of the circle. The other deer's ears perked up and, also sensing danger, they sprang away.

One deer was not as swift. Cloud Eagle notched an arrow on his bow and sent it into the animal's side.

For a moment the deer staggered, then it dipped its head so that the right antlers touched the earth.

Finally the animal fell on its side, breathing heavily.

The deer's mournful eyes looked up at Alicia. Blood trickled from its mouth, and a stillness filled the air.

Alicia could hardly stand watching the animal die a slow death right before her eyes. She was glad when Cloud Eagle made the deer's end swift by plunging his lance deep into the heart of the animal.

The deer had earned as much respect.

A second later, it was over.

It was then that Alicia and Cloud Eagle both noticed that not only was Cloud Eagle's arrow lodged in the deer's side, but another arrow as well.

Clutching a bow, his dark eyes proud, an Indian warrior stepped into the clearing.

He was almost as handsome as Cloud Eagle. His facial features were sculpted, his body muscled. His bronze skin glistened in the morning air; his only attire was a breechclout and moccasins.

Cloud Eagle quickly recognized Thunder Roars, a neighboring Apache. He stepped up to him. "We share a kill today," he said, clasping his hands onto Thunder Roars' shoulders. "I view this shared kill as a sign of fellowship—of friendship."

"I, too, see it that way," Thunder Roars said, nodding.

"Let us vow today that we will be devoted friends forever," Cloud Eagle said.

"Destiny has made it so," Thunder Roars said, smiling at Cloud Eagle. "Friends forever."

Cloud Eagle stepped away from Thunder Roars and they both went to study the deer.

Alicia stood behind them, marveling over how quickly they had become friends, and why. As each day passed, she saw the genuine kindness of Cloud Eagle.

She looked at Thunder Roars. He seemed kind too, and genuine. She thought back to all the terrible things that she had heard about the Apache when she was in school in Saint Louis. She was seeing for herself how wrongly the historians had depicted them.

Of course, she knew that there were some Apache who had fought, and were still ready to fight, any white man who crossed their paths.

Again she found herself grateful and relieved

151

that Cloud Eagle had chosen the peaceful path with the white man. Had he not, she might at this very moment be lying dead or held in captivity.

Instead, Cloud Eagle was protecting her with every fiber of his being.

She welcomed this protection and did not feel as though she were a weakling because of it.

She enjoyed being a woman for the first time in her life.

"Thunder Roars, each half of this deer's skin will make a vest worthy of a warrior," Cloud Eagle said, kneeling down beside the deer. He ran a hand over its smooth fur. "Since the kill was shared, also must the skin be shared."

Thunder Roars nodded and knelt down on the other side of the deer while Cloud Eagle took out his knife and cut the skin down the middle.

Alicia turned her eyes away as the pelt was taken from the animal. And while the meat was taken from the animal, she listened to the shared conversation between these two Apaches. She smiled to herself when Cloud Eagle invited Thunder Roars to his village for a celebration of newfound friendship. That was just like Cloud Eagle. Generous and friendly to the very core of himself.

She was not at all surprised when Thunder Roars accepted the invitation; he seemed to have been made from the same mold that had formed Cloud Eagle's personality.

After the deer meat was evenly divided and made into bundles tied in yucca cord, then secured to their horses, Cloud Eagle and Thunder Roars approached Alicia.

Cloud Eagle had seen Thunder Roars eyeing Alicia for some time now and had not questioned his reasons. He knew without asking. Not only was she a white woman, she was on the hunt with Cloud Eagle although it was taboo for her to be there.

"This is my woman," Cloud Eagle said, pride in his eyes as he gestured toward Alicia. "Her name is Alicia. But I call her *Ish-kay-nay* because of how she looked and acted when I first met her."

He gestured toward Thunder Roars as he smiled at Alicia. "Alicia, this is my friend, Thunder Roars," he said with much pride. "He is from a neighboring Apache stronghold. He will return to the village with us. There he and I will share a smoke, then the whole stronghold will celebrate their chief's newly found friendship."

There was a moment of silence.

"You bring a woman on the hunt?" Thunder Roars then blurted out.

"That is so," Cloud Eagle said matter-of-factly. "And do you not see? She brought luck to the hunt."

Thunder Roars kneaded his chin as he measured the worth of the white woman.

Then his lips formed a slow smile. "She is welcomed as my friend because she is yours," he said, in his eyes a keen admiration of what he saw in Alicia.

Cloud Eagle placed a possessive arm around Alicia's shoulders. "She is more than a friend," he said, wanting to make his possession of Alicia perfectly clear to this Apache who might find her more than intriguing. "She will soon be my wife."

Alicia's heart fluttered with surprise, then moved into a quiet rhythm of happiness as she beamed up at Cloud Eagle.

His wife.

There. He had finally said it.

They would soon be married, and with this marriage would come a new life for her, one that she welcomed. She had not realized how alone she had been since her parents' deaths until she found such happiness and contentment with Cloud Eagle. They seemed to fill each other's every need.

They mounted their steeds and rode off with strips of venison hanging from their saddles. Alicia beamed as she rode proudly beside Cloud Eagle. She felt as though she belonged there. Everything in her past life was now only a faint memory. Her expected future of happiness outweighed anything that she had ever experienced in the past.

Gray leapt up and nipped playfully at Alicia's feet. "You can feel my happiness, can't you, sweet coyote?" she said, laughing into the wind.

Chapter Thirteen

Alicia had bathed in the river after arriving home from the hunt. She had washed her hair with yucca suds and it now lay in a satin sheen across her shoulders.

She gazed admiringly down at the clothes Cloud Eagle had given her to wear for the celebration of his new friendship with Thunder Roars. It was another treasure from the trunk that held his beloved mother's clothes.

Alicia put on the skirt and blouse of deerskin. The fringed skirt extended from the waist to the knees. The blouse and the skirt were both ornamented with bits of bright metal and glass. And she wore the usual moccasins now instead of those she had worn on the hunt.

Alicia stepped outside into the cool breeze of evening. The sky was just now darkening overhead. Her eyes were drawn to the gathering of Apache around a huge outdoor fire. They sat on

155

blankets, leaving room enough between them and the fire for dancers to perform. The celebration had already begun.

Alicia's eyes shifted to Cloud Eagle. He stood with Red Crow and Thunder Roars away from the crowd, laughing with his friends over some shared joke. Except for brief breechclouts, their sleek bodies were revealed, the muscles bulging at their shoulders, arms, and legs.

A feeling of contented bliss swept through Alicia at the sight of Cloud Eagle. He had shared her quick bath farther downriver from the village. They had shared many kisses and long embraces, but because of the lack of time, they had not made love.

The thunderous beats of her heart were counting out the minutes until they could be alone again. After the celebration, they had the long night ahead of them. If they wished, they could make undying love until morning. And they could do this every morning of their lives. She was going to be Cloud Eagle's wife!

Smiling, feeling deliciously happy, Alicia went to Cloud Eagle and edged herself between him and Red Crow so that she could stand beside the man she loved.

"After taking so much time with your hair, do you feel pretty enough so that I can show you off to my people?" Cloud Eagle teased, placing a possessive arm around her waist. He smiled from Thunder Roars to Red Crow. "Is not my woman something very special?"

When neither offered a response, Alicia experienced a sudden feeling of renewed apprehension over being there. And although the Apache chief's word reigned supreme above everyone else's, she felt as though she were an alien to the Apache, ruining what she had felt might be an evening of fun and happiness.

Cloud Eagle's jaw tightened and his eyes narrowed as he stared at his friends. "She is going to be my wife," he said sternly. "I expect you to treat her as though she already were."

Thunder Roars was the first to respond. His frown was replaced by a smile. He faced Cloud Eagle and gripped his shoulder with a hand of friendship. "She is most beautiful," he said, his eyes dancing into Alicia's. "Bring her to my stronghold anytime for my people to see and become acquainted with. Although she is white, the fact that you have chosen her for your wife will make her welcome in this Apache's stronghold whenever you wish to bring her."

Thankful tears burned at the corners of Alicia's eyes. She whispered a thank-you and wiped the tears away just as Red Crow took Thunder Roars' place at Cloud Eagle's side.

"This Apache, who has fought side by side with you and who has laughed and cried with you, will no longer show his displeasure over your choice of women," Red Crow said, clasping a hand to his chief's shoulder. "Bring her to my lodge. Let her become acquainted with my wives. She needs Apache women friends in order to survive the life of a white Apache wife."

"Thank you," Alicia said, wiping tears from her cheeks. With Red Crow's show of allegiance and friendship, she felt as though she had won a great victory. "I will be happy to come to your lodge. I am anxious to make the acquaintance of your wives."

Red Crow stepped away from Cloud Eagle and

nodded toward the crowd of Apache. His eyes stopped when he found his wives. "Sweet Rose and Laughing Eyes. Do you see them as they both cast looks over their shoulders at their husband? And do you see my children? Two sons. I am a most lucky man."

Alicia followed his stare and found the two Apache women to whom he was referring. His wives were petite and pretty and had smiles that proved their happiness. She found this hard to understand—how any woman could be happy sharing a man's love with another. She recalled Cloud Eagle's wives and how jealous they had been of her.

But that was because she was white, she thought to herself.

She glanced quickly over at Cloud Eagle. Should he find another Apache woman to his liking, would he take a second wife?

The thought petrified Alicia, not only because of how the Apache felt about her, but because she would never accept another woman in Cloud Eagle's life. She could never share him or their home.

"They are quite lovely," she finally murmured, her gaze now on the babies who were sitting on the blanket next to Red Crow's wives. Children. His wives had given him children.

Cloud Eagle, too, was gazing at the children with a look of fondness. Yet there was a sadness, a longing in the look. She could tell that he was being eaten away by this want for children. There seemed to be some sort of urgency in this need—an urgency that frightened her. What if she couldn't give him a child? She could be discarded just as easily as his first wives.

The sound of the drums reverberating through the night air drew Alicia's attention. People were joining hands and dancing around the fire, their feet thumping in time with the rhythm of the drum, as rattles shook out their own strange sounds for the dancers.

"Come," Cloud Eagle said, taking Alicia's hands. "We will dance." He nodded at Thunder Roars. "Join us. We share my woman in the dance."

Red Crow had already gone to his wives and had chosen one of them to join the dancing, leaving the other behind to care for the children.

Laughingly, Alicia ran hand-in-hand with Cloud Eagle and Thunder Roars into the dancing frenzy. She became filled with the joy of the moment as she followed Cloud Eagle's lead and lifted her feet and bobbed her head rhythmically with the music. She enjoyed Thunder Roars' company. He was good-natured, his eyes laughing as he gazed into hers.

For hours the celebration continued, until the moon passed its zenith and began its descent. The older Apache retired, but the young remained outside.

Exhausted by the energetic dancing, Alicia flopped down onto the blanket with Sweet Rose and Laughing Eyes and accepted a platter of food which they offered her. She enjoyed the cakes made from mesquite bean and acorn meal. She feasted on roots, berries, nuts, and seeds of grasses, washing these down with water sweetened with honey.

Pleasantly full and exceedingly happy, Alicia pushed the empty platter aside and watched several young Apache braves gather in a tight circle, which was then surrounded by a larger circle of girls.

The throb of the drum stopped, and as one of the girls stepped forward to select the young man with whom she would dance, the lonely, thin wail of the *flageolet*, a small wood flute, carried through the moonlight.

After saying a farewell to Thunder Roars, Cloud Eagle sat down beside Alicia and watched the dance with her. He knew this dance well, and the meaning behind it. He had at one time participated in such a dance himself. Lost Wind had chosen him that night to dance with her. At the end of the dance, he had presented Lost Wind with a special present, a Navaho blanket.

He remembered her well that night. She had been beautiful and sweet in her costume of white deerskin and flashing beads.

But sometime since then she had lost her sweetness and had become a nagging, spiteful woman. Even if she had given him children, he doubted he could have kept her as his wife. She was someone now he did not know, and no longer cared to.

Spellbound, Alicia watched the young people. The young girls selected the braves with whom they would spend the rest of the night, dancing. The braves seemed shy. The girls seemed just as timid.

On and on the dancing continued. Alicia was bone-tired, yet she did not complain. Staying and observing the dancing ritual seemed the proper thing to do. The lovers' dance went on and on until the moon was paled by the sun's rising.

Alicia leaned forward, her eyes wide, when at the end of the dance, the young braves presented the girls with gifts. Each gift was different and seemed special. The girls' eyes shone as they clutched them to their bosoms and ran away to their lodges, while the young braves broke apart and went to their own tepees.

The crowd that had stayed the full night began to disperse. Alicia had not expected the celebration to last this long and somewhat resented not being able to spend the time as she had planned—making love with Cloud Eagle. But she *had* enjoyed the night.

She clung to Cloud Eagle as they walked toward their lodge, then stopped when they saw someone coming into the village on horseback.

"Is that Thunder Roars?" Alicia asked, shielding her eyes against the brightness of morning with the back of her hand.

Cloud Eagle forked an eyebrow when he noticed that Thunder Roars was not riding straight-backed in the saddle. Instead he was slouched over. His insides grew cold. "He appears to be in pain."

"Oh, Lord, no," Alicia cried. "I hope he wasn't ambushed."

Alicia and Cloud Eagle broke into a run and met Thunder Roars' approach. When they reached him, they stopped and stared, stunned at his appearance. There were no bullet wounds, but there were many red and inflamed welts covering his powerful chest, his arms, and his face. His eyes were so swollen, they appeared to be only slits in his skin. His cheeks were puffed out. His ears and lips were twice their size.

Thunder Roars slid easily from the saddle, then lifted a deer sack from the back of his horse.

Alicia stared dumbfoundedly at what it contained. She now knew what had caused the stings all over his body. The sack was heavy with crushed honeycomb.

"This gift, which is highly regarded by our people, is yours," Thunder Roars said, handing the deer sack to Cloud Eagle. "This gift truly seals our new friendship. Also I give it to you to acquire real merit among your people."

Alicia had heard that honey was the Apache's main store of sweets and was greatly desired for *pinole,* which was a flour made of mesquite beans and acorns. The very cakes that she had eaten tonight had been made from this flour.

"This chief is humbled over the gift and the sacrifice you made in acquiring it," Cloud Eagle said, hugging the deer sack to his bosom. His eyes raked over Thunder Roars' body again. "You have hardly been left untouched by the bees. Come to my lodge. I will prepare a herbal medication that will remove the pain and help take away the swelling."

Thunder Roars nodded, then groaned as he began walking his horse toward Cloud Eagle's tepee. Alicia could see him shivering and knew that he must have a fever. It was obvious that this Apache was allergic to bee stings. She felt that he might have a miserable several days ahead of him regardless of whatever Cloud Eagle did to try to make him more comfortable. She was also allergic to bee stings and avoided the creatures at all costs.

"Alicia, could you take Thunder Roars' horse to the corral?" Cloud Eagle said, stopping just before he entered his lodge.

Alicia nodded and took the reins.

When she returned to the tepee, she sat down away from Cloud Eagle and Thunder Roars and watched Cloud Eagle's gentle ways of medicating the welts.

When Thunder Roars was led to the pallet of furs upon which Cloud Eagle and Alicia had made love more than once, Alicia pitied him. He could not straighten his back, nor could he see. His eyes were now totally closed. When he stretched out on the furs, he groaned.

"Do you wish a shaman?" Cloud Eagle asked, as he leaned close to Thunder Roars' ear.

"No shaman," Thunder Roars mumbled through his swollen lips. "Sleep. All I need is sleep."

"When you awake, the welts will be all but gone," Cloud Eagle reassured him. "The herbs I used on them will ensure that."

Cloud Eagle stepped away from Thunder Roars. He went and stood over the fire and stared into the flames. Alicia sidled up next to him and placed her arms around his waist. "I'm worried about something," she murmured.

"He will be all right," Cloud Eagle reassured her, still staring into the flames.

"I am concerned about Thunder Roars, but my main concern is for you," Alicia said, causing his eyes to turn to her. "Isn't the duel today? This morning?"

"In a matter of moments," Cloud Eagle said solemnly.

"Cloud Eagle, you have been up all night without any rest," she said, her voice breaking. "Darling, because of the celebration I forgot about the duel. How could I be so thoughtless? I should have encouraged you to go to bed long ago."

"Do not fret so," Cloud Eagle said, framing her face between his hands. "I purposely lingered at the celebration, not only because I am the chief, but also because I knew that if I went to my bed, I would not sleep. It is not a pleasant thing to think about—losing a valued warrior. And that I will today. I never lose at duels. Anticipating that loss with sadness would have caused sleep to elude this Apache chief."

Alicia flung herself into his arms and clung to him. "I still feel responsible," she murmured. "Tell me again that I am not."

"Ten Bears is the one responsible for his own untimely end," Cloud Eagle said, gently stroking her back through the buckskin blouse. "It is as though he wishes to enter the land of the hereafter before his time."

"A death wish," Alicia whispered, shuddering.

"But fear not, my *Ish-kay-nay*," Cloud Eagle quickly reassured her. "Should I be the victor, my plan is to spare Ten Bears' life, not take it."

"But only moments ago you said that . . ."

"There are other ways to take a warrior's life than killing him."

"I don't understand."

"You shall see. You shall see."

Chapter Fourteen

The sun was directly overhead when Cloud Eagle and Ten Bears stepped into a clearing just outside their stronghold. They were dressed only in breechclouts and faced each other with their left wrists and elbows banded to small oxhide shields, their bared knives flashing in the morning light.

Anticipating the duel, there was a hushed silence as everyone watched from both sides. Alicia stood between Red Crow and Thunder Roars, her heart pounding with fear for the man she loved. She kept telling herself over and over again that Cloud Eagle would win the duel. She had feared that losing sleep might cause him to falter. But Ten Bears had not slept either during the night-long celebration.

Her gaze swept over the crowd, stopping at Lost Wind. Alicia could see the dread in her eyes. This told Alicia that Lost Wind did not have much faith in her brother's ability to fight Cloud Eagle.

Alicia's eyes shifted downward and her lips parted in a light gasp. Lost Wind clutched a buckskin bag. Had she already packed for her journey from the Apache stronghold? Did she understand already that she was going to be banished along with her brother, who would not be victorious this morning?

Alicia's gaze went back to Cloud Eagle and Ten Bears, who were still only facing each other, not fighting. She had to wonder if Ten Bears had known all along that he could never win today. If not, she was confused as to why he had challenged Cloud Eagle to a duel.

Then she realized why. Ten Bears had no choice but to accept a challenge from his chief or he would have lost face and would have been humbled in front of all of his people.

Alicia's breathing came more evenly. Her heart even resumed its regular beats. Her beloved Apache chief would come through this unscathed.

She clasped her hands behind her when Cloud Eagle and Ten Bears sparred for an opening. Cloud Eagle held his war shield shoulder-high and slightly to the left, his knife lower to the right, blade down. He rocked sideways as he stepped around Ten Bears, the weight on the outside of his feet, his toes turned in. Both Ten Bears' and Cloud Eagle's bodies were relaxed. There was no tension or bunching of muscles.

Then the fight began. As they jabbed at the wind with their knives, and as they missed each other, they pressed together toward the edge of the trampled space. Their bodies gleamed with sweat like those of snakes that had sloughed off their skin.

Cloud Eagle leaped back to avoid a viper thrust

almost invisibly swift from Ten Bears' knife, then jumped forward again. He thudded the earth with his bare feet.

Shields crashed; feet tramped in rhythm.

Ten Bears leapt again to attack.

Cloud Eagle stepped aside and swung around.

As swift as a lightning strike, Cloud Eagle flung himself forward and struck like a leaping bobcat as he lifted a leg and with his foot knocked Ten Bears' knife from his hand.

Ten Bears took a step backward, but he was not fast enough. Cloud Eagle pounced on him and wrestled him to the ground. He pinned Ten Bears to the ground as he knelt over him, the point of his knife at the hollow of Ten Bears' throat.

"Do not spare my life only so that I can be humiliated and ridiculed," Ten Bears growled up at Cloud Eagle when he saw Cloud Eagle's hesitation.

Cloud Eagle was aware of someone softly crying. He looked away long enough to see Lost Wind, her eyes filled with tears as she gazed back at him.

Cloud Eagle locked his eyes with Lost Wind's for a moment longer, then turned his attention back to Ten Bears.

"Killing you would be easy because you have gone against your chief in words and deeds," Cloud Eagle said as he glared down at Ten Bears. He inched his knife away from Ten Bears' flesh. "But your sister needs you for her protection."

Again he placed the knife to Ten Bears's throat and leaned down into his face. "Give your word to me that you will look after Lost Wind," he hissed.

"She should still be your responsibility," Ten Bears snarled back.

"You will show disrespect to your chief with spiteful words while your chief holds a knife to your throat?" Cloud Eagle said, searching for enough willpower not to plunge the knife into this warrior's flesh. "The knife would end your words quickly."

"That is what I wish," Ten Bears said, trying to strain his throat closer to the knife. "I have no wife. Only a sister. She can find another husband to look after her. Kill me, Cloud Eagle. I do not wish to carry disgrace with me throughout the rest of my miserable life."

"Your sister is barren," Cloud Eagle argued back. "No man but a brother would have her."

"You are sure it is my sister who is barren?" Ten Bears taunted. "Or are you void of seed that would make a child grow within my sister's womb?"

An angry flush rose from Cloud Eagle's neck. His self-control was at its end. And had Ten Bears's words reached farther than Cloud Eagle's ears, it would have been a swift end for the Apache warrior.

But Ten Bears had said the spiteful remark in a low hiss, meant only for Cloud Eagle to hear. And Cloud Eagle knew that there was a chance that what Ten Bears had said might be true.

Two barren wives.

It did eat away at Cloud Eagle's gut to think that he might be the cause. He had never thought that anyone else might consider this possibility. He was surprised when Ten Bears had the courage to speak of such a thing.

Tired of the arguing, and wanting to thrust Ten Bears from his sight and away from his stronghold so that he could not share his thoughts with others, Cloud Eagle moved away from him.

"Get on your feet," he said, motioning with the knife towards Ten Bears. "Take your sister and leave. I will spread the word that you are not welcome in any other Apache stronghold, that you are unworthy of lodging among our people."

Alicia scarcely breathed as Ten Bears slunk away from Cloud Eagle.

Her gaze moved to Lost Wind, who broke away from the crowd and ran to Ten Bears and clung to him, her eyes wide as she watched Cloud Eagle.

There was a strained silence among the Apache people as Ten Bears and Lost Wind walked away. Everyone turned and watched until they were only a tiny movement along the horizon.

Thunder Roars was the first to break the silence. He went to Cloud Eagle and clasped a hand on his shoulder. "You did well," he said thickly. "It took much courage and self-discipline not to silence that man's words and heartbeat. I admire you, Cloud Eagle, for saving his life, especially since it was for the sake of his sister."

"He was once a brave and valiant Apache warrior," Cloud Eagle said, turning to Thunder Roars. He slipped his knife into its sheath. "But now, except for caring for his sister, he is worthless."

Alicia ran to Cloud Eagle and flung herself into his arms. "I'm so glad it's over," she cried. She looked up at Cloud Eagle as he swept an arm around her waist. "You spared him. How noble of you."

"As I forewarned you, it was never my intention to kill him," Cloud Eagle said. "There are more ways than one to lose a warrior. In the back of my mind there was always Lost Wind and her welfare. It is not a good thing to send wives away.

But when you do, it makes one feel better to see that she is being taken care of by someone of her kin. Her brother was all that remained of her family. She became his responsibility when I cast her from my life."

Alicia glanced toward the crowd. They were looking at Cloud Eagle with utter adulation, including Spring Dawn. She wondered about *her* welfare. But she did not voice this concern out loud to Cloud Eagle. This particular Apache woman seemed capable of taking care of herself.

And perhaps one day some man would take pity on her, whether or not she could bear a child, and take her into his household so that she could serve him in ways other than mothering children.

A thought came to her that made her insides quiver with dread. What if that thought entered Cloud Eagle's mind? What if his pity for Spring Dawn urged him to bring her back into his lodge to do the cooking, mending, and cleaning? Alicia could not stand the thought of sharing anything with another woman.

Especially her man!

And she was very capable of caring for Cloud Eagle without any interference.

"I must now ride to my stronghold," Thunder Roars said, groaning as he ran a hand over his swollen arm.

"I wish my herbal medications could have done more for you," Cloud Eagle said regretfully. "My shaman should have been called."

Thunder Roars smiled at Cloud Eagle. "I will always remember what you have done for me, Cloud Eagle," he said, nodding a thank-you to a brave as his horse was brought to him. He had stashed his deer meat high in a tree before gathering the honeycomb from the same tree. If the night creatures had not found it, he would have more than a bee-stung warrior to take back to his people.

"Return often," Cloud Eagle said, helping Thunder Roars onto his horse. "Share a smoke and plenty of talk."

"That I will do," Thunder Roars said. He shifted his eyes to Alicia. "You are a pleasant, beautiful, and gentle woman. You are good for Cloud Eagle." He shifted his gaze to Red Crow. "You are a dedicated warrior, my friend. You do your duties well for your chief."

Then he slowly encompassed them all, his eyes warm as they lingered on them one at a time, his lips curved into a smile. "One and all, come to my stronghold," he said. "My chieftain father will open his arms to everyone. We will entertain with a great feast and much dancing."

"The invitation will be remembered," Cloud Eagle said. He patted Thunder Roars' horse on the rump. "Ride well, my friend."

Cloud Eagle paused, then said, "Keep watch for renegades and outlaws. They spring up out of the depths of the sand, it seems, to attack passersby, be they red or white-skinned."

Thunder Roars nodded, then rode away, trying to straighten his shoulders, but obviously unable to because of the burning welts on his chest and back.

"There goes a fine man," Cloud Eagle said, feeling warm inside to have found a solid friendship with Thunder Roars. "If only Ten Bears could have been as fine."

"Do not labor over Ten Bears," Red Crow said,

stepping up to Cloud Eagle's side. "He is gone from sight. Allow him to be gone from your memory as well."

"I may regret not having killed him," Cloud Eagle said.

"He will wander far, Cloud Eagle, to get away from the shame of banishment," Red Crow said. He patted Cloud Eagle on the back and laughed beneath his breath. "My wives await my arrival in my lodge. It has been a long night and morning. They will have our bed prepared. There we will linger for the rest of the day. Tomorrow comes too soon with chores neglected today."

Cloud Eagle waved a farewell to Red Crow, then turned to Alicia. "It has been a long night and morning," he said, his eyes dancing into hers. "But somehow I cannot concentrate on sleeping. Is there not something left unfinished between us?"

"I think so," Alicia said. She swung to his side and locked her arm through his.

"Shall we, darling?" she said, giving him a sideways, smiling glance.

The crowd had dispersed back to the stronghold and their lodges. Even the children and the village dogs were quiet. "It seems everyone is ready to sleep," Alicia said. She circled around the tepees at the edge of the clearing with Cloud Eagle. His lodge was in sight only a few feet away.

"Not everyone," Cloud Eagle said, turning to her. He suddenly swept her up into his arms and nestled her close to his chest. "My woman, today I taught you how I fight to retain my right to have you. Now let me teach you more about how this Apache makes enduring love."

Snuggled in his embrace, Alicia felt her entire body grow limp with passion, all her senses yearning for the promise that he was offering her. Each step he took promised more, assured fulfillment. She clung around his neck as he carried her into his lodge. Their lips met in a frenzied kiss as they flung themselves down on the pallet of furs beside the glowing embers of the fire.

Their hands became just as frenzied as they hurriedly undressed each other.

Alicia sighed with pleasure as he moved over her, nudging her thighs apart with his knee.

There were no preliminaries. There was only the urgent need to become as one.

He entered her in one deep thrust, then began his rhythmic movements within her as she met him with lifted hips, her legs wrapped around his hips.

Cloud Eagle placed his hands beneath her and lifted her even closer. His mouth slid from her lips and covered one of her breasts, his tongue flicking around her nipple.

Alicia tossed her head back and forth, her eyes closed as she felt the rapture spreading within her. She felt as though she were glowing, so alive and filled with fire. Tremors cascaded down her back as Cloud Eagle withdrew his manhood and leaned away from her, to make a path down her body with his tongue.

She inhaled a shaky breath of ecstasy and found herself becoming weak all over with pleasure as his tongue sought and found the pulsing bud of her womanhood.

Surges of warmth flooded through Alicia's body. She had never felt anything as wonderfully delicious as his tongue moved over her, his fingers parting her fronds of hair to make her more accessible for this forbidden way of making love.

The more he caressed her, the more she became mindless with bliss. She caught her breath, not daring to breathe, for she was too close to the ultimate of pleasure.

She wanted it to last longer—perhaps until the stars filled the heavens with their miniature twinkling lamps.

Then once again he shifted his weight and moved inside her, his manhood magnificently filling her. She twined her arms around his neck and drew his mouth to her lips. They kissed sweetly and passionately. Their bodies strained together.

Cloud Eagle was hardly able to hold the energy back much longer, when the ultimate of pleasure would explode through every cell in his body. He held onto the moment, savoring the way their naked flesh was fused, their bodies sucking at each other, flesh against flesh in gentle pressure.

He trembled and felt the passion growing, growing almost to the bursting point when she thrust her tongue into his mouth and flickered it in and out, then moved it along his lips.

"Now," he whispered against her lips. "I feel it coming now. Share with me, my love, the wonders of paradise."

There was a great shudder in his loins. He gripped Alicia hard within his arms. His lips covered hers in a maddening kiss as the flood of rapture swept raggedly through him and she strained her hips up at him, crying out at her own fulfillment.

They clung for a while longer, then Cloud Eagle rolled away from Alicia and lay on his back. His eyes closed, he panted hard.

"While I am with you, it is such paradise, darling," Alicia murmured. She turned on her side and caressed his muscled, hairless chest. "I never knew that loving a man could be so sweet. I am filled with a quiet bliss, with a splendid joy. How do you feel at this moment, Cloud Eagle?"

He turned to her and engulfed her within his powerful arms and drew her against him. He lay his cheek against hers, now breathing easily. "I want you to be my wife," he said huskily. "You have said that you want to stay with me forever. Say that you will stay as my wife."

"I want nothing more than that," she murmured. She leaned away from him and traced the hard line of his jaw with her fingertip. "Yes, Cloud Eagle. I want to be your wife. Whenever, wherever you wish. I love you more than I ever imagined I would love anyone. You are the world to me."

Yet, in the back of Alicia's mind, there was a fleeting moment of doubt about becoming his wife. She knew that difficulties might arise by her living the life of a white Apache, as she might be called if she married an Apache chief.

And there was her brother, Charlie. If he came looking for her and found her, he would try and convince her that this was not the life that she should lead; he would demand that she leave Cloud Eagle.

But no brother and no prejudices would keep her from loving and staying with Cloud Eagle.

"My *Ish-kay-nay*, the marriage will happen soon," Cloud Eagle said, his face a mask of desire as he gazed intensely into her eyes. "First there are preliminaries. You have much to learn in order to adapt to the life of the Apache."

"My father always said that I was an astute student," Alicia said, crawling atop him. She straddled him, sucking in a wild breath of pleasure when she felt him hot and ready to enter her again. "I will learn quickly so that our marriage will not have to be delayed for long."

Desire shot through her and she held her head back so that her hair hung down to Cloud Eagle's thighs when he thrust himself up and into her.

She closed her eyes and rode him, bounce by bounce, floating, drifting, thrilling.

High in the mountains, Ten Bears began eagerly building a protective lodge for Lost Wind as she stood by, quietly watching. He made the dwelling from materials that were available to him. It was called a *wickiup*, a cone-shaped dwelling on a framework of slim, sturdy tree limbs covered with the leaves of the yucca plant.

"You will stay here until I return," Ten Bears ordered.

Unable to stay quiet any longer, Lost Wind stepped up to Ten Bears. "You will abandon me here?" she said, her voice breaking. "Why did you fight for my honor, then abandon me? Or was the duel with Cloud Eagle for more than your sister?"

Ten Bears turned to Lost Wind. He took her by the wrists and yanked her close. "Do not question your brother about anything that he does," he shouted. "Just obey."

She winced and jerked herself free. "You are not my keeper," she said in a hiss.

Ten Bears shrugged. "Then walk away," he said. "See how long you can exist without your brother."

"If you are gone, I will be forced to see to my needs anyhow," Lost Wind shouted back. "You are a thoughtless brother. I hate you."

Ten Bears ignored her. He finished the wickiup, went inside, and shaped rocks in the center for a fire pit.

Since he had been forced to leave the stronghold without any of his weapons, he only had the knife that Lost Wind had brought with her in her belongings.

He fashioned a spear out of a long, thin stick and tied the knife at the end.

With this weapon he left and was gone long enough to kill a deer so that Lost Wind would have meat for several days in his absence.

He dropped the deer just outside the wickiup door.

Lost Wind came out and stared at it.

"I leave now," Ten Bears said. He removed the knife from the stick and shoved it toward Lost Wind. "You have chores to do. Dress the deer. It is yours for the length of my absence."

Lost Wind cast him an angry frown, then dropped to her knees and began taking the pelt from the deer. She gave her brother a worried glance as he turned and began walking away.

"You will not get far without a horse," she shouted after him.

"I will steal the first one I see," he shouted back, over his shoulder.

"Why are you doing this?" she cried, tears splashing from her eyes.

"Vengeance," he snarled back.

A tremor of fear soared across Lost Wind's flesh. She knew whom her brother would be targeting with thoughts of vengeance. Cloud Eagle.

She set her jaw and flung her long hair back across her shoulders. "Cloud Eagle deserves what he will get from my brother," she hissed out.

She smiled wickedly as she continued preparing the deer for the many lonely days ahead.

Chapter Fifteen

When Alicia brought the breakfast dishes from the river, she found Cloud Eagle outside his lodge with an elderly man whose body was bent and twisted, but whose face was radiant with kindness as he smiled at Alicia's approach.

She returned the smile and stepped to Cloud Eagle's side. Her gaze looked past the elderly man's disability at the way he was dressed and his features. His hair was gray; long and thin, it lay over his bent, frail shoulders. His eyes were no longer a brilliant dark brown, as she assumed they had been in his youth; they had faded with time to a dusty, indistinct color.

He wore a full-length, fringed buckskin robe that turned and twisted with the curvature of his body. It was decorated with beads of brilliant colors which depicted desert flowers.

"*Ish-kay-nay*, He Who Knows Much has come at my request to be your teacher," Cloud Eagle said. He took the dishes from Alicia's arms. "You will learn the Apache language and all the Apache customs under the tutelage of He Who Knows Much."

"I am glad to make your acquaintance, He Who Knows Much," she said, extending a hand of friendship to the lame Apache. "And I am eager to learn all of the ways of your people."

"He Who Knows Much takes pride in teaching my chief's woman," he returned.

"He Who Knows Much's life was altered by a fall from a horse when he was a mere boy," Cloud Eagle said softly. "He is a lame Apache whose prowess is in the mind."

"I'm sorry about the accident," Alicia said, yet knew that he would not appreciate pity. He seemed well adjusted to his lot in life. Happiness radiated from him, like warm rays from the sun.

And as Cloud Eagle talked about and looked down at He Who Knows Much, he seemed not to see the twisted body. Instead he saw an Apache who had earned the title of warrior in other ways besides proving himself on the battlefield or in youthful games when skills were tested before a brave became a warrior.

"The accident was long ago," He Who Knows Much said, patting Alicia's arm. "Now let us proceed with your schooling. Let us go inside and sit by the fire. I shall teach you a little each day until your knowledge of all that is required of you is complete and you can live among the Apache as one heart and soul with them."

Alicia cast Cloud Eagle a smile across her shoulder as He Who Knows Much took her by the arm and led her into Cloud Eagle's tepee.

Once inside, she looked around, expecting to find some sort of books or writing tools.

But she soon discovered that the teachings were going to come directly from He Who Knows Much's storehouse of memories. Intrigued, she eagerly sat down beside him. She crossed her legs beneath the buckskin skirt and gazed at him. His eyes grew more alive as he began his teachings.

Cloud Eagle came into the lodge and set the dishes down, then left again.

Alicia had been hardly aware of his presence. She was listening intently to He Who Knows Much, whose voice had an almost mystical quality about it. She leaned closer, taking in his every word. She filed everything in her memory and would use this knowledge when it became necessary to prove that she did deserve to be the wife of a powerful Apache chief.

"*Tloh-ka-dih-nadidah-hae* means 'rise from the grass', another word for Apache," He Who Knows Much said, careful to pronounce the Apache phrase so that Alicia could remember it without asking him to repeat it. "Among the Apache, *tloh-ka-dih-nadidah-hae* is the art of surprising another within three or four feet, a form of play from babyhood. The one surprised or taken off his guard is in disgrace."

He paused and nodded at Alicia, gesturing with a twisted hand for her to repeat the word and the teachings. "*Tloh-ka-dih-nadidah-hae*," Alicia said slowly, then repeated its meaning.

He Who Knows Much's eyes and smile showed his approval of her swiftness to learn and her willingness to participate. "The young men, one at a time, are taken out on moonless nights and released to find their way back to the camp," he said. In his eyes there was a sudden haunted look, as though he was reliving the time he had experienced what he was telling. "In coming to a strange ridge, the boy is told to stop and study it from a distance, then from halfway, finally from close up. That way it is imprinted in his mind. He finds his way back to camp that way."

He paused and reached over to pat her knee through her skirt. "I tell you this so that when you have a son, you will understand why he is taken far away and left to find his way home," he said, again smiling. His gaze raked slowly over her, then he looked into her eyes. "You will not disappoint my chief as did his first two wives. You will give my chief many sons, and perhaps a dainty, pretty daughter in your image."

She smiled back and wondered how he would feel about her if he knew that her skills were more manly than feminine. Would he then call her dainty?

She gave him a smile and moved closer as he talked again about the Apache's customs. She was glad when he took the teachings away from the discussion of children. It gave her a fretful ache around her heart when she allowed herself to think of what might happen if she did not bear this chief a child.

It was obvious that everyone dwelled on the subject!

"Quail is the master," He Who Knows Much said, causing Alicia's eyebrows to rise. "To the Apache, the quail is one of the highest forms of bird life."

He patted her knee once again, then drew his limp hand back to rest it on his lap. "*Na-tse-kes* means to think, to turn something over and over again in the mind—to meditate," he said, nodding. "It is an Apache's mental process."

He leaned toward the fire and shoved a piece of wood into the flames, then folded his arms across his chest. "Cloud Eagle is a beloved chief. A chief among men is one who does the thinking for other men," he said, his eyes always twinkling when he mentioned Cloud Eagle. "His brain is like an invisible magnet sweeping over iron filings."

He continued talking. Alicia took everything in.

"It is not enough to have thoughts," He Who Knows Much said. "Thoughts must be carried into action."

He paused, rubbing his fingers as though they were paining him, then continued. "It is not only a matter of sitting still, but of thinking still, of emptying the mind," he said. "If you do not wish your adversary to know your plan, you must not even think it when he is near until the instant of *coup*. This is a far deeper fold of the game than a mere motionless huddling against a rock. It has to do with the science of invisibility mentioned in high medicine lore. To die on the warpath is a calamity."

He Who Knows Much burst into sudden laughter. His eyes danced as he looked over at Alicia. "So often I forget that the one I am teaching is a woman, not a brave who hungers to become a warrior," he said, again patting her knee. Then he pushed himself slowly up from the floor of the tepee. "I will teach you more later on the language and customs of our people. This old, twisted man is bone-weary. He must go and rest before attempting further teachings."

Alicia scrambled to her feet, relieved that her

leg no longer pained her and that she was free to move about without limping. She placed a hand on He Who Knows Much's elbow and helped him to his feet, then slipped an arm around his frail waist and walked him outside, into the blazing sun of morning.

"Thank you for the lessons you taught me today," Alicia said as he limped away from her.

Cloud Eagle and Red Crow sat just outside the lodge, carving new bows. Alicia sat down beside Cloud Eagle and watched his skill in carving designs on his new bow.

"Did you learn much today, *Ish-kay-nay?*" Cloud Eagle said, giving Alicia a glance. "He was not with you for long."

"He seemed in pain," Alicia said, turning her eyes just in time to see He Who Knows Much enter his lodge in a bent-over fashion.

Then she looked at Cloud Eagle, her eyes wide. "But I did learn enough, I think."

She wet her lips with her tongue, sat up straight, and repeated the two words that she had been taught today. "*Na-tse-kes*, to think, to turn something over and over again in the mind," she said. "And *tloh-ka-dih-nadidah-hae*, to rise from the grass."

She waited anxiously for Cloud Eagle's reaction.

He laughed and laid his bow aside. He took her hands. "If you can remember the Apache phrase for 'to rise from the grass' so easily, you will not have any problem with the rest of He Who Knows Much's teachings. That is a phrase that is hard to grasp."

Red Crow rose to his feet. "I must leave you

now," he said, slinging his bow over his shoulder. "A hunting party is planned. I am a part of it. Do you wish to join us, Cloud Eagle?"

"No," Cloud Eagle said, rising to his feet. He offered Alicia his hand, which she took. She rose and stood at his side. "There are other important issues on your chief's mind today."

Red Crow frowned at Alicia, then turned and sauntered away.

"He may never truly like me," Alicia said sadly. "Although he has invited me to his tepee to visit his wives, I know the invitation was not given to me from his heart."

"In his eyes you may forever be white," Cloud Eagle said, shrugging. "It matters not. In mine, you are everything."

He raised the entrance flap, and Alicia went inside. He followed.

When the flap was lowered, Cloud Eagle went to Alicia and placed his hands at her waist and lowered her to the pallet of furs. "What else did He Who Knows Much teach you today?" he whispered, brushing kisses across her ear.

Alicia shivered with desire and opened her legs to him as one of his hands snaked up inside her skirt, leaving a heated trail in its wake as he moved toward her throbbing center.

"He taught me ways of boys and men," she whispered, shimmering with ecstasy when his hand found her open and ready for his fingers. She became mindless beneath his caresses.

She twined her fingers through his long, thick hair and drew his lips to hers. "Do I still behave like a boy, my darling?" she whispered.

"Did you ever?" he said, chuckling as he drew a gasp from her when he thrust a finger deeply within her moist woman's place.

"I think not," she said, sighing.

Their kiss was filled with fire. His hands were quick to lift the skirt of her dress and to lower his fringed breeches. He was inside her more quickly than lightning could flash across the sky.

She moaned with pleasure and again blessed the heavens for having sent him to her.

Ten Bears crouched behind Red Crow's tepee. He had watched the two wives wander to the river with their children.

He had seen Red Crow enter his lodge, then leave.

He had even witnessed Red Crow leave the village with several warriors on horseback.

This gave Ten Bears the opportunity to use Red Crow's lodge for a distraction so that Ten Bears could steal a horse without getting caught.

But first, he would steal himself a weapon.

An Apache without a weapon was empty of soul!

Looking from side to side, making sure that no one saw him, Ten Bears crept around the tepee toward the front. When he saw that the way was clear, he ran inside Red Crow's lodge.

He stood just inside. His eyes took in everything as he looked for Red Crow's supply of weapons. His gaze stopped at the painting of a woman, wondering why it was there.

And the woman's likeness that was painted on the canvas was Cloud Eagle's white woman!

He shrugged.

He had more urgent things on his mind than a painting.

He smiled when he found the store of weapons

at the back of the tepee, partially covered with blankets.

Moving stealthily, he went to the weapons and chose a rifle and a knife.

He turned and stared at the fire, smiling. That was the way he was going to find an easy escape. He would set fire to the lodge. While everyone was rushing about trying to put it out, he would very easily get a horse without anyone noticing him.

All eyes would be on the fire. All hands would be busy throwing water on it.

He knocked everything aside and pushed his way to the very back of the tepee. Chuckling beneath his breath, he cut a hole large enough for him to crawl through.

Then he turned and crawled to the fire pit. He placed a blanket over the fire and watched the flames take hold.

When it was fully engulfed, he laid the blanket on a pile of clothes and brushed the dried grass that was spread across the floor into the flames. Then he lunged outside and ran toward the trees where he would hide until he found it safe enough to steal a horse.

"Fort Thomas," he whispered as he found a large tree and hunkered down behind it. "This Apache is riding to Fort Thomas. The white pony soldiers will be told a few things that will work against Cloud Eagle . . . and his white woman."

He sneered when someone shouted "Fire!" and the whole community ran to save Red Crow's lodge.

Ten Bears moved quickly. He went to the corral and sorted through the horses until he found his own mighty steed. In one leap he was on its back.

Riding bareback, he led his horse to the fence, where it jumped it as though it were as limber as a deer.

Lying low over the horse's mane, Ten Bears rode hard across the land. He looked over his shoulder. When he saw that no one was following, he laughed into the wind. It gave him a feeling of power to know that he had tricked Cloud Eagle and had gotten away with it.

Now to continue with his plan of revenge!

Chapter Sixteen

The cry of "Fire!" wrenched Cloud Eagle and Alicia apart. They scurried into their clothes and rushed outside. When Cloud Eagle saw that it was Red Crow's lodge that was burning, a cold fear spread through him. Red Crow was gone. But were his wives and children in the lodge?

Blinded with anxious concern, he shoved his way through the crowd of people who were already carrying water to the fire and rushed into Red Crow's lodge.

He was instantly assaulted by intense heat and smoke. Coughing, he covered his mouth with his hand. His eyes burned as he searched for Sweet Rose and Laughing Eyes and the children.

People shouted at Cloud Eagle from outside, urging him to leave. The buckskin covering was now totally engulfed in flames. The poles holding it up were smoldering. There was a threat that everything would soon come tumbling down, and no one wanted their chief to die an unglorious death.

Hands grabbing at his arms caused Cloud Eagle to look quickly around. The pit of his stomach tightened when he discovered Alicia there in the tepee with him, tears streaming from her eyes from the smoke burning them.

"You must leave this place, Cloud Eagle," Alicia screamed at him. She tugged frantically on his arm. "Come on. It's unsafe. Red Crow's family are safe. They were at the river when the fire broke out."

Choking on the smoke and afraid for Alicia, Cloud Eagle turned to leave, but stopped when Alicia suddenly made a mad rush through the smoke, more deeply into the tepee.

"*Ish-kay-nay!*" he cried.

Stumbling over burning debris, he went after her, puzzled as to why she had gone ahead into the threat of the fire instead of retreating outside with him. She had come for him. She had begged him to leave. Why then would she stay herself?

"Stop!" he shouted. "Come with me outside!"

Although her throat burned from the smoke and her eyes felt as though they were aflame, Alicia stopped and knelt down before a painting that she had seen through the veil of smoke.

Her heart skipped a beat and her insides went weak when she grabbed the painting and held it up before her eyes. She was oblivious to the smoking frame that was near to exploding into flames. She was aware only of the gnawing ache circling her heart.

This was the painting of herself that had hung above the fireplace mantel in her family home in Saint Louis. Her brother Charlie had painted it.

She gulped back a sob that lodged in her throat, a sob not brought on by the stiflingly hot smoke. It was because she knew that her brother would never willingly part with this painting. He had always boasted that this was the best that he had ever done and had enjoyed capturing his sister in oils when she had looked her loveliest.

Seconds turned into minutes as she stared at the painting. The fire popped, crackled, and hissed on all sides of her now. The heat was intense. The smoke was blinding. But none of this matched the rage that now filled her.

Her jaw tight, clutching the painting, she turned her eyes up to Cloud Eagle. "How?" she cried, thrusting the painting out for him to see. "How would Red Crow have this? How, Cloud Eagle, except that it must surely have been taken when my brother's wagon train was ambushed! Cloud Eagle, he was on his way out here to see to my welfare. When did you ambush him? When?"

Cloud Eagle stared disbelievingly at the painting. He had no idea how Red Crow had it in his possession. He had no answers for Alicia!

A lodge pole fell away from the buckskin covering and crashed in flames close beside Cloud Eagle and Alicia. Cloud Eagle flinched and forgot everything but getting Alicia to safety. He swept her into his arms while she still clung to the painting and carried her outside.

Cloud Eagle ran past those who continued to throw water on Red Crow's tepee and carried Alicia toward those who were only watching.

"Let me down, you liar, you swindler, you murderer," Alicia screamed, kicking her legs in a futile effort to be set free. "How could I ever have trusted you? You killed my brother or how else

191

would one of your warriors have this painting? My brother would never have parted with it except by force. My brother was in the Arizona Territory to find me. This painting in Red Crow's tepee has to mean that Charlie will never find me. He was ambushed. He was murdered."

Embarrassed by Alicia's tirade, and puzzled over why Red Crow had the painting, Cloud Eagle carried Alicia farther away, to the far edge of the stronghold. When he set her to her feet, he stared down at her anger and the hate in her eyes.

"I know nothing of how this painting came to be in the possession of Red Crow," he said, reaching to wipe the smudges from her face.

She took a quick, angry step away from him and glared up at him with a look of bewildered mistrust.

"You lie so easily," Alicia whispered, her heart aching over so many things. Over realizing that Cloud Eagle could be a double-crossing liar, and that her brother was now more than likely dead.

Her beloved Charlie.

How could she accept that he was dead, or *how* he had died?

Cloud Eagle, the man with whom she had shared so many beautiful moments. He or Red Crow had surely killed her very own brother.

"How could you have such little faith in this man who has given you his heart?" Cloud Eagle said thickly. "Cloud Eagle is known for his honesty. His peaceful ways. And you can so easily condemn this chief without listening to reason?"

He took a determined step toward her and gripped her shoulders so tightly no matter how much she squirmed, she could not get free. "When

I say that I knew nothing of this painting being in Red Crow's possession, then you must believe me," he said. The sudden tears flooding Alicia's eyes washed away his anger. "*Ish-kay-nay*, I *have* seen the painting before. But only to admire it. When the man who owned it refused to make trade, this Apache chief rode off and left it in his possession."

Alicia's lips parted. "Then you did see my brother?" she gasped.

"If the man who had this painting in his possession was your brother, yes, then I saw him," Cloud Eagle said. He felt her stiffen even more beneath his grip. "Your brother was alive when I last saw him."

"How can you stand there and lie so easily?" Alicia suddenly screamed. "If my brother were still alive when you left him, why then did Red Crow have the painting? He followed your commands. He would not take the painting unless ordered to. This has to mean that my brother—"

The tepee having now burned to the ground, everyone's attention had turned to their chief and his screaming woman.

Turtle Crawls, one of Cloud Eagle's most trusted warriors, stepped to Cloud Eagle's side. "There is confusion over the painting?" he said to Cloud Eagle, then shifted his gaze to glare at Alicia for showing such outward distrust and disrespect for his chief.

"Much," was all that Cloud Eagle would offer.

"You wonder how it happened to be in Red Crow's lodge?" Turtle Crawls said, turning his eyes back to Cloud Eagle.

Frowning, Cloud Eagle turned to Turtle Crawls. "You know the answer?" he said.

"In Red Crow's absence, yes, I will speak for him," Turtle Crawls said, nodding. "This painting was taken from Sandy Whiskers' office. I was there with Red Crow when he offered payment for the painting to the Englishman. He wanted to bring the painting to you for a surprise gift, since he knew that you had admired and had wanted it when it was in the possession of the man who had painted it."

Alicia listened with a pounding heart and could not believe one word of what was being said. She saw this as a ploy, all planned out should she ever discover that the painting was among the belongings of one of Cloud Eagle's warriors.

It had all been practiced.

A dirty, rotten scheme meant to trick her into believing that the Apache had not taken the painting from an innocent man in a terrible ambush.

It made her dizzy with anguish to believe that her brother had come to such a horrible end. He had been one of the most gentle men she had ever known. Firearms were never a part of his attire. He had loved and trusted everyone and everything. His trust had gone too far this time, it seemed.

"And Sandy Whiskers parted with it after Red Crow made payment?" Cloud Eagle said, feeling warm thoughts about his friend, Red Crow.

"No, he would not accept any payment," Turtle Crawls said.

This confused the issue even more.

This convinced Alicia more than ever that there were too many lies here that sounded far-fetched and practiced.

To her it made no sense whatsoever that Sandy

Whiskers would part freely with a painting that he could sell to the highest bidder.

No, she was convinced that Cloud Eagle had known all along that Red Crow had the painting. It had been kept hidden in Red Crow's lodge purposely, for one look at the painting would be proof enough that she was the artist's subject and that she would know that the painting had come into the possession of the Apache in the wrong way.

This was being kept from her purposely so that she would be pulled into more deceit by Cloud Eagle. He would marry her while all along knowing that he had killed her very own brother!

"Then how is it that Red Crow had the painting if the Englishman would not willingly part with it?" Cloud Eagle asked.

"Knowing your want of this painting, Red Crow left the Englishman's outpost after he had made a good trade for the woman's mail sack, then went back later and stole the painting when Sandy Whiskers was gone," Turtle Crawls said matter-of-factly. "Red Crow was going to present the painting to you later as a special gift."

"He is a trusted friend," Cloud Eagle said, slowly nodding. Then he placed a hand on Turtle Crawls' shoulder. "Did Red Crow question Sandy Whiskers as to how he had acquired the painting?"

"He asked. Sandy Whiskers bragged about having taken it from a white man," Turtle Crawls said softly. "But he did not say whether or not he had left the man dead or alive."

Alicia took several shaky steps away from Cloud Eagle. Tears streamed down her face, making paths through the smoke smudges. "I've heard enough," she cried. "Enough lies. Enough deceit. Enough talk of my brother! You know as well as I that everything you are saying is a lie. You know as well as I that my brother is dead! How could I have ever put my trust in you, a dreaded Apache?"

Then she hissed out as she glared at Cloud Eagle, "You lowdown, thieving, damn sonofabitch."

Gasps reverberated around Alicia. Her insides shook with alarm as she turned and stared at the people who were horrified by what she had said and by her behavior—but mainly by her accusations.

She felt suddenly threatened.

The painting dropped from Alicia's hands when Cloud Eagle came to her and grabbed her up into his arms and carried her away from the stunned Apache people.

Infuriated, she pummeled his chest with her fists. "Let me down!" she screamed. "I hate you. Do you hear me? I hate you. You damn Injun. You murdering Apache, let me down, or do you plan to murder me too now that you've been caught with your pants down?"

Her words pierced Cloud Eagle's heart as though arrows were being shot into it. Her insults sank deeply into his soul.

But he knew that part of her mindless attitude was the result of believing that her brother might have been killed by ambushers. The very fact that the painting had been in Sandy Whiskers' possession was perhaps all the proof one needed to know the fate of its owner.

Alicia continued fighting Cloud Eagle, then

grew quiet when he took her to the corral and slammed her onto the back of his frisky roan and swung himself into the saddle behind her. She had no chance to get away. His arm was there too quickly around her waist. He held her as though she were in a vise, not budging to her continued demands and insults. He sent his horse into a gallop through the gate as one of his young braves opened it for him.

"Where are you taking me?" Alicia cried, her eyes wild. "Please just let me go. I promise not to bring the army back to arrest you for having killed my brother. But please tell me where his body is. He needs a decent Christian burial."

Cloud Eagle still did not respond. He knew that anything he might say to her now was wasted. It was up to someone else to prove his innocence.

His eyes were filled with a determined anger. His jaw was clenched tightly as he sent his roan into a hard gallop across the land, intent on proving his innocence. There was only one way, and he was going to take it, even if it proved Red Crow's guilt for having stolen the property that Sandy Whiskers had claimed as his.

It was time, anyhow, to break ties with the murdering English scoundrel. It was no longer safe to link his name with someone who so blatantly killed and stole.

Cloud Eagle could no longer turn his eyes the other way.

Sandy Whiskers was out of control.

Fearing the worst for her brother, that he was indeed dead, tears trembled down Alicia's cheeks. She no longer had the strength to strike back at Cloud Eagle. Her emotions had totally drained her.

Chapter Seventeen

The sun cast its flames of color onto the small outpost that sweltered in the middle of a barren strip of land. Only a few trees whispered and trembled in the dry breeze around the high white wall that hid the activities of the outpost behind it.

In sweat-stained buckskins, Sandy Whiskers sat at his desk, which faced a window over which the shade was drawn, except for a small slit left open at the bottom. That was enough to let Sandy Whiskers see the courtyard and front gate of his outpost.

He chewed aimlessly on his cigar. He rolled it around and around between his thick lips as he watched Cloud Eagle enter the wide gate on horseback.

He leaned closer to the window and squinted out. Cloud Eagle was not alone. A woman was on the horse with him. She looked familiar.

Grunting beneath his breath, he pushed his bulbous body out of the chair and went to the window. Slowly he lifted the shade to get a better look at the woman.

"Well, I'll be damned," he whispered to himself. "It *is* Alicia. Alicia Cline from the stage station." He idly scratched his brow. What the hell was she doing with an Apache? And why did he sense that she was not here under her own volition?

His eyes squinted beneath a shadowing of thick, sandy-colored eyebrows as he shifted his gaze to the guards, who stood just inside the gate. They had allowed Cloud Eagle's entrance. They knew the Apache chief well and had been instructed that no questions should be asked when he arrived at the outpost. Sandy Whiskers and the Apache had sealed a bargain that worked in both their favors. Only recently had the Englishman seen cause for one or the other to make a final break in their relationship.

Red Crow. He was the cause.

"As for Red Crow," he said to himself, snickering, "that sonofabitch will never steal from anyone else again, especially *me.*"

Sandy Whiskers lowered the shade again. Wheezing from the effort it took to move, he went back to his chair and eased himself into it.

The chair squeaked and swayed beneath the weight of the short, fat Englishman. The leather of the chair had split long ago, and the stuffing was hanging down on both sides.

The room was hazy with cigar smoke. A lone kerosene lamp spread its golden light through the smoke. Sliding a thick hand across the top of his desk, Sandy Whiskers shuffled papers aside. His breath came in heaves as he reached for a bottle of tequila.

He placed his half-smoked cigar in an ashtray and placed a glass beside the bottle. Half watching the door and half watching what he was doing, he slopped tequila half into the glass and half onto his desk. Shoving the bottle aside, he lifted the glass to his lips and downed the tequila in a few quick gulps.

Then he flattened his hands on the top of the desk and smiled crookedly as one of the bearded men under his command brought Alicia and Cloud Eagle into his office.

Sandy Whiskers dismissed the bearded man with a nod, then gazed from Cloud Eagle to Alicia, then back at Cloud Eagle.

"My outpost has been frequented lately by more Apache than usual," Sandy Whiskers said and lifted his fingers to his thick, sandy-colored mustache and toyed with it. He twisted the ends around his finger, his pale gray eyes squinting at his visitors. "But never before have you brought a lady. What's the occasion today, Cloud Eagle?"

Cloud Eagle squared his shoulders. He fought to keep his composure, but it was hard. The Englishman had brought disharmony into his life when things had just become perfect between Cloud Eagle and his *Ish-kay-nay*.

Now it was as though Cloud Eagle and Alicia were strangers. And it was all because of this stocky Englishman who sat smugly in his chair, reeking of tequila, cigars, and dried perspiration.

"I have come today with this woman so that the truth can be told about the painting that Red Crow saw in your possession," Cloud Eagle said, his voice tight. "He not only saw this painting, he bargained with you for it."

Sandy Whiskers offered no response.

Silence dragged on, demanding a reply.

"White man, answer me or regret your silence," Cloud Eagle warned, his teeth clenched.

"I know of no painting," Sandy Whiskers said. Lies always came easily for him.

Sandy Whiskers grabbed the bottle and poured himself another glass of tequila. He drank it in one fast swallow, then shoved the glass away.

"You lie," Cloud Eagle said, placing his palms flat on the Englishman's desk to enable him to lean into Sandy Whiskers' face. "You had the painting. Red Crow bargained for it. There was a witness. Turtle Crawls. He also saw the painting in your possession."

Sandy Whiskers lit his cigar again and worked it over into the corner of his mouth. "Why such interest in a damn painting?" he said, knowing the answer.

He stared up at Alicia, recalling that the painting showed her exact likeness. When he had seen it with the white man, he had seen the resemblance. He knew then that he had to have it.

And although he had never seen Alicia in anything besides men's clothing, he had known what surely lay beneath them and had secretly hungered for Alicia since the first time he had seen her.

He just had not approached her yet. He had too much to hide that she might discover.

She worked for the government. Because of this, she was a threat. He could not take any more chances that what he did behind a wall at the back of his outpost would be discovered.

Sandy Whiskers also knew that he could not tell Cloud Eagle the truth about how he had acquired the painting in Alicia's presence, or everyone would know that he was responsible for the latest massacre on the California Road.

Thus far the United States Government was unaware of his marauding ways. In fact, they were more apt to defend than to ridicule him. There was a peaceful truce between them.

"You play games?" Cloud Eagle said, enraged by Sandy Whiskers' lies. He reached over the desk and wrapped his fingers around the Englishman's throat.

The cigar popped from Sandy Whiskers' mouth and fell to the desk on the stack of papers. The papers began smoldering.

"Your words are like a whisper borne by the mourning winds," Cloud Eagle hissed between clenched teeth. "Now tell the truth. Where did you get the painting? What happened to the man in whose possession you found it?"

"I . . . know . . . of no painting," Sandy Whiskers managed to get out in a strained whisper. "Let me go, Cloud Eagle."

Cloud Eagle squeezed the Englishman's throat more tightly.

Sandy Whiskers gagged. His eyes bulged.

"My warrior Turtle Crawls is a man of honor and truth," Cloud Eagle snarled. "He said that Red Crow took the painting from your cabin. I know this is true. Now you tell the lady the truth. Tell her that you stole the painting from her brother."

"I cannot tell her something that I know nothing of," Sandy Whiskers said, looking wildly over at Alicia. "I am innocent. Tell this crazed Indian to let me go."

Alicia had stood by, silently watching, trying to measure the truth between these two men, and found it hard to believe Cloud Eagle's story over the Englishman's. She saw no reason for Sandy Whiskers to lie so blatantly about the painting. What did he have to gain?

She turned on a heel and rushed from the room, hell-bent on getting away from Cloud Eagle. She ran outside, but he was soon there, stopping her by grabbing her wrist.

"You believe the Englishman over me?" Cloud Eagle said, searching her face for some semblance of the love that she had shown for him until the painting was rescued from the fire.

Deep within his heart, he was not only condemning the Englishman for this estrangement with Alicia, but also Red Crow. If Red Crow had left well enough alone, and had not stolen the painting, then there would be no reason now for the woman he loved to turn on him.

He doubted if he could get her feelings turned around again. The only way he could show her absolute proof of his innocence was to bring her brother face to face with her.

But he saw that as impossible. Her brother was surely dead. The Englishman would not be foolish enough to leave anyone behind who might tell the truth about his illegal activities.

And as far as Cloud Eagle and the Englishman were concerned, it was war!

"All I saw today was one lie being stacked onto another," Alicia sobbed. She tried to jerk her wrist free, but Cloud Eagle would not allow it. She went limp and pleaded with her eyes. "Just let me go.

I'm so weary of all of this. My brother. My poor brother. Because of me and my stubborn decision not to return to Saint Louis, he is probably lying dead out there somewhere in the desert." She hung her head. Her body trembled as she cried in earnest. "He's dead. I know he's dead."

Cloud Eagle wanted so badly to draw her into his arms and comfort her but knew that she would not allow it. Instead he lifted her into his arms and carried her to the horse. This time she did not fight him. She saw it as useless.

Mounting the roan behind Alicia, Cloud Eagle glanced at Sandy Whiskers' window and scowled when he saw that he was peering out at him with a glint in his eyes. "You will pay for your lies," he said, making sure to mouth the words distinctly enough for the Englishman to see and understand. "*Pindah-lickayee dis-ay-go, dee-dah-tatsan.* White-eyed man, you will soon be dead."

Sandy Whiskers glared back at Cloud Eagle and understood each of the words being mouthed, even those spoken in Apache.

"*Excremento*," he muttered, a curse he used frequently when referring to the Apache. "Soon *you* will die, filthy Apache. I will get even with you. Savage, I have tolerated your interference long enough."

The sky was sprinkled with sequins of stars, and the moon was so bright that it sent a soft white sheen across the land as Cloud Eagle rode into his stronghold with Alicia.

As he rode past the charred remains of Red Crow's lodge, he was filled with many emotions. He was sad over Red Crow and his wives' loss.

Yet he could not place his anger aside when he thought of the painting that had been found in the fire. He kept reminding himself that Red Crow had stolen the painting with the best of intentions—to please his chief with a special gift.

He stiffened when he rode up to his lodge and saw the painting resting against the buckskin covering. It was hard to recall when he had first seen the painting and had wanted it for his own. Now he wished he had never seen it and would never see it again. It meant anything but good in his life.

Alicia had slept fitfully in Cloud Eagle's embrace for the past several miles. The crying and grieving over her brother, and over being so disappointed at Cloud Eagle's deceit, had drained her of energy.

As Cloud Eagle drew his roan to a shuddering halt, Alicia awakened and looked around her. She was again engulfed with the pain that cut deep into her heart when she saw the painting that rested against the outside of Cloud Eagle's lodge. The painting stood for many things now, most hurtful.

Gray romped from the tepee and stood patiently waiting for attention when Cloud Eagle dismounted. He grew frisky at Cloud Eagle's feet when Cloud Eagle reached for Alicia.

Alicia allowed Cloud Eagle to help her from the horse. She was weak. She felt empty through and through.

When her feet reached solid ground, she eased away from Cloud Eagle and walked in a dazed state toward the painting. Lifting it, she carried it inside Cloud Eagle's lodge. She sat down beside the lodge fire, which had burned down to glowing embers. She had enough light from those embers to see the familiar signature of her brother on the painting in the right lower corner.

Trembling, her fingers traveled over the signature. It was as though she were touching her brother.

With Gray at his heels, Cloud Eagle entered his lodge. He stood over Alicia. "Allow me to help you put your grief and anger behind you," he said, kneeling down beside her. He reached a hand to push back loose strands of hair from her face and flinched when she slapped his hand away.

"I don't want you ever to touch me again," Alicia said, although saying the words cut to the very core of herself.

How could love turn to hate so quickly? Though she felt that all guilt pointed directly at Cloud Eagle, a part of her would never let go of loving him. What they had shared had been so beautifully sweet. She wanted it back again the way it was before she had found the painting in Red Crow's lodge!

But she knew that was impossible.

Cloud Eagle was a thief.

He was a liar.

More than likely, he was a murderer.

"You say what you do not mean," Cloud Eagle uttered softly, his voice filled with pain. "In time, you will see that. For now I will leave you alone with your grief. I will also think through how you feel about this Apache chief. If you will allow yourself, you will know that I am not guilty of that of which you accuse me. I know there is no more proof than my word, my beautiful *Ish-kay-nay*. If that is not enough, then all is lost between us."

Alicia cast him a glance, and seeing him look so beaten almost made her throw all doubts aside and rush into his embrace.

It would be so easy.

He was there. He needed her. She needed him.

Yet she could not find it in herself to go against the feelings that nagged at her insides. She could never love a man who had killed her brother!

She turned her eyes quickly away.

Cloud Eagle gazed at her for a moment longer, then he left to see if Red Crow had returned from the hunt. He had much to say to him! He would thank him for being thoughtful enough to steal the portrait for him. He would scold him for causing so much heartache because he stole it!

Cloud Eagle found Turtle Crawls sitting beside the communal fire. "My friend, has Red Crow returned yet from the hunt?" he asked, settling on his haunches beside Turtle Crawls.

"The hunt must be good," Turtle Crawls said, smiling over at Cloud Eagle. "They have not returned yet."

Cloud Eagle stared into the fire. "Turtle Crawls, the Englishman lied," he said, his voice hollow. "In the presence of my woman, he lied. He said that he knew of no painting. Nothing made him change his mind. My woman believes him over me."

"Then she is not deserving of you," Turtle Crawls said.

"I do not see it that way," Cloud Eagle said. He looked over his shoulder at his tepee, then stared at the fire again. "She is white. All whites have little trust in the Apache. Just because she learned to love me does not erase that suspicion entirely from her heart. She is a victim of prejudices taught her as a child. How can I blame her for that which someone placed inside her heart

207

when she was only a child? Her reaction now over seeing the portrait in the Apache's possession is only natural. In time she will learn to trust this chief again."

Gray tried to get Alicia's attention, and when she ignored him, he sauntered outside and sat down beside Cloud Eagle.

Alicia stared at the painting a moment longer, then laid it aside and stretched out on the pallet of furs. She was exhausted. She needed sleep. In the dark void of sleep, she could forget all that she had lost, if only for the moment.

Then she sat up quickly and stared at the closed entrance flap. She listened to the muted sounds in the village. Everyone was going about their own business. If ever she were to escape, this was perhaps the best opportunity. She now felt more like a prisoner than she had at the beginning.

Feeling the urgent need to place miles between herself and Cloud Eagle, she moved to her feet. Making plans, her mind traveled quickly. She knew that the horses were carefully guarded, so she would not be able to use one for her escape. She would have to take her chances on foot.

She turned and gazed at the weapons, then chose a knife which she placed in a leather sheath at her right side.

She stared at the rifle, then without further thought, also grabbed it.

Her gaze then fell upon something shiny beneath a roll of blankets. Her eyes brightened with recognition. "My pistol," she softly cried. She picked it up and tucked it into the waist of her skirt.

Tears streamed down her cheeks, and she

fought the memory of her nights with Cloud Eagle as she tiptoed to the entrance flap.

Grasping the rifle with one hand, she eased the flap slightly aside. Peering outside, she caught sight of Cloud Eagle on his haunches beside Turtle Crawls, and remorse filled her in a deep, painful rush. At this moment she knew that no matter what, she would always love Cloud Eagle. Nothing could take away those feelings that were locked within her heart as though branded there.

She loved him deeply. Reverently. Forever.

Then she rushed from the tepee and circled around behind it. She looked toward the corral. As she had guessed, a warrior guarded it. She would have no chance to steal a horse.

She welcomed the darkness that stretched out before her, yet she feared it. She hoped she would come across travelers who would take pity on her and give her a ride. She had many miles to travel until she reached Fort Thomas. That was her destination. It tore at her gut to think that she could be the cause for Cloud Eagle's eventual arrest.

She ran onward into the darkness, her eyes cautiously darting on all sides of her. Only when the stronghold was a vague shadow in the distance did she allow herself just one last look.

A sob lodged in her throat to know what she had left behind.

Her heart.

Her very reason for being.

Again she turned. She stumbled listlessly along and cringed when distant wolves and coyotes barked and bayed at the moon. She was reminded of Snow. Was she among those restless animals tonight?

And Gray?

Alicia already missed Gray with all her heart.

When the wolves seemed closer, she broke into a mad run, and was soon exhausted. She found an overhang of rock and sought shelter beneath it. Limply she sank to the ground and fell into a deep, heavy sleep.

Chapter Eighteen

The morning came with the harshness of desert light and the blistering sun, awakening Alicia with a start. She rose on one elbow and looked around her. She felt suddenly empty again when she realized where she was, and why. She had lost everything in the world that meant anything to her.

Cloud Eagle had betrayed her.

Her brother was more than likely dead.

She grabbed the rifle and rose slowly to her feet and moved out of the shade of the towering rock overhang. Her thirst was so intense that her mouth felt as though it were filled with cotton.

She ignored the gnawing at the pit of her stomach. Food was the last thing she was interested in. She had to quench her thirst, then be on her way. She had no idea which way to travel to reach the California Road, where she might be rescued and taken to Fort Thomas, or to her stage station, where Milton was surely proudly taking charge.

She doubted that scalawag had even sent word to the fort that she had disappeared. He had said more than once that he would be glad to be rid of her.

"Looks like you got your wish, Milton," Alicia whispered to herself. She then laughed beneath her breath. If she made it back to civilization alive and discovered that he hadn't sent someone to look for her, he'd pay dearly for that little deception.

Half stumbling over strewn rock, she placed a hand over her eyes and shielded them from the sun in her search for the sheen of water.

When she discovered that she was close to a small stream that snaked across the land, she sighed with relief and made her way toward it.

She tried to block out all thoughts of Cloud Eagle. She could never forgive him.

And he would soon see how she got her revenge against someone who had wronged her. She would see that he was arrested and brought to trial for the disappearance, and possibly the death of, her brother.

The thought of Cloud Eagle swaying in the wind with a hangman's noose fitted around his neck made tears sting the corners of her eyes. She stubbornly brushed them away, knelt over the water, and began cupping the deliciously cold liquid into her mouth.

The sound of his Apache people leaving their tepees to begin their morning chores awakened Cloud Eagle. He rolled his blanket away and looked slowly around.

Pangs of sadness struck him when he realized

why he had chosen to sleep outside his lodge instead of inside. Since Alicia had been so withdrawn and angry the prior evening, he had decided to give her the privacy of sleeping alone, if for only one night.

Today he would somehow convince her of his innocence, even if it meant having to return to the Englishman's outpost to drag him away into the desert and force the truth from him in Alicia's presence.

There were ways to make the truth easier for a man to say than to make him suffer the pain and humiliation of being tortured.

Yes, Cloud Eagle thought. If it was required, he would take many of his warriors to the Englishman's outpost and fight for his right to have his woman with him again.

Discovering many eyes looking at him quizzically and realizing that his people knew that he only slept outside when he was unhappy with his women, Cloud Eagle rose with much dignity from the ground and went back inside his lodge.

Although the sun was pouring its mighty fire from the sky, its brilliance did not seep through the buckskin sides of the tepee.

And the lodge fire gave off no light.

It had gone completely out.

The only light inside the tepee was that which sprayed downward from the smoke hole in the ceiling. But that was enough light for him to see that something was very wrong inside his lodge.

Alicia was not on the pallet of furs beside the firespace.

His heart racing, he moved farther into the dwelling, his eyes slowly searching the dark corners.

Still he saw nothing.

He stopped and listened with his keen ears. His pulse raced and his heart began to hammer out a message inside his brain. He could not hear her breathing from somewhere in the shadows where she might be angrily hiding.

There was only one answer.

She was gone.

She had more than likely fled into the night while he had trustingly slept outside, away from her.

His morning calm turning into an angry inferno, his hands circled into tight fists at his sides. Her faith in him had been so weak that she had felt the need to flee from him? Hadn't their moments together, when they had spoken words of love to one another, meant anything to her?

How could she trust him, or his words, so little?

He would have trusted her to the ends of the earth!

Now all that he could think about was to find her and bring her back with him. He would tie her up to hold her there if required to keep her while he raided the Englishman's outpost to abduct Sandy Whiskers. Cloud Eagle would tie the Englishman to posts on the ground in the middle of the desert, then go and get Alicia. He would take her to witness how he got the truth from his enemies.

Then if she still wanted her freedom, so be it. He would place her from his mind as quickly as she had slipped into it.

He would begin his life anew without her.

But he could not leave this thing unfinished. He would prove his innocence. His honor was of the utmost importance to him, perhaps even more than the white woman had ever been!

Cloud Eagle was an expert tracker. At a determined gait, he left his lodge and searched for Alicia's footprints.

When he found them, he smiled.

Then his eyebrows arched. There were also the prints of his coyote blending in with Alicia's. It was apparent that Gray had discovered her gone and had gone after her. This made him feel somewhat better. Gray would be of some protection to her.

He traced the footprints, thinking they would lead to the horses. He was puzzled when he discovered that Alicia had gone past the corral without getting a horse for her travels.

"She travels on foot," he said, alarm grabbing his insides. "If her destination is Fort Thomas, it will take her days, possibly weeks. She will face much danger. Perhaps more than she or Gray can handle."

Cloud Eagle bolted back to his stronghold. He gathered together a good number of his warriors.

"My woman and my coyote are gone," he shouted to them. "We will search for them. Arm yourselves well. The outlaws and renegades might find her first. If so, we must find them. A battle may ensue to take her away from them."

He did not tell them of his plans to go for the Englishman. That would come later—after he had Alicia and Gray back safe with him.

He turned and went back inside his lodge. He took his arrows from their quiver and inspected each of them. The flint arrowheads held fast and the fletching was trim.

He returned the arrows to the quiver, slipped it over his shoulder, and secured it.

Then he went to his store of weapons. When he discovered that one of his rifles was missing, a ray of hope penetrated his heart. If Alicia had taken a weapon with her for protection, surely between the rifle and Gray she would be safe enough until he found her.

He sank to one knee. From his blanket roll he removed two parts of a Sharps rifle. It was a buffalo gun capable of bringing down big game at long range. It would most certainly take two renegades or outlaws at a time.

He assembled the rifle and chose several cartridges from a leather pouch, one of which he placed in the chamber, the heavy breechlock sliding open with oiled and silent precision.

Carrying the rifle, his bow slung across his shoulder, Cloud Eagle stepped outside and gazed heavenward, where the sun flung crimson banners across the sky. He whispered a prayer to the Great Spirit, then ran to the corral, where his men were already mounted on their proud steeds, waiting for him.

A young brave had saddled Cloud Eagle's frisky roan and held out the reins to him as he approached.

His heart pounding within his chest, Cloud Eagle swung himself into the saddle. He lifted the rifle into the air and let out a loud war whoop; then he rode off, his warriors following him.

They rode at a slow pace, Cloud Eagle's eyes never leaving the tracks that led away from his village, into land that could be very unfriendly to a white woman who traveled on foot and a coyote that had chosen one master over another.

"Keep her safe, Gray," Cloud Eagle whispered to himself. "Keep her safe."

Alicia leaned over the water and splashed it onto her face. As she wiped her eyes free of the water, she lingered a moment longer over the stream, dreading leaving it. Too often water was scarce and there was more sand than grass as one moved farther away from the mountains.

She leaned over to look at her reflection as she fussed with her hair, twining it into braids to make it easier to handle.

When another reflection appeared in the water, next to hers, she gasped, then laughed and turned to Gray and hugged him as he nudged her fondly with his nose.

"Gray," Alicia cried, now stroking his fur as she gazed into his trusting eyes. "You missed me and came for me. How sweet."

Gray whined and looked over his head in the direction of the stronghold, then back at Alicia again.

She got his message and her smile faded. "No, Gray," she murmured. "I'm not going to return to Cloud Eagle's stronghold. He proved to be someone I don't know, nor want to. He lied to me, Gray. He deceived me." She swallowed hard. "He may even have murdered my brother."

She gave Gray another fond stroke, then nodded toward the stronghold. "Go," she said, motioning with her hand. "Return to the stronghold. You belong to Cloud Eagle, not to me."

Gray refused to budge. He kept looking up at her with his trusting gray eyes.

Alicia sighed. She could tell that he was not going to leave her. He had become too devoted to allow her to travel alone. He was a smart coyote. He had followed her trail and had found her easily enough.

Her eyes widened and a sudden panic filled her. "If Gray found me, then so can Cloud Eagle," she said, her words running together in a rush. "Lord. I mustn't allow it. I must hurry onward."

She also knew that she couldn't get much farther without food.

But she would have to take her chances. The Apache were known for their skill at tracking. Cloud Eagle was an Apache. He was more skilled than most at everything.

He could even now be on her trail!

Half stumbling in her haste, Alicia moved onward. Clouds of gnats and sand flies darted about. The wind lifted whirls of sand and rattled brittle brush and sage. It strummed a thin whine through the cottonwood's leaves beneath which Alicia sought a moment's reprieve from the scorching sun. It was intensely oppressive today and glared like a shield of red-hot brass.

Then she moved onward, Gray loping trustingly at her side. She found a scarcely traveled road. It was covered with a fine and almost impalpable dust, containing an abundance of alkali. She choked and gagged as the dust blew into her mouth, nostrils, and eyes.

As she tried to travel away from the road, terrible cactus thorns and the pointed leaves of the Spanish bayonet soon covered her legs with blood. She regretted not having put on the high-top moccasins instead of the ones that she had chosen to wear.

A red racer scooted across the ground and caused Alicia to emit a sudden, sharp scream.

Then, remembering her father's teachings, she stopped dead in her tracks.

"Snakes do not strike in anger," he had told her. "They strike at movement. Be still and they will go away."

She scarcely breathed as she watched the snake slither away across the dusty land.

Then she moved onward, especially when she noticed how nervous Gray had become. He would stop and gaze over his shoulder, then speed up and romp at her side again, his ears stiff, his tail between his legs.

"What is it, boy?" Alicia asked, stopping to kneel down beside him.

She gazed into the distance, then on all sides of her. She was near a canyon where anyone might be lurking and waiting for innocent passersby.

She stared at it for a moment, then something else caught her eye.

A fringe-toed lizard's tail protruded between rocks close beside her. Something else scurried under the stone.

Curious, she knelt beside the stone. She laid her rifle aside and placed a cheek on the ground and poked a stick under the stone.

A startled grasshopper mouse made a terrified dash into the open, causing Alicia to start, then giggle.

"Gray, it was only a mouse," she said, tossing the stick over her shoulder.

She started to push herself up from the ground but stopped when Gray turned and began to snarl and show his fangs, then pounced away barking and yelping.

Alicia froze on the spot. She was afraid to move or look to see what was causing Gray's sudden change in mood. If it was Cloud Eagle approaching, Gray would not have become antagonized.

That had to mean that it was someone Gray did not know, or welcome. . . .

The sudden thundering of horses' hooves made Alicia's heart stop. She grabbed for her rifle, but was not quick enough. A loop from a lariat shot out and fell over her head and around her neck. The breath was knocked out of her when the rope was yanked hard, causing her to fall to the ground.

She grabbed at the rope, choking and fighting as she was dragged across the ground. She could hear much mocking laughter. She looked through the dust and discovered that she had been lassoed by an outlaw; other renegades and outlaws rode alongside the one who was dragging her.

Out of the corner of her eye she saw Gray lying still on the ground. He looked dead. When she was dragged past him, a sob lodged in her throat.

"Gray," she cried. "Sweet, innocent Gray."

Chapter Nineteen

Alicia's whole body ached. Feeling bruised all over, her moccasins having fallen from her feet as she was being dragged, Alicia held back from screaming for the outlaw to stop. She would not give those who were laughing boisterously at her the satisfaction of hearing her beg for mercy. She closed her eyes and gritted her teeth, then went limp when the horse finally stopped.

Everything became suddenly quiet. The men were no longer laughing. As Alicia lay on the ground, one massive throbbing pain, all that she could hear was the harsh breathing of the horses—and perhaps her heart thudding wildly within her chest.

Slowly she opened her eyes. She achingly drew herself into a fetal position when she found one of the men kneeling down beside her, staring at her.

The man gathered her hair in one of his hands

221

and gave it a hard yank, positioning her face so that she had no choice but to look up at him.

"You are the white woman who came to Sandy Whiskers's outpost with the Injun, eh?" he growled out, his thick mustache bobbing above his lips as he spoke.

Afraid, yet too stubborn to act upon such fear, Alicia spat into the man's face. Rage filled the man's dark eyes. He drew his free hand back and slapped Alicia hard across the face. "You whore!" he hissed, then wiped the spittle from his face and mustache with a handkerchief that he yanked from his back breeches pocket. "I should kill you for that. But Sandy Whiskers has other plans for you."

"Sandy Whiskers?" Alicia gasped, her insides turning cold.

"Yeah, Sandy Whiskers," the man said. He dropped his hands from her hair, then grabbed her by a wrist and jerked her to her feet. "Come now, whore. Sandy Whiskers is waiting."

"What does he want with me?" Alicia asked, fearing the answer.

"Soon you will see," the man said. He threw her across the back of his horse and tied her wrists together, then her ankles. She was left to hang over the horse like a sack of potatoes. Quickly the blood rushed to her head, dizzying her.

Yet she was rational enough to think through things that flooded her with guilt and regrets. She had been proven wrong about Cloud Eagle. What he had said about the Englishman was true, or else why would Sandy Whiskers give orders to abduct her?

She had to wonder if this outlaw gang would have gone as far as entering Cloud Eagle's village to abduct her. If so, who else would have been taken captive?

When the horse broke into a lope across the parched land, Alicia was given one more glance at Gray as the outlaws rode past his body, and this time she noticed the blood on his matted gray fur.

He had been knifed.

He was more than likely dead.

She squeezed her eyes closed, but that did not trap the tears behind her lids. They seeped from the corners in silver rivulets down her dust-covered face.

Because of her, Gray was dead.

Because of her inability to trust Cloud Eagle, everything had changed.

Not only for herself, but for Cloud Eagle.

As the horse rode onward, Alicia could not help but grunt and groan with each of its movements. As each minute passed, she discovered a new pain, a new ache.

But she welcomed the discomfort. As long as she could concentrate on that, she was not plagued so much with guilt over Cloud Eagle or Gray.

She was even temporarily able to set aside her worries about her welfare once she reached Sandy Whiskers' outpost.

It came to her in splashes of anger that if what Cloud Eagle had said was true, what he had tried to prove to her by taking her to the Englishman's outpost was true, that meant that Sandy Whiskers *was* the one responsible for her brother's disappearance and possible death.

Not her beloved Cloud Eagle.

A sob lodged in her throat when thoughts of

Cloud Eagle seeped into her mind somewhere amidst her pain and misery and guilt.

If she had only believed him.

If she had only trusted him.

And what of her brother? What sort of end had he met at the hands of the renegades and outlaws?

What they had just put her through had been terrifying.

And she was a woman.

Charlie was a man, and they might make his death even more insufferable. . . .

When she glanced over her shoulder and saw that they were approaching Sandy Whiskers' outpost, anger turned to fear.

She recalled a wall at the back of Sandy Whiskers' cabin. She had often wondered why it was there and how it was used. She was afraid that she was soon to find out.

Watching guardedly as well as she could from her position on the horse, Alicia saw the gate as the outlaw gang rode their horses through it.

Once inside, several other armed men on foot surrounded the horse on which she was held captive. They laughed and poked at her with the butts of their rifles.

She winced with pain as one jabbed her on her leg that was almost healed but now throbbed like a dozen toothaches.

She stifled a cry of wrenching pain when one of the rifles glanced across her head.

Then she scarcely breathed when the horse stopped.

She watched as the man on whose horse she had traveled dismounted and came to yank her from the horse in one jerk.

Moaning, she fell to the ground in a heap.

She fought back tears, then sucked in a wild breath when she suddenly saw Sandy Whiskers, standing over her, his fists on his hips.

"So, pretty lady, you have come to visit Sandy Whiskers again so soon?" he said, chuckling beneath his breath. "This time you do not bring your Apache friend? What a shame."

Hating him with a passion, Alicia glared up at him. She could not help but cry out when one of the outlaws kicked her in the back. She tried to move away from the offender, but was stopped when Sandy Whiskers placed a heavy foot on her stomach.

"Pretty lady, you aren't going anywhere," he snarled. "You brought me big trouble when you gave the Apache chief cause to come and ask questions about the painting. For this you will pay."

Alicia trembled and watched Sandy Whiskers as he shouted commands to his men. She had wanted to tell him what she thought of him, but some of her usual spunk and energy had been drained from her by the shock of having been treated so cruelly, and from the realization of how wrong she had been about Cloud Eagle.

She wanted to scream at Sandy Whiskers and ask him about her brother.

But she could not find the courage.

She feared hearing Charlie's fate in his answer.

Her breath was knocked from her when another outlaw kicked her in the stomach, then untied her ankles and wrists and yanked her up from the ground by the arm.

Struggling to regain her breath, Alicia inhaled

shakily, then stumbled as one of the men gave her a shove.

"Walk ahead of me," he said brusquely. "Do not falter again or you will be sorry."

Alicia gave him a sour look over her shoulder, then determinedly took each step with caution. Her eyes grew wide and her heart skipped a beat when she was pointed in the direction of the wall behind Sandy Whiskers' cabin. She felt helpless and she feared for her next moments of life. Being Sandy Whiskers' prisoner most certainly differed from having been Cloud Eagle's when he had forced her to go with him to his stronghold after he had found her injured on the California Road.

An armed guard flung the gate open. Alicia was shoved through it. She walked onward. Seeing nothing suspicious somewhat alleviated her fear. Squatted behind the wall was a long building made from logs. It seemed innocent enough until a mind-wrenching scream from the building broke through the silence of the morning. It caused the hair to rise at the nape of her neck. The scream was feminine. It had sounded as though it came from someone who was being tortured.

Alicia swallowed hard and again became cold inside with fear as she listened for more screams.

But everything was now strangely quiet.

Birds no longer sang in the cluster of cotton-wood trees near the building.

It was as though the woman's screams had silenced the whole world.

An armed guard with a face shadowed with dark, wiry whiskers opened the door that led inside the long building.

Alicia was shoved inside.

When she steadied herself, and her eyes grew accustomed to the dark room, panic filled her.

The building was divided into two parts. She could see down one side. The full length of that part of the building was wide open, and she could see everything in it. Her insides recoiled at her discovery.

Cages. Many cages filled the room.

And to her horror, they were filled with women, both white and red-skinned!

Built of cedar, the cages were set on sturdy tables placed against the wall. From a quick calculation she surmised that the small cages were about four feet high, four feet long, and four feet wide.

"And so, pretty lady, you see my collection?" Sandy Whiskers bragged as he stepped to Alicia's side. "I think you'll look even prettier in such a cage yourself."

He nodded at the guard, who promptly grabbed Alicia by the arm again and pushed her toward the caged women.

Panic-filled, Alicia yanked herself free, shoved the guard aside, and ran toward the door.

Sandy Whiskers blocked her way. He drew his heavy pistol and aimed it at her as Alicia slowly backed away from him. "Do as you are told, Alicia, or my guard will kill you instead of just locking you up."

The blood rushed from Alicia's face and her heart skipped a beat. "What?" she gasped. She stopped and stared at Sandy Whiskers.

"The women?" Sandy Whiskers said, waving toward the caged women with his gun. "They have been impregnated by my men."

"Good Lord," Alicia said, her knees growing weak.

"The women are held until they become pregnant," Sandy Whiskers said, obviously getting a delight out of telling Alicia what her future held for her. "The pregnant women then bring a high price with the purchaser, anticipating a birth that will add to his wealth."

"I should have listened to Cloud Eagle," Alicia hissed, her eyes narrowing as she glared at Sandy Whiskers. "He warned me about you."

Sandy Whiskers threw his head back in a fit of laughter, then sobered and grabbed Alicia by the shoulders as he stared into her defiant eyes. "He thinks he knows so much," he growled. "But he does not know about my breeding program. I do not sell all of the pregnant women that you see in the cages. I keep many to use in my breeding program, with a birth goal of four children per woman. The children are sold to rich ranchers in New Mexico and to rich mine owners, who raise the children to use in the copper mines."

"You are sick," Alicia said, her voice hollow.

"You can call me anything you wish," Sandy Whiskers said, shrugging. "It doesn't matter. There's no one here who cares what you say about anyone or anything."

He motioned with his gun again toward the guard. "Get her in a cage and if she keeps mouthing off, gag her," he said. He gave Alicia a mocking smile. "Perhaps it will be *I* who will impregnate you. It will be my pleasure, pretty lady. I've had my eyes on you for quite some time. You see, I looked past your man's breeches and shirt. I knew what lay beneath them had to be something special. Perhaps I shall soon see *how* special."

"I'll kill you first," Alicia said, then pain flooded her senses when the guard knocked her across the back of the head with the butt of his rifle.

She fell to the floor, senseless, only half aware of what was then happening to her.

She could hear women crying on all sides of her.

She could hear them begging Sandy Whiskers to set them free.

She knew that she was being dragged, then lifted.

Alicia opened her eyes and through the haze of pain saw that she was being placed in one of the cages. She was aware enough of what was happening to realize that the cage was designed for no freedom of movement. She could neither stand nor lie down. She remained in a folded position.

She moaned as her hands were lashed behind her and her head was forced between her knees. She scarcely heard Sandy Whiskers as he taunted her. His voice seemed to come from some deep, dark tunnel.

His parting laughter rang in her ears.

She heard this until it became only a faint sound as she slipped into a black void of unconsciousness.

His roan traveling at a slow trot, Cloud Eagle continued to follow Alicia's and Gray's tracks. It was the dry season. The grass that had been trampled did not "come back," but gradually became flattened, dried, and turned, finally to dust.

And he knew every spring, water hole, canyon, and crevice. A skilled tracker such as he was as clever as the most erudite scholar who traced, read, and translated the choreography of past ages in his cold, dark cubicle.

Suddenly Cloud Eagle drew a tight rein and stopped. Shielding his eyes from the sun, he gazed ahead to where he had noticed something lying still in the sand.

"Gray," he said, numb at the sight of his coyote lying so apparently lifeless beneath the beating rays of the sun.

Then his heart faltered and the pit of his stomach grew weak as he looked quickly on all sides of Gray for Alicia. When he did not see her, he was torn with feelings. If she was not there, then she might still be alive.

Yet if she was, where was she?

And why had she abandoned Gray?

He knew the affection she felt for his coyote.

"Follow me!" he cried, motioning with his hand to his warriors.

He rode hard until he reached Gray. He drew his horse into a shuddering halt and leapt from the saddle.

Gnats and flies buzzed around Gray, and the dried and matted blood on his pet coyote's fur sent Cloud Eagle's heart to reeling.

After shooing the gnats and flies away, Cloud Eagle knelt beside Gray and checked to see if there was a pulse at the base of his throat.

He heaved a sigh of relief when he found one, then inspected the wound. It was a clean knife wound that had obviously just missed Gray's heart.

Although Gray had lost a good amount of blood, Cloud Eagle felt as though his pet coyote had a chance of surviving if he was cared for right away.

He gave abrupt orders to two of his warriors.

One of them picked Gray up in his arms and carried him to his horse. Gently laying him over the saddle in front of him, the warrior mounted, then rode away toward his stronghold.

Cloud Eagle walked slowly around and checked all the hoofprints that had seemed to stop at Gray, then went in another direction away from Gray.

He went stone cold inside when he found Alicia's footprints, then noticed strange long marks that followed along behind one of the horse's prints.

"Someone was dragged behind a horse," Cloud Eagle said, more to himself than anyone else.

Then it hit him like a thunderclap who it must have been.

Alicia!

She and Gray had been traveling together.

Gray had been knifed.

Surely Alicia's life had been spared by her assailants, but her fate was now in question.

He wandered onward for a while longer, studying the tracks, then concluded that he was right to believe that Alicia was the one who was being treated so cruelly, and the one who was carried away on a horse.

He glared in the direction of the tracks and concluded where they would eventually lead.

"Sandy Whiskers," he hissed between clenched teeth. "She has been taken to his outpost."

He turned and faced his men. He told them his conclusions, then said, "We will attack Sandy Whiskers' outpost in the early morning hours when his men will least likely be on guard."

He moved into his saddle in one leap and waved his rifle in the air. His warriors followed him. The air trembled with the shriek of war whoops.

Chapter Twenty

Alicia was awakened with a start when a scream filled the air. Her eyes jerked open in time to see a burly man unleash the cage door beside her. With one powerful, practiced motion, he jerked the woman from the cage and slammed her onto the floor.

Alicia was aware that somehow she had managed to sleep through the night. The room was dim in the early morning light, but not so dark that she could not see what was happening. As the woman lay on her back, looking up at the man, Alicia's gaze froze on her. Her calico blouse and skirt had been ripped down the front. It fell open, revealing copper skin and small rounding breasts with delicate nipples. An ugly blue knot had formed over her left cheek where someone had struck her. Her eyes revealed nothing. She wore a glaze of stoicism that hid whatever lay behind the black pupils.

Alicia was almost certain that the woman was Apache, and she soon discovered that she was right. When the woman spoke angrily at the vile man, it was in the Apache tongue.

Although He Who Knows Much had not had the opportunity to teach Alicia more of the Apache language and customs, she had been in Cloud Eagle's stronghold long enough to be able now to put words and phrases together that helped her understand the language.

"Apache squaw, it isn't smart to speak to your master that way," the man growled. "It will give me much more pleasure when I set the brand to your flesh."

Alicia's color faded. "Brand?" she whispered, squirming to try and get more comfortable in her small quarters. She cried out with pain. Moving even slightly sent spasms through her bound wrists and cramped legs. She scarcely breathed when the man stepped up to her cage and leaned into her face.

"Yeah, pretty woman," he said, leering at her. "A brand will mark not only the copper skin of the Apache, but also yours." He kneaded his whiskered chin. "The brand I use is an *A*, to stand for Apache. That will also be what will identify you, for you were living with the Apache, weren't you?"

He threw his head back and laughed, then forked an eyebrow as he gazed at Alicia again. "Why were you running away from the Apache chief?" he asked.

When Alicia offered no response, he shrugged and turned his attention back to the Apache woman, who had managed to crawl to the far side of the building. The man stamped toward her and when he reached her and was about to stoop to grab her, he jumped back just as the woman's feet grazed his pants leg, narrowly missing his groin.

His face red with rage, he slapped the woman across the face and dragged her back to the cages and dropped her there within eye range.

Turning to Alicia, he emitted a feral snarl and unlatched the door to her cage. He grabbed her hair and yanked her sprawling onto the floor. Keeping hold of her, he dragged her until she lay alongside the Apache woman.

Alicia's heart hammered wildly. She cowered away from the man and reached a trembling hand to her mouth. It was swollen and caked with blood. The wound that had all but healed on her leg now throbbed unmercifully. Her whole body ached.

She turned her eyes quickly when Sandy Whiskers entered the building. She glared up at him when he came and stood over her and the other woman, his fists on his hips. "And now, pretty women, how do you enjoy my hospitality?" he said, laughing softly.

He jumped and took a quick step away from Alicia when she spat on his moccasins.

"Those who do not cooperate are always sorry," Sandy Whiskers said, then shifted his gaze to his hired gunman. "This must be done quickly. Both these women are trouble. They will escape at the first opportunity. Get them branded and back in their cages quickly."

The man nodded.

"You must also have men prisoners. Where are they? And how do you treat them?" Alicia shouted. "They cannot bear you children that can be sold. My brother—what did you do with my brother?"

Sandy Whiskers stared at her for a moment, then gave her a slow, knowing smile and turned and walked away.

"You killed him, didn't you?" Alicia cried after him. "You sonofabitch cold-hearted bastard!"

Hearing such crude words coming from the mouth of a woman made Sandy Whiskers stop. He turned and stared at Alicia. He took a step toward her, his mustache trembling as his lips lifted into an amused smile. "I like you," he said, stroking his beard. "You have a spirit that is usually lacking in women. Your children will be spirited as well. They will bring me much more money."

"I will find a way to kill any man who tries to force himself upon me in that way," Alicia cried back. "You will see that you have brought the wrong woman to your breeding post this time."

"I do not see you stopping anything that has been done to you at my breeding post yet," Sandy Whiskers said, then walked away, his laughter loud and sharp as a whip crack in Alicia's ears, even as he stepped outside.

Guardedly, Alicia turned her attention to her true threat—to the man under Sandy Whiskers' command. He was a big man. She knew that she would never be able to defend herself against anything that he might try with her—unless she could manage to get his knife from its sheath.

She eyed the knife hungrily; then her vision was blocked when he knelt down between her and the Apache woman. She cried out with pain when his fingers locked in her hair as his other hand grasped the Apache woman's. Alicia gagged and choked when he lifted her head, and soon had her head and the Apache's in a headlock.

Alicia squirmed and moaned as he rose with them and dragged them into a room at the far end of the building.

The man flung Alicia and the Apache like two sacks of grain forward onto the floor.

Alicia groaned and turned slowly over and looked around. The room was small. It had one window from which came a fluttering of light.

The floor was stone. In one corner, a blacksmith's pit was flued by a stone chimney. Across the low ceiling, a long pole was suspended by a chain at each end, looped around the pole and fastened to the ceiling.

A large wooden tub filled with water was the only furnishing.

Alicia scooted closer to the Apache woman. They huddled together, wide-eyed and helpless, as the man walked to the blacksmith's pit and pumped energetically at a bellows until red glowed through the charcoal. He chose two iron bars and nestled their heads in the red coals.

Quickly, he returned to them, his knife drawn from its sheath.

He slashed the hand ties of the Apache woman, then rolled her to her back and bound her hands in front.

Moving to Alicia, he did the same.

His eyes glazed with the pleasure that he was soon to get from the women, the man jerked the Apache woman upward. He leaned into her face as sweat rolled down his cheeks and into his beard. "All Apache women are pretty," he said thickly. He glanced over at Alicia. "And also those of my own kind. Today I will get *double* pleasure."

He laughed throatily as he seized the Apache woman by her wrists, jerked her upward, and grabbed her around the waist in a bear hug. In a quick rush he slammed her against the stone wall.

With one hand he lifted the horizontal pole out of its chain loop; with the other he raised her bound hands, then slipped the pole between her arms and raised the end of the pole back into the looped chain.

She was suspended, hands around the pole, her feet barely grazing the floor.

He turned and gave Alicia a slow smile, then just as quickly had her disabled in the shackles alongside the Apache.

Grinning, white teeth flashing beneath a thick, black mustache, the man slid his knife under the clothing of the Apache woman. He slit her dress, front and back, until she was naked.

His breath came more quickly now, and his free hand trembled as he ran the flat side of the knife over the woman's slender, supple bronze body, which was stretched upward toward her bound hands.

"You filthy bastard," Alicia hissed, disgusted by the lust she saw in the man's eyes and by how he was taking advantage of the Apache woman. And she knew that she would be next.

He ignored her.

After taking many liberties with the Apache woman, he took a rope from the wall and, looping the left ankle of Alicia and the Apache woman, drew their left legs outward and upward, tying the end of the rope to the pole.

He took an iron from the coals with tongs held in one hand and advanced toward the Apache woman.

Alicia's eyes widened and her pulse raced fearfully as she gazed at the iron bar. It was a branding iron and the *A* was glowing red.

Just as he started to lower the brand to the Apache woman's leg, something stopped him.

He turned and gazed at the door and dropped the branding iron to the floor.

"Apaches!" he cried, stumbling backward as the war cry of the Apache rang out, clear and distinct outside in the courtyard.

He also now heard the thundering of hoofbeats. He paled and fell across the branding iron, sprawling on his back on the floor.

Having caught the guard beside the gate dozing, Cloud Eagle rode squared-shouldered in his saddle into the courtyard. In fresh vermilion worn in long streaks along his cheekbones, he rode at the head of his mounted, excited, charging warriors, his aspect fierce and repellent.

Cloud Eagle raised his rifle with one hand above his head and waved it. As he shook his weapon for all to see, a sound began deep in his throat and scaled to a high-pitched scream.

"*Eeeeewaaaah!*" he cried—the war cry of the Apache.

All the warriors joined in a confusion of screams and chants as they raced on their steeds throughout the courtyard, killing and maiming.

Some of the Apache horsemen, in charging the enemy, held fifteen-foot lances with strong, sharp points, above their heads with both hands, controlling their horses with their knees.

Others fired their rifles rapidly.

Rifle shots exploded, scattering over a wider and wider area.

After Cloud Eagle's first kill, he lowered his rifle

and turned his face to the sky like a coyote, savage and mournful. *"Haaaaooooh,"* he cried, crying out the death call.

Then he rode onward, dealing out death at every turn. His eyes searched for any signs of his woman and the Englishman.

One he would save.

The other he would kill!

Then he saw the wall at the rear of the outpost. He watched as several of his warriors dismounted and went to open the gate.

Cloud Eagle paused for only a moment, then rode like thunder through the gate and slid from his saddle.

His eyes narrowed as he studied the long cabin.

He gripped his rifle more firmly and stalked carefully toward the door.

Inside Sandy Whiskers' cabin, the Englishman had watched the attack from his window. Realizing that he did not have the manpower to stop the Apache, he saw that there was only one other recourse.

Escape.

For now he would escape, and to hell with the women prisoners—and the men. The men would remain incarcerated in the cavern cells that had been dug beneath his outpost. He would leave them there to die if he did not have the chance to come back for them later. He knew that the women were lost to him. The Apache would free them.

Recalling Alicia, whom he would have to leave behind, waves of anger and regret rushed through him.

"Her brother," he whispered to himself. "If she

knew that he was below, in the cavern cells . . ."

He went to the trap door that led beneath his cabin to the caverns. He had made sure that when the cabin was built over the caverns, the floor boards had been made without hinges, so that when the trap door was lowered after his escape, if one was ever needed, no one would know to follow.

And if fire was set to the cabin, the second trap door made of steel would not cave in. Instead it would hold steady and become hidden beneath the ashes.

The gunfire and the constant screams of the Apache came from all sides of his cabin now. Sandy Whiskers lifted the first trap door, then the second. He wheezed as he fit himself through the small hole and awkwardly placed his foot on the top rung of the ladder.

Sweat pearling his brow, he lowered the wooden door back in place. He moved lower on the ladder, then reached overhead and lowered the steel door back in place.

Now all that he could hear was the muffled sounds of the gunfire overhead and the moans of the men in the cells below him.

Wriggling his way down the ladder, he was met at the bottom by two of his most trusted guards. They helped him down from the ladder, their eyes filled with silent questions.

"The Apache," Sandy Whiskers said, wiping his brow free of sweat with the back of one of his hands. "They have come." His jaw grew tight. "Alicia Cline. It's because of her that the Apache have gone against us."

He lumbered to the cells, then stopped at one in particular. He stared at Charlie Cline, who was shackled to the wall, his torn and tattered clothes reeking of perspiration and his own filth.

Charlie looked empty-eyed back at Sandy Whiskers. His face was gaunt. His naked chest was striped from beatings. One of his arms was missing.

"You are a most stubborn man," Sandy Whiskers grumbled. "Those who cooperate and go to the silver mines without causing us problems are treated much better. Seems you needed convincing."

Sandy Whiskers grabbed the bars and leaned his face against them. "Alicia? Your sister?" he said, catching a sudden flicker of light in Charlie's eyes at the mention of his sister. "She is even less fortunate." He shrugged. "Her disobedience caused her an early death." He laughed throatily. "But I enjoyed her body before I slit her throat."

Remorse filled Charlie, making his heart feel as though it were being wrenched from inside his chest. The wrist of his one arm strained against the steel rings that held it to the wall as he tried to pull it free. He glared at Sandy Whiskers. "If ever I get free, it won't be to work in the silver mines," he growled. "It will be to kill you."

When another loud volley of gunfire spat out overhead, Sandy Whiskers looked up at the rocky ceiling of the cavern, then walked hurriedly away from Charlie.

Charlie turned his eyes upward and hope sprang forth within him. Someone had arrived. The outpost was being attacked!

He looked quickly at Sandy Whiskers, who was retreating into the darker depths of the cavern.

"Coward!" he shouted. "Run or die, eh? I swear,

if I ever get free, I will find you and kill you myself!"

Sandy Whiskers shouted over his shoulder at his guards. "Follow me!" he cried. "We must escape now! The Apache chief might be smart enough to find the trap doors."

"But what about the prisoners?" one of the guards said. He broke into a run and followed Sandy Whiskers.

"The women are lost to us," Sandy Whiskers shouted back. "Perhaps we can return later to get the men and deliver them to the copper mines for payment." He stopped long enough to get his breath. "If not, we will start anew somewhere else. We will have to return to Mexico, far enough away from the Apache chief Cloud Eagle."

Charlie listened with interest. Sandy Whiskers had mentioned women. Did that mean that perhaps Alicia wasn't dead after all?

Again he tried to pull his wrist loose as men on all sides of him were shouting at Sandy Whiskers to set them free. They were begging for food.

Charlie's insides grew cold. Although he and the other prisoners had not been fed well, at least they had been fed enough to keep them alive from day to day. Without the outlaws there to supply food, they could die!

Realizing that dying of hunger could be slow and torturous, Charlie hung his head. Behind the veil of his tears, in his mind's eye he was seeing Alicia as he had last seen her in Saint Louis.

Ravishing. Vivacious. Spirited.

And stubborn. . . .

"Alicia, oh, Alicia," he moaned. "What have you gotten us both into this time? Where are you? Are you dead or alive?"

*   *   *

Hearing the rapid shooting outside and seeing how frightened the guard was, Alicia gazed intently at the door of the small room. "Cloud Eagle," she whispered, her heart beating soundly. "Oh, darling, is that you? Am I going to have the chance to tell you how sorry I am for having doubted you?"

The light from the door was suddenly shut out. Alicia blinked her eyes and stared at the man standing there. He completely filled the doorway.

His knife in his trembling hand, Sandy Whiskers' gunman rose slowly to his feet, having seen the large figure looming at the doorway. There was no doubting whether it was foe or friend. The man wore only a breechclout, and his bronzed skin was sleek with sweat.

"Get out!" the man spat between clenched teeth. "Get out!" He edged backwards when the Apache did not move, but spoke in a slow, dignified manner, in English, to the women.

"Have you been harmed, *Ish-kay-nay?*" Cloud Eagle asked.

"I'm fine," Alicia said, eyeing first Cloud Eagle, then the guard.

Cloud Eagle asked the Apache woman the same. She replied the same.

"Thank God you came," Alicia cried. "Forgive me, Cloud Eagle, for having doubted you. Please forgive me."

Cloud Eagle nodded, then fastened his gaze on the man who held his knife threateningly before him, pointed at Cloud Eagle.

In the distance, rifle fire still popped and cracked and exploded.

In the small cubicle of the room, the branding iron now lay gray and lifeless on the floor between Cloud Eagle and the man.

Cloud Eagle moved slowly toward the man.

The guard backed slowly away.

Cloud Eagle followed. He kept only a short distance between himself and the other man. They were watching each other's eyes.

Suddenly the man lunged toward Cloud Eagle, the knife making a straight path toward his chest.

Cloud Eagle was quicker. His hand moved faster than the guard's. It grabbed the wrist of the knife hand. The grip tightened.

The man swung his left fist at Cloud Eagle's face. He too soon felt his left wrist seized. The knife fell with a hollow ring to the floor.

They stood with bodies pressed tightly together.

Slowly Cloud Eagle forced the guard's hands upward. He still gripped the wrists. The man's face and beard were wet with sweat as he tried to get his wrists free. He screamed as his arms cracked like dried sticks beneath Cloud Eagle's pressure.

Cloud Eagle then released the man.

His arms broken, the guard fell to the floor, crying in pain.

Cloud Eagle leaned over the man and grabbed a fist full of his hair. With his free hand, Cloud Eagle took his knife from his sheath and held the knife blade before the man's eyes.

"For your sins," he hissed.

With a quick motion Cloud Eagle ran the knife across the man's throat. He died without a sound.

The gunfire had stopped outside. Several warriors ran into the room where Cloud Eagle was already setting Alicia free. Turtle Crawls went to the Apache woman and released her from her shackles and soon had a blanket around her bare shoulders.

Alicia flung herself into Cloud Eagle's arms as her shackles fell away from her. Sobbing, she clung to him with all of her might. "It's been so horrible," she cried. "And the women, Cloud Eagle. Did you see all of the women in the cages?"

"They are going to be set free," Turtle Crawls said, his arm around the waist of the Apache woman.

Cloud Eagle held Alicia close. He looked over his shoulder at Turtle Crawls. "Did you kill Sandy Whiskers?" he said.

"He has disappeared," Turtle Crawls said, his eyes filled with rage. "We searched. We did not find. We burned his cabin. Nothing, Cloud Eagle. There is nothing but what you have seen already."

"For now that is enough," Cloud Eagle said. He framed Alicia's face between his hands and felt icy currents of remorse flood his insides to see her face so damaged. "Had you not fled, you would not have suffered so."

Alicia lowered her eyes. "I know now so much more than before," she said, swallowing hard. She looked slowly up at him. "I shall never doubt you again."

Then a fresh stream of tears flooded her eyes. "My brother," she said, biting her lower lip as she paused before saying the dreaded words. "I am almost positive now that he is dead. Sandy Whiskers' interest lay in keeping women alive, not men."

She quickly explained the breeding program to Cloud Eagle. He was stunned, but not altogether surprised. It did seem now that the Englishman might be capable of anything.

He cradled Alicia close. "Let us return home, where you can forget these things that have brought heartache into your life," he said, stroking her back. "We will take those women with us who have been locked away in cages. We shall return them to their rightful people."

"But the children they will bear?" Alicia asked, a chill encompassing her at the thought of the men forcefully impregnating the women. "What will become of them?"

"It will be up to the women," Cloud Eagle said. He placed an arm around her waist and walked her out of the room, through the room of cages to the outdoors that was filled with the scent of gunpowder and death.

Alicia took one look at the death scene, then looked away. She stumbled along until Cloud Eagle led her to his horse. He helped her into the saddle.

"Stay. I will see to everyone else's welfare, then we will return home," he said. "We will not look back at what has been, but ahead, at what will be."

Alicia swallowed hard. She flicked tears from her eyes and nodded. Then she sat in the saddle, numb, as she watched the activity around her. A long string of mules and horses were led from the corral. The Apache loaded the mules with the war weapons of the enemy. Next came food from the dwellings, then bolts of cloth, tools, and clothing.

The sun was shifting its way downward in the

sky as the last mule was loaded. The women were helped onto horses and mules. The warriors mounted.

Cloud Eagle slipped into the saddle behind Alicia and placed a protective arm around her waist. With a silent wave, he led his warriors out of the outpost, the horses snorting at the smell of blood and death. No death had come to the Apache today. Only to those who deserved it.

After they were outside, on open ground, Cloud Eagle turned his frisky roan in the direction of his stronghold. The warriors followed. Everyone was quiet. The sky was bright.

Cloud Eagle looked heavenward and saw something that broke the tranquility of the turquoise, cloudless sky.

Buzzards.

Spiraling buzzards.

His shoulders and back tightened, knowing that there were two unmistakable signs of trouble on the plains.

Black, billowing smoke and spiraling buzzards.

Both were signs of death.

Cloud Eagle appointed two other warriors to ride with him, to see what the buzzards were after.

Not wanting to see any more death, Alicia turned and clung to Cloud Eagle, her face pressed against his powerful chest. She could hear the rapid beat of his heart as he drew his horse to a sudden halt. She could hear anguish in his voice as he shouted into the wind the name.

"Red Crow!" he cried.

"Red Crow?" Alicia whispered, unable not to follow Cloud Eagle's gaze, not after hearing the

247

utter shock in the depths of his voice over what he had seen.

The blood drained from her face and she felt dizzy with her own anguish when her gaze fell upon the five bodies that were hanging lifelessly from the limbs of several cottonwood trees, their necks broken, enormous black clouds of blowflies covering their naked bodies.

Now everyone knew why Red Crow and his warrior companions had not returned from the hunt. It was not because their hunt had been good. Instead someone else's hunt had been successful—more than likely Sandy Whiskers'!

Cloud Eagle rode up to Red Crow, and while Turtle Crawls stood waiting, he cut the rope that held Red Crow's body on the limb.

Turtle Crawls dutifully caught him, then lay him peacefully on the ground. Others shooed the flies from his body.

This was repeated until all of Red Crow's warriors lay side by side on the ground.

Alicia stayed on the roan as Cloud Eagle slipped from the saddle.

His eyes moved from Red Crow to the others, then back to Red Crow. He knelt beside Red Crow, his head bent.

Alicia could not stand to see him suffering alone. She dismounted and went and knelt beside him. She placed an arm around his shoulders. "I'm so sorry," she murmured. "Darling, I'm so sorry."

"I grew up with Red Crow," Cloud Eagle said, his voice hollow. "My heart strings are bound around my friend. And he had to have died nobly. Never have I seen fear cross the face of my friend!"

Cloud Eagle's fury knew no bounds. "At whatever cost to my own safety and comfort, I will demand just satisfaction for the death of my best friend," he then said, his eyes filled with fire. "The Englishman is responsible for this. I will hunt him down. One day I will find him. He will wish that he had never come to the land of the Apache!"

Alicia clung to Cloud Eagle, his hurt and anger melding with hers. She wanted revenge also. And against the same man. As Cloud Eagle avenged the death of his kindred, especially that of his best friend Red Crow, she would avenge the death of her beloved brother. She now knew for certain that her brother had been slain by the wicked Englishman.

"We shall find a way, Cloud Eagle," she murmured. "We will find Sandy Whiskers and make him pay."

"Not we," Cloud Eagle said, placing a gentle hand to her cheek. "You will be protected at all cost from coming face to face with that fiend again. This is our fight, that is true. But it is for this Apache alone to see that revenge is carried out and that you are kept safely from it."

Alicia listened, and she wanted to please him. But she was torn with feelings. That part of her which always met challenges head-on did not want to allow someone else to fight her battles for her.

Yet on the other hand, she did not want to disappoint Cloud Eagle again.

"Do you hear me well?" Cloud Eagle said, his eyes narrowing. "*Ish-kay-nay*, you understand what I just said? That you will not interfere in my sought-for vengeance?"

Alicia innocently nodded, yet was still not

sure which way it would be for her when the time came.

"Good," Cloud Eagle said, yet doubted that Alicia was being altogether truthful. He knew that it would take time for her to forget her willful, stubborn ways.

And he understood. Her fiery nature was still attractive to him.

He rose to his feet and gave Red Crow a lingering look.

He then gave orders to make enough travois for the return of the bodies to their homes.

Cloud Eagle lifted Alicia into the saddle, then swung himself up behind her. The sun was now setting. The twilight had deepened. The evening coolness and shadows fell over Alicia and Cloud Eagle as they rode onward, in silence, she with her feelings, he with his, yet intertwined as one thought, as one wish.

To see the Englishman dead.

Chapter Twenty-One

The moon was high in the sky when the procession of Apache entered their stronghold. Alicia stirred awake in Cloud Eagle's arms when he slowed the pace of his horse. She looked quickly around. Firelight struck the tepees from within, turning their skins translucent. As Cloud Eagle's people became aware of horses' hooves entering the stronghold, they emerged from their lodges.

The flames of an outdoor fire leapt high into the sky, as the Apache people's eyes anxiously scanned the faces of those who were arriving, understanding that not only were their warriors returning, but also several women, white and red-skinned. And it was obvious to everyone that several of the women were huge with child.

Cloud Eagle rode on ahead and dismounted. He put his people as a whole at ease when he explained about the attack on Sandy Whiskers' outpost and that not one of their warriors had been killed or wounded.

As the people broke away and ran to greet their warriors, Cloud Eagle reached his hands to Alicia's waist. She leaned into them as he gripped her and helped her to the ground.

They embraced for a moment, then Alicia stepped aside so that Cloud Eagle could attend to his chief's duties.

She watched him go to those who had been released from the dreadful cages, joining his warriors who were helping the women from the animals. The white-skinned and those of copper skin were treated alike.

The weak, thin, and gaunt, and those who were large with child, were led to the fire. Soon they were resting on blankets, accepting food and water.

Then Red Crow's wives came into sight. Alicia and Cloud Eagle saw them at the same moment, exchanged quick glances, then went to them.

Alicia stood at Cloud Eagle's side as he drew the women together, side by side, then placed a comforting hand on each of their shoulders.

Alicia dreaded hearing Cloud Eagle reveal the truth to them. They had erected a new lodge, to have it ready for Red Crow when he returned from the hunt. And now Red Crow would not return to see the labors of their love for him. He had been unmercifully murdered.

And then there were the others who were yet to be told about the warriors who had died with Red Crow.

"What is it, Cloud Eagle?" Laughing Eyes blurted out. "Why do you treat us as though we have lost a husband in battle? I see no casualties.

You said that your ambush was a success. And, Cloud Eagle, Red Crow did not ride to fight this war with you. He is still out on the hunt."

The horses dragging five travois behind them came in view at that moment at the far edge of the stronghold. A muted hush fell over everyone. They watched the slow procession come closer, their eyes on the travois. It was puzzling to everyone how their chief could speak of no casualties when proof of such casualties was brought before their very eyes!

Those wives whose husbands were not among those who had left for the ambush, but who had been gone longer than they should have on the hunt, stepped forth, then began running alongside the travois, sobbing.

Laughing Eyes and Sweet Rose broke away from Cloud Eagle. When they reached the travois, the horses dragging them had stopped.

Cloud Eagle rushed to them and one by one uncovered the bodies. Then he stood back and allowed the wives to kneel down beside them, chanting as their losses were discovered.

The rest of the people shoved closer, their eyes filled with sudden despair and grieving.

"On our way home from victory against the Englishman, these valiant warriors who you see lying motionless on the travois were discovered hanging from trees," Cloud Eagle shouted. He raised a fist into the air, then lowered it to place it over his heart. His voice was filled with remorse and pain. "I am not certain who is responsible, but I feel in my heart that it is the Englishman, Sandy Whiskers. I will avenge the deaths of our warriors! I vow to you that they have not died forgotten men."

Low chants began.

Shivers ran up and down Alicia's spine. The voices of the Apache in their mourning sounded like the low moaning of the wind.

This moaning increased in volume. The voices rose higher and higher in pitch.

It made Alicia feel the sadness twofold in her own heart over her own loss and also Cloud Eagle's.

She lowered her eyes and said a soft prayer, then looked up again quickly when she heard an even louder cry of grief.

Her mouth opened in a mortified gasp as she watched Laughing Eyes and Sweet Rose tear at their flesh with their sharp fingernails. Blood rolled in streams from the wounds.

Their hair was assaulted next.

Several of the wives in mourning snatched their knives from sheaths attached to their thighs beneath their skirts, and were soon snipping their long braids off.

Alicia ran to Cloud Eagle's side. She grabbed him by the arm, her eyes wide as the various wives kept assaulting themselves in ways that were strange to Alicia.

"It is their way to show their mourning," Cloud Eagle explained when he saw Alicia's puzzlement. "If I should die, it would also be expected of you in the eyes of my people."

Alicia looked up at him, then moved into his arms. "If you should die, I would not only cut my hair and punish my flesh, I would want to die alongside you," she sobbed. She hugged him tightly. "I never want to be parted from you again. Tell me you still want me."

"Had I not, you would still be in the Englishman's cages, his brand on your lovely flesh," Cloud Eagle said, comfortingly stroking her back through the thin buckskin fabric.

Alicia leaned away from him and looked over at the women who were sitting beside the fire. Only a short while ago, they were captives. They all wore Sandy Whiskers' brand.

"On the morrow the women will be taken to their proper strongholds," Cloud Eagle said, following Alicia's gaze. "Their future is their own again."

"But the white women?" Alicia asked. When she glanced their way, their vacant eyes tugged at her heart. "How can they ever be reunited with their loved ones?"

"I will interview them all," Cloud Eagle said, frowning. "They can tell me which city they are originally from. My warriors will take them to the stagecoach station. From there the women will travel in all directions, back to their original destinations. There will surely be some kin they can seek shelter with, and pity."

"Some are so large with child," Alicia worried aloud. "They won't be able to travel far."

"It is up to the white community to see to their welfare, not the Apache," Cloud Eagle said. "The Apache have done their part by rescuing them. It is up to the white community to do the rest."

"Are you going to report to the white authorities what happened at the Englishman's outpost?" Alicia asked, worry building upon worry.

"When the women are taken to the stagecoach stations, they can explain themselves what has happened to them, and how they were rescued," Cloud Eagle said. "It will be proof enough to the white pony soldiers that Cloud Eagle fights for the rights of their people as well as his own."

"As for Sandy Whiskers, what are you going to do about him?" Alicia asked softly.

"He has gone into hiding," Cloud Eagle acknowledged. "And so let him hide for now, thinking that he has eluded Cloud Eagle. Cloud Eagle has duties to his warriors first to tend to."

He turned and watched as each of his fallen brothers was carried away, their burial rites ahead of them. "In my eyes, they all were heroes," Cloud Eagle said. He gave the instructions to his warriors about the released women, saw that his horse was taken to the corral, then turned and with a hung head walked toward his lodge.

Alicia went ahead of him and opened the entrance flap. She then followed him into the dark tepee, shivering as the damp coldness of midnight seeped into her pores.

She hugged herself as Cloud Eagle prepared a fire.

When the flames were eating at the logs, she sat down beside the fire and held her hands close, her flesh soaking up the warmth.

She looked quickly up when an Apache woman brought a basin of water into the tepee, and another brought a fresh dress and moccasins.

When they left, Alicia turned to Cloud Eagle and smiled. "I did not hear you give the command to look after my comforts," she said, hugging the soft dress to her bosom.

"I do not always speak my commands through my lips," he said. He stood over her and softly stroked her face with his hands. "The women of my stronghold watch my eyes and my gestures. They respond quickly to my silent commands."

"As do I," Alicia said, smiling up at him.

He ran a finger over her swollen lip, then brushed a soft kiss across it. "He will pay for everything evil that he has done to you and to my people," he growled. "If he would have placed the brand to your lovely flesh, he would have been branded a hundred times over with the same brand. Not one inch of his flesh would have been spared his dreaded *A*, which stands for Apache in the eyes of the evil Englishman."

Cloud Eagle then proceeded to gently wash Alicia's face. She closed her eyes, melting inside with rapture over being with him again. She would not allow herself to think of what might have happened if he had not cared enough to rescue her.

Although she had threatened to kill the bastards if they tried to impregnate her, she knew they had ways to keep a woman from being able to defend herself. They could have raped her, time and time again, while she was shackled to the wall.

She would have been forced to endure the pain and the humiliation not only of rape, but also of giving birth to one of their children.

The child would then have been forced to live a life of degradation at the silver mines.

She shuddered at the thought of all of this that would not leave her mind.

Cloud Eagle noticed how she shuddered. He laid the cloth in the water in the wash basin and framed her freshly washed face between his hands. She opened her eyes and gazed into his.

"What were you thinking about?" he asked softly.

"Things I never want to speak of again," she said, her voice breaking. "Some day I shall surely forget." She twined her arms around his neck and drew his lips closer. "Help me forget, darling? Please help me forget?"

When he kissed her, she was not even aware of the pain that his lips brought to hers with the kiss. The throbbing of her swollen lip seemed to blend with the throbbing of her heart, so happy to be there, to be with him forever.

When he drew his lips away and removed her soiled clothes, Alicia was perfectly content to allow him to wash the sweat, dirt, and stains from her body.

As the damp cloth came to the rips and tears on her legs, which she had gotten while escaping her beloved, she winced, but was glad when the blood was finally washed from her flesh.

Cloud Eagle knelt over her and leaned her hair into the water. He washed it in the suds of the yucca plant, then dried it with a buckskin cloth.

Alicia combed her hair back from her eyes with her fingers, then leaned back so that her hair tumbled in wet strands down her back.

When Cloud Eagle kissed the hollow of her neck and cupped her breasts within the palms of his hands, she moaned with ecstasy.

"I need you," he said huskily. "But my need must wait until later."

Alicia opened her eyes, disappointed that they could not make love this very moment. She felt as though being held within his arms while he was loving her might momentarily help her forget the anguish she was feeling over the loss of her brother. Nothing would ever cause her to totally forget her brother. His memory would remain sweet in her heart, but only after she accepted that he was truly dead.

"I understand," she murmured. She moved to her knees and reached for the cloth in the water.

"Let me at least do this for you now," she said, gently washing the yellow war paint from his face. It was too much of a reminder of the bloody scene they had left behind at the Englishman's outpost.

Although she saw the outlaws and the renegades as the lowest form of humans on the earth, death to any human being was never something she accepted without remorse.

Those men had surely been raised with hardships, and perhaps without love. Or why else could they have turned into such hardened criminals?

Yes, they were to be pitied, the whole lot of them.

After the last of the paint was removed, Cloud Eagle drew Alicia into his arms. His eyes devoured her face, his fingers again gently touching her bruised lip. "Never again will anyone treat you wrongly," he said thickly.

He dropped his hands and turned his eyes to the fire. "I am responsible for too many things," he said, his voice filled with torment. "I am almost certain that the Englishman ordered Red Crow's hanging. Had I not gone and confronted Sandy Whiskers about the painting, to prove my innocence to you, the Englishman would have never known that Red Crow was responsible for the theft. But had I *not* gone for answers from Sandy Whiskers, you would have left me."

He paused and gazed over at her, his eyelids heavy over his dark eyes. "But you left me anyhow when the Englishman would not reveal the full truth to Cloud Eagle," he said, his voice tormented.

Alicia reached for a blanket and draped it around her shoulders. She knelt before Cloud Eagle, her hands on his cheeks. "You are wrongly blaming yourself," she murmured. "Red Crow is dead because of *me*. Had I trusted you in the first place, none of this would have happened. Please stop blaming yourself. Allow me to carry the burden instead of you."

She nodded toward the closed entrance flap. "Hear the chants of your people?" she murmured. "They need you. They will always need you."

She leaned into his embrace, sighing with pleasure when he enwrapped her within his powerful arms. "So shall I always need you, Cloud Eagle," she whispered. "I love you so."

He stroked her long, wet hair, then she drew suddenly away when she heard a whimpering sound coming from the dark shadows of the tepee, back where blankets and equipment were stored.

"What is that?" she asked, her eyes widening.

The same sound wafted toward her. She gasped and her pulse raced as she looked up at Cloud Eagle, hope in her eyes. "Can that be Gray?" she asked, her voice breaking. "Oh, Lord, how could I have forgotten about Gray? When I last saw him . . ."

Her words broke off. She did not want to even think about how she had last seen Gray, blood matted on his fur.

"When I was searching for you, I found Gray," Cloud Eagle said. He rose to his full height and took Alicia's hand. She clutched the blanket around her shoulders. Her heart pounded as she was taken to Gray, who lay on a thick pallet of furs, his fur shaved in a small area, his wound covered with medicinal herbs.

Alicia swung the blanket away from her shoulders and fell to her knees beside Gray. His eyes looked trustingly up at hers. She stroked his head.

"Gray, Gray," Alicia sighed, tears streaming from her eyes. "Thank God you are alive."

Gray pushed himself up from the furs and settled onto Alicia's naked lap. Laughing softly, Alicia looked up at Cloud Eagle. "He remembers me," she said, a grateful sob lodging in her throat. "He still loves me."

"Who could not love you after having known you?" Cloud Eagle said. He knelt down beside her and kissed her on the cheek. "As for Gray—his bonding with you is more than it is with Cloud Eagle. Now that you are here, he no longer broods. This is the first time he has made an effort to move since I brought him home after he was wounded. In his eyes and heart, he felt responsible for your absence. Look at his face and into his eyes, *Ish-kay-nay*—do you not see that he is smiling?"

Alicia giggled and hugged Gray as Cloud Eagle walked away and left the tepee. "Now if only Snow would come home," she said. "Our little family would be complete—at least until I give my husband his first child."

Her smile faded. Always there was that fear nagging away at her consciousness that she might be as barren as Cloud Eagle's first wives. It was a thought almost as unbearable as recalling how it had felt to be shackled to the wall at the Englishman's outpost.

261

Chapter Twenty-Two

The low beats of the *esadadnes,* the hoop drums, throbbed mystically in the early morning light. Alicia lay on her bed of furs beside the fire, Gray snuggled next to her. She awaited word that Cloud Eagle had finished preparing Red Crow's body for burial.

According to the Apache way, the preparing of the dead fell to the nearest male relative. Red Crow had no father or brothers. His wives had come to Cloud Eagle at daybreak, asking him, Red Crow's most devoted friend, to prepare their husband for his long walk in the hereafter.

For his friend, and his wives, Cloud Eagle had agreed.

The wives and children had vacated their lodge, where Red Crow had been laid out. They had returned to the lodges of their parents.

If this were a normal preparation for the burial rites, and Red Crow's lodge still contained everything he owned and wore, instead of having burned in the earlier ravages of the fire, his wives would have given away all of their husband's belongings and kept nothing for themselves.

This was the way of the Apache—so that no Apache could benefit from the death of a family member lest desiring that death for material riches might enter and weaken his spirit body.

As it was, nothing but the clothes that he had worn on the hunt, and his war knife that had been sheathed at his waist, remained of Red Crow's wealth.

The tepee in which Red Crow was being readied for burial would be burned after the ceremony.

Alicia stood up and slipped the buckskin dress over her head, then sat back down again beside the fire and began braiding her long hair.

She gazed listlessly into the fire. She was filled with much sadness, knowing that now she would never get the opportunity to see that her brother had a proper Christian burial.

Even if Cloud Eagle somehow found the Englishman, she doubted that Sandy Whiskers would tell anyone where her brother was killed, or what had happened to his body.

A shudder engulfed her and tears flowed freely from her eyes. Gray sensed her sadness. He lifted a paw and gently scratched at her arm.

Alicia wiped the tears from her face with the back of her hand and placed an arm around Gray and hugged him. The wound on his back would heal with time.

"The pain in one's heart takes much longer to heal than those of the flesh," she whispered to Gray, the light of the fire leaping into her eyes, turning them golden.

"Thank God I have not been left totally alone on this earth," she said, sighing heavily. "I have Cloud Eagle's forgiveness and love."

His insides gnawingly empty with remorse, Cloud Eagle knelt over Red Crow's body, which lay in repose on a white doeskin blanket void of any design or beads. Red Crow should have been dressed in his most colorful war garments. But those had been destroyed in the fire the day his tepee had burned to the ground.

Cloud Eagle had brought his own special war garments and was gently, devotedly, placing them on Red Crow.

Cloud Eagle could not keep his eyes from wandering to Red Crow's face. It was as though he were asleep and would soon awaken with a big smile and a warm embrace for his best friend.

But one shift of Cloud Eagle's eyes, locking now on the scar and contusions that wound obscenely around Red Crow's neck, and the way his head lay crooked on his shoulders, made Cloud Eagle more than aware again of how Red Crow had died.

A rope had snapped his neck and had squeezed the life from his best friend.

"I vow to you, my friend, that the one responsible for this disgrace to your body will pay," Cloud Eagle said, lifting a pouch of paint into his hands.

He dipped his fingers into the paint that had been made from the earth and various flowering plants. He placed streaks of yellow beneath each of Red Crow's eyes, so that his friend would not lose sight of the sun on his journey to the hereafter.

Cloud Eagle set the pouch aside and wiped the excess paint from his hands on a cloth, then lowered his eyes and began a low chanting as the paint on Red Crow's face dried.

Cloud Eagle became lost in the moment of chanting songs that were sad. They came from the heart, his feelings flowing from deeply within and helping him exorcise those feelings that were like festering sores. Those feelings would be revived later, when he began his search for the Englishman.

Now he wished only to think of his friend, of their past times together. They had enjoyed the hunt. They had enjoyed games. They had even enjoyed sharing tales of their prowess with women when they had just discovered that their bodies spoke in ways unfamiliar to them, which soon led them to discover that women were of the utmost importance in their lives.

Cloud Eagle looked slowly up at Red Crow, his eyes wavering. "My friend, never again shall we share anything of this earth, but my love for you is enduring, even in death," he whispered. "As you walk on the long road of the hereafter, I will be there with you, in spirit. We can laugh. We can sing. There will be no deep sadness that I am suffering now. Once you are laid to rest, and your spirit separates from your earthly body, then again you will know me and embrace me as I walk with you, forever in your shadow."

He paused, then added, "Free from the body, the spirit of the good is without pain. Free from the body, the spirit sees more clearly."

The throbbing beats of the hoop drums were growing more intense now, drawing Cloud Eagle's eyes to the closed entrance flap of the dwelling.

His mind was a naked nerve. He sensed the emotions of his people. *His* feelings were as clean and sharp as a thunderclap.

The others.

His favored warriors who had died with Red Crow.

They were perhaps ready now for their journey to the burial cave where they would all be buried together, as they had ridden and fought and hunted together as trusted warriors and friends while they were alive.

Knowing that he could not delay the ceremony by dwelling on thoughts that kept him closer to Red Crow, Cloud Eagle reached for a heavy red woolen blanket and wrapped it around Red Crow.

Cloud Eagle's eyebrows forked as he searched frantically around him for Red Crow's war knife. It was the only weapon that had been laid out with Red Crow's body. Now it was gone.

After searching in every nook and corner and beneath the sweet grass that had been spread on the ground, Cloud Eagle's jaw tightened. He knew for certain that the knife had been with Red Crow when he had seen him hanging from the tree. It was still in its sheath at his side, the bandits not having taken the time to take it from him, perhaps because they had been frightened away too quickly to gather up the weapons of the dead.

But the knife *had* been there.

And now it was gone.

"Someone has stolen from my dead friend," Cloud Eagle hissed through clenched teeth. "It has to be one of my warriors. No one else has been near the dead since they were released from the death ropes, except for the Apache."

A sick feeling swam around inside him to think that one of his very own men might be so despicable as to steal from Red Crow when Red Crow had already suffered so much at the hands of his enemy.

This man who stole from him was no less his enemy.

And he was Apache!

A gentle hand on Cloud Eagle's arm drew him quickly around. When he discovered Alicia there, he pulled her into his arms. "I know it is time," he said thickly. "I have taken longer with Red Crow because our friendship was so special. Also, I have taken time to look for his war knife. Someone has stolen it, *Ish-kay-nay*. It cannot be buried with him."

Alicia drew away and stared up at him. "Who would do such a thing?" she gasped.

"Now is not the time to ponder over the loss," Cloud Eagle said, glancing at Red Crow's body. "He will be buried without the knife. But once it is found, the thief will have the responsibility of placing it with Red Crow, even though Red Crow will be buried behind tons of rock."

"Buried behind rock?" Alicia asked, her voice drawn. "You don't bury your dead in the ground?"

"This is not an ordinary burial," Cloud Eagle said, gently clasping her shoulders. "The warriors will be buried together in a cave. The entrance will be blocked by boulders so that animals can not enter and defile the bodies of the dead.

"Come outside with me," Cloud Eagle said, taking Alicia by the hand. "Wait there until the procession is readied. Then walk with me at my side. Your presence will make these last moments with Red Crow less painful."

Alicia went outside and watched as a young brave brought a horse to the entrance of the tepee. It was not Red Crow's best horse, for that horse had been taken on the day of his death by those who had killed him. But Red Crow had owned many horses and this was his next favorite.

Cloud Eagle went inside the tepee and picked Red Crow up and carried him to his horse and laid him across his saddle. He tied him there so that he would not fall as he was being taken to the cave a short distance from the stronghold.

Cloud Eagle then stood back as Red Crow's wives and children came and wept and chanted over the body.

Alicia turned with a start when four other horses, bearing bodies and weapons, came up behind her. She stepped aside, then was glad when Cloud Eagle took her hand and drew her to his side.

The procession toward the cave began. The sun was hidden behind a veil of clouds. An eagle swept and soared overhead, as though following the dead to their burial spot. A wolf howled in the distance, followed by the cry of a coyote, causing Alicia to wonder about Gray. He had followed her from Cloud Eagle's tepee when a young brave had come for her, but she had not seen the coyote since.

Her attention was drawn from her worries when Cloud Eagle began chanting Red Crow's deeds as a warrior as he clutched Red Crow's horse's reins and led him far up a canyon.

Alicia turned and gazed around her as other chants rose from the warriors who led their fallen brothers' horses in the dull gray of morning.

Alicia then looked away from them and stared straight ahead. Everything seemed so unreal today.

The useless deaths.

The preparations for the burials.

The mourners' chants reaching clean into her heart, as though an extension of her own sadness which she kept locked inside.

Perhaps, she thought, if she lifted her voice to the heavens in a cry of desperation, she might even feel less burdened, less saddened.

Yet in her society, mourning was done in a quiet, private way. As one's heart broke, tears were the only way that anguish could be expressed. She had stood over more than one casket in the parlor of the deceased, knowing the empty, remorseful feelings that came with losing a loved one.

"My sweet Charlie," she whispered to herself, a sob lodging in her throat. "I shall miss you forever."

The canyon was a deep cleft among tall walls of reddish-gray rock. The wind sang and whistled through the passage that narrowed as the funeral procession traveled farther into it. A hawk swept low, its wings shadowing Red Crow's body, then swept up again and landed on a nest that clung precariously to the sides of the canyon.

The sun came from behind the clouds, a single ray shining on a cave that was suddenly revealed at the side of the rock-strewn path; boulders were stacked on each side of the entrance.

Cloud Eagle led Red Crow's horse to the cave entrance. Alicia stepped aside as he untied the ropes that held Red Crow in place on the horse, as other warriors did the same for their fallen comrades.

269

The dead were placed inside the cave, along with their weapons.

Wide-eyed, Alicia watched as the warriors' horses were led into the cave. She gasped when there was enough light in the cave for her to see Cloud Eagle and four other warriors stand beside the horses, their rifles raised.

She clasped her hands over her ears when the gunshots rang out, mortified to see the lovely horses being shot and laid beside their dead warriors.

His head hung, his rifle smoking, Cloud Eagle came from the cave and went to Alicia's side as others began placing the boulders over the entrance of the cave.

Alicia leaned closer to Cloud Eagle. "Why did you shoot the animals?" she whispered.

"The horses remain with their fallen masters for the warriors to ride to the land of their ancestors," Cloud Eagle said, his expression solemn as he watched to see that the entrance was completely covered. "I already miss him."

He paused and sucked in a quavering breath, then said, "Red Crow will lie in the cave. The pines will sing low around him as he waits to begin his journey to the land of the hereafter."

He paused again and nodded. "There lie my valiant warriors within this cave, at peace with themselves and all enemies they may have acquired during their lifetime," he said. "It is time for them to begin anew where there is no more suffering. It is something that perhaps one can envy, is it not?"

His tone of voice, his attitude, sent shivers up and down Alicia's spine. "Please don't talk like that," she said softly. "Although I believe in heaven and what God offers me there, I am in no hurry to die. I don't envy the dead. There is much to live for, Cloud Eagle. There is so much for us to share. Please think about our future. Our future together. It will be so wonderful, Cloud Eagle."

Cloud Eagle gave her a slow, sweet smile, then walked away from her when those who had helped bury the dead moved together.

Alicia watched, puzzled again by the custom they were practicing. Each man who had had contact with the dead brushed himself all over with wisps of green grass, in a sense disinfecting his clothes and body. He then lay those tufts of grass on the ground before the cave in the form of a cross, like the tombstones white people used to mark the deceased's grave.

She was glad when the ceremony was over and everyone turned back in the direction of the stronghold. Alicia and Cloud Eagle were joined by Red Crow's wives and children. They returned to the stronghold together.

Once there, Cloud Eagle escorted each of Red Crow's wives and children to their parents' lodges, where they would stay until the mourning was over.

Then, in due time, they would marry again and begin a new life, a new family.

Alicia was glad when they finally returned to Cloud Eagle's lodge. She sat down beside the fire and watched him. He was in a fretful mood, and it seemed to stem from more than having lost a dear friend and four favored warriors.

Yes, she thought, it was because someone had stolen Red Crow's knife. He would not rest easy until he found the thief.

She watched as he removed his clothes, then,

stark naked, burned them, a piece at a time, in the fire.

She went to him and knelt beside him and ran her hands over his tautly muscled back. "What can I do to help alleviate some of your pain and anger?" she murmured.

"Tonight I must carry the burden alone," he mumbled. He watched the last of his garments burn into dark ashes. "Tomorrow I shall bring you into my life again."

He rose away from her and flung a blanket around his shoulders. "I must go to the river and cleanse myself," he said, giving her a heavy-lashed look.

"Can I go with you?" Alicia asked softly, feeling as though she shouldn't leave him alone for a second. Never had she seen him so despairing. So empty-eyed. He looked as though he might not be able to come out of this well of sadness in which he seemed to be drowning.

Cloud Eagle did not respond right away. He gazed at her at length, and she was glad when she was able to see some sparkle enter his eyes again, and a softness come to his jaw that meant that he was emerging somewhat from his dark void of unhappiness.

"Yes, come," Cloud Eagle finally said, opening the blanket for her to enter it with him. "Tomorrow is too far away to bring you into my life again. I need you today."

Sighing with relief, Alicia hurried to him and melted inside when he wrapped her into the blanket with him.

They did not leave right away. Instead, Cloud Eagle bent his lips to Alicia's and gave her a long, soft kiss, careful not to cause the wound on her lip to break open and bleed again.

"My *Ish-kay-nay*," Cloud Eagle whispered, his muscled arms holding Alicia to him. "You fill my life with sunshine when there are too many thunderheads trying to overshadow my very existence. You are good for me. You give me reason to look ahead instead of allowing myself to sink further into my unhappiness over my friends' deaths, and into anger over the theft of Red Crow's knife when he was not alive to defend himself against such a thief."

"The lowdown, no good, sonofabitch thief," Alicia said, then giggled when she saw the look on Cloud Eagle's face at her return to speaking in such an unladylike fashion. "Sorry, Cloud Eagle. I'll try and watch myself more carefully when I get riled up over anything." Her eyes twinkled into his. "But Cloud Eagle, whoever stole Red Crow's knife *is* a—"

He placed a hand over her mouth and stopped her flowery expressions. "Let us go to the river," he said, his eyes dancing into hers.

"Where you can wash my mouth out with soap for having said things that displease you?" Alicia teased, glad to find at least some lighthearted moments among the heavy hours. "When I was small and I let slip a word that I had heard my father say, but which was too delicate for a child to repeat, my mother washed my mouth out with soap."

"Perhaps she should have used the suds from the yucca plant," Cloud Eagle teased back.

Clinging, and finally able to feel at least a small measure of contentment, they started to leave the tepee.

Then Alicia stopped and grabbed Cloud Eagle's

arm. "Gray," she gasped. "Have you seen Gray? I haven't since I left the tepee to join the burial rites."

This was enough to cause their moment of lightheartedness to turn to weariness again as they broke apart and searched the tepee.

They searched beneath the blankets and behind the store of weapons and bundles of clothes.

They met by the fire, their eyes troubled.

"He's gone," Alicia murmured. "But why, Cloud Eagle?"

Cloud Eagle shook his head and sighed heavily.

"Is he well enough to fend for himself?" Alicia worried aloud.

Cloud Eagle turned and gazed toward the closed entrance flap, not voicing his concern out loud to his woman. Gray was not like Snow. He had never ventured far from the stronghold. He had learned to depend on man for all of his needs.

"Should we go search for him?" Alicia asked, following Cloud Eagle's troubled gaze.

"It would be useless," Cloud Eagle said, his voice drawn. "Gray has not been among those of his own kind for many moons. Who is to say that once he finds a pack that will accept him, he might not turn against his friends and see them as enemies?"

"So we just let him go, the same as Snow?" Alicia asked weakly.

"That is the way of nature," Cloud Eagle said. He swung the blanket around Alicia's shoulders again, drawing her into its cocoon with him. "Perhaps Gray will find his way back to us. Perhaps not. It is just another thing that we are forced to accept, whether it makes us sad or happy."

Alicia nodded. She placed an arm around Cloud Eagle's waist and walked with him outside to a gray, cool, and misty day. The aroma of food cooking in a tepee close by made her realize that she had not yet eaten today.

She glanced up at Cloud Eagle. For now he was all that she needed to sustain her. She felt lucky to be with him. She had come so close to losing him, and along with him her sanity.

The shine of the river was inviting. And even though she knew that it would be cold, she savored the thought of bathing with Cloud Eagle in the river, where she could become reacquainted with his ways of making her feel deliciously wonderful.

Her footsteps quickened. He gave her a knowing smile and walked more quickly alongside her.

Chapter Twenty-Three

Day had turned into night and night had given way to dawn. Strong hands moving over her body awakened Alicia. She felt as though she were floating, yet she knew she wasn't still in the river. She and Cloud Eagle had returned home after their swim and long embraces in the water. They had fallen asleep in one another's arms, their satiated bodies intertwined.

Now she was being awakened in the best way imaginable. His lips were now on her body, brushing soft kisses everywhere that was sensitive. His hand moved to that wonderful magic place between her legs, and suddenly there was nothing to mourn. Their love was propelling them to that place where sadness was left behind and there was only light, a dancing light of magical moments.

As Cloud Eagle caressed her throbbing center, he bent low over her and kissed her everywhere, then licked her.

She held her head back and moaned, her hips gyrating against his hand that pressed into her trembling spot.

Cloud Eagle rolled on top of her.

Alicia reached down to guide him inside her.

He kissed her long and deep and moved slowly, powerfully within her. He squeezed her breasts, pulling, rotating the stiff, resilient nipple against the palm of his hand.

Her hips rocked. Her pelvis reached up and pushed against him, bringing him more deeply within her.

She twined her arms around his neck, wrapped her legs around his hips, and thrust her tongue between his parted lips.

A tremor went through her body when his tongue met hers in a soft dance; his hands, now at her hips, lifted her more tightly against him.

She opened herself wider to him and her hips responded in a rhythmic movement.

She clung and rocked with him.

His mouth left her lips and moved over one of her breasts, his tongue lapping the nipple into a throbbing hardness. Breathing in the sweet scent of her body, his tongue and lips skillfully teased her taut breast.

His lips brushed her throat as he moved slowly toward her mouth. His hands pushed her hair from her face as he kissed her, his mouth searing into hers, leaving her breathless and shaking.

The sudden onslaught of passion captured them both, the tremors beginning from deep within them. Cloud Eagle swept his arms around Alicia and anchored her fiercely still as he thrust himself more intensely into her, then groaned

277

against her lips when the ultimate of pleasure was felt.

Their bodies strained together hungrily as they quaked together.

They kissed.

His fingers ran down her body, caressing her.

Afterwards they lay perfectly quiet, clinging.

Alicia's soft laughter bubbled from deep within her as Cloud Eagle rolled away from her. She turned to him and placed her hands at his cheeks. "Darling, did you hear?" she murmured. "I can laugh again. After all we have been through recently, I can actually laugh."

She snuggled close to him and pressed her head against his powerful chest. "Because of you, I am for a moment able to put all sadness behind me," she murmured. "I wish we could stay together like this forever and keep everything and everyone else locked out. Wouldn't it be wonderful, Cloud Eagle? To live forever just for each other?"

"That is the way it is for me, no matter what else I do through the day," Cloud Eagle said, hugging her close to his taut body. "You are always with me. Your lips. Your smile, the touch of your delicate hands goes with me while I am away from you."

"It is the same for me," Alicia said, sighing. "You are now a part of me. You are my very soul, Cloud Eagle. I could not exist without you."

Cloud Eagle placed his hands to her cheeks and directed her eyes up to his. "Never depend fully on Cloud Eagle for your existence," he said gravely. "You have seen recently how quickly things can change, how quickly one's life can be snuffed out. Should I die, you must not look back. You are a woman with much strength. You could carry on without Cloud Eagle. Without *any* man."

"I'm not as strong as you think," Alicia said softly. She blinked her eyes up at him. "I've learned that since I met you. Like most women, I have many weaknesses." She flung herself into his arms. "I so adore being a woman, with womanly feelings and desires. Never do I wish to be as I was before I met you. You've changed me. I love how it feels to be changed. Everything to me looks different. I see the beauty of life. I feel it."

"There is much ugliness in life," Cloud Eagle said, moving away from her. He rose from his pallet of furs and pulled on his breechclout. He frowned down at Alicia. "The man who stole Red Crow's knife? I believe I know who it is. I will go now and see if I am right."

Alicia leaned up on an elbow. "How could you know?" she asked, forking an eyebrow.

"One watches others to see if their behavior changes or stays the same after a theft is discovered in the Apache stronghold," he said. He combed his fingers through his long black hair and flipped it over his shoulders. "I have watched. This quickly I know who behaves differently."

"Perhaps this person is behaving differently because he is touched deeply by the recent deaths of your warriors?" Alicia said, rising from the pallet. She slipped her buckskin dress over her head. "If not for you, *my* burdens would be many, Cloud Eagle. Not everyone has someone like you to help remove the sorrow from their heart. Perhaps this person you suspect for the theft needs your council, your understanding . . . your guidance."

"This warrior knows that he has all of this from his chief, if he wishes it," Cloud Eagle said, tying a headband around his head. "Still he avoided my eyes yesterday during the burial rites. I could not go to him then. In respect for my fallen warriors, I delayed until now what must be done. Their day was yesterday. Today is also theirs while everyone mourns. But today I make wrongs right for Red Crow!"

"But if you are wrong, Cloud Eagle?"

"Very rarely am I wrong about these things."

He turned to Alicia and swept her into his arms. "When I return, I will bring food," he said. "But beginning today, you must learn to prepare food for your man who will soon be your husband."

Alicia smiled wanly across his shoulder, at the cooking paraphernalia lined against the wall. During her growing-up years she had been too occupied with her father, being taught ways of young boys, instead of being with her mother, being taught ways of girls. Cooking would be more of a challenge for her than that first time she had picked up a rifle and took aim with it.

"I might disappoint you," she said, easing from his arms. She locked her hands together behind her. "What if I do, Cloud Eagle?"

His eyes danced into hers as he twined a hand through her hair and brought her lips close to his. "Food is not that important to me," he said huskily against her lips. "What else you do is enough to sustain this Apache chief."

"You say that now, but what about later, when I scorch everything I cook and your stomach growls and aches with hunger?" she said in a softly pleading tone.

He shrugged casually. "Then I shall have to bring another wife into my lodge," he said matter-of-factly.

Alicia paled. "You wouldn't," she said, gasping.

When his lips curved into a slow, teasing smile, she knew that he was jesting with her.

She laughed softly, but deep inside where her fears were formed, she knew that she must learn to cook, or he *might* be forced to depend on another woman for the preparation of the meals. If he did this, he might find it simpler to bring her into his household to live. Alicia could become second in his life.

"I shall learn to cook quite well," she said, stubbornly firming her lower lip. "Just you wait and see. I shall conjure up all sorts of delicacies to tease your palate."

He leaned a soft kiss to her lips. "I shall help you," he said. "While on the hunt, away from wives, I have done quite well at warming my belly with food. If I must warm yours also with my cooking, so be it."

He stepped away from her, grabbed his rifle, and walked toward the entrance flap. "What I must do now will not take long," he tossed over his shoulder. "Pity Running Free if my suspicions are founded."

"Running Free?" Alicia whispered, unfamiliar with that name. She watched Cloud Eagle leave, then sat down beside the glowing embers in the fireplace. Slowly she began adding wood, her eyes again moving to the cooking paraphernalia. She knew not one pot or container from the other, or how they should be used.

But by damn, she thought, she would learn!

Cloud Eagle sat outside his tepee with his firing piece resting across his knee, shining the barrel. He cast occasional suspicious glances at Running Free, who sat outside in the shadows of his lodge, fashioning a short bow from a cholla stick.

Running Free nervously glanced Cloud Eagle's way, his hands trembling as he twisted the guilla fiber to string his bow. Laying the bow aside, Running Free fumbled while making an arrow. Using reeds, he split the ends and precariously secured a pointed stone at the tip.

Cloud Eagle continued to watch Running Free, waiting and watching him with a spidery patience. He stiffened when he heard the low, haunting sound of an owl. He watched it as it flew just past Running Free's face, then rose into the air and disappeared into the low-hanging fog of morning.

Cloud Eagle's eyes moved to Running Free again and frowned. Never had he seen one of his warriors look so frightened and nervous and guilty. He was certain now that Running Free was plagued with "ghost sickness." Behavior of this sort always pointed to the guilt of a warrior who had kept something of a dead relative, fearing that the ghost of the departed might come back to claim it. Running Free might even believe that the owl was Red Crow, having returned to haunt him into revealing that it was he who stole his beloved knife.

Having seen enough, his suspicions confirmed, Cloud Eagle laid his rifle aside, rose to his feet, and sauntered over to Running Free, where he stood with his arms folded across his chest. Yet he said nothing. His eyes bored into Running Free, forcing him to look up at him.

"My chief comes early to the lodge of Running Free," the guilt-laden warrior said, inching slowly to his feet. "Why do you look at me with anger in your eyes, and suspicion? What do you think me guilty of? Allow me at least to profess and prove my innocence."

"Can you do those things?" Cloud Eagle said, his voice a low rumble. "Can you both profess and prove your innocence to this chief who has seen enough to know that you are suffering from the ghost sickness?"

Running Free's eyes wavered. He brushed his hands nervously down his fringed buckskin attire, then wove his fingers gingerly through his waist-length, coal-black hair. "Ghost sickness?" he stammered, his hands now idle at his sides, clenching and unclenching into fists.

"You saw the owl?" Cloud Eagle said, his eyes squinting even more angrily into Running Free's. "You deny the cause of the owl's presence?"

"The owl?" Running Free stammered. "Yes, I saw the owl. It has its days and nights mixed up. That is the reason for its flight of confusion this morning. Running Free is most certainly not the cause."

"You steal, then you stand there and lie so easily to your chief?" Cloud Eagle said, rage building within him.

Running Free stared at Cloud Eagle for a moment, then lowered his eyes. He became silent. He offered no more lies or explanations, yet not the truth that Cloud Eagle had tried to pull from him.

Cloud Eagle drew in a jagged breath, then brushed past Running Free. He entered the warrior's lodge. Running Free did not yet have a wife. His tepee was cold and dark. There was no fire in the fire pit, only a glow from dying embers.

The light seeping in through the smoke hole at

the top of the tepee was enough for Cloud Eagle to see while he searched Running Free's belongings for the knife.

Running Free came into the lodge. His breathing was harsh as he watched his dwelling being torn apart. His eyes shifted to a thick layer of grass just past his roll of blankets. He shuddered visibly with fear when Cloud Eagle stepped on the grass, his bare foot feeling the distinct outline of the knife against its sole.

Running Free turned to run away, but Cloud Eagle's voice, firm with a command, stopped him.

"You stay," Cloud Eagle said, then bent over and brushed the grass aside and took the knife from beneath it.

"That is Running Free's knife," the young warrior said, adding lie upon lie. "It is identical to Red Crow's because we traded at the same time for them, from the same traveler." He took a brave, awkward step toward Cloud Eagle. "Give it to me."

Keenly disappointed in Running Free, not only over the theft, but because of his ability to lie so easily, Cloud Eagle grabbed him by his hair with one hand, while thrusting the point of the knife against the flesh of his throat.

"You fear Red Crow's spirit?" Cloud Eagle hissed. "You best fear your chief who has caught you in lies and thievery!"

"Do . . . not . . . kill me," Running Free pleaded, his eyes wild.

"Now you even beg for your life?" Cloud Eagle said, stepping away from Running Free. "You do not deserve to be called Apache."

Running Free placed his hand to his throat,

where he felt a trickle of blood oozing from the wound that Cloud Eagle had made with the knife. He slowly backed away from Cloud Eagle, fear locked in his expression.

"You have no more to fear from me," Cloud Eagle said, stroking Red Crow's knife as though it were his friend. "But you still have much to fear from Red Crow's spirit. As you know, since he was buried without his war knife, he is not yet able to begin his long journey to the hereafter."

"This I know," Running Free said, swallowing hard.

"Then you will see that his journey begins today," Cloud Eagle said. He slapped the knife into Red Crow's unwilling hand.

"What will you have me do?" Running Free gulped, the knife heavy in his hand.

"You will be punished for what you have done," Cloud Eagle said, folding his arms across his chest. "You will go to the burial cave. Without assistance, one by one, you will remove the boulders until the bodies are revealed to you. You will go into the cave. You will place the knife with Red Crow."

The Apache experienced great horror in the presence of a corpse after it has been buried. Running Free stiffened and tossed the knife to the floor. "No," he cried. "Kill me. That will be my punishment. I cannot do this other thing that you command."

"Killing would be too easy," Cloud Eagle said, a slow smile forming on his lips. "No. You must do as I have commanded. You have no choice. You as well as I know there is no other way. Even if I killed you, you would still be plagued with ghost sickness. Your soul would never rest. You would not be allowed to travel the road to the hereafter while such guilt was your companion."

Cloud Eagle stooped over and picked the knife up again. He held it out for Running Free. "Take it and do as you must with it," he said. "Then move onward, away from my stronghold. Never return. In your chief's eyes, you have lost the privilege of living among your Apache brethren."

"You banish Running Free as you banished Ten Bears and his sister?" Running Free said, his voice drawn. "How many more Apache will you send from your village?"

"As many as is required to cleanse our stronghold of those who are not fit to live among us," Cloud Eagle said firmly. He raised a hand and motioned toward the entrance flap. "Go. Red Crow awaits the return of his war knife."

Running Free cowered for a moment beneath Cloud Eagle's steely stare, then turned and fled from the lodge.

Cloud Eagle looked slowly around him. No one would want to possess anything that had even remotely touched Running Free's life. Cloud Eagle saw no choice but to destroy the lodge. That would erase from all of his people's lives even the slightest memory of such a man as Running Free.

Cloud Eagle left and went to the large outdoor communal fire. Bending, he withdrew a log that was only half burned, the fire still eating away at one end.

Determinedly, and with people staring at him with wonder, Cloud Eagle took the flaming log and tossed it into Running Free's tepee.

Soon flames engulfed it, roaring and sending spits of black soot into the sky.

Alicia heard the commotion outside. She soon discovered the smell of fire and could hear the crackling of flames. Rushing outside, she gasped when she saw the lodge totally engulfed in flames. She looked over at Cloud Eagle. Never had she seen him look so fierce, so filled with loathing.

Then she had to guess whose lodge was burning, and how it had started.

She ran to Cloud Eagle and clung to his arm. "Why did you see the need to set his lodge on fire?" she asked. She looked into the distance and got a glimpse of Running Free as he walked away toward the canyon.

"Now I am totally free of Running Free," Cloud Eagle said. He gazed down at Alicia. "As I suspected, he was the thief. He takes the war knife even now to return it to its rightful owner."

"He is going to roll the boulders away and place the knife with the corpse?"

"That is the only way."

"But Cloud Eagle, shouldn't you go with him, to see that it is actually done?"

"It will be done," Cloud Eagle said. "Running Free now fears death more than life while the knife is in his possession."

Cloud Eagle took Alicia's hand and walked her back to his lodge. "My heart is weary," he said thickly. "Food will be brought to you soon. But my body does not need the nourishment from food. It is my spirit that needs to be fed. I must go and be alone, to commune with the Great Spirit. I will send a warrior to stand watch over you while I am gone. You are forever in my protection, *Ish-kay-nay*. Nothing will ever harm you again."

Alicia wanted to go with him. But this time she knew that it would not be proper to ask him to allow it. She understood his need to pray. Privacy was needed for such meditations. She did not feel that she should interfere.

She crept into his arms and hugged him. He led her inside the tepee, embraced her again, then left.

She had only gotten comfortable beside the fire when a tray of food was brought to her. She thanked the lovely Apache woman.

After the woman left, Alicia eyed the different variety of foodstuffs, but did not have the appetite just then to eat. Without Gray or Cloud Eagle there, she felt too alone. She looked guardedly toward the closed entrance flap when a figure outside shadowed it.

Then she sighed. This was her assigned guard.

She fingered the food, sorting out strips of venison to nibble on. Yet she still could not relax. Something seemed to be nagging at her consciousness.

"A warning?" she whispered. "But what about?"

She leaned back, her heart pounding, but attributed her uneasiness to all that had happened, making her wary of what might still happen. She didn't feel as though she could let her guard down.

Not yet, anyhow.

She wondered if she ever could while living the life of a white Apache.

It seemed as though someone or something was always there to complicate their lives.

Chapter Twenty-Four

Cloud Eagle had sought his usual place for meditation, on a small hill that was surrounded with the whispering and sighing of cottonwood trees.

Still lost in prayer and meditations, he turned his eyes to the turquoise heavens. As the birds sang in the treetops, and while small animals played among the branches of the trees behind him, Cloud Eagle poured forth his remorse to his Great Spirit and asked that his burden be lightened. He offered a prayer to the sun, the source of all fire and light.

He closed his eyes and bowed his head for a moment, then opened his eyes, ready to return home. His eyes swept over his stronghold below him in the distance. He had only one regret that nagged at him. He wished now that he had brought Alicia with him so that she could have released her agony to the wind, the sky, and the mountains.

Yet he understood that she had her own god to go to in time of sorrow, and he expected that she was even at this moment reaching out to this god in her moment of privacy. When he returned to her, they both could put the bitter past behind them and begin their future with no regrets or sorrows. The future was theirs for the taking.

Suddenly Cloud Eagle stiffened. He was aware that everything had gone silent around him.

And then he heard a sound that made his heart falter in its beats—the sound of a twig breaking behind him and the snorting of a horse not far from where he rested on his haunches.

He had not brought his horse.

That had to mean that . . .

Before he could react to the danger he had sensed, a rope fell over his head and tightened around his upper arms, rendering him helpless.

Ten Bears yanked on the rope and caused Cloud Eagle to fall clumsily to the ground, on his side.

Cloud Eagle glared up at Ten Bears. "You would do this to your chief?" he snarled.

A soldier suddenly appeared. He tied Cloud Eagle's hands behind his back.

"The moment you banished me from your village, you were no longer my chief," Ten Bears said. He yanked on the rope, causing it to eat into Cloud Eagle's flesh. "You disgraced me before my people. I disgrace *you* now."

"You disgrace yourself over and over again by your careless deeds and actions," Cloud Eagle said, attempting to stand.

Ten Bears gave him a shove that made him fall to the ground once again.

Cloud Eagle turned livid eyes up to Ten Bears. "You will never walk the peaceful path of the hereafter," he said, his teeth clenched. "If you should die today, you would be trapped in a place where there is only fire and pain. And what about your sister? How does she fit into your plan?"

"She is safe," Ten Bears mumbled. "She is better off without you."

"Never is she safe while she is in the care of a brother who goes against his own people," Cloud Eagle said.

"Not my people as a whole, only one man," Ten Bears corrected. He looked over his shoulder and motioned with his free hand toward the trees.

Cloud Eagle watched incredulously as several more blue-coated soldiers appeared from hiding in the shadows of the trees and surrounded him.

Cloud Eagle eased to his knees and looked from man to man, their rifles reflecting the sun into his eyes. He recognized many of them. They were from Fort Thomas. Until now, he had considered them to be friendly.

But with their eyes filled with hate and their rifles aimed at Cloud Eagle, he saw just how mistaken he had always been to trust the white eyes.

"You join in the vengeance of an Apache who has been banished from his tribe and is worthless?" Cloud Eagle said, his words slow and measured as he looked from soldier to soldier.

"His vengeance is not our concern," a soldier said as he stepped forth, his shoulder-length blond hair fluttering in the breeze. "But what he has told us is."

"And what does he say that you listen to and believe?" Cloud Eagle said, squaring his shoulders. He winced beneath his breath when Ten Bears gave a hard yank on the rope, causing it to eat more deeply into the flesh of his arms. He held himself too rigid to be forced to the ground again.

"He tells me that you and your warriors have led many raids along the California Road," the soldier said, his hands resting on his holstered pistols on each of his hips. He had not drawn them. He was being backed up with the soldiers under his command.

"And I say that he lies," Cloud Eagle responded quickly, fighting to keep his dignity as Ten Bears kept maliciously yanking on the rope. "Did not Cloud Eagle send many freed white women to Fort Thomas after finding them incarcerated at Sandy Whiskers' outpost? Sandy Whiskers is the guilty one. He raided the California Road often. He even stole and incarcerated Indian women at his outpost."

"Yes, the women told us of Sandy Whiskers' abductions and program of impregnating them, *and* that you released them," the soldier said. "But the true reason, the *only* reason you set them free, was to recapture the white woman whom you had initially abducted, yourself, from the California Road. Do you deny that you stole a white woman from the California Road a short while ago? How many more have you abducted? Have you killed?"

Cloud Eagle's eyes lit with fire. He gave Ten Bears an angry stare, then looked at the soldier again. "Cloud Eagle has abducted no one from the California Road, nor has he ambushed or killed anyone," he said in a slow, measured way. "The woman you speak of is at my stronghold willingly. When she was abducted by Sandy Whiskers' outlaw band, yes, I went to rescue her. While doing so, I discovered the outrage at Sandy Whiskers' outpost. It should be *he* you are questioning. Not Cloud Eagle."

He grew tense when a white man out of uniform stepped out of the shadows.

"Alicia wouldn't go with Injuns willingly," Milton Powers said, half staggering as he reached for a bottle of whiskey that he had shoved into his back pocket earlier. He unscrewed the lid, bent the bottle to his lips, took a deep swallow, then placed the lid back on the bottle and stepped closer to Cloud Eagle. "Admit it. You stopped her for the mail sack, then when you saw that she was a woman, you took her as well."

Milton laughed loosely and staggered closer to Cloud Eagle. "This Apache here tells us that you sent his sister away and you took your white captive into your lodge with you to be your wife." He laughed fitfully again, then leered down into Cloud Eagle's face. "There ain't no man on this earth except a stupid Injun who'd want that woman for a wife. Are you blind, or what? She's more man than female."

Cloud Eagle was ready to jump to Alicia's defense, then held his words guarded inside himself, knowing that he had to be careful of what he said where Alicia was concerned. If he shouted to the world that she was more woman than any he had known before, then the white pony soldiers and this man stinking with whiskey would know that they had been together sexually. If they thought that he had raped her, then his life would end almost as quickly as the words spewed from his mouth. And if he were dead, Alicia would have no one to protect her from these foul men.

He pressed his lips together tightly, refusing

to incriminate himself any further with words that might be misconstrued. He would wait until he reached the fort. General Powell had always listened to reason when Cloud Eagle had spoken. General Powell always saw truth when it was laid out before him.

Milton Powers took another step closer to Cloud Eagle. He leaned into his face. "You and your warriors' marauding days are over, Apache," he said darkly. "And as for Alicia— I'm goin' right now with some soldiers to take her from your stronghold. I have my own plans for that feisty lady."

Cloud Eagle's gut twisted at the thought of his woman being taken from his lodge forcefully, for he knew that was how it would be if this drunken white man had anything to do with it. His brain soaked with firewater, he would not listen to Alicia when she spoke of her feelings for the Apache and said that she wished to stay. He might even see her as a traitor and treat her as such. This thought sent spasms of anguish and fear for Alicia through him, yet he could not go to her defense.

"You will be met at my stronghold by many warriors," Cloud Eagle growled out. "They will determine who enters and who is turned away."

"If they are caught off guard, the only way they will react will be with surprise," Milton said, filling the air with his drunken laughter.

Milton stumbled away. He soon emerged from the shadows of the tree on horseback, leading another horse behind him.

Ten Bears forced Cloud Eagle onto the horse, then mounted his own.

Cloud Eagle eyed Ten Bears' horse, realizing

now that he had managed to circle back and steal his own horse from the Apache corral. He had been planning this disgrace to his chief and the Apache people from the moment he had been ordered from their stronghold.

Cloud Eagle was taken away by Ten Bears and several soldiers, while several others rode away with Milton in the direction of the stronghold.

Panic filled Cloud Eagle. He tried to wrestle himself free of the ropes, but this only caused the ropes at his wrist and the one around his arms to tighten and bite into his flesh even more.

He looked down and saw blood trickling from the rope burns on his arms, then looked straight ahead. His eyes were void of expression, but his heart ached to know that he was not there to protect Alicia, as he had promised her. And if his warriors were taken off guard, not even the one left to guard Alicia could stop what Ten Bears had started by his lies to the white pony soldiers.

"Ten Bears, *dee-dah tatsan*, you will soon be dead," he whispered beneath his breath.

Somehow, some day, Cloud Eagle would see that this threat was carried out.

Many Apache warriors were at the river on the outskirts of the stronghold. They were collecting stones to make *metates* for their wives—the slightly hollowed hard stone, upon which the women soaked maize and then reduced it to paste to make bread.

The soldiers approached the Apache, then separated. Several went to the river and cornered the warriors there, while others went to the stronghold and surrounded it.

Milton Powers was at the lead. He rode into

the center of the stronghold and dismounted as the Apache men, children, and women clustered about, staring.

Having heard the commotion outside and the arrival of many horses, Alicia crept to the entrance flap and slowly drew it aside to take a look. She couldn't see around the warrior who still guarded her.

Alicia's heart skipped a beat when she heard gunfire down by the river. She edged away from the entrance flap, her knees suddenly weak. She looked over her shoulder at Cloud Eagle's store of weapons, but she did not have a chance to reach them before a gun blast just outside the tepee drew her eyes around in time to see the guard fall backward into the tepee, clutching a wound in his chest.

Numb from surprise and terror, Alicia stared down at the warrior.

Terrible screams and cries and the spattering of gunfire outside the lodge made Alicia's head begin to reel with fear.

She turned and started to run to the store of weapons again but was stopped when a familiar voice spoke through the horrifying cries of death and confusion outside the lodge.

"Alicia?"

Alicia turned with a start just as Milton Powers stepped clumsily over the dead Apache into the tepee. Her gaze fell to his rifle. It was smoking.

Then she looked bitterly at Milton Powers again, the realization just sinking in that he had a part in the massacre that was taking place in the stronghold.

"Why are you a part of such a dastardly thing

as this?" Alicia asked, her fists at her sides. "Milton, why?"

Milton's gaze moved slowly over her, then he smiled devilishly as he looked into her eyes. "So the Injun made you into a woman, eh?" he said mockingly. His eyes raked over her again. "Just look at you. You look like an Apache squaw."

He kneaded his chin. "Hmm," he said studiously. "I don't see no ropes holdin' you captive. Why, I do believe that Cloud Eagle may have been tellin' the truth after all. You're at his stronghold because you want to be, not because he dragged you here by the hair on your head."

Alicia paled and took a shaky step toward him. "Oh, Lord, Milton," she said, her voice drawn. "Where is Cloud Eagle? What have you done with him?"

"He's been arrested and is on his way even now toward Fort Thomas," he said.

"Why did you arrest Cloud Eagle?" Alicia asked. She looked past him, startled by the sudden silence outside the lodge. It was as though the whole world had come to an end and no one was left on it. "Why did you come and kill the innocent Apache people? What have they ever done to you?"

Her eyes widened. "Lord, no," she gasped, placing a hand to her throat. "This all didn't happen because of me, did it? Because you thought I was taken captive by Cloud Eagle? Please tell me that I'm not the cause, Milton. Please?"

"What does it matter, anyhow?" Milton said, slowly lifting the rifle to aim it at her. "You've nothing to say about it. When I look at you I see just another Apache. Come on, Alicia. Step outside. You are going to join the survivors to be incarcerated at the fort."

"What?" she gasped.

"Do as you are told, white Apache," Milton said, motioning with his rifle for her to leave the tepee. "I'm glad now that I decided to come lookin' for you. It took some time to think on it, though. Without you, life has been more peaceful for me. And I like bein' in charge of the mail station."

He spat at her feet. "Yep, glad I came for you," he said, his eyes squinting into hers. "Now I'll be rid of you for sure. I'll see to it that you stand beside your Apache chief lover when the hangman's noose is slipped over your head."

"Good Lord, Milton," Alicia said weakly. "What did *I* ever do to you to deserve such treatment?"

"Got in my way, that's for sure," he growled out. He placed his finger on the trigger. "Now don't give me any excuse to shoot you dead right now, do you hear?"

Alicia trembled as she stepped over the bodies of the warriors who had been faithful to Cloud Eagle's command. She went outside and tears streamed from her eyes when she saw the death and devastation that lay sprawled on the ground on all sides of her. The soldiers had not been at all merciful.

A soldier came and looked at her with a puzzled look on his face. "Milton, is this the white woman who was taken captive by the Apache?" he asked, scratching his brow.

"Yeah, but she's no Injun captive now," Milton said smugly. "Arrest her. She should be a prisoner of the United States Army."

"Why, Milton?"

Milton laughed and shoved Alicia toward a

horse. "'Cause she turned into an Apache," he snarled. "That's why."

The soldier asked no more questions. He took Alicia by an elbow and led her to a horse. He tied her hands together behind her before lifting her into the saddle.

Alicia glared down at him. "You are making one helluva mistake, soldier," she said, then turned her eyes straight ahead, her fears for Cloud Eagle mounting. If he gave the soldiers any excuse to kill him, it would happen so quickly!

She saw movement at her far side in the brush and saw the flash of copper skin in the sunlight, as well as weapons in the warrior's hands.

Farther still, hidden behind boulders, she caught a hint of horseflesh. Knowing that some of the warriors had escaped sent a measure of relief through her.

She sighed heavily and looked straight ahead again. She smiled, yet only slightly, for she was not sure if just a handful of warriors could do the work of many. She closed her eyes and said a soft prayer.

Chapter Twenty-Five

Standing before the commandant at Fort Thomas, chains heavy on his ankles, Cloud Eagle stood stoically and with dignity before General Powell's desk, as the general stared up at him while he nervously drummed his fingers on the top of his desk.

"Cloud Eagle, you have been accused of many things," General Powell said, easing back into his chair. He placed his fingertips together. "I'll give you this one chance to speak in your own defense. If what you say does not satisfy me, I shall see that you hang before sunup tomorrow. As for the other warriors who accompanied you on these raids, they will soon be brought here to join you in the cells. Later your women and children will be rounded up and shipped off to a reservation."

The mention of his people made Cloud Eagle's heart turn cold to know that he was not the only target of hate today. His whole stronghold was surely even now lying in shambles, death spread across his hallowed land.

And Alicia? he despaired. What of Alicia?

His gut twisted at the thought of what may have happened to her. The drunken white man who had accompanied the soldiers today had seemed adamant about Alicia, even anxious perhaps to see to her downfall.

And Ten Bears was the cause. It did not seem that someone of Cloud Eagle's stronghold could be this evil, this calculating.

But Ten Bears would one day regret having chosen the wrong path on which to travel and the wrong people to whom to give his loyalty.

Lost Wind came like a thunderclap to Cloud Eagle's mind. How could he blame her for what her brother did? He was torn as to what he would do about her once Ten Bears was dealt with.

And now was not the time to allow Lost Wind to enter his mind. There was much more at stake here than the safety of a spiteful, jealous woman!

"Have you nothing to say, Cloud Eagle?" General Powell said, leaning forward. "Your silence will condemn you. Is that the way you want it to be?"

Cloud Eagle found it hard to respond to a man who had been a friend until Ten Bears had accused Cloud Eagle of things he knew were not true. He glared down at the general. He wore a freshly laundered uniform, the golden buttons shining against the blue fabric of the garment. He looked much older than his age of forty-five. His well-groomed gray hair lay just above his shirt collar, his thick, gray mustache scarcely revealing a straight line of lips beneath it. Wrinkles lay like well-traveled paths across his face.

"White eyes, I have been falsely accused," Cloud Eagle began. "I am not a bad man. I do not rob and steal. I speak the truth always. The Great Spirit gave me an honest heart and a straight tongue."

He squared his shoulders proudly and continued. "Yes, my skin is red," he said. He placed a hand on his breast, over his heart. "There is no guilt there. I can look you in the face like a man and say that my heart is big and that my tongue is not forked."

"Then why does one of your own Apache come to the fort and tell things that incriminate you?" the general said, fidgeting with a pen, rolling it back and forth between his fingers. "Do not all Apache profess to have been taught to be honest? Who am I to believe? You or Ten Bears? What does he have to gain by lying?"

"Cloud Eagle has a lot to gain by telling the truth," he said, then his eyes flickered like burning coals down at the general. "Ten Bears gains vengeance by lying."

"Oh?" the general said, easing back in his chair again. "And why is this vengeance sought against his very own chief?"

"In a duel, Ten Bears was the loser," Cloud Eagle said. "And then it was I who banished him and his sister from the Apache village. This brought much humiliation into the life of Ten Bears. Hunger for revenge then was the only thing that remained in his heart."

"I see," the general said, nodding.

Cloud Eagle leaned over and placed his palms

against the top of the desk, bringing his face closer to the general's. "The Apache have bad men among them, but your soldiers who wrongly entered my stronghold today have always been considered my friends," he said. "Friends and brothers."

"Friends, yes," the general said. "But we are also soldiers who must do our duty. The raids on the California Road must be stopped. You have been accused of these raids. Therein lies the cause for friends to become enemies."

Cloud Eagle straightened his back and placed his arms tightly to his sides, his hands doubled into tight fists. "My heart is heavy and wounded that the white pony soldiers would believe that this Apache could be guilty of raids against people to whom this Apache has offered protection for so many moons."

Cloud Eagle glared down at the colonel. "You look cross-eyed when you search for those who are guilty of these crimes for which you lay blame on Cloud Eagle and his warriors," he said. "Go. Go to Sandy Whiskers' outpost. Take a long, searching look. You will see the cages where prisoners have been held and some have surely died. Sandy Whiskers—the man you looked past as though he were a mere dot of sand in the desert—is responsible for most of this of which you accuse Cloud Eagle."

"The women you freed from the Englishman's outpost told us about what he is guilty of. But that does not clear your name. You may have made similar raids and ambushes."

"You do not want to see my innocence," Cloud Eagle accused. "You would rather take time arresting me and my warriors than to go out

303

beneath the hot rays of the sun to search for Sandy Whiskers."

"You have been arrested because Ten Bears said that you are guilty of the crimes accused," General Powell argued back. "And as for Sandy Whiskers—he is long gone. We can search no further for him."

"You can allow him to go free that easily? After what he was guilty of?" Cloud Eagle said, his voice drawn. "My woman was recently abducted and incarcerated there. Cloud Eagle and his warriors released her and the others. Now death should come to Sandy Whiskers. Yet you waste time raiding my people? Innocent, peace-loving people?"

General Powell toyed with his mustache. "If what you say is true . . ." he said, his words breaking off when Cloud Eagle interrupted him.

"Sandy Whiskers thinks he is lucky to have escaped," Cloud Eagle said, his lips clenched. "But when he is found by the Apache, his death will be much worse than had it been done quickly at the outpost."

The general rose from his chair and began pacing. "I'm not sure what I must do about all of this," he said, kneading his chin.

"What of my people?" Cloud Eagle said. "Did your soldiers leave death behind at my stronghold? If so, where lies the blame? Did you order such a massacre?"

The general turned abruptly and faced Cloud Eagle. "No massacre was ordered," he said. "I would not give such an order, Cloud Eagle. All that I wanted was for you to be brought in for questioning, and the white woman released."

"The drunken white man was out of place

among your soldiers," Cloud Eagle said. "He could entice others into doing that which was not originally ordered by you. If this happened . . ."

"If that happened, then he will pay, as well as the others who might be responsible for careless, callous behavior," General Powell said. "As for now, Cloud Eagle, I have no choice but to place you behind bars until I can investigate everything more completely."

Cloud Eagle's blood ran black with anger, yet he practiced the restraint that he had been taught as a child and kept his anger at bay. "You are wrong to place this Apache chief behind bars," he said in an even tone. "Your people came to our country. You were well received by the Coyotero Apache. We watched you pass by ones, by twos, by threes across our land. You went and came in peace. We believed your assurances of friendship and we trusted you. Why do you now distrust this chief who has offered you nothing but friendship?"

"It is the law," General Powell said, his eyes wavering into Cloud Eagle's. "If *any* man, no matter if his skin is red or white, is accused of performing heinous acts against others, he must be incarcerated until proven guilty or innocent of the crime."

"You know that an Apache behind bars is an Apache without dignity," Cloud Eagle said solemnly. He leaned into the general's face. "White man, your tongue is forked, and your heart is black, like a snake's."

"I would be careful who you call names," General Powell said, his face reddening with anger. He slapped his hands behind him, clasping them tightly together. "There is one more thing that I have failed to question you about. The white woman. You took her captive, did you not? If not, how can you explain her presence at your stronghold?"

A sudden commotion in the corridor outside the general's quarters caused Cloud Eagle's and General Powell's eyes to move toward the closed door that led to the corridor.

Cloud Eagle was taken aback when he recognized Alicia's voice. He smiled slowly as he heard her using a few choice unladylike words while shouting at those who were bringing her to the general's quarters. It made relief flood his senses to know that she was all right and still filled with a fiery spirit, enough to stand up for herself against those who might have humiliated and offended her.

He wanted to go to her and grab her away from the soldiers, but the chains heavy at his ankles rendered him helpless.

He glared down at them. They were an abomination of the worst measure in the eyes of an Apache.

He looked slowly up and his eyes rested on the keys that lay on the edge of the general's desk, yet too far away for him to reach.

The door burst open. Alicia was flanked on each side by two brawny soldiers. She was jerking and yanking in an effort to wrench herself free, her curse words flying forth from between her delicate lips like hornets on wing.

"You damn ingrate sonsofbitches, let me go," Alicia screamed, her hair flying around her face as she continued to struggle. "You have no right to treat me like this. I've done nothing wrong."

When she caught sight of Cloud Eagle standing there with chains on his ankles, all of the fight left her. The color faded from her face and her knees grew weak. The pit of her stomach felt as though someone had doubled up a fist and hit her.

"Cloud Eagle?" she whispered, the words faint now as they passed across her lips. Tears sprang from her eyes. "Oh, Lord, Cloud Eagle."

"Alicia?" General Powell said, surprise in his eyes. "My God, Alicia Cline. Milton Powers failed to tell me the name of the woman who had been taken captive. He just called you by—eh, other choice names since he did not seem to think too highly of you."

"Yes, it's me," Alicia said, yanking herself free at last as the soldiers lost their grip. "And I'll have you know, *sir*, I think even less of Milton Powers and you for what you have done today to the Coyotero Apache." She turned soft eyes to Cloud Eagle. "Especially Cloud Eagle."

"Cloud Eagle was arrested because he has been accused of certain crimes," General Powell said, going to Alicia. He tried to place a hand to her cheek, but she slapped it away. "As for you, dear, you should be glad that I sent someone to set you free. No white woman should suffer disgrace at the hand of any Indian, even if the Indians have professed to be friends to all white people."

Alicia slung her hair back from her face and placed her hands on her hips. "I was not being held captive at the Apache stronghold," she spat out. "I will soon be married to Cloud Eagle. I will then gladly go by the name of white Apache. And, *sir*, you will live in disgrace and shame the rest of your life for having ordered the massacre at Cloud Eagle's stronghold. Many innocent Apache—women, children, and men alike—died needlessly today. What have you to say for yourself, *sir,* to know that your orders were carried out? Much blood seeps into the Apache soil even now, as I speak."

There was a strained silence in the room.

Cloud Eagle was instantly numb from the realization of what had happened to his people.

General Powell was stunned.

Then a roar, much more loud than any lion could set free from the depths of its throat, filled the room. It was Cloud Eagle's voice, filled with despair and rage.

He then stumbled toward the desk and grabbed the key. Before the soldiers could stop him he unlocked the irons at his ankles, then threw them across the room.

Then he lunged across the desk and grabbed the general by the throat.

When Alicia heard the click of triggers on each side of her, she moved as though she were a whirlwind. She kicked one rifle from one of the soldiers and swung around and grabbed the other one. She aimed the rifle at the soldiers.

"I wouldn't try anything if I were you," she said, her eyes daring them to.

Chapter Twenty-Six

The general grasped at Cloud Eagle's fingers and tried to pull them away from his throat. "Let me go," he said, his voice faint and raspy. "You don't know what you are doing."

"Cloud Eagle knows very well what he is doing at all times," Cloud Eagle growled between clenched teeth. "You said that you did not order a massacre of my people. Again you speak with forked tongue. My woman brings news that blood has been spilled in my stronghold—spilled by your blue-coated soldiers."

"It was not carried out . . . as a result of a direct command from me," the general said, his face reddening as he gasped for breath. "Good Lord, Cloud Eagle. I had no reason to give such a command. I wanted you for questioning. And I wanted to be sure the white woman was released from captivity. That's all. You've got to believe me."

"Cloud Eagle, it seemed that things got out of control," Alicia said over her shoulder as she held a steady aim at the soldiers. "I believe it was because Milton Powers incited the soldiers to violence. I saw enough to truly believe that after one shot was fired, perhaps carelessly, it began something that could not be stopped. I hold General Powell responsible, only because he has lost some control of those under his command, not because he actually ordered the raid."

"Is that so?" Cloud Eagle said, leaning his face into General Powell's.

"Seems I have lost some strength as a commander," the general said, his eyes wavering. "Never would I have ordered a raid on your people, Cloud Eagle. Many of them are my friends."

"Yet you would condemn me and would hang me so quickly?" Cloud Eagle said, relentlessly keeping his fingers locked on the colonel's throat.

"If you were guilty of that which you were accused, yes," the general sputtered out. "I would have no choice. I must set a good example, or else others would take up raiding. What then, Cloud Eagle?"

"You set a good example by being so lax a leader that your soldiers kill and maim innocent Apache?" Cloud Eagle demanded.

"I'm sorry about that," the general said, his voice now only a hoarse whisper.

Cloud Eagle glared into the general's eyes a moment longer, then yanked his fingers from his throat. He moved back to the other side of the desk to Alicia's side, his eyes never leaving the general in case he might try and draw the firearm that was holstered at his waist.

It amused Cloud Eagle to see the general, now

cowering beneath Cloud Eagle's steady stare, rubbing his red, raw neck.

"Those soldiers who brought death and destruction to my stronghold must be punished," Cloud Eagle said. He took his eyes off the general long enough to stoop and pick up the rifle that Alicia had kicked away from the soldier. Quickly Cloud Eagle straightened his back again and leveled the rifle at the general's chest. "You must give your word that reparation will be made or I will return and make sure it is done myself," he warned.

"I will see that those responsible are punished," the general said, his voice drawn.

Alicia's eyes wavered up into Cloud Eagle's. "Darling, your people, those who lived through the massacre, are on their way to this fort by foot," she murmured. "They are being treated as captives. Those who died . . ."

The sound of sudden, repeated, and rapid gunfire outside the general's quarters caused Alicia's words to falter. She had not had time to tell Cloud Eagle everything—that several of his warriors had fled so that they would not be killed or taken prisoner. They must have arrived. They had come to take back what was theirs, especially to save the life of their beloved chief.

"What now?" the general said. He took two wide steps and stood at the window, aghast at what he saw. "My God. Where will this all end? Now *we* are being attacked by *Apache*."

Cloud Eagle was momentarily taken off guard. He was afraid that there would not be enough of his Coyotero Apache to withstand the gunfire of the soldiers. He could envision all of his warriors being dead at the close of this day.

When he realized that the firing had stopped

abruptly, Cloud Eagle grabbed Alicia by her free hand and ran with her from the general's quarters, followed by the general and his men.

They were all surprised to see the outcome of the Apache attack on the fort. It had apparently come as a total surprise. Leaderless, the soldiers had surrendered without a single casualty.

The soldiers had been ushered into a tight circle in the courtyard, their hands raised above their heads, the Apache on horses encircling them.

Beyond the walls of the fort, more Apache on horseback encircled Fort Thomas, their rifles drawn.

"So many Apache," Cloud Eagle gasped. "There are more Apache warriors than ever I could lay claim to. They outnumber the soldiers ten to one."

Alicia's gaze roamed over those Apache who were within the walls of the fort, stopping at one in particular when she quickly recognized him.

She grabbed Cloud Eagle's arm. "Look," she said, smiling up at him. "Thunder Roars is there, among the Apache. It is *his* warriors who have joined yours in the attack on Fort Thomas."

Cloud Eagle's gaze moved searchingly over the warriors. A broad smile spread on his face when Thunder Roars turned his eyes to Cloud Eagle at the same moment that Cloud Eagle recognized him. "He is staying true to our vows of friendship," he said gratefully.

Thunder Roars dismounted and went to Cloud Eagle. They embraced, then stepped apart, their eyes locked.

"It is with a sad heart that the blue coats saw cause to interrupt the serenity of my friends' lives," Thunder Roars said, lifting a hand to

Cloud Eagle's shoulder. "Your surviving warriors brought the news to me of the disaster at your stronghold. They sought my help. I came not only to see that you and your woman were released, but to seek justice for the Coyotero Apache."

"It was a good day when two arrows felled the same deer and brought two warriors into a bond of friendship," Cloud Eagle said. "This friend thanks you, Thunder Roars."

"I freely gave my skills to see that your woman was freed from the greedy clutches of the white pony soldiers. You both are free to go now and forge ahead with plans for your future."

"And I thank you for what you have done for me, but mostly for Cloud Eagle and his people," Alicia said, placing a gentle, appreciative hand on Thunder Roars' arm. A shudder overtook her at the memory of the death scene at Cloud Eagle's stronghold. "I just wish I could have done more for them. It all happened so quickly."

"And now what are we to do with these captive soldiers?" Thunder Roars said, looking from soldier to soldier. "Perhaps we should kill them and be done with it."

Alicia searched among the men, too, looking for Milton Powers or Ten Bears. But they were nowhere to be seen. Their luck had held for a while longer. They had escaped.

"No, we will not kill these men," Cloud Eagle said, turning to gaze at the general. He smiled at Alicia, then at Thunder Roars. "They will ride with us to once again see proof of a true enemy to the white people. They will see exactly how far an enemy will go to feed his greedy hungers."

Cloud Eagle paused, then addressed the general. "Sandy Whiskers," he uttered, "is the worst kind of an enemy. After you witness the extent of his operation, you will realize that Cloud Eagle and his warriors are innocent. Our names will be cleared."

He glared at the general with squinted eyes. "You and your soldiers must look upon the Apache cages," he said, his teeth clenched. "Then you will admit to this Apache chief that you were wrong to accuse the Coyotero Apache of the raids on the California Road."

"But Cloud Eagle," Alicia asked, gazing up at him. "Sandy Whiskers may have destroyed all of the evidence. He may have returned and destroyed all of the cages. What proof, then, can we show the soldiers?"

"No one can that quickly totally destroy all evidence of such a large slavery and breeding program," Cloud Eagle reassured her. "Especially since Sandy Whiskers knows that he takes his life into his own hands should he surface and return to his outpost. And he would not destroy all of his equipment. It would be too costly."

"Even if leaving everything intact might incriminate him?" Alicia questioned.

"He is a greedy man," Cloud Eagle rumbled. "It is a chance that he would take."

"I hope you're right," Alicia said softly.

Cloud Eagle took two horses from the hitching rail. He handed one set of reins to Alicia, the other to the general. He nodded toward one horse. "Mount up," he said flatly to the general. "Then ride over to your soldiers and tell them to get their horses and follow. Also warn them not to bring any firearms. There have been enough needless deaths today."

His shoulders slumped, General Powell did as

he was told. As he gave orders to his soldiers, Cloud Eagle went to Alicia.

"*Ish-kay-nay*, you make Cloud Eagle proud to say that you are his woman," he said, framing her face between his hands. "Never lose your savage spirit. That, among other things, is what separates you from all other women I have ever known."

"What I did today was for you," Alicia said, rising on tiptoe to brush a kiss across his lips. "I would do anything for you. Anything."

She clutched the rifle tightly in her hand as Cloud Eagle placed his hands at her waist and lifted her into the saddle. "One day we can return to an ordinary life," he said. A frown suffused his handsome face. "But not very soon. There is much mourning among my people. There are many burials to see to."

Alicia hung her head. "I cannot help but feel responsible," she murmured. "Had I never entered your life, none of this would have happened."

"Never forget that it was I who introduced you into the life of my people," he said, giving her a fierce look. "If blame is to be cast, cast it my way."

"Never can you be blamed for all the wrong that has come to your people of late," Alicia said, blinking tears from her eyes. "Never could they have had such a devoted, loving leader as you."

"The soldiers are ready to ride with us to Sandy Whiskers' outpost," Thunder Roars said, urging his horse next to Alicia's, and leading Cloud Eagle's roan, which he had brought with him from the stronghold.

Cloud Eagle turned and gazed at length at the double line of soldiers, the general at the lead. He checked with a more careful eye for the shine of weapons, relieved when he saw none.

Then he mounted his frisky roan and rode away.

He stopped and edged his horse close to the general's. "Is everything understood?" he said, his dark eyes watching for the general's acquiescence.

"Understood," General Powell said, nodding.

Alicia snapped her reins and nudged the flanks of her horse with her heels, then grew pale and breathless with horror when she caught sight of the shine of the barrel of a rifle from the shadows at the side of the soldiers' barracks. The flash of copper skin caught her eye as the man stepped more into the open, his aim leveled at Cloud Eagle.

It was Ten Bears!

"Cloud Eagle!" Alicia cried, her scream muffled by the loud blast of rifle fire.

Chapter Twenty-Seven

Alicia felt faint when she realized that not one gunshot but two had rung out. Someone else had seen Ten Bears.

It all happened in an instant. But surely not quickly enough to save Cloud Eagle. The shots had exploded at the same time. Almost paralyzed with fear at the thought of her beloved possibly being mortally wounded, Alicia placed a hand at her throat and stared at Cloud Eagle. She expected him to fall from his horse at any moment.

To her relief, he did not budge—except to lower his smoking rifle to his side as he glared at Ten Bears. She then realized that Cloud Eagle had been the one responsible for the second gunshot. He had shot Ten Bears!

Alicia turned quick eyes back to Ten Bears just as he crumpled to the ground, clutching his chest.

"Thank God," Alicia breathed. Cloud Eagle's aim had been more exact than Ten Bears'. Ten Bears had been shot mortally in the chest. He was breathing hard, his gaze on Cloud Eagle as Cloud Eagle slid from his saddle and walked stiffly toward him.

Thunder Roars was suddenly there, standing over Ten Bears, smoke spiraling from the barrel of his rifle. In one movement, he kicked Ten Bears' rifle away.

Thunder Roars gave Cloud Eagle an assured, pleased smile as Cloud Eagle came to him.

"We fired at the exact moment. Again we share in a kill," Thunder Roars said to Cloud Eagle. He gazed down at Ten Bears. He gazed at the two bullet wounds, blood seeping from them. "He will be dead soon, Cloud Eagle."

Alicia dismounted and went to Cloud Eagle. She was amazed at the irony of what had happened. The gunfire that she had heard had not been from Ten Bears' firearm at all. Thunder Roars and Cloud Eagle had chosen the same instant to shoot Ten Bears.

Yes, they had shared another kill, for Ten Bears' breaths were now numbered as he lay gasping and struggling for each as though it were his last.

Cloud Eagle thrust his rifle into Alicia's hands, then knelt beside Ten Bears. "You die without honor, snake," he said coldly. "Your spirit will never rest. Instead it will wander aimlessly through time. You will never be reunited with your loved ones. Was it worth losing the wonders of the afterworld in an attempt to get revenge on Cloud Eagle?"

"Should . . . you . . . have died, it would have

318

meant everything to this Apache," Ten Bears managed to say between shallow breaths.

"I have told you before that you have relinquished all right to call yourself Apache," Cloud Eagle said. "Snake. Forever you will be no better than a snake. Your spirit will crawl on its belly and never find peace."

Ten Bears closed his eyes in an attempt to block Cloud Eagle from not only his sight, but also his mind. He gasped for air and clutched desperately at his chest again. "Leave me be," he begged. "Just leave me be."

Cloud Eagle lifted Ten Bears' face closer to his. "Your sister," he said, his teeth clenched. "Where have you left her? She is without protection?"

Ten Bears' eyes opened at the mention of his sister. With his free hand he grasped Cloud Eagle's arm. "Lost Wind!" he gasped. "She *is* alone. She *is* without protection. I would have returned for her, but now . . . but now . . ."

Again he closed his eyes, breathing much more slowly.

"Where is she?" Cloud Eagle demanded.

Wide-eyed and trembling, Alicia watched Cloud Eagle's interrogation, worrying about his motive. Had he missed Lost Wind since her banishment? Did he still love her?

Or was Cloud Eagle's concern for her truly only because he feared for her life, since her brother would no longer be there to see to her welfare?

Alicia knew that Cloud Eagle had warned Ten Bears to care for his sister. And now that he hadn't, she wondered if Cloud Eagle would send for her and take her into his own life again.

Cloud Eagle's heart was good. She doubted that he could allow even one of the Apache women of

319

his stronghold to face danger alone, even if she was a spiteful, unlikable person.

Surely Cloud Eagle was going to just see that Lost Wind was brought back to his stronghold to live a life of safety, Alicia thought to herself. Not as his wife.

Spring Dawn was still in the stronghold. She was no threat. Alicia would not allow Lost Wind to become a threat, either.

If Lost Wind was ever found to bring back to the stronghold, she thought.

Guilt spread through her when for a moment she found herself wishing that Lost Wind might never be found.

When she heard Ten Bears manage to breathe out where he had left his sister, Alicia knew that she had much to think over and accept, should Cloud Eagle send for Lost Wind now that he knew where she was.

"Go for her, Cloud Eagle," Ten Bears whispered harshly. His eyes grew wide; he clasped harder to Cloud Eagle's arm as his body went into a spasm, then subsided limply on the ground.

Cloud Eagle placed his fingers over Ten Bears's eyes and slowly closed them. He bowed his head for a moment, remorse filling him for this fallen warrior who had lost his way in the world of the Apache.

Then he lay Ten Bears' head back on the ground and rose to his full height over him. He stared at Ten Bears for a moment longer, Alicia watching him.

Then out of the corner of her eye, she caught another movement that no one else seemed to have noticed. Everyone seemed focused on the death scene—not on other survivors besides Ten

Bears who might be lurking in the shadows.

Wheeling around, Cloud Eagle's rifle clutched in her hands, Alicia aimed at the man who was sneaking behind the building on her left.

"Stop right there!" she shouted. "Don't go another step or I'll blow a hole clean through you."

All eyes turned at once when Milton Powers stepped into view and dropped his weapon and raised his hands quickly into the air.

"Damn it, Alicia, it's only me," Milton shouted back. "Turn that firearm away from me. Do you hear?"

"Milton?" Alicia said, her eyebrows forking. "Lord, Milton. Did you hate me so much that you—?"

"I sure as hell don't like you," he said, interrupting her. He inched toward everyone. "You ain't never been anything but trouble for me. And now that you're an Injun lover, I doubt I'll ever be able to stand bein' around you."

"You won't have that to worry about," Alicia said, keeping her aim leveled on him. "And not because I don't plan to return to work at the stage station, either. But because you are going to be in jail. You are going to stand trial for your part in the Apache massacre. There's no way you can lie your way out of this, Milton, so don't even try."

General Powell dismounted and came to Alicia's side. He nodded to two of his soldiers. They also dismounted and went to Milton.

"Take him away and lock him up," General Powell said, bending to pick up Milton's rifle. He thrust it into the hands of one of his soldiers. "Stay with him and question him. If you get any answers from him about Sandy Whiskers,

321

catch up with us as we head out now for Sandy Whiskers' outpost."

"I don't know nothin' about Sandy Whiskers," Milton cried as he was half dragged away. "Alicia, for pity's sakes, tell them I usually tend to my business. Only when you came up missin' did I stray from my usual duties at the stage station."

Alicia just glared at him.

"You're wrong!" Milton shrieked as he was dragged further away. "I meant no harm, Alicia, in what I did at the Injun village. It was the soldiers. It was their fault. They just went crazy once that first gun was fired. Alicia, tell them that I'm innocent."

"Like hell you are," Alicia said, then turned her eyes from the pitiful sight of the blubbering weakling.

General Powell took one last look at Ten Bears. Then he turned his gaze toward Cloud Eagle. "I think in the end I will have so much apologizing to do, I won't know where to begin, or how," he said thickly.

"You have enough information now to know of my total innocence, yet I feel that you still should accompany me to Sandy Whiskers' outpost," Cloud Eagle said. Alicia gave him his rifle. He turned to his horse and slipped his firearm into its gunboot.

Then he turned and looked quickly toward the gate of the fort. His throat went dry as he watched those Apache of his stronghold who had survived the massacre now being forced by gunpoint to enter the courtyard.

He felt as though he were strangling with despair and guilt. He felt that he had let his people down. A very brave and successful chief would win distinction for his band, would give it prestige, so that ambitious young warriors would desire to join it.

Always before there had been safety under his leadership, so that the Apache nation as a whole had come to know and honor his wisdom and prowess.

But he worried about having lost prestige today. There was a real democracy among the Apache. It was for the people as a whole to decide upon a given course of action. As long as a chief was strong enough to protect his followers and courageous enough to lead them to victory against their foes, he held sway over them.

When a chief failed to make good, an abler man took his place.

Would his people demand his replacement?

He would know soon.

Words would not have to be spoken.

It would be in the eyes of his people as they gazed at him.

Alicia gasped, her color quickly paling when she turned and also saw the sad procession of men, women, and children.

The children were crying and clinging to the skirts of their mothers. The men walked stoicly, their eyes empty. The women held their chins high, their faces void of emotion.

His agony over what he saw was so intense that Cloud Eagle felt as though his insides were being torn apart.

He watched his people for a moment longer, then turned angry eyes at General Powell. "This is how my people are treated in time of peace between Chief Cloud Eagle and the white father in Washington?" he demanded. "There is nothing you can say or do to fully return the dignity to my people after they have been forced at gunpoint to march like animals across the land of our ancestors. Where are the papers of peace that protect my people from such treatment? To have arrived at Fort Thomas this quickly, they had to have been forced to run at times. Have they not suffered enough already?"

General Powell's mouth was agape with humiliated surprise. He stared at the marching Apache, then turned to Cloud Eagle. "As was the massacre not of my doing, so was this also not ordered by me," he said. "Cloud Eagle, I shall make this up to you. Somehow."

"You can begin by ordering your soldiers away from my people," Cloud Eagle said, giving General Powell an angry stare. "Then you can supply them all—men, children and women alike—with horses for their return to our stronghold. Is that understood?"

"That's the least that I can do," General Powell said. He rode off and drew rein beside his soldiers.

Alicia walked with Cloud Eagle as he stepped before his people. They slowly gathered about him. His eyes filled with them, with their misery, with their shame.

He then glanced at the sun, where it burned in the sky, and offered a prayer. He raised his hand and the glow of the sun upon the flat of his forearm caught the eyes of his people. Low gasps wafted through the air at the sign that had been sent to them from the sun.

Hope filled the eyes, hearts, and souls of his people as Cloud Eagle began moving among them. He took the time to embrace each one.

The children clung to him and cried. The women lingered in his embrace. The men gave him a quick hug, then stood tall and proud as horses were brought to them.

Cloud Eagle felt as if the weight of the world had been released from his shoulders when he saw that his people still looked to him as their leader. There was respect and admiration in their eyes. They understood that none of this was of his doing. It was the fault of white men whose hearts and minds were twisted.

After everyone was ready for traveling, Cloud Eagle looked from one to another. "Return to our stronghold and begin preparing our dead for their burial rites," he said solemnly. "I have other duties which will separate us for a while longer. But soon I will join you. We shall make all wrongs right together at our stronghold."

As the Apache people rode away, Alicia watched, tears flowing from her eyes.

Then she followed Cloud Eagle's lead as he swung himself into his saddle. She was just as quickly in hers. Proud to be a part of this noble Apache's life, she rode beside Cloud Eagle as they left the fort.

General Powell and several soldiers rode on ahead.

Before Sandy Whiskers' outpost came into view, columns of smoke were visible in the air.

Alicia edged her horse closer to Cloud Eagle's. "The bastard *did* return," she said angrily. "He's returned and burned everything. I doubt there will be any trace left of those damnable cages."

"Sandy Whiskers may have burned the proof, but that does not change the truth," Cloud Eagle said as he looked heavenward and watched the smoke blending into white puffy clouds. "I will hunt him down. Justice will be done only when he is dead."

Thunder Roars edged his steed close on Cloud Eagle's other side. "See smoke yonder?" he said, gesturing with a hand. "The fire will destroy all proof."

"Fire and smoke will soon fade away to nothingness and along with it the physical proof," Cloud Eagle said, smiling at Thunder Roars. "But Sandy Whiskers cannot disappear in a burst of smoke. We will find him. If I have to turn over every grain of sand in the desert to find him, I shall."

Cloud Eagle sank his heels into the flanks of his horse and rode away. Thunder Roars and Alicia exchanged quick glances, then rode after Cloud Eagle.

When the outpost came into full view, the smoke had turned to shifting, hazy sheets of gray. Cloud Eagle rode through the opened gate, everyone following. He yanked his reins and stopped his horse abruptly, his gaze slowly taking in the total destruction which lay around him.

"He can't have gotten far," Alicia said. "This fire was set not all that long ago."

Cloud Eagle slid out of his saddle. Alicia and Thunder Roars followed his lead. They walked with him toward Sandy Whiskers' destroyed cabin. It had burned during the Apache attack on the outpost, and its ashes were now cool.

Cloud Eagle walked around the outer fringes of the remains of the cabin, his moccasins scattering ash into the wind.

He looked farther still, at the remains of the building at the far back of the courtyard.

Nothing could be left of the cages. But the branding irons could not have burned. They could be handed over to General Powell as evidence. The brand *A* was one certain way to incriminate the Englishman!

He turned to walk away, to go and search in the ashy remains for the branding iron, but stopped and gazed over his shoulder at the remains of Sandy Whiskers' cabin when he got the distinct feeling that he had heard someone shouting from that direction. It was a strange sound, as though it came from the deep depths of a well.

Alicia's insides quivered strangely as she turned abruptly and stared down at the ashes of the cabin. She had also heard something. She held in her breath in an effort to hear better. She was almost certain that she had heard someone shouting from somewhere beneath the rubble and ash.

Even Cloud Eagle had heard it. He was there now, his eyes searching the ashes.

"Did you also hear?" Thunder Roars said, moving to Cloud Eagle's side. "It was a voice, was it not? But from where?"

Cloud Eagle nodded and hurried into the ashes, following the sound of a voice crying out to be saved.

It was beneath him.

Below the ground.

Alicia hurried after him. "Cloud Eagle, the voice is coming from beneath us," she said, studying the burned-out floor of the cabin as Cloud Eagle began shoving the ash aside with his moccasined foot.

Then a thought came to Alicia. "There must be an underground tunnel," she said. She moved to her knees and began sorting through the ash with her fingers. "It has to be here somewhere. It sounds as though we are just above the person who is shouting."

When the voice began fading in strength, Alicia moved her hands more desperately through the ash. When her palms came in contact with something smooth, she gave Cloud Eagle a look of alarm.

"Here, Cloud Eagle," she said, as her fingers traced the outline of a trap door. "It's a door. I've found a door."

Cloud Eagle came to her. She scooted aside as he cleared the ash from the steel door. Everyone came and hovered around them as he placed his fingers beneath the edge of the door and slowly lifted it.

"Help!" the voice cried. And then there were others making the same plea.

The door lifted and steps were revealed that led downward. Cloud Eagle made his way down the steps.

Alicia followed, and then Thunder Roars and General Powell.

When Alicia placed her feet on the cold, damp ground, she wheeled around and could not believe her eyes. The light from the trap door was enough to make out that she was in an underground cavern in which many men were manacled to the wall. Most were nude, yet some of the men wore tattered clothes.

All of the men were emaciated, and their scarred bodies revealed that they had endured many whippings.

Alicia was horrified by the sight and stench that filled the place.

She covered her mouth with one hand when a sick feeling flooded her senses. She started to turn her head away from the terrible scene of pain and torture, but the sound of someone speaking her name ever so weakly made her heart skip a beat.

Then it began thumping wildly within her chest as she sorted through the thin, gaunt faces and empty eyes. When she found her brother among those who appeared to have been the most cruelly tortured and saw that one arm was missing, a spinning blackness seized her. Her legs went limp, and she sank to the floor in a dead faint.

"Alicia," Charlie cried. "Oh, God, Alicia."

Cloud Eagle bent over Alicia and picked her up in his arms. He held her close as he gazed over at the man who had spoken Alicia's name. A flickering of remembrance grabbed at his senses. Could this be the man who had refused to sell him the painting? He saw scarcely a resemblance to that man who had sat painting the sunset the day Cloud Eagle had briefly made his acquaintance. The red beard and hair were the identifying features. It surely was him!

And it was obvious that Sandy Whiskers' men had not spared him their evil torture. Cloud Eagle wondered if he had even arrived in time to save the man's life.

Thunder Roars went to Charlie and released him from his chains. Charlie fell to the floor, too weak to stand on his own. General Powell found a blanket and took it to him and wrapped it around his thin shoulders.

Trembling, Charlie gazed up at Cloud Eagle. "My sister," he whispered. "Bring her to me."

Cloud Eagle took Alicia to Charlie. He knelt

329

down with her in his arms so that her brother could get a good look at Alicia.

"She is all right," Charlie said weakly. "That's all that matters."

He ran his thick tongue over his parched lips and reached a trembling hand to Alicia's face. "Yes, she's all right," he said, his voice breaking. "I had thought that perhaps that mangy Englishman had taken her as his captive."

"She was his captive, but Cloud Eagle set her free," Cloud Eagle said. He ran his fingers over the fine features of her face. "She will soon awaken. The shock of seeing you has momentarily taken her into a place where horror is more easily accepted."

"You have seen to her welfare?" Charlie asked weakly. "You? An Apache?"

"I did and I always shall," Cloud Eagle said, glad to see Alicia's eyelids flutter. "She is my woman."

Everything became suddenly quiet.

Charlie stared at Cloud Eagle.

Cloud Eagle accepted the stare, understanding it.

All around them, others were set free from their bonds. One by one they were taken from the dungeon.

Alicia opened her eyes slowly. When she saw her brother again, tears streamed down her cheeks.

Cloud Eagle placed her on her feet, and she knelt before Charlie and engulfed him within her arms.

"Oh, Lord," she cried. "Charlie. My sweet Charlie."

Cloud Eagle stepped away from them and stood

at General Powell's side. "Have you seen enough?" he said, his voice drawn.

General Powell was pale and shaky. "More than enough," he said. "I'll search for that sonofabitch until I find him. A noose isn't enough for that Englishman."

Chapter Twenty-Eight

As Alicia fed her brother a nourishing broth, she turned occasional glances toward Cloud Eagle. He sat beside the fire pit in his lodge, brooding, so much in his life now a turmoil.

Outside his lodge, rawhide drums beat slowly and mournfully. Many within the sound of the drums wailed to the heavens while others worked diligently at building themselves new lodges.

The dead had been buried in a quick mass ceremony. Moon Shadow had performed his healing powers over the ill and wounded.

But those tasks had thus far not come near to making things right in the world of the Coyotero Apache.

Especially for Cloud Eagle, their leader.

Alicia knew that Cloud Eagle felt drained from the recent tragedies. He had confided in her and had told her that he felt out of control, as though he could not see to the welfare of his people as a chief was required to do.

She feared that he might even be considering handing the title over to somebody else, even though no one could have foreseen what was going to happen to his people. He was human, unable to perform miracles.

Nor could any other Apache.

Since the white man had arrived in the land of the Apache, nothing had been the same.

Alicia would even understand if Cloud Eagle's feelings for her turned into a silent loathing, for her skin was white.

So was her brother's.

She looked back at Charlie. Her own grief over how he had been treated came to her again, knocking the breath from inside her. Charlie was not an Apache, and look at how the white men had treated him!

Surely, she thought to herself, as astute as Cloud Eagle was, he would see this and not cast blame where it should not be cast.

Alicia's eyes were drawn to Cloud Eagle when he rose to his feet and suddenly left the lodge.

Her eyes wavered as she turned them back to her brother. Not wanting to worry Charlie, she held a sob deep within her throat. But deeply within her, where her emotions were born, she felt as though she were suffocating. Only days ago, she had been so wonderfully content as she and Cloud Eagle had spent time laughing and being carefree.

And oh, Lord, when they had made love!

It was as though she had floated into the heavens, the pleasure had been so sweet and wonderful.

And now it had all changed.

She doubted that it would ever be the same.

"Alicia, I can see that you are going through something deep and agonizing," Charlie said, reaching his hand to her cheek. "Honey, don't worry about me. I'll get my strength back soon. Nothing can hold me down for long."

"You've been through hell, yet you can still speak with so much hope?" Alicia said, resting the spoon in the bowl as her gaze swept slowly over her brother. Even through his thick red beard, she could see how gaunt his face was. On his scarred chest the stripes left from the whippings were oozing with infection.

A sob she did not want to set free jumped from her throat when she once again looked at the stub that had been Charlie's left arm.

"Now, now," Charlie said, watching the trail of her eyes over him. "Remember what mother used to say? It'll all come out in the wash?"

"You can joke at such a time as this?" Alicia said, wiping a stream of tears from her cheek. She forced a smile. "Keep it up, Charlie Cline. It's best to laugh about things instead of cry."

"I feel lucky that I even *survived* the cruelties at the outpost," he said, easing his hand to his side to support himself as he moved to a more comfortable position on the pallet of furs. "Of course, I lost one of my arms. But God, Alicia, at least I was spared my right arm. If I were left-handed, my career as an artist would be ruined. As it is, I can paint again soon and lose myself in my world of brushes and oils."

"You lost all of your supplies in the raid," Alicia said solemnly.

"There are plenty more where those came from," Charlie reassured her. "I only brought half of what I owned with me. The rest are in my office back at the art museum in Saint Louis. And if I had lost everything, I'd just start fresh. I'd buy out Jackson's once I returned to Saint Louis. You know that I have always loved browsing in artist-supply stores. They always liked seeing Charlie Cline coming."

"You'd best eat more broth then," Alicia said, lifting the spoon to his lips again. "These next several days I've got to fatten you up, or no one back home will ever recognize you."

He reached out his shaky hand and eased the spoon aside. "You're going to go home with me," he said, more in a command than a question. "I won't stand for your staying behind. Not after what I've been through. You could be next, Alicia. Damn it, you could be next."

"Nothing is going to happen to me," Alicia said, firming her lower lip. "Most of those responsible for your incarceration are either dead or in jail." She gazed hauntingly toward the entrance flap. "Except for . . ."

Charlie interrupted her. "There," he said flatly. "Don't you see? You know that Sandy Whiskers is out there somewhere, wreaking havoc. Who is to say that he won't gather together more outlaws and renegades and start his hellish raiding all over again? I'm sure he won't forget *you*. He'll come for you, Alicia. You can't be here, if he does."

"I can't leave Cloud Eagle," Alicia said, watching her brother's expression. "I love him. I will risk everything to be able to stay with him. Even my life, Charlie. Even . . . my life."

Charlie managed to lean up on his elbow. "You can't be serious," he gasped. "You? Live like an

Indian? You would willingly become one of the Apache's squaws?"

"A woman in the Apache stronghold is not referred to as a squaw," Alicia quickly corrected him. "That word is misinterpreted by the white man. To an Indian woman, the name squaw is insulting."

"Whatever," Charlie said, sighing heavily. "Just listen to me, Alicia. This isn't the sort of life you were raised into. Back home many comforts await you. Many available, unmarried gentlemen await your return. You could have your choice of admirers, Alicia. You could marry someone affluent who could give you the world."

Charlie's pleas were interrupted when Cloud Eagle returned. Alicia smiled at Cloud Eagle as he sat down beside her. She gazed then at a small wooden bowl, in which she could see a green mixture.

"I collected herbs and mixed them with river water for the sores on your flesh," Cloud Eagle said. He sank two fingers into the mixture, swirled them around until they were covered, then carefully applied this to Charlie's chest. "The herbs have much healing power. Then, if you wish, I shall bring my shaman to you for healing rituals."

As Charlie watched Cloud Eagle apply the medicine, marveling at how cooling it felt on his burning flesh, he was at first tense, then relaxed and eased his back down onto the furs and closed his eyes.

"No," he said thickly. "No shaman."

Charlie then slowly opened his eyes. "Cloud Eagle, I want my sister to return with me to St. Louis once I am well enough to travel," he said. He stiffened when his words brought a quick anger to the depths of Cloud Eagle's eyes.

"Because of white men, this chief has already lost too much," Cloud Eagle said, not missing one stroke of his fingers as he continued spreading the herbal mixture on Charlie's sores. "Do you think I would allow you, a white man, to take anything else from me? Especially not my woman!"

Charlie swallowed hard. "But Cloud Eagle, Alicia's skin is white," he dared to say. "How can you separate her from the rest of us who are white?"

"Cloud Eagle does this easily," he said, his voice tight. "Her *heart* is Apache."

Charlie's eyes widened. "You are wrong," he said. He glanced at Alicia, who sat quietly by, watching and listening. "Nothing *about* her is Apache."

"The moment she gave herself to this Apache chief, she became Apache," Cloud Eagle said. He wiped the herbal mixture from his fingers with a buckskin cloth now that he had totally covered Charlie's festering sores.

A coldness spread through Charlie. He gazed at Alicia. The mere fact that she did not lower her eyes in shame over what Cloud Eagle had just revealed to him made him see that she had changed a lot since he had last seen her in Saint Louis. She had matured in many ways.

To realize that she had slept with the Apache made Charlie want to retch, for he had never been able to cast prejudices from his heart since he had first read about Apache slaughters in the Saint Louis newspapers.

He doubted that he ever would. Not even if Alicia stayed with Cloud Eagle and had children with him. To him an Apache was an Apache. An Indian was an Indian. To him they were all savages.

Charlie had to believe that Cloud Eagle was only treating him civilly because of Alicia. If not for her, he was almost certain that he would have been left to die.

"Charlie?" Alicia said. She took his hand and squeezed it fondly. "Don't be alarmed by what Cloud Eagle said. I love him. You would also grow to love him if you were around him for long. Charlie, his personality is so much like our father's. He is one of the kindest, gentlest men I have ever known. I'm going to be his wife, Charlie. I'm going to bear his children. Say that you accept this. Please tell me that you will give me your blessing." She hung her head, then looked slowly up at him again. "Besides Cloud Eagle, you are all that I have left of family."

"Besides Cloud Eagle?" Charlie said incredulously. "You refer to him as family?"

"He is family, Charlie," Alicia said stubbornly. "You'd best accept that now. As are you a part of *his* family now. It doesn't take a piece of paper to join people as family. It is in the heart. It is in their feelings for one another."

Charlie turned his eyes away. "God," he choked out.

"Charlie?" Alicia pleaded.

"Just leave me be," Charlie said, his voice breaking. "I need to sleep. At least in sleep I can escape the cruelties of reality."

"Oh, Charlie, I'm so sorry you feel that way," Alicia said. When he refused to respond, she moved away from him. She set the soup bowl and spoon with the other dishes that needed washing later in the river, then went and sat down beside Cloud Eagle as he added wood to the fire.

"He didn't mean to insult or hurt you," Alicia said gently. "It's just that suddenly he has so much to accept that is hard. Can you imagine how it must feel to suddenly have lost an arm? Perhaps, though, losing me to you might even be worse for him. Oh, how I wish I knew how to make him understand."

"Understanding one's feelings sometimes is hard and complicated," Cloud Eagle said, turning to her. He took her hands in his. "*Ish-kay-nay*, this Apache chief hopes you can understand what *he* has to do and not resent it."

"What are you talking about?" she said, searching his eyes.

"I must go and find Lost Wind," Cloud Eagle said, his words slow and measured, as though testing her. "Our stronghold will not be complete while one of our people is out there alone, away from the protective shield of our warriors, at the mercy of white outlaws and Indian renegades."

"You feel duty-bound to go for her since her brother was killed?"

"It is not fair to force her to live under the cloud of fear each day and night when there is safety in numbers at our stronghold," Cloud Eagle tried to explain. "Her only crime is owning a spiteful tongue and having been burdened with a brother who disgraced his people. It is not right for her to suffer for the sins of her brother, nor for the foolishness of her tongue."

"You would bring her here as your second wife?" Alicia asked weakly, fearing the answer.

"Never," Cloud Eagle said, firming his jaw. "She

would just be one woman among the others at our stronghold."

Alicia lowered her eyes. "I'm so sorry about Spring Dawn," she said softly. She gazed up at Cloud Eagle again. "It's terrible that you found her among the dead when we returned to the stronghold. I had not even thought to look for her at the fort when your people were ushered into the courtyard."

"Nor did I," Cloud Eagle said, nodding. "There were many more important things on my mind than Spring Dawn. And now she is dead. Her spirit is set free in the hereafter." He nodded again. "I am sure she is much happier there than here."

"I truly wouldn't want the same fate to come to Lost Wind," Alicia said, sighing. "I think it is best that you go for her."

Cloud Eagle framed Alicia's face between his hands. "You of good heart could say nothing else," he said lovingly. He smiled at her. "But of course you know that it was easily said because you know the power of my love for you. No woman but you will ever again warm my blankets at night. You are the very wind beneath my feet as I leave you now."

Alicia twined her arms around his neck and kissed him passionately, then eased away from him and watched him leave. There were no reservations now in her trust of this wonderful Apache chief. She knew that she had his love. She would be sure he received hers, twofold.

"How can you trust what he says?" Charlie said, drawing Alicia's quick attention. "This woman he goes for? Surely his feelings are stronger for

340

her than you realize. Or else why would he go for her?"

Alicia knelt beside Charlie. She ran caressing fingers across his brow. "Because that is the sort of person he is," she murmured. "Caring and big-hearted. He would never rest if he did not bring Lost Wind under the protective wing of his people. And once she is here, he will have no cause to think about her ever again."

"Is she pretty?" Charlie persisted.

Alicia drew her hand slowly away. She did not have to answer Charlie. He knew the answer by the way her eyes wavered at his question. He knew that even though he could not see how it was possible, perhaps the Apache woman's beauty challenged Alicia's.

"Charlie, Cloud Eagle loves only me," Alicia said, then left him and went outside and peered into the distance. She wished now that she had insisted on going with Cloud Eagle. He would be with Lost Wind alone. Lost Wind might even use her feminine wiles on him and lure him back into her arms.

Alicia felt the urge to flee now and go after her beloved Apache chief.

But for two reasons she decided not to.

She had to prove to Cloud Eagle that she trusted him.

And Charlie needed her, although he seemed hell-bent on tormenting her into doubting Cloud Eagle enough to return to Saint Louis with him.

"I shall never leave this place," she whispered to herself. "I shall fight for Cloud Eagle, tooth and nail, if I am forced to."

She looked slowly around her and guilt spread through her for thinking only of herself when there were so many who had lost so much. She watched the men and women working together to assemble new tepees.

She felt that perhaps she needed some respite from her brother's nagging. She went and offered her help and soon lost herself and her worries in the task of fitting buckskin on the poles of one tepee, and then another.

She kept casting her eyes into the distance, wondering if Cloud Eagle had reached Lost Wind yet.

Chapter Twenty-Nine

The sun was making its descent in the sky, casting spirals of pink onto the mountain peaks. The air was cooler as night approached.

But as Cloud Eagle had not felt the heat of the day, he also did not feel the sting of the wind as it blew through the canyon through which he was traveling.

When his horse whinnied, he patted him fondly on his powerful neck.

"It won't be long now," Cloud Eagle reassured his stocky roan.

His eyes narrowed and his spine stiffened as he watched a thin trail of smoke as it reached into the heavens.

"Her campfire is near," he whispered.

Cloud Eagle had mixed feelings about coming face to face with Lost Wind again. Although she was beautiful to look at, he felt nothing except irritation when he was with her.

"She will be most surprised to see me," Cloud Eagle said, patting his horse again. "I wish it could be a more pleasant meeting than I expect. There is no doubt in my mind that she detests me."

He rode onward and became quiet, his eyes never leaving the spiral of smoke that reached heavenward. He knew that he had time to turn around and return to his stronghold without Lost Wind. Deep in his heart, this was what he wanted to do most of all.

Yet he could not allow Lost Wind to remain alone when her solitude was of his own doing. He had cast her from the fold of the Coyotero Apache. It was up to him to give her the opportunity to return.

"Perhaps she will refuse," he said, wishing it would be so. "Then my heart will be free never to worry about her welfare again because it will have been her choice to live away from her people."

He grabbed his reins with both hands again. He nudged his roan with his moccasined heels and made a turn which gave him now a full view of the campfire a short distance away.

He drew a tight rein and stopped his roan. As he slipped out of his saddle, another thought came to Cloud Eagle which made him almost retreat and forget that Lost Wind ever existed. He recalled the taunts she had thrown at him. She had said that he might be the one who was responsible for her being unable to conceive. If she carried these suspicions back to his people, they could humiliate him.

Cloud Eagle was torn with what to do. It would be easy to get back on his horse and ride away and leave Lost Wind's spiteful tongue behind him.

And he was almost ready to place his foot in a stirrup when something at the campsite caught his attention. He stopped and stared, his jaw agape, when he discovered that Lost Wind was not alone.

There was a man placing wood on the outdoor fire.

Lost Wind was now beside the man.

Cloud Eagle's eyes widened when he saw Lost Wind and the man embrace and kiss!

"How could this be?"

He studied the man more closely as Lost Wind and the stranger drew apart. When the man turned and offered Cloud Eagle a look at his profile, he gasped.

"Running Free?" he whispered harshly. "Running Free and Lost Wind are together as lovers?"

From this distance, he was able to see something else that shocked him.

Running Free was lifting Lost Wind's skirt. Lost Wind held the skirt up at her waist as Running Free placed his hands on the small round ball of her stomach.

Cloud Eagle felt dizzy from the discovery that Lost Wind was with child! And it was apparent that she was more than a few weeks pregnant. Her loose garments had hid the presence of the child from his eyes while she had been at the stronghold.

"It must be mine!" Cloud Eagle said, his heart pounding at the thought.

He smiled and wanted to shout to the heavens that Lost Wind's pregnancy was all the proof he needed to know that he was virile enough to father a child. For so long now, he had felt guilty for blaming his wives when silently he had worried that he might be the one who was responsible for their not becoming heavy with child.

And now he could see that he was wrong. It made him proud to know that his *Ish-kay-nay* would one day be carrying his offspring.

He lifted happy eyes to the heavens and uttered a soft prayer of thanks. Filled with such relief, he wanted to shout to the sky, the trees, the rocks that he was a virile warrior who would have many sons to follow after him.

"And beautiful daughters," he whispered, envisioning daughters in the image of their mother—his *Ish-kay-nay*.

"Out of all the recent sadness comes some sunshine," he whispered. "And I shall bask in it!"

Then his thoughts turned grim and his eyes became dark pools of resentment. He glared at Lost Wind. As Running Free bent before her on one knee and placed his ear to her stomach, she giggled and ran her fingers through his thick black hair.

"She is carefree now," Cloud Eagle whispered harshly. "But wait until I appear before them with anger flashing in my eyes. She has deceived me in the worst way by not telling me about the child!"

Then another thought came to him that made his insides tighten. She was with Running Free. It was obvious that they cared for one another. What if she had been with Running Free before she had left the village? What if they had had secret liaisons and she was carrying *his* child?

This caused him to move quickly into action. He grabbed the rifle from its gunboot, secured his horse in the mesquite, then carefully and stealthily moved toward the campsite. He kept himself hidden in the shadows as he drew closer. He hid behind a boulder, then inched himself along against the high wall of rock.

When he was close enough to hear what they were saying, he hugged his back against the rock and listened, his breathing shallow.

"It is good that you came along when I was feeling so alone," Lost Wind said, dropping her skirt. She twined her arms around Running Free's neck and pulled him close. "Am I beautiful, Running Free? Even growing larger with Cloud Eagle's child, do you find me beautiful?"

"Running Free has always viewed you from afar and has watched and hungered for you," he said thickly. He placed his hands at her waist and yanked her closer. "Had I known that you also watched me from afar and desired me, not even the fact that you were my chief's wife would have stopped me from pursuing you."

"But you saw Cloud Eagle sleeping each night outside our lodge," Lost Wind whined. "Did you not know then that Cloud Eagle no longer desired me as his wife?"

"It had to be something more than that which caused him to look away from you," Running Free said. "Who could not want to take you between the blankets? And now that I have seen your ways of giving back to a man while making love to him, I am even more puzzled as to why Cloud Eagle turned away from you."

"There are reasons I wish not to discuss," Lost Wind said, lowering her eyes. She slowly looked up at him again. "But because he turned his back on me, I did not share the news that I was with child when I knew that I was."

"And why did you not tell him the blessed news?" Running Free asked. "Would not that have gotten him back with you between your blankets? Any man would want children with you. The children will be handsome warriors and beautiful women."

"Lost Wind is stubborn at times," she confessed. "And I know that I might have saved my marriage if I had told him, except that when the white woman came into our lives and he showed her special attention that he no longer gave me, I decided then not to tell him."

"He would have cast her to the wind had he known about his child," Running Free insisted.

"He cared too much for her, and I would never share my husband with a white woman," Lost Wind hissed. "So let him have white children." She shrugged. "I no longer care about anything that he does. Not now that I have you with me."

She looked past him into the far distance. "I wish my brother would return to me," she said solemnly. "I worry about him."

"Where did Ten Bears go?" Running Free asked. He took her hand and led her down onto a blanket beside the outdoor fire. "You have yet to confide in me as to why he left you alone."

"I am not sure I should tell you," Lost Wind said, giving him a guarded look. Then she shrugged. "I don't know why I shouldn't. Cloud Eagle banished you from our village as well as me. You must hate him as much as I and my brother do."

"No, I do not hate him," Running Free said, lowering her to the ground. He moved over her, straddling her. His hand sneaked up the skirt of her dress. "I do not think about him at all since he sent me away."

"You should never have stolen Red Crow's knife," Lost Wind said, gasping then when he began stroking her at the juncture of her thighs.

"If you condemn me for stealing, why do you give to me now that which I am after?" Running Free said huskily.

"Because I want you as badly," Lost Wind said. She spread her legs farther and gave him easier access to her throbbing center.

"Tell me where your brother has gone," Running Free said, brushing soft, teasing kisses across her lips.

"To kill Cloud Eagle, I am sure," Lost Wind said nonchalantly.

Running Free drew quickly away from her. He bolted to his feet and stood over her, his eyes accusing. "You condone what your brother is planning?" he asked, his fists on his hips.

"Do you not also want Cloud Eagle dead?" Lost Wind asked, looking innocently up at him. She reached a hand out to him. "Come. Make love to me. Why worry about Cloud Eagle? He cared not for you or he would have not sent you away."

"Stealing from the dead is cause enough to be banished," Running Free said, taking her hand. He started to kneel over her again but stopped when he suddenly sensed a presence. He started to rise, then stopped when a gunshot rang out.

Cloud Eagle stepped out into the open, his rifle smoking. Slowly he aimed his firearm at Running Free's heart. He glared down at Lost Wind. "Get up," he said flatly. "Both of you get up and face me."

Wild-eyed, Lost Wind scrambled to her feet beside Running Free. She scooted close to Running Free and grasped one of his hands.

"And so I see you found your way to Lost Wind," Cloud Eagle said, his eyes accusing Running Free as he glared at him.

He turned slow eyes to Lost Wind. "And I see that you did not hesitate to accept him into your camp."

"I was alone," Lost Wind said, her voice trembling. "I was afraid. My brother . . ."

"I know why he left you stranded here alone," Cloud Eagle said stiffly. "And he is now dead. I thought it best to come for you and take you back to live among our people. Now I see that I needn't take the trouble of coming to you with this offer. You have someone who can care for you now. I would say that was good riddance, except that I now know about the child you are carrying, and that it is mine."

"My brother?" Lost Wind said, taking a shaky step toward Cloud Eagle. It did not seem yet to register in her mind what Cloud Eagle had said about the child, and that he knew. "He is dead? My brother is dead?"

"And rightfully so," Cloud Eagle said, nodding. "To go against your own kind is sinful—almost as sinful as keeping the knowledge of being with child from the child's father."

Still Lost Wind seemed focused on only one subject. In her grief over her brother's death, she began pulling her hair. She scraped the flesh of her arms with her sharp fingernails, drawing blood. She wailed and moaned.

Cloud Eagle understood her need to mourn, yet he had needs of his own. He went to her and shook her until she stopped crying and damaging herself with her fingernails.

"The child," he said, looking squarely into her

eyes. "You will return with me to my stronghold until the child is born. Then you will leave again. I pity you no more."

Running Free stepped up to Cloud Eagle's side. "She is now my woman," he said, his chin lifted. "She stays with *me*."

Cloud Eagle turned glaring eyes to Running Free. "She is not your woman until the womb is empty again and ready for *your* seed," he said, his jaw clenched. "You may wait here for her if you wish. When my child is in my arms, only then will Lost Wind be free to come to you." He smiled at Running Free. "If you will want her then."

Finally realizing what was happening, Lost Wind turned and began running away.

Cloud Eagle went after her. He grabbed her by a wrist and stopped her. He swung her around so that again their eyes were locked in an angry stare. "You are no longer my wife," he hissed. "But the child is mine. So you shall return with me until the child is born."

"No," Lost Wind cried. "Never will I give up my child."

"You do not hear clearly enough," Cloud Eagle persisted. "You lost claim to the child the moment you decided not to share the news of my offspring with me, the child's father. The child will be raised by my wife."

Lost Wind pleaded with Running Free with her wide, tear-pooled eyes. "Tell him that you won't allow this," she cried. "Running Free, if you love me, you will stop him."

Running Free made not a movement or a sound.

He then turned and walked away, past the campfire, past the wickiup.

Cloud Eagle held onto Lost Wind to keep her from going after Running Free when Running Free left the campsite and became lost to sight.

"He loved you so much?" Cloud Eagle tormented, laughing in Lost Wind's face.

Lost Wind turned her eyes away. "I shall never have this child for a white woman to raise," she murmured. "I will take it from myself somehow."

"I thought you might threaten to do that," Cloud Eagle said. He gave her a slight shake, causing her to look up at him again. "You will be watched every minute of the day and night. Someone will always be with you. At night, when you sleep, you will be watched. During the day, when you take your bath in the river, you will be watched. You will regret ever having deceived Cloud Eagle."

Lost Wind stared up at him for a moment longer, then a slow smile quavered across her lips. "The white woman you think you know so well?" she said mockingly. "She will not want to raise a child that is not her own. She will not have milk in her breasts to offer the child should she agree to mother him. What then, mighty Apache chief? What then?"

"She will take a child that is born of my seed, no matter the color of the skin," Cloud Eagle hissed back. "And as for milk, there are plenty of women in our stronghold who will willingly share their breast with the child of their chief!"

"The child will never be yours," Lost Wind said, her eyes narrowing into his. "Running Free will come for me. He will steal me away. He has cause to. He has lain with me between blankets. He has tasted my lips. He will return for me."

"I have lain with you and I have tasted your lips, yet did I not send you away?" Cloud Eagle said. "You are beautiful, and I could have loved you forever. But you are incapable of being the woman a man cares to have around. Did you not see how quickly Running Free gave you up to me? Does not that tell you something?"

Lost Wind's eyes wavered. Then she looked with hate up at Cloud Eagle. "I will forever hate you," she spat out. "And I *will* give the child to you willingly. I do not want anything ever to remind me of you once I am set free from your bondage."

"No matter how hard you try, you will never be free of Cloud Eagle," he said solemnly. "Wherever you are, whoever you are with, you will always remember the man who gave you everything, only for you to lose it."

He brushed the rocks that surrounded the campfire into it, then smoothed dirt onto the flame, extinguishing it.

When he saw Lost Wind turn and run, he was quickly there, again stopping her.

"Why do you waste your time running?" he said, his fingers clutched onto her shoulders. "Just give in to what fate has handed you. Time will pass more quickly for you."

Sullenly, she walked beside him to his horse. When he lifted her into the saddle and his hands brushed against the swell of her abdomen, he could not help but feel proud.

Now he had to share the news with his *Ish-kay-nay*. That filled him with concern. The fact that he was bringing Lost Wind back to the stronghold had been hard enough for his woman to accept.

That Lost Wind was with child, *Cloud Eagle's*

child, was another thing, another reason for concern!

If Alicia could not accept the child, then he would be forced to choose!

His child?

Or his *Ish-kay-nay?*

Chapter Thirty

The Apache stronghold was quiet. No one stirred as Cloud Eagle arrived with Lost Wind. With his arm locked around her waist, he rode at a slow lope toward the corral. The glow of the moon revealed many new lodges spread across the land, some that were only poles in their half-built state.

Beneath those poles lay Apache families who were starting life anew since everything had been taken from them during the raid.

But Cloud Eagle knew that their pride was still intact. In the end, when they met their maker face to face, that was what mattered.

Cloud Eagle shifted his gaze to his own lodge, which had not been destroyed by the blue-coated soldiers. Within it a fire still burned. It cast a dancing light along the inside walls of the tepee, soft and alluring.

A stinging despair grabbed at Cloud Eagle's

heart. He wished that he had only to go to his lodge and take his woman into his arms. But there were obstacles that made him feel as though he had a high wall to climb before he could ever be with his woman again in the way that he wanted.

Her brother lay in the lodge on the pallet of furs that had cradled Cloud Eagle and his *Ish-kay-nay* while they had made love.

There was also Lost Wind. Her presence in the stronghold might cause his *Ish-kay-nay* to leave with her brother and never return. He was afraid that Alicia might not accept a pregnant Lost Wind, a woman who would bear a child for Cloud Eagle.

He lifted his eyes to the stars, the moon, and the heavens, and whispered a soft prayer to himself that Alicia would understand this that he had to do. If she forced him to choose between her and the child, he was not sure how he could give up either!

"And so you have returned me to our people," Lost Wind said, drawing him from his troubled thoughts. She turned spiteful eyes to Cloud Eagle.

"Will you take me between your blankets and leave the white woman out in the cold?" she said sarcastically. "Or will you share your blankets with both of us? Who will you draw next to your body? Who will you caress?"

Cloud Eagle gazed down at her. In the moonlight, her loveliness was something that would make any man's loins heat up to an inferno.

But for him her cool beauty only caused a silent fury to creep through his veins. She was nothing but an interference in his life. If not for the child that she carried within the cocoon of her womb, he would be tempted to take her out into the middle of the desert and abandon her!

As it was, he could see ahead for himself many sunrises and sunsets of verbal altercations with her, and he dreaded it. And he knew that she would not hesitate to torment his *Ish-kay-nay*.

He had to find a way to keep this from happening.

A smile fluttered across his lips. He knew the perfect solution to his problem.

Cloud Eagle would take Lost Wind into Turtle Crawls' lodge. His wife was a willful, outspoken person herself and would know how to keep Lost Wind in her rightful place.

If Lost Wind spoke in a spiteful tongue to Purple Blossom, Purple Blossom would return it twofold.

And Turtle Crawls was the perfect warrior to ask to guard Lost Wind. Not only because he would not hesitate to obey his chief, but because Turtle Crawls had had his own experiences with Lost Wind. He had seen her for her spiteful self long before Cloud Eagle had discovered her true personality.

Turtle Crawls had had many private liaisons with Lost Wind before Cloud Eagle's eyes had been drawn to her. When Cloud Eagle chose her for a wife, Turtle Crawls had kept silent about having discarded her himself because of her spiteful tongue.

He had not wished to show disrespect toward his chief by telling anything that might embarrass him because of his wrongful choice in women.

Only after Lost Wind had been sent away had Turtle Crawls confessed all of this to Cloud Eagle.

Cloud Eagle had listened, then they had both had a laugh about two warriors whose hearts had been blinded to the truth about the same woman. It was something they could share in private while smoking—their tales of a woman whose beauty made the loveliness of stars dim in comparison, but whose flashing eyes and quick tongue made her uglier than a snake!

"You do not answer me. Is that because you stare at me? You see my loveliness?" Lost Wind taunted. "Does it steal your breath away as it did when you first courted me? Do I make your white woman look ugly in your eyes? Why not send her away? You no longer need her. You will finally have your child. This child comes from the womb of Lost Wind, not the one you call your *Ish-kay-nay*."

"You are there, and yes I see you, yet I see you not," Cloud Eagle said, drawing a tight rein beside the corral. "When I look your way, all that I see is the child. Now speak no more of my woman who will soon be my wife and who will be the mother of all future children born to this Apache chief. Stay away from her. Do not say spiteful things to her. If you do, your mouth will be sealed closed. The buckskin gag will be removed only when you eat and drink." He leaned his face closer to hers. "Do you understand?"

Lost Wind looked blankly up at him for a moment longer, then turned her eyes quickly away.

Cloud Eagle did not feel proud to treat a woman in such a way, especially a woman whom he had once had strong feelings for.

But she deserved no better treatment. She had

earned every bit of his antagonism. She was blood kin to the shrew, for sure.

And the sooner the next months passed, the better for everyone. He would then take her to a neighboring Apache stronghold and ask pity of them to take her in and see to her needs. Perhaps some warrior might enjoy a woman of her personality. He might see her as a challenge to be overcome.

As for himself, he had enjoyed conquering less troublesome foes! He would leave her for those who had more time for trivial pursuits.

Those types of pursuits were not for a powerful chief!

He slid from the saddle and gave the reins to the warrior who stood guard over the horses tonight. He ignored the wonder in Brown Bison's eyes as his warrior gaped openly at Lost Wind. Instead he lifted her from the saddle and led her away with a firm grip on her elbow.

"And how do you think your white woman will receive this pregnant Apache wife?" Lost Wind said, smiling wickedly up at Cloud Eagle. "Did you not see the surprise in Brown Bison's eyes?" She placed her free hand on her stomach and slowly stroked the tiny ball through the buckskin fabric of her skirt. "How good it will be to see the white woman's horror at seeing me with child, knowing that it is yours."

She winced and cried out when Cloud Eagle grabbed her wrists and swung her around to face him. He gripped her tightly and drew her so close that when he spoke, his breath was hot on her face.

"Listen this last time to what I say, spiteful woman," Cloud Eagle hissed from between clenched teeth. "Never refer to yourself again as my wife. Never flaunt your pregnancy in front of my *true* love. You will wear a loose dress so that no one, especially my woman, can stare at my disgrace."

"Your disgrace?" Lost Wind said, gasping. "If this child is your disgrace, why then do you lay claim to it? Why do you not let me go to Running Free so that I can be his woman? He wants me."

"He would soon learn how to despise you as much as I," Cloud Eagle said, then yanked her even closer. "And hear me well when I say this only once to you. The child is not a disgrace to me. The woman who is carrying it is."

Lost Wind's lips pursed tightly as she glared up at him, then her expression softened. "Should I have been sweeter, and should I have guarded my tongue well, would you have loved me still, Cloud Eagle?" she asked, her eyes searching his.

"Perhaps," he said, then swung her away from him and led her on into the village. He paused and looked from his lodge to Turtle Crawls', wondering which he should go to first. If he could, he would hide Lost Wind from Alicia's eyes forever!

But he knew that was not possible. She must be the first to be told of the child. If she heard it from someone else, he could lose her and her trust.

Determination in his steps, he forced Lost Wind toward his lodge. He paused for only one moment to catch his breath before entering, then shoved Lost Wind inside the tepee, following quickly behind her.

Inside, in the light of the lodge fire, Lost Wind

stood in front of him so that Cloud Eagle was not aware of what she was doing.

But Alicia saw quite distinctly how Lost Wind pulled her dress tightly across her abdomen, and what she was revealing to her.

Dressed in a loose and flowing buckskin robe, Alicia scrambled to her feet, aghast to learn that Lost Wind was pregnant. Wide-eyed, her heart feeling as though it had sunk to her feet, Alicia slowly backed away from Lost Wind and Cloud Eagle. Her brother, awake now, silently witnessed everything.

Cloud Eagle saw Alicia's reaction and did not see it as a natural one. Alicia had known that he was going for Lost Wind. She had been given much time, in his absence, to prepare herself for Lost Wind's arrival.

It was hard, then, for him to understand why she was acting so mortified at the sight of Lost Wind. It made no sense, unless . . .

He stepped quickly around Lost Wind, and his jaw tightened when he discovered what Lost Wind was doing. She was defying all that he had warned her against. She was purposely flaunting her pregnancy to Alicia.

Never in his lifetime had Cloud Eagle hit a woman. But at this moment, he had to hold himself back to keep from slapping Lost Wind. He reached deeply within himself for the willpower to get him through these next moments without harming Lost Wind.

He clasped his fingers into tight fists at his sides, then turned his back to Lost Wind and went to Alicia.

Gently gripping her shoulders, he stopped her from stepping away from him any farther.

He gazed lovingly down at her, his dark eyes imploring her.

"She is with child?" Alicia said, her voice trembling and soft with despair. "It is your child?"

"The child will be *ours, Ish-kay-nay*," Cloud Eagle said, forcing his voice not to break with emotion. "We will raise it as our own with the other children who will be born of our union."

"No," Alicia choked out. She turned her eyes from him. "I can't."

He framed her face between his hands and directed her eyes into his again. "You must," he said. "Or we will be forced to say a final farewell."

He paused, then said, "Is that what you want, *Ish-kay-nay?* To say farewell to all that we have known between us and shall have in the future? A small child would stand in the way of such happiness that we know between us?"

"Not a child," Alicia said, gazing over his shoulder at Lost Wind. "*Her*, Cloud Eagle. The child's mother." Her eyes wavered into his. "Don't you see? She will always be there in our thoughts if the child is a part of our lives. And . . . and how can you separate a child from its mother? That would be cruel."

"Do you not see it as cruel that this woman was never going to reveal to me that she carried my child?" Cloud Eagle said, his voice drawn. "Had I not had pity on her and gone to find her, never would I have known that I had impregnated this woman. She lost her right to the child the moment she chose to deceive its father."

Alicia slowly shook her head back and forth. "I don't know," she murmured. "I just don't think I can accept this. I despise Lost Wind, yet I cannot see taking her child from her."

"You would rather Lost Wind stayed among our people and shared motherhood with you?" Cloud Eagle asked.

Alicia leaned closer. "I despise her so," she whispered to Cloud Eagle.

"And so is she despised by most who know her," Cloud Eagle said, shrugging.

"The child's welfare is at stake here," Alicia said, torn with all that was swirling around inside her head. "If you allow Lost Wind to stay, I imagine I could make the sacrifice of having to be around her, for the child's sake."

"Your heart is big," Cloud Eagle said, yanking her into his arms. He hugged her tightly. "It is good that your feelings are pure, instead of filled with jealousy. This is another reason why I love you so much, my *Ish-kay-nay*."

Alicia clung to him, then stepped away and gazed up at him. "Where is she to sleep?" she asked warily.

Cloud Eagle gently took one of her hands. "I take her now to Turtle Crawls' lodge," he said, smiling reassuringly down at her. "There she will stay until the child is born. Then I will see that a lodge is prepared for her. But even then, I will have her watched day and night. Never shall she have the opportunity to run away with my child."

"Her existence will be miserable," Alicia said, shuddering at the thought.

"Her existence is how she has made it for herself," Cloud Eagle said, unmoved.

He turned from her and went to Lost Wind. He took her by an elbow, but she jerked quickly away. "I heard all that you said about me and what my future holds for me," she said. She lifted her chin proudly. "You can force me to stay only as long as I am with child. Then, Cloud Eagle, Lost Wind leaves your stronghold. I do not wish to stay near you, a man I despise, any longer than I must. I even relinquish my child to you willingly."

Alicia stifled a gasp behind her hand. When Lost Wind turned toward her and gave her a mischievous smile, Alicia felt a coldness seize her insides. She dreaded the coming months.

Cloud Eagle quickly ushered Lost Wind from the tepee. Alicia stared blankly at the closed entrance flap. Her world seemed topsy-turvy and she wondered if it would ever be any other way if she stayed with Cloud Eagle.

Doubts crept in like fire spreading across an open prairie. And when Charlie spoke behind her, what he said made her die a slow death inside.

"If Cloud Eagle truly loved you, he wouldn't force that woman's child on you," her brother said. "Nor would he force that spiteful wench upon you. Honey, you've got to get out of this mess. Return to Saint Louis with me. Forget you ever knew Cloud Eagle. He's nothing but trouble for you."

Alicia turned slow eyes to Charlie. "Cloud Eagle isn't forcing Lost Wind's child on me," she said, her voice tight. "In his eyes, it is only *his* child. And since she is willingly giving the child up to him, then I also see it as only his. And furthermore, Charlie, I understand that things are looking a mite difficult for me now, but I will get through it. For Cloud Eagle, I must. He needs me now. I would never turn my back on him."

"But another woman's child?" Charlie persisted. "You can honestly say that you wish to raise another woman's child?"

"Charlie, I don't think you are hearing what I say at all," Alicia said, sighing deeply. "The child is Cloud Eagle's. That's what makes all the difference in the world to me. I shall love this child. I know it. Because it will be of Cloud Eagle's flesh and blood."

"You have several months to think this through," Charlie said, groaning as pain shot through the scars on his chest and the stump of his arm. "And in the end, I am certain that you will wish that you were back in Saint Louis. Little sister, you need your big brother's protection."

Alicia saw the pain that he was in. She knelt beside him and began smoothing a fresh mixture of the medicinal herbs that Cloud Eagle had prepared for the sores. "Big brother, I think you need me more than I need you," she murmured. "Oh, Charlie, I thank God every day that you are alive. You've been through hell and back, and all because of me."

"Another reason why you should return with me," Charlie said, gazing up at her. "You owe me, sis. You owe me."

Her brother had never resorted to blackmail before, and Alicia was taken aback by his tactics now.

Yet what he had said had hit a nerve.

Torn with emotions and guilt, she continued spreading the herbal mixture along his scarred flesh.

And then suddenly Cloud Eagle was there.

Alicia's breath was stolen when he grabbed her up into his arms and carried her from the lodge.

"Where are you taking me?" Alicia asked.

The moon's glow revealed a steely, determined expression in Cloud Eagle's dark eyes.

When he did not respond to her, she wiped the remaining herbal mixture from the tips of her fingers onto her dress, then rested her cheek against his bare chest and asked him nothing more.

She knew where he was taking her.

Where they could be alone.

Where they could make maddening, enduring love beneath the stars.

Where they could forget at least for the moment those things that stood in the way of their total happiness.

Chapter Thirty-One

The darkness had a bluish quality. And although the wind was brisk and chilly on the hilltop where Alicia and Cloud Eagle stood, neither noticed. As they took turns disrobing each other, their bodies were warmed under the caress of each other's eyes.

Her eyes sheened by moonlight, the soft glimmer of her red hair draped across her pale shoulders, Alicia tossed her last garment aside.

Cloud Eagle reached his arms out for her, beckoning her to him. She smiled up at him and willingly melted into his embrace.

Their bodies strained together as they kissed heatedly. Cloud Eagle's fingers gripped Alicia's buttocks, bringing her closer so that her body was molded more perfectly against his.

Alicia moaned with pleasure, and her senses swam when she felt the heat of Cloud Eagle's manhood swelling against the throbbing juncture

of her thighs. She hungered for him, to be filled
by him, to be caressed and taken to another world
where there was only beauty and bliss.

She had found these things before with him
and she knew that she could again.

With him there was only the moment.

There was only their enduring love.

No one could enter their little world while they
embraced. Their minds were occupied only by the
wonder of their passion, of their commitment to
each other.

When Cloud Eagle held onto the soft flesh
of Alicia's buttocks more tightly and lifted her
from her feet, she followed his silent bidding and
wrapped her legs around his hips.

Her breath quickened with yearning when she
felt him probing at the entrance of her desire.
She emitted a soft cry of passion against his lips
when he found his way and buried himself deeply
inside her. She moaned throatily against his lips
when she felt the slow thrusting of his pelvis as
he pushed himself even more deeply into her.

As an incredible sweetness swept through her,
Alicia clung to Cloud Eagle and kissed him fervently as he began his rhythmic strokes within
her, his powerful hands holding her against him.
The pleasure began to spread a slow, delicious,
tingling heat through her.

Cloud Eagle was propelled by a drugged passion. His heart pounded more excitely with each
thrust inside her. Her lips were voluptuously
warm against his. Her breasts were like soft
petals of flowers as they brushed against his
chest while she rocked with him in rapture's
throes.

He fought the rising heat, wanting to prolong

this precious moment. While he was with her, he forgot everything but the wonder of their love.

Needing to touch and kiss her everywhere, Cloud Eagle withdrew his throbbing member and laid Alicia on the ground, where he had prepared a lover's lair earlier.

Having planned these private moments with her even before he had decided to go and bring Lost Wind back to his stronghold, he had come to this hill and had spread a cushion of cedar boughs beneath a blanket.

He had been anticipating this time with Alicia even while he had performed the dreadful task of going for Lost Wind.

Now that anticipation had become reality. She was there with him. Her body was like wildfire beneath his caresses. Her lips were like the morning dew, clinging and beautiful.

Leaning on his knees over Alicia, his legs straddling her, Cloud Eagle smiled as he pushed her hair from her face.

"My *Ish-kay-nay*," he said huskily, his gaze moving slowly and seductively over her.

His hands followed the trail of his eyes, her skin warm, smooth, and a little moist.

In a state of suspended animation, awaiting the one moment when he would ride on clouds of rapture with Alicia again, his hands cupped her breasts. He squeezed them gently, pulling, rotating the stiff, resilient nipples.

His hands then moved downward.

He smiled again when he felt the quiver of her stomach against the palms of his hands.

He closed his mouth over her lips and kissed her wildly as his hand moved over one of her breasts and softly kneaded it, while his other

369

hand proceeded downward, following the curve of a buttock, around then, to run his fingers along the inside softness of her thigh.

He then moved his hand to that wonderful moist place between her legs. His fingers sought and found her mound of pleasure and caressed it.

Spasmodic gasps arose from deeply within Alicia as the pleasure began to build into something magical and wonderful. She whimpered when his mouth slipped down and moved over a breast. His tongue was wet and wonderful as it flicked around the nipple.

Afraid that the ultimate of pleasure would spill over within her while Cloud Eagle was not inside her, Alicia reached for his manhood and guided him to that place where his hands had created such magic.

Once more he kissed her long and deep. His body moved rhythmically against hers, moving slowly, powerfully, wonderfully into her.

Her hips moved with him, rocking, her pelvis pressed against him.

Gripping her shoulders, Cloud Eagle's mouth brushed her cheeks and ears and lightly kissed her eyelids.

Then he placed his cheek against hers and burrowed closer against her and moved into her in an even wilder, more dizzying rhythm.

Feeling the pleasure building, Cloud Eagle moved his face from hers and gazed down at her, watching the hidden flames behind her eyes as she smiled seductively up at him.

Never wanting her as badly as now, and needing the final release that was burning like hot coals in his loins, Cloud Eagle placed his hands at her waist and held her as though in a vise.

He plunged over and over again inside her.

His need was a sharp, hot pain within his loins.

The excitement was rising, building, ready to spill over within her.

Again he kissed her, then reverently breathed her name against her lips as their bodies began to quiver and quake.

Alicia clung around Cloud Eagle's neck and drew his lips to hers again. She moaned as his body hardened and tightened, then shook like thunder into her.

She absorbed the bold thrusts. The surges of pleasure that rushed through her came in exquisite explosions of ecstasy.

And then it was too soon over, leaving them hungering for more.

Cloud Eagle rolled away from Alicia and turned her on her side to face him. "We could stay here until the night fades into morning," he said huskily.

"Yes, let's," Alicia whispered, placing a gentle hand to his smooth copper cheek. "Let's never leave this wondrous place. Everything is so sweet here, so magical. I never want the loving to stop. I love you so, Cloud Eagle."

"You never need to express in words how you feel about this Apache chief," Cloud Eagle said, taking her hand and kissing the palm. "Your body speaks very well of it to me."

"Am I truly enough for you, Cloud Eagle?" Alicia dared to ask, afraid that she might break this beautiful spell they were caught up in.

But something always made her ask this dreaded question again. It never seemed to stop haunting her. Now that they weren't embracing and caressing each other, the real world had suddenly emerged again, and with it the consummate worry that Cloud Eagle might someday see a need for more than one wife.

"You should never have the need to ask this question again when I tell you quite adamantly that this Apache chief will never need more wives than you," Cloud Eagle said as he drew her lips close.

He kissed her, then lowered his lips to her breasts, taking one nipple, then the other between his teeth.

Alicia twined her fingers through his hair and drew him closer. She closed her eyes and trembled sensually when his tongue lapped the nipples to sharp peaks, his fingers kneading the breasts.

She was hardly aware of what she was doing when she guided his lips downward.

She was hardly aware of him changing positions.

Not until she felt his tongue on that wonderful place between her legs, where her heartbeat seemed to be centered. Her mound pulsed pleasurably against his tongue.

She sucked in a wild breath when his tongue crept farther and plunged into her pulsing cleft.

She tossed her head from side to side, her hair flailing like a whip. Her gasping breaths were like lightning flashes in the dark. Her body was heating up, the pleasure spreading through her like warm waves of sunshine.

Cloud Eagle placed his hands beneath her and lifted her even more closely to his mouth. He pleasured her until he felt her tremble and cry out, then he moved over her and thrust his manhood deeply inside her and began his strokes within her in a frenzied rhythm.

He held his head back and gritted his teeth, the sweat pearling on his brow the closer he grew to his final explosion of ecstasy. The sensations were searing. His hunger was unending, ferocious in his need to have her tonight, over and over again.

They would never forget this night.

Tonight he would make a child within her womb!

Alicia ran her hand down his back, then around where she could get an occasional touch of his pulsing satin hardness.

When he realized what she sought, he withdrew and guided her hand to him. He sucked in a breath of pleasure when she shifted to her side and her fingers moved on him.

His whole body seemed fluid with fire when he felt the warm wetness of her tongue as it was suddenly there on him, and then her lips.

He turned over onto his back so that she could have more freedom with what she was doing. As she knelt over him, giving him what she felt might be a forbidden pleasure, he positioned her so that he returned the pleasure in kind.

His hands clutched her breasts.

His tongue flicked.

His manhood pulsed.

When he felt that he was too close to that edge of rapture, he lifted her away from him and placed her on her back, then straddled her and entered her in one deep thrust.

He pressed into her, his mouth wild upon her lips as he kissed her. He pressed endlessly deeper. He clutched her waist and molded himself perfectly to the curved hollow of her hips.

A sensual shock then engulfed them both.

There was a great shuddering in Cloud Eagle's loins.

A flood of ecstasy swept through Alicia. She strained her hips up at him and cried out at her fulfillment.

The pleasure found for a second time tonight, their bodies subsided exhaustedly together.

Alicia brushed her lips across Cloud Eagle's cheek, her hands touching him everywhere, for she did not feel that she could ever have enough of him tonight. She did not want to relinquish him to the everyday world of sorrow and worry.

Tonight was everything to her.

Cloud Eagle was hers tonight. All hers.

Cloud Eagle slipped away from her and stretched out on his back.

Alicia was soon on top of him, straddling him. She leaned over and took one of his nipples into her mouth, her tongue flicking it. Her hands moved slowly and teasingly over him again, stopping only when she found his limp manhood resting against his thigh.

She raised her eyes to him. She smiled slowly as she circled her fingers around his manhood. "Shall I?" she whispered. "Or is it impossible to make love again? A third time?"

The fact that she felt him growing within her fingers was all the answer she needed. She gently kneaded him until her fingers were filled with his throbbing flesh.

She leaned over and kissed him as she slowly slid him inside her again.

When he began pushing himself rhythmically

within her, she threw her head back in a throaty sigh. His powerful thighs lifted her. Her emotions were endless, like the thrust of waves. She cried out when she reached that ultimate of pleasure again, sobbing from the sheer bliss of the moment.

Cloud Eagle's loins shuddered into her. He closed his eyes as the pleasure consumed him. He heaved himself into her, over and over again.

Then, spent, he lifted her from him and cuddled her to his side and held her. His fingers wove through her hair and directed her lips to his. He trembled as he kissed her, then held her only slightly away so that he could gaze at her blushed cheeks.

"Ish-kay-nay," he said thickly. "They say that women tend to beauty with child, that a woman is never more beautiful than while she carries a child within the cocoon of her womb. But never could any woman be more beautiful than you are at this moment. You are radiant. The sun does not shine at this moment, yet I see it in your face and eyes. There is such a warm peace, *Ish-kay-nay*, about you."

"You are the cause," Alicia whispered back, stroking his back with her hand. "You have changed so much in my life, Cloud Eagle. I feel blessed to have met you."

"I wish to change more in your life," Cloud Eagle said, slipping his hand to her abdomen. Almost meditatingly he laid his palm against her soft flesh. "One day I hope to see you growing with child. Then you and I will both be blessed. *Twice* blessed."

Alicia smiled up at him. She wanted to tell him that she thought she might be pregnant, yet held back. She did not want to tell him that she was carrying his child until she knew for certain that she was. She had only missed her monthly flow by a few days. The excitement in her life during these past weeks might be the cause.

But she had experienced much excitement in her lifetime and never had she missed a monthly flow, nor had she ever been late even one day. She always kept track of when it was due so that she would be ready with the cloths that she wore to save herself embarrassment.

"You seem deep in thought," Cloud Eagle said, brushing a strand of her hair back from her eyes.

"My silence is only because of my contentment while lying here with you," Alicia said, covering his hand which still lay on her abdomen. "And I too hope to carry a child within my womb one day soon. It will be my gift to you, Cloud Eagle, for all that you have done for me."

"The gift of a child will belong to us both," he said, brushing a kiss across her lips. "And if it should be in your image, ah, how beautiful a daughter we will have."

"A son," Alicia whispered. "The first child born of our union will be a son."

She closed her eyes tightly to thoughts that crept in to pain her. If Lost Wind's first child was a son, Alicia despaired, it would take away the importance of a son born to herself and Cloud Eagle!

She would wait with an anxious heart until Lost Wind finally gave birth.

Chapter Thirty-Two

The activity in the Coyotero Apache's stronghold was back to normal in only a few weeks. The need to replenish their cache of food had forced them to leave their mourning behind before they wished to, for it was now late autumn. While the Apache women combed the slopes for piñon nuts and juniper berries, the men stalked deer and antelope and mountain sheep. Apache boys had to be nearly grown before they were allowed to hunt large game. It was said by the elders that a young boy's heart would not be strong enough to stand the hunt; it would make him ill, or even kill him.

The river and lagoons were infested by wild ducks, arriving in greater flocks every day. Preparations were being made to catch a good number of the fowl.

Marveling at how this was done, Alicia sat beside the lodge fire. She watched Cloud Eagle scoop the insides out of a gourd, while other gourds that had already been emptied sat beside the entranceway.

"Cloud Eagle, do you mean to say that you are actually going to fit that over your head?" she said, as Cloud Eagle continued to dip a wooden spoon in and out of the gourd. She straightened the buckskin cloth upon which the seeds and flesh of the gourd were being placed.

"In the river bottoms and lagoons, the gourds grow big but the pith is not good to eat," Cloud Eagle said, casting a smile at Alicia, then at Charlie, who sat beside him, also watching and listening. "But the gourds make handy water vessels."

Subconsciously, Charlie rubbed the stump of his arm as he listened to Cloud Eagle. During the past weeks, he had come to admire and like the Apache chief. He understood well enough why Alicia wanted to marry him. Cloud Eagle was a gentle man of good heart.

Charlie was well enough to travel now but had chosen to stay a while longer to attend his sister's wedding. Now he did not mind seeing her stay behind with a man who seemed to worship her every movement.

Also, Charlie felt confident enough that his sister would be well cared for and safe with Cloud Eagle. It was evident that Cloud Eagle would willingly lay down his own life if that meant that Alicia's life would be spared.

Charlie's gaze shifted to Alicia's waist, then her abdomen. Both were thickening. He did not believe it was from her diet of Indian food. She sometimes only picked at it as she ate.

But he thought that she just might be pregnant.

That somewhat irked him, for she had not yet shared vows with Cloud Eagle. The reason for delaying the wedding had been explained to him, yet he still was not happy with the circumstances. The mourning period for the dead had interfered with most of the Coyoteros' lives. *No* wedding ceremony had been performed, nor had there been any celebrations.

Today would be the first feast shared by those who had survived the raid by the soldiers from Fort Thomas. Charlie felt confident that one day soon there would be a wedding ceremony between his sister and Cloud Eagle.

Only after Cloud Eagle was totally committed to his sister would Charlie proceed with his own life. Now that he was one-armed, everything that he did was clumsy. But nothing would interfere with his painting career.

He dropped his eyes and swallowed back bitter bile when he thought of those who had come trustingly with him from Saint Louis to find Alicia. None besides himself had survived the attack by Sandy Whiskers' renegades and outlaws.

He would have to carry that guilt with him all of his life.

Worst of all, he dreaded having to spread the news to the families of those who had died. At least he would make sure that the wives of those who had died would live comfortably for the rest of their lives. He had enough wealth to share with them all. And he would. Until his last cent was gone, if need be.

He wiped tears from his eyes and looked again at Cloud Eagle as he continued explaining how the birds would be caught today.

"Several uncarved gourds will be taken to a nearby lagoon," Cloud Eagle said, reaching his fingers inside his gourd to gather the last of the seeds which stubbornly clung to the sides. "Those gourds will be set adrift on the windward side of this lagoon."

He proceeded then to carve out holes in the gourd, reminding Alicia of the pumpkins that she and Charlie had carved on Halloween when she was a child. Cloud Eagle was creating two eyes, a nose and a mouth on the face of the gourd.

Alicia raised an eyebrow when Cloud Eagle picked up another gourd and began carving a face on it. He had said earlier that each person who participated in this strange ritual would need only one gourd with a face. She had to wonder who he was carving this second one for.

As he continued talking, she forgot her questions and again attentively listened.

"The wind will gradually propel the gourds until they reach the other side of the lagoon, where the ducks are gathered," Cloud Eagle said. "At first the ducks will be suspicious of the strange floating objects. Soon the ducks will get used to the gourds and pay them no further attention. Then my people will fit the gourds they have prepared for the hunt over their heads. Armed with bags, they will enter the water, which is not over five feet deep in any part. Exactly imitating the bobbing motion of the empty gourds upon the water, they will succeed in getting close enough to the ducks to catch them by the feet."

"How clever," Alicia said, taken aback when he handed the second carved-out gourd to her. She turned it around in her hands, finding the face on this gourd different from the other one. Cloud

Eagle had cleverly carved out eyelashes that looked feminine, as well as beautifully shaped lips and eyes.

"That is *your* water vessel mask," Cloud Eagle said, wiping his spoon and then his knife clean on a buckskin cloth. "You will hunt at my side in the water to replenish our stores of meat. Too soon the cold winds from the mountains will bring ice that seals the rivers closed and makes travel sometimes impossible."

Alicia paled as she gazed at Cloud Eagle. "You expect me to help catch ducks?" she said incredulously. "Cloud Eagle, since I have never done this before, I will more than likely frighten them away."

"I will be at your side to teach you how it is done in the proper way," Cloud Eagle said. He pushed himself up from the pallet on which he had prepared the gourds. "After the hunt, there will be a great feast. It will be good to hear and see my people laugh again."

Alicia slipped a hand over her abdomen. She was now absolutely certain that she was pregnant. At least two months. She had planned to tell Cloud Eagle tonight.

But now she wondered if she should tell him right away. She was afraid that this sort of activity, the strain of catching the ducks, might cause her to miscarry.

Then she scoffed at such a worry. She would perhaps have to endure worse activities than this during her pregnancy. Nothing about living the life of an Indian was simple.

And if Apache women could be involved in all sorts of hard labor and still gave birth to healthy children, then so could she. She had to prove not only to herself, but also to Cloud Eagle, that she was the Apache women's equal in every way. She never wanted to give Cloud Eagle any reason to be disappointed in her.

"That sounds exciting," she said, forcing her voice to sound lighthearted. "The hunt *and* the feast."

Charlie held on to the stump of his arm as his muscled legs managed to get him to his feet. "Alicia, are you sure you should help catch the ducks?" he said, his eyes heavy with concern.

"Big brother, I'm a grown woman and still you worry about me as though I were that six-year-old sister who got into more fights than most boys my age," Alicia said, laughing softly.

She set her gourd aside and moved to her feet to embrace Charlie. "You can be sure, my sweet Charlie, that I've learned many lessons these past months," she reassured him. "I will be careful with what I choose to do, especially now."

"Especially now?" Cloud Eagle said, forking an eyebrow.

Alicia eased from Charlie's arms and turned to Cloud Eagle. The slip of her tongue had caught his attention. And she did not want to tell him about the child now. She had planned a private time, when Charlie took his usual long walk in the evenings, to tell Cloud Eagle about her pregnancy. They always took advantage of Charlie's absences to make love. Tonight there would be more than lovemaking. There were secrets to be shared! She had delayed long enough. She had waited this long to be absolutely sure that she was pregnant. She never wanted to disappoint Cloud Eagle, especially when it came to children.

"Especially since I have found you, darling,"

Alicia said quickly enough. She went to Cloud Eagle and embraced him. "My darling Apache chief, now that our wedding day is drawing near, do you think I would allow anything to interfere? I want nothing more than to be your wife."

Charlie's presence was no longer a deterrent to shows of affection between Alicia and Cloud Eagle. When they wished to embrace and kiss, they did so without hesitation.

As now, Charlie smiled and watched his sister enjoy being kissed. He did not even resent it when she moaned with pleasure. Her happiness had been one of his goals ever since his parents had allowed him to witness her birth.

This had formed a special bond between him and Alicia. He would never forget that very first cry from her lungs.

His only regret was that he would not be at her side to hear the first cries of *her* child.

Then again, he thought to himself as he pulled absently on his red beard, just perhaps he *could* manage to be there. If the weather cooperated, and the good Lord was willing.

The excitement was growing outside. The children were laughing and playing. The men and women were talking excitedly as they left their homes for the lagoon.

Alicia swung away from Cloud Eagle. Her eyes danced into his as he placed her gourd in her hands. She was pleased when Charlie got into the fun of the occasion as he bent over and got Cloud Eagle's gourd and handed it to him.

And so Alicia was not at all surprised when Charlie grabbed two blankets and flung them over the crook of his arm as he left the lodge with Alicia and Cloud Eagle. She knew that he was worrying about her discomfort when she left the lagoon. The air was crisp. The water would be bone-chilling. The blankets would warm her.

The thought of entering the water did not alarm her. She had already gotten used to its sting when she bathed each day.

Cloud Eagle sent several young braves into his lodge to collect the other emptied gourds into a bag for him. They soon brought the heavy bag out to him, then darted away, excitement dancing in their eyes.

Feeling carefree for the first time in weeks, Alicia smiled and walked in a half skipping fashion between Cloud Eagle and Charlie as they left the stronghold behind and headed toward the lagoon. The sun was burning a path through a thin layer of clouds overhead. An occasional rabbit hopped into view, then scampered off just as quickly to take refuge in taller grass.

Alicia looked ahead at the women walking with their warrior husbands. Alicia realized then that she was not going to be the only woman to enter the water in pursuit of the ducks. Several of the Apache women carried their prized gourds. The children were carrying buckskin bags to put the ducks in after they were caught in the water.

She looked toward Cloud Eagle. He was dressed in buckskins. He toted his heavy bag of gourds, and several buckskin bags hung from his waistband, where he had thrust them for safe-keeping. From the looks of things, he expected to capture many ducks today. Alicia would have a hot pot of stew cooking every day, the broth rich.

When they reached the lagoon, at least a hundred ducks were swimming gracefully in the water on the other side, occasionally foraging for food as they ducked their heads beneath the surface.

Everyone became quiet. Alicia stood back and watched the Apache release their emptied gourds into the water, keeping their carved ones so that they could place them over their heads at the appropriate time. There were so many gourds in the water now that Alicia did not bother to count them.

Wide-eyed, she watched the wind do its duty as it began propelling the gourds across the lagoon, directly toward the ducks.

The gourds bobbed and swayed.

In alarm, some of the ducks flew away, while others took wing only briefly, then settled back into the water again and went about their business, ignoring the intrusion of the gourds.

A hand on Alicia's arm drew her attention from the ducks. She looked over at Cloud Eagle and giggled when she discovered that he had placed the gourd over his head and was staring at her through the carved eyes. His nose was only barely exposed, as were his lips.

Charlie chuckled. "Well, sis?" he said, his eyes twinkling. "You're next."

The smell of the gourd made Alicia's nose twitch. And the thought of the raw, wet insides of the gourd getting all over her hair and skin made her flinch. But she noticed that many of the men and women were already in the lagoon, the children watching breathlessly.

She had no choice but to act now, or not at all. Cloud Eagle was patiently waiting, but his patience would run out. He wanted to be there when everyone else began catching the ducks, or those left untouched might fly from fright, leaving none for Cloud Eagle's store of food.

Alicia's insides tightened and she held her breath as she slipped the gourd over her head. When it was finally in place, she looked through the small holes Cloud Eagle had carved out for her eyes, then broke into soft laughter when she realized how funny she must look. She turned to Charlie and saw it in his eyes. She could tell that he was holding back his laughter.

Sighing, she hurried to Cloud Eagle's side. She took the bag he handed her, then moved slowly into the water. The coldness grabbed at her as her wet clothes clung to her flesh. Her teeth chattered. Her toes felt quickly numb.

But still she went deeper into the lagoon, her eyes now focused only on the ducks that she and Cloud Eagle were approaching. The ducks' bluish-green feathers shone like silk beneath the rays of the sun. Their beady eyes glistened as they guardedly watched the gourds approaching them. But they did not move away. They continued swimming in a half circle, watching the gourds.

"Now!" Cloud Eagle said suddenly. "Grab one of the duck's feet. Drag it under the water. Slip it inside the bag."

Alicia was clumsy with the first duck. But after it was caught, and the bag was tied together at the top so that it could not escape, she gave it to a young brave who had come to assist them. She then caught another duck and then another.

When she and Cloud Eagle left the water, they had caught ten ducks between them. Only a few ducks remained in the lagoon that had not flown or been captured.

Charlie came to Alicia to drape a blanket over her shoulders. It felt warm. She trembled. Her teeth would not stop clicking together.

"Your lips are purple," Charlie said, frowning down at her. "You've got to get those wet clothes off and get warmed by a fire."

Alicia nodded.

Cloud Eagle nodded his approval. "Go to our lodge and get warmed," he said. "I will come later. Then we will join the celebration together."

Charlie drew Alicia next to him, his arm around her waist holding the blanket snugly against her. Alicia walked away with him, savoring these moments with him that she knew would soon end.

But she also looked forward to the celebration today. It would be a time of harmony and peace with the Apache people. She had lived with them long enough now to have grown fond of them all. They were generous, kind, and very sociable. Always after the chief meal of the day, which was usually eaten in the evening, they sat about the outdoor communal campfire. They talked endlessly about the happenings of the day, or exchanged tales of past deeds in raids and battles.

She had even come to know that every Apache was a gambler. Man, woman, and child, there was nothing they would not stake, from their horse to their shirt.

She also knew they had little desire to create things of beauty. Their most notable achievement was their basketry, but there were two kinds— burden baskets and water jugs. She had learned that to the Apache, beauty was subordinated to function.

When distant horsemen came into view, and Alicia saw that they wore the blue coats of the soldiers from Fort Thomas, wariness surged through her. She stopped quickly and turned to see if Cloud Eagle had seen the approach of the soldiers.

Of course he would have, she thought. He did not miss a sound or a movement that might bring harm to his people.

"What the hell do they want?" Charlie said, also watching the soldiers' approach. "From what I have seen of the soldiers in this area, they are negligent, worthless sons-of-bitches."

"They are worse than that," Alicia said. She broke away from Charlie and ran to Cloud Eagle. She stood devotedly at his side as they waited to see why the soldiers had come this time. She knew that she might never witness a true peace between Cloud Eagle and the soldiers.

When General Powell drew a tight rein before Cloud Eagle, the few soldiers accompanying him following his lead. Cloud Eagle did not offer any gesture of welcome to the commandant.

Nor would he until he knew the reason for the blue-coated pony soldiers' interference in the life of his people again.

Chapter Thirty-Three

General Powell slid easily from his saddle.

Alicia stood her ground as Cloud Eagle took a step toward the general.

"Why have you come to Cloud Eagle's stronghold?" he said, his shoulders rigid. "There are no plans for council between us tonight."

"My visit is for two reasons," General Powell said, extending a hand of friendship toward Cloud Eagle and nodding a welcome to Alicia. "I wish to set up a council meeting with you—let's say, day after tomorrow?"

Cloud Eagle's eyes leveled with General Powell's as he paused, then accepted the handshake that was being offered him. "Yes, after two sunrises it will be good to have council with you," he said, shaking General Powell's hand with a firm grip, then easing his hand to his side. "But only if it can be held within the perimeter of Cloud Eagle's stronghold instead of Fort Thomas."

"That suits me just fine," General Powell said, resting a hand on the pistol holstered at his right hip. "I shall arrive shortly after sunup with several of my soldiers to share a smoke and a talk with you."

Cloud Eagle nodded, then his eyes narrowed. "Your second reason for being at Cloud Eagle's stronghold?" he asked, aware of his people moving in behind him, solemnly quiet. "What is it?"

Although the air was filled with the tantalizing aroma of duck roasting over many open fires, the celebration had come to an abrupt halt. Those sitting at the drums and those who held rattles in their hands were as though frozen as they watched their chief.

General Powell shuffled his feet nervously and clasped his hands tightly together behind him as his eyes wavered into Cloud Eagle's. "It's about Sandy Whiskers," he said guardedly. "He was found and arrested."

The news made Cloud Eagle's heart skip a beat. Not so much over hearing that Sandy Whiskers had been caught and jailed, but because it had not been *he* who had found and dealt with the man in ways that he thought were more effective than the white man's judicial system. The white man's ways of punishing a man seemed no punishment at all compared to those used by the Apache.

"He is at Fort Thomas?" Cloud Eagle said, a plan forming in his mind. He would take some of his most trusted warriors and abduct Sandy Whiskers from the jail. He would take the Englishman far out in the desert . . .

His thoughts and plans were interrupted when General Powell slowly shook his head back and forth. "No, he is not imprisoned at Fort Thomas," he said. "The clever bastard got away. That's why I have a full battalion with me tonight. We're on Sandy Whiskers' trail. We should have him captured and back in our jail by daybreak."

The news made a soft smile flutter across Cloud Eagle's lips. He would find Sandy Whiskers before General Powell did.

Cloud Eagle would have searched high and low for Sandy Whiskers before now except that his duties to his people had come before vengeance. Now his stronghold was rebuilt with new lodges. There was cause for a celebration tonight as ducks roasted over the outdoor fires.

There was once more a semblance of peace for his people.

He now felt free to go after Sandy Whiskers and end the yearning for revenge that had eaten away at him since the very day that the Englishman had captured his woman. That had been a deed that had even then marked the Englishman for death.

Sandy Whiskers' days were now numbered, Cloud Eagle vowed to himself.

"And so you see, my friend, I must be on my way," General Powell said, mounting his horse. "I shall see you soon. I look forward to our council."

"Talk and smoke is good between friends," Cloud Eagle said, nodding. "It makes way for an even more enduring friendship."

"And that is important between us, Cloud Eagle," General Powell said, his eyes locking with Cloud Eagle's. "We don't want any more crazy misunderstandings between us, do we?"

"Crazed people cause crazed misunderstandings," Cloud Eagle said solemnly. "Choose whom

Cassie Edwards

you listen to more carefully, and misunderstandings will be less likely to happen between us."

General Powell nodded and smiled. "The smell of duck is heavy in the air and is inviting," he said, looking past Cloud Eagle at the ducks dripping their juices into the flames of the fires. "Were it not for Sandy Whiskers' flight, I might invite myself to dinner with you tonight." He shrugged and gave Cloud Eagle a quick glance. "As it is, I must be on my way."

General Powell turned his gaze to Alicia. "And Alicia, it has been good seeing you again," he said. "It is good to see you looking well."

"Thank you," Alicia said, her hands subconsciously going to her abdomen. Her pregnancy was the reason she looked healthier than before.

She had so badly wanted to tell Cloud Eagle about the child tonight. But Sandy Whiskers' escape might change everything. She saw the look in Cloud Eagle's eyes as he turned and gazed at her. She could see a restlessness, an eagerness.

Also within them she could see a guarded rage, which could only be there because of Sandy Whiskers.

"Please, Cloud Eagle," Alicia said, going to him. She placed a gentle hand on his cheek. "Please forget about Sandy Whiskers. Let the soldiers deal with him."

"You know me well and you read my thoughts accurately," Cloud Eagle said as he took her hand and fondly held it. "I *am* going for Sandy Whiskers. I *will* find him before the soldiers have the chance to. Finally I will have my revenge. I will have it in my own way, not as the soldiers would want it."

"Cloud Eagle, the celebration," Alicia said, looking over her shoulder at the people quietly watching and waiting. Whatever he chose to do tonight would affect his people, perhaps forever.

The delay in the celebration was only a minor problem. The chance that he might bring the wrath of the soldiers down upon him and his people was a far worse problem than putting off talk and laughter and eating roasted duck.

"The celebration can continue without me and a few of my select warriors who will ride with me to track down Sandy Whiskers," Cloud Eagle said, already walking away from the crowd toward his lodge.

Alicia hurried alongside him, her eyes filled with concern. "Please don't do this," she pleaded. "There are more important things on this earth than revenge. Cloud Eagle, I had something to tell—"

She immediately stopped her flow of words. This was not the time to tell him about the child. She wanted a quiet setting, a romantic mood. She wanted the moment to be perfect for them, not fraught with worries about Sandy Whiskers.

Cloud Eagle's steps faltered. He turned and clasped his fingers to her shoulders. "You will ride with me and see the Englishman's end as I have it planned," he said. "We will return then and truly have cause to celebrate."

Again Alicia slipped a hand to her stomach. Should she ride while she was pregnant? Could there be danger in it for the child? A miscarriage now would devastate her.

Yet she did want to share as much as possible with Cloud Eagle. And even though she dreaded

393

the way Cloud Eagle might kill Sandy Whiskers, she nodded.

"Yes," she said. "If you insist on going, take me with you."

Cloud Eagle smiled and brushed a kiss across her lips, then shouted out orders to his warriors to ready their horses and weapons and to bring a saddled horse for his woman!

The campfires were behind them now, but the sound of the drums and rattles echoed and followed the Apaches on horseback as they followed the path of the moon across the land.

Alicia rode proudly at Cloud Eagle's side, her fringed buckskin skirt hiked above her knees. "Do you truly think you are going to find Sandy Whiskers?" she asked, breaking the silence that had fallen between her and Cloud Eagle since they left the village.

"The blue-coated soldiers' search took them in the opposite direction from the path I feel Sandy Whiskers will be traveling," Cloud Eagle said, gazing over at her. "They think he will hide in the mountains. I think he is headed for Mexico, where he can take refuge. There he could also begin his practice of slave trading again. A man like him would not take long to find those who would follow his command. I imagine that Mexico could soon become a target of Sandy Whiskers' raids, instead of the Arizona Territory."

"I hope we can find him and stop him," Alicia said, brushing her hair from her eyes with the back of her hand as the wind continually whipped it around her face. "He well deserves being shot." She choked back a sob when she envisioned the way she had found her brother and the others at the Englishman's outpost. If given the chance, she would get her own vengeance tonight!

"I do not intend to allow Sandy Whiskers to be killed by bullets," Cloud Eagle said, his voice cold.

Alicia cast him a questioning glance. "Then how, Cloud Eagle?" she asked. "If you find him, what *do* you plan to do?"

Cloud Eagle laughed into the wind. "He will die a slow death, and as he dies, he will beg for mercy," he said, his eyes narrowing at the thought of what he had planned for Sandy Whiskers.

Shivers of dread ran down Alicia's spine. She stared at Cloud Eagle, wondering about this man whose mind seemed intent on torture. He was usually so gentle, so caring. It did not seem like him at all to be considering killing someone in an inhumane way.

Yet she reminded herself that Sandy Whiskers was scarcely human. It did seem only right that he would die slowly and mercilessly.

Gripping the reins in her hands, Alicia asked no more questions. Her gaze was intense as she looked into the shadows of the night. The moon was now behind the clouds. Everything in the distance seemed dangerous and threatening.

Fear crept into Alicia's heart and she rested a hand on the holstered pistol at her waist. She was reminded of another night when she was on horseback. The ambush had happened so suddenly. It could come as quickly tonight.

The only difference tonight was that she was not alone. The thundering of horses' hooves behind and beside her gave her a sense of well-being, of camaraderie. Nothing could penetrate or overtake the shield of warriors who rode with her.

Breathing more easily, Alicia rode onward.

When Cloud Eagle raised a hand in a silent command for everyone to stop, she drew a tight rein. Her horse shimmied to a quick halt beside Cloud Eagle's. Alicia questioned him with her eyes.

"There is a lone rider a short distance ahead of us," Cloud Eagle said as his warriors circled around him, listening. "We will overtake and surround the rider and stop him. If it is Sandy Whiskers, you know what the next move is to be."

Alicia wanted to cry out and demand that he tell her what he had planned for the Englishman. It was obvious that everyone else knew.

But she did not want to show disrespect to Cloud Eagle by insisting that he tell her. If he had wanted her to know beforehand, he would have confided in her.

This made her believe that what he planned might be worse than anything she could imagine, and for a brief moment, she wished that she was back among the Apache, where roast duck was being eaten and where there was much laughter and lightheartedness.

But it was too late for regrets. She held her chin high and rode beside Cloud Eagle as the Apache divided into two columns and made a wide circle in the sand so that both sides could close in on the rider at the same time.

Breathless, her heart pounding, Alicia rode hard with Cloud Eagle.

Then she felt her knees weaken with fear when suddenly before her was the rider, the other half of the Apache riders closing in on his other side.

The moon came out from behind the clouds, casting its light brilliantly across the land—and upon the lone rider. Alicia was not at all surprised when she realized that the rider *was* Sandy Whiskers. He looked helpless as he was quickly surrounded by Apache warriors.

Sandy Whiskers held his hands away from his weapons and looked guardedly around him, studying one Apache face and then another.

When his gaze locked on Cloud Eagle, only glancing briefly over Alicia, he snarled like an animal.

"You may have fooled the bluecoats, but never the Apache," Cloud Eagle said. "You had to know that in time we would find you."

Cloud Eagle waited to dismount after his warriors had disarmed the Englishman.

Only then did he slip out of his saddle and go to Sandy Whiskers. He reached a hand to the Englishman's belt, unbuckled it, and gave a hard yank which pulled Sandy Whiskers from his horse.

Sandy Whiskers groaned with pain when he fell on the ground, one leg twisted awkwardly beneath him.

Cloud Eagle gave the Englishman a swift kick, which straightened him out on the sand, on his back.

Sandy Whiskers' eyes were two slits of hate as he glared up at Cloud Eagle, then slowly at the other Apaches who came to stand around him.

Cloud Eagle began handing out orders to his warriors. "Place stakes in the sand in the appropriate places!" he shouted. "You who have brought the bag of rattlesnakes, bring it forth.

You who were assigned to bring rope, it is time now to use it!"

Alicia's heart seemed scarcely to beat as she watched what seemed a ritual.

Rattlesnakes?

Rope?

Stakes?

It came to her like a flash of lightning what Cloud Eagle had planned for Sandy Whiskers.

She took a step away from the sudden flurry of activity as Sandy Whiskers' horse was taken away and the stakes were hammered into the ground.

With a dry throat she watched Sandy Whiskers squirm in an effort to get away from the Apache as two warriors took him by the arms and dragged him over to the stakes.

"You can't do this!" Sandy Whiskers cried, paling. "Good Lord, Cloud Eagle, only savages treat people like this. You have always preached against being called a savage. Don't behave like one now!"

Sweat poured from Sandy Whiskers' face as first one wrist was secured to a stake, then another. He turned pleading eyes Alicia's way. "Stop him!" he begged. "If you don't, you are no better than a savage yourself! What they have planned for me ain't Christian! Stop them, Alicia. Oh, God, stop them."

Alicia bit her lower lip nervously as Sandy Whiskers' legs were spread wide apart and his ankles were tied to stakes.

A bitterness rose in her throat when Cloud Eagle took his knife from its sheath and rapidly slit the Englishman's shirt and breeches in front, down the middle.

As the clothes were spread open, leaving Sandy

Whiskers' body fully exposed, Alicia clutched her hands together behind her and started to look away, but her gaze locked on a bag that one of Cloud Eagle's warriors had set down on the sand beside Sandy Whiskers.

Alicia stifled a gasp behind her hand when she heard the sound of rattles inside the bag. Rattlers. There had to be several rattlesnakes waiting to be released from the bag. She held her breath when the bag was untied and placed close to Sandy Whiskers' face.

Everything happened quickly then.

Cloud Eagle helped Alicia into her saddle.

He swung himself into his own.

The warriors mounted their horses in a flash.

When the first rattlesnake crawled from the bag, and then a second, Cloud Eagle gave the command for everyone to ride away.

They stopped a short distance away when the first throaty scream from Sandy Whiskers proved that the rattlers had begun to work on him.

"Lord have mercy," Alicia whispered, a shudder engulfing her at the thought of the rattlesnakes inflicting their bites all over Sandy Whiskers' face and chest.

"*Haiiieee,*" Cloud Eagle cried and raised a fist into the air. "The deed is done. Now let us return home to join the celebration!"

Alicia rode off beside Cloud Eagle. She took only one quick glance over her shoulder when one last blood-curdling cry pierced the shadows of night.

Then she looked straight ahead, understanding Cloud Eagle's decision to kill Sandy Whiskers in such a way. No other punishment would be severe enough for him.

And this punishment was final.

The poison had surely traveled throughout Sandy Whiskers' veins by now, stilling his evil heart forever.

Glad that it was over, Alicia inhaled a quavering breath. The settlers arriving in the Arizona Territory could now find some measure of peace on the California Road.

With a lifted chin and a soft smile, she rode suddenly on ahead of Cloud Eagle.

When he caught up with her, he grabbed her reins and stopped her horse as he drew his to a shuddering halt. He gave Alicia a wondering stare.

"Why did you break away from Cloud Eagle and his warriors to ride alone?" he asked. "Is it because you are displeased over the way I chose to kill the Englishman?"

"No, darling, that is not the cause," Alicia said, smiling over at him. "It is only because I am anxious to return home, to *our* home, in your stronghold. There is so much to look forward to."

"The marriage between us?" Cloud Eagle said, returning her smile. "There will be three sunrises and then we will become as one. Does that suit you?"

A sensual tremor swept Alicia at the thought of finally being married to this handsome, noble Apache. "Yes, and I am already anxious for these next two days to pass." Her eyes danced into his. "Besides the marriage, there is more I want to share with you."

Cloud Eagle's eyes shifted and rested on her abdomen.

She gasped softly, wondering if he already knew that she was with child.

His knowing smile as he looked into her eyes made her realize that, yes, he was astute enough to know that her body had changed. The fact that he had not questioned her about it puzzled her. Was he not glad to know that she was carrying his child? Before, it had always seemed so important to him!

He edged his horse closer to hers. "You are beautiful with child," he said thickly.

"You have known all along?" Alicia gasped.

"A man who does not know his woman's body well is no man at all," he said. Reaching a hand to her abdomen he stroked it lovingly. "This child is the world to me."

"If you knew, why didn't you say something?" Alicia said softly.

"The knowing was all that was necessary to make this Apache chief's heart swell with joy," Cloud Eagle explained.

"I was waiting for the right moment to share my secret with you, and you knew all along," Alicia said, laughing softly. "My handsome Apache chief, I should have known I could keep no secrets from you for long."

He reached over and twined his fingers through her hair and drew her lips to his mouth. He kissed her passionately, then drew away and whispered into her ear. "You please me so in every way," he said huskily.

Chapter Thirty-Four

A roaring fire burned in the center of the council ring. Alicia at his side, Cloud Eagle faced General Powell, who sat in the council with several of his soldiers.

Thunder Roars had been invited to participate in the peace council. He sat close by, flanked on each side by a beautiful wife who held a newborn child on her lap. Turtle Crawls sat among the circle with his wives and children. Lost Wind sat just behind him with Red Crow's widows and children.

Those who sat at their drums at the far edge of the stronghold and those who held rattles awaited the moment when Cloud Eagle would send word to them that the celebration could begin.

Food lay piled high on platters beyond the council ring.

Ears of corn roasted slowly in the hot coals of

the lodge fires, sending delicious aromas through the air.

Young braves stood over the food, shooing flies and hungry, sniffing dogs away.

Dressed in his breechclout, with eagle feathers in his hair, Cloud Eagle had already greeted General Powell and had offered him and his soldiers seats on pallets of buckskin. He then had taken his seat at the center of the council.

The sun was gliding slowly up from behind the mountains, sending an orange splash across the turquoise sky. Fog lay like a heavy shroud over the river, and the air was crisp and cold. The promise of a cold winter was revealed in the black, thick coats of the caterpillars.

A young brave brought Cloud Eagle his large calumet pipe, feathers hanging colorfully from the bowl. After lighting the pipe, Cloud Eagle passed it over to General Powell. He waited as General Powell took the first smoke from the pipe, then handed it back to Cloud Eagle.

Cloud Eagle held the pipe with one hand on the stem, the other on the bowl. He sucked in a breath of smoke, then slowly exhaled it into the wind.

He blew smoke to the east, the west, the north, and the south, to the four corners of the earth.

Then he gave the pipe to Thunder Roars, and thereafter the pipe was passed around until a cloud had been blown between them all and everyone had shared in the smoke.

The pipe was handed back to a young brave, who took it away to Cloud Eagle's lodge.

Alicia sat stiffly beside Cloud Eagle. She had noticed from the first moment of General Powell's arrival that there was something different about him.

His smiles seemed forced. His jaw was tight. His eyes seemed wary as he gazed at Cloud Eagle.

A warning shot through Alicia at the memory of Sandy Whiskers lying spread-eagled on the sand.

If the general had found Sandy Whiskers . . .

"Cloud Eagle, my search for Sandy Whiskers took my regiment from the mountains when we did not find him," General Powell began. "We then rode in the opposite direction."

Alicia blanched. She twined her fingers tightly together and nervously placed them on her lap, her legs crossed beneath her fringed buckskin dress.

Her heart pounded as her fears built within her. If the general had found Sandy Whiskers, and blame was cast Cloud Eagle's way, how might the general react?

Breathlessly she listened.

"We searched the mountain passes for Sandy Whiskers, and when we did not come up with even a hint of his whereabouts, it came to me suddenly that perhaps he went south instead of north," General Powell said, his eyes locked on Cloud Eagle, watching the play of his expression. "I'm sure he was headed for Mexico. But he didn't quite make it, did he, Cloud Eagle?"

There it was, Alicia thought to herself, stiffening. The general did not come right out and accuse Cloud Eagle, but instead toyed with him.

She looked quickly over at Cloud Eagle, awaiting his reply.

"You found him?" Cloud Eagle said, showing no emotion in his voice or on his face.

"I sure as hell did," General Powell said. He stretched his legs out before him and crossed them at his ankles. He drummed the fingers of one hand on one knee. "And the way we found him? I'd say the way he died had the earmarkings of an Apache kill."

"He was swollen much from the sting of the rattlers and the heat of the sun?" Cloud Eagle asked nonchalantly.

"Very," General Powell said, shifting his glance to Alicia. Then he stared at Cloud Eagle again. "You took the law into your own hands, Cloud Eagle, instead of giving me a chance to see that justice was done in the appropriate manner."

"How many days did you search in the mountain passes for Sandy Whiskers?" Cloud Eagle said blandly, his face still void of emotion.

"One full day and most of the night," General Powell replied.

"That was too much time," Cloud Eagle said. "He was headed south for Mexico the very first day of your search. Had I not stopped him, you never would have found him."

"And that gave you the right to condemn him to death before he had a trial?"

"There would have been no trial. He would have been under the protective custody of the Mexicans."

"Still, I . . ." General Powell began.

Cloud Eagle interrupted him. "That man was responsible for many deaths along the California Road, and now he is dead," he said flatly. "It should not matter how, or by whose hand. He will no longer kill and maim innocent people. The greed that grew on him like a cancer was removed the moment that first rattler inflicted that first wound on his flesh. Now I wish to say nothing more about it. You have come to have a big talk. Let us have council. Let us speak of peace and eternal friendship. The time for counseling is good. It is the waxing of the moon."

General Powell squirmed uneasily on his pallet of buckskin. He looked nervously from side to side, at his soldiers, then slowly around the circle of Apache. Since Thunder Roars had brought many of his warriors to take part in the peace talks, joining with those of Cloud Eagle's Coyotero Apache, the soldiers were outnumbered two to one.

General Powell had no choice but to resume the peace talks. To talk of arresting Cloud Eagle might be the same as condemning his soldiers to death.

Sandy Whiskers was not worth it.

"I am as much in favor of peace as anybody," General Powell said, clearing his throat nervously. "I came today with hopes of making total peace between you and the citizens of the United States, and of thus saving lives and property."

"White-eyed brother speaks well, and it is good to hear you make such an offer," Cloud Eagle said. "The Apache were once a numerous tribe, living well and at peace. White men came to this land like locusts in summer. Many of my ancestors were taken by treachery and murdered. Are you saying now that Cloud Eagle can trust that this will never happen again?"

"I vow to you, Cloud Eagle, that you have nothing to fear from my soldiers ever again," General Powell said sternly. "And there will be no more men like Milton Powers who come and entice my soldiers into fighting and killing your people. I am sorry for the grief the raid brought your people. Never shall it happen again."

"Lessons learned together are not quickly forgotten," Cloud Eagle said, his eyes locked with
the general's.

"Lessons learned together are well learned and
long remembered," General Powell offered in
return.

Alicia stifled a sob of happiness behind her
hand. Tears stung the corners of her eyes. She
crept a hand over and clutched onto one of
Cloud Eagle's, his fingers willingly intertwining
with hers.

Cloud Eagle gave a nod, and soon the air
was filled with the rhythmic beating of the
rawhide drums and the resonant throbbing of
the pebbled-gourd rattles.

Alicia joined the women who began serving
the food on wooden platters to the soldiers,
then to the visiting Apache, and then to their
own people.

With a platter for herself, Alicia sat back down
beside Cloud Eagle. She ate ravenously, her eyes
watching something that seemed to be brewing
between Thunder Roars and Red Crow's two
widows.

Alicia quickly noticed that even Lost Wind
had managed to go and sit among them, using
her dark, alluring eyes on Thunder Roars as
he silently admired her, her pregnancy hidden
beneath a full, fringed smock.

Alicia nudged Cloud Eagle. When he looked at
her, she nodded over at Thunder Roars who had
set his food aside and was talking earnestly to
the three women, his two wives sitting idly by,
seemingly trusting him.

"He has eyes for more wives, it seems," Cloud
Eagle said, chuckling. His gaze stopped at Lost

Wind. His smile faded and his eyes narrowed. "He knows Lost Wind. He knows I sent her away with her brother. Yet he speaks with her in an interested way. Could he possibly be considering taking her for another wife? I can see and understand why he would take Red Crow's widows. They are worthy of being his wives. They were married to a noble warrior. But Lost Wind? Her brother disgraced our people. So did she, by deceiving her very own chief!"

"Perhaps he thinks he will be helping you by taking her off your hands?" Alicia whispered back.

"Only because he does not yet know that she is pregnant with my child," Cloud Eagle said, his eyes burning with a building rage. "It is time someone told him."

When he started to get up, Alicia stopped him by grabbing his arm. "Wait, Cloud Eagle," she softly encouraged him. "Perhaps he is only being polite. If he does prove that he wants to take her with him, and he still wants her when he hears that she is with child, why not allow him to take her?"

"Because she *is* with child," Cloud Eagle said, his eyes narrowing into hers as he gazed down at her. "And not just any child. *Mine*. I will let her leave our stronghold only after the child is born. Not before."

Alicia stared at him, wanting to understand his reasoning, but feeling jealous because he wanted to keep a hold on Lost Wind.

Oh, Lord, Alicia despaired. If *she* had a say in the matter, she would be rid of Lost Wind in a minute. She was growing to despise her more each day.

And she trusted her even less!

She did not feel safe with Lost Wind near. If not for Cloud Eagle holding her close in his arms every night, she would be afraid to go to sleep. She was afraid that Lost Wind might come in the middle of the night and thrust a knife into her heart!

"Cloud Eagle, is the child she carries more important to you than I am?" Alicia blurted out, feeling the color draining from her face when she realized what she had said.

Everything happened quickly then. Cloud Eagle took her by the hand and led her away from the celebration, where dancers had just begun to perform and where the soldiers and the Apache warriors were laughing and carrying on together. He led her inside his dwelling, then gently took her by the wrists and pulled her against his chest.

"My *Ish-kay-nay*," he said, his voice soft with understanding. "No child, not even the one that you carry within your belly, is as important to me as you are. Do you not know by now the extent of my love for you?"

"I believe I know, yet when it comes to Lost Wind, I cannot help but be filled with doubts," Alicia said, hating this jealousy that was tearing her apart inside. Yet she could not shove the feelings aside as though Lost Wind and the child she was carrying were not there.

"What would it take to make you accept this life that I offer you?" Cloud Eagle said, brushing her hair back from her face. He framed her face between his hands and lifted her lips to his.

"Do you wish that I send her away?" he asked huskily. "If so, I will ask this of my friend Thunder

Roars. It was in his eyes that he was taken by her loveliness. I am certain that he will look past her pregnancy and see her as she will be once the child is born. She will again have a wasp-like waist. She will be as beautiful as before."

Alicia emitted a soft cry against his lips as he kissed her heatedly. She did not protest the way he kissed her, but his declaration about how lovely Lost Wind was.

But the longer he kissed her, his hands kneading her breasts through the buckskin fabric of her dress, the more she found it hard to concentrate on her worries. She twined her arms around his neck as he pressed her down onto the pallet of furs beside the lodge fire. She sighed with pleasure as he lifted the skirt of her dress and began caressing her woman's center, where she throbbed with need of him.

She kissed him long and hard, and when she felt his manhood slip inside her, she shuddered with ecstasy and wrapped her legs around him.

Thrust for thrust, she met him with lifted hips.

She flicked her tongue across his lips, then closed her eyes with rapture when he lifted her dress past her waist and his lips closed over a breast, his tongue moving urgently around the nipple, his teeth nipping.

Her senses reeled in drunken pleasure as his tongue left a warm, wet trail downward, his lips greedily absorbing the sweet taste of her flesh.

And then he kissed her lips again as he swept his arms around her and enfolded her within his solid strength. His mouth forced her lips apart. His tongue swept inside her eager mouth and surged between her teeth.

She moaned and met his tongue with her own, then seductively sucked his until he pulled away and once again drew a taut nipple between his teeth and softly tugged on it.

Outside the excitement was building, seemingly matching the excitement that was growing at a rapid pace in the privacy of Cloud Eagle's lodge.

The drums were beating with a more rapid rhythm.

The sound of the rattles reverberated around Alicia and Cloud Eagle.

The laughter and the singing and the thump-thump of the moccasined feet dancing around the great outdoor fire became more profound.

Alicia's breathing came in sharp gasps. Her passion was like a hot fire, scorching her insides. Her body tightened and hardened, absorbing Cloud Eagle's bold thrusts.

Cloud Eagle's sensations were searing as great surges of passion swam through him. His tongue brushed her lips lightly. His breath teased her ear. He reverently breathed her name.

The fires of passion leapt higher between them. Then they took flight together. Their bodies quivered. They clung. They rocked. Their bodies pulsed as though they were one heartbeat. Cloud Eagle thrust deeply within her and moaned when his seed shot into her.

Soon they pulled apart. Alicia was aghast when she looked down at her attire. It was terribly wrinkled. She gazed at Cloud Eagle as he attempted to pull his breechclout back in place.

There would be no disguising from anyone what had transpired in Cloud Eagle's tepee. The celebration there had been far different from the one in which everyone else was participating outside.

Cloud Eagle finally got himself presentable.

He eyed Alicia with amusement, then went to the trunk where his mother's clothes were stored and withdrew a beaded shawl from it. He took it to Alicia and placed it around her shoulders, then wove his fingers through her hair, to make it smooth and lovely again.

"What will everyone think?" Alicia said, blushing as she peered into Cloud Eagle's eyes. "You know that they have to realize why we stayed away from the celebration for so long."

"They will think this Apache chief very lucky," Cloud Eagle said, his eyes twinkling, "to have such a woman as you. All men will be jealous."

"What kind of a woman *am* I?" Alicia asked, moving into his gentle embrace.

"Such a woman as will make this Apache chief never look past her at other women," he said. He placed his hands on her cheeks and guided her eyes to his. "Now let us talk no more about Lost Wind or her child. If you wish, I will relinquish all claim to the child. Our child will be the beginning of our family. I will not consider Lost Wind's child mine in any way."

"Even if it is a son and I do not give you a son?" Alicia asked, unable to cast all of her worrying aside.

"Do you wish that I relinquish claims on this child that Lost Wind carries?" he persisted, ignoring her question about a son.

In his heart, this child that Alicia was carrying was that son, the one who would one day lead his people.

In his heart he now knew that this child that

Lost Wind was carrying truly seemed no more to him than an extension of his resentment for Lost Wind.

"No," Alicia gasped. "I would never ask that of you."

He smiled and brushed a kiss across her lips. "Only you could be this unselfish," he said.

Then he took her hands and drew her close again. "My darling *Ish-kay-nay,* I have decided not to lay claim to Lost Wind's child after all," he confessed. "The child would only bring confusion into our lives. I want nothing but peace and harmony to be brought into our marriage. And I do not want to put a strain on our children by having to make space in their lives for Lost Wind's child. Our children will have true sisters and brothers to fill their lives. Is that not so, *Ish-kay-nay?*"

Tears streamed from Alicia's eyes. "I would hope so," she murmured. She flung herself into his arms. "Oh, how I do love you."

A voice speaking Cloud Eagle's name outside the dwelling drew Alicia and Cloud Eagle apart.

Cloud Eagle shoved the entrance flap aside.

General Powell stepped inside. He stretched out a hand toward Cloud Eagle.

"It is time for us to say farewell," he said to Cloud Eagle. He shook Cloud Eagle's hand, then clasped a hand onto his shoulder. "We must meet again soon in council."

"When the moon is full, during the moon of the great snow, let us sit in council here again," Cloud Eagle said, nodding.

"I will be here," General Powell said. He slipped his hand into his front jacket pocket and brought out something wrapped in buckskin.

"A present, Cloud Eagle," he said, shoving the gift into Cloud Eagle's hand.

Alicia's eyes were wide with wonder as Cloud Eagle unfolded the buckskin, soon revealing several matches. She looked quickly up at General Powell.

"Cloud Eagle, you told me once that the gift you appreciate most is matches," General Powell said, watching as Cloud Eagle sorted through them with his fingers, pleasure in his eyes.

Cloud Eagle smiled and thanked General Powell, then went to his trunk and lifted the lid. He extracted a buckskin pouch from inside the trunk and took it to General Powell, pushing it into the general's hands.

"My gift to you," Cloud Eagle said.

General Powell opened the pouch and withdrew a square of buckskin from it. He stuffed the pouch into his pocket and proceeded to unroll the square of buckskin, which being unrolled, disclosed another square of buckskin. The unwrapping continued until five pieces had been unrolled, displaying a handsome leopard-skin pouch, in which was a parchment with several signatures by well-known white leaders.

"I recognize this," General Powell said, looking quickly up at Cloud Eagle. "This is the peace treaty signed between you and our United States Government leaders when you first became chief."

General Powell looked down at the signatures again, then up at Cloud Eagle. "You are sure you want me to have this?" he said, his voice filled with emotion.

"Yes, take it," Cloud Eagle said, closing General Powell's fingers over the buckskins. "This is proof always for you that I have celebrated a treaty of peace with the United States."

"Thank you," General Powell said, his voice breaking.

Cloud Eagle moved his hand away as the general slipped his gift into his pocket.

"I shall have returned to you soon a newly written treaty on paper signed by the President of our United States," General Powell said. "I will have it placed in a frame. You can hang it here in your lodge to show those who come and have a smoke with you."

Cloud Eagle smiled widely. "I do feel that peace is solid between us now," he said, clasping a heavy, friendly hand on the general's shoulder.

"The feast was good," the general said, his compliment genuinely said.

"Yes, good," Cloud Eagle agreed. "But feasting every day is not good. One grows like the duck on the bank, too heavy to take wing."

General Powell laughed softly.

Cloud Eagle walked the general outside, Alicia beside him.

When the soldiers were gone, Thunder Roars came to Cloud Eagle with his wives, and those he wished to have for his wives, trailing behind him.

"I wish to lighten your burden today," Thunder Roars said. He turned and gestured toward Red Crow's wives and children, then gave Lost Wind a lingering look. "I wish to take Red Crow's wives and children into my lodge. Also I wish to take on the responsibility of Lost Wind and the child that she carries."

He turned slow eyes back to Cloud Eagle. "If you wish that Lost Wind's child be brought to you upon its birthing, so be it," he said. "But if you would rather that I raise the child as my own, you know that it could never find a better home, or father, except for you."

"You know then that the child Lost Wind carries is mine?" Cloud Eagle said, frowning at Thunder Roars.

"Yes, she was truthful about the circumstances of the child," Thunder Roars said, nodding.

"And you still want her?"

"If *you* do not want her, Cloud Eagle."

"Take her then, and be warned that she has a spiteful tongue."

"And the child?"

"We will have children of our own. I will need no more," Cloud Eagle said, his chin held proudly high, his arm embracing Alicia.

He could feel the venom in Lost Wind's eyes, and he ignored it.

Alicia's insides warmed into a pleasant sort of bubbling feeling. Cloud Eagle had just gone beyond what was expected of a man who wanted to prove his love for a woman!

Feeling as though she were walking on air, Alicia went with Cloud Eagle to join the celebration again. As they sat down among the Apache people, black-masked dancers representing the benevolent mountain spirits called *gaan* performed, to drive away evil and to guard against illness.

Her thoughts flying ahead to her wedding day, Alicia was only half aware of the performance.

Chapter Thirty-Five

Alicia was enjoying her finest hour. She had finally reached that most special day in her life, the day when she would be wed.

Her brother was ready to leave as soon as he witnessed the ceremony. He was strong enough now for the journey, and he would be heavily escorted by the Apache on his journey to Fort Thomas.

A drummer was beating an oxhide drum behind Alicia's tepee.

Many women were attending her as she prepared herself to meet Cloud Eagle in the large lodge that had been prepared for the wedding.

She had been told that the actual ceremony, where she and Cloud Eagle exchanged vows of total commitment, would be short. What led to that special moment was all a part of the wedding ritual.

As one of the women slipped the tribal robe

of beaded buckskin, with paintings of bright red and blue dye upon it, over her head, she was told that the yellow buckskin ceremonial dress was the color of pollen, a symbol of fertility. A beaded, T-shaped necklace was placed around her neck.

She smiled when she allowed herself to return in her thoughts to the prior evening.

She had been purposely left out of Cloud Eagle's private "bachelor party," but he had told her about it later, when he had held her close after making love. He had told her that the old warriors and the young men had gathered in the newly constructed ceremonial lodge. While the younger warriors had listened, those with much life behind them had recounted adventures and exploits, each man telling his own, for he knew them best.

They had drank *tizwin,* a beverage that had the same effect on the Apache as the white man's "firewater" had on them.

Cloud Eagle had come to her after the party, singing and swaying. When they made love, he had been like a man possessed. The way he had loved her had been intoxicating to Alicia. She had returned his eagerness.

But while he was gone, enjoying his bachelor party, Alicia had been placed in the hands of the old wives and was instructed in the duties of married women. She was told that wisdom was won from much sorrow, and that experience, knowledge, and the secrets of handling a man were the life's work of a woman who married into the Apache culture.

She had listened attentively as the hair of her eyebrows had been plucked, and seven thin red lines had been painted from her lower lip to the base of her chin.

She had not questioned the old wives. She had just listened and allowed them to do whatever they saw fit with her, knowing that this would please Cloud Eagle.

The dress finally lying smoothly along her body, her hair combed until it was shining and sleek, Alicia thought of how Cloud Eagle would see her only moments from now.

Bright ornaments were displayed to the best advantage on the fringes of her buckskin dress and along the sides of her moccasins.

She had bells on, as well as tinsel, beads, and bracelets. There were also faded symbols of dark red made from the dried blood of a beef-heart painted on the dress.

She was suddenly aware that the drum no longer beat out its steady rhythm behind her tepee. Instead, she could hear many drums, as though they were coming from a deep tunnel, as they thumped inside the ceremonial lodge in the center of the stronghold.

Pure Sky handed a cane to Alicia, who eyed it warily.

"This is a ritual cane," Pure Sky softly explained. "It is decorated with eagle feathers to ensure health and oriole feathers for a good disposition. The cane is made of hardwood in order to last into your old age, to support you when you become frail."

Alicia smiled at Pure Sky. "Such a beautiful custom," she murmured.

"It is now time," Pure Sky said, as she took Alicia by a hand. "Come. Cloud Eagle waits for you."

Alicia grasped the cane. Her heart pounding, she looked from woman to woman. She was glad when she saw approval in their eyes, and also admiration as their gazes swept over her.

"I do look all right, don't I?" she asked suddenly, needing verbal assurance.

"You look beautiful, even though your skin is white," Pure Sky teased back.

The rest spoke almost in unison as they told her that she was pretty.

Alicia went from woman to woman. As she hugged them, she thanked them. She now truly felt as though she belonged, that she was a part of the Apache people.

Then once again Pure Sky came to her and clutched her hand. "We must not keep Cloud Eagle or our people waiting any longer," she said, pulling on Alicia's hand.

Fringed, beaded, and combed, Alicia left the tepee with Pure Sky, the other women following behind them.

Her eyebrows rose with surprise when the women, all but Pure Sky, suddenly ran around her and entered the lodge ahead of her. Yet she still did not ask questions. She was learning by doing.

The sky was brilliantly turquoise overhead. Although winter was fast approaching, the day had seemed made especially for two lovers. Not one cloud floated across the sky. The sun was deliciously warm. There was scarcely a breeze fluttering through the golden leaves of the cottonwoods.

Again her attention was drawn to the pulsing of the drums and the throbbing of the rattles. They were more pronounced. The beat was faster, almost maddening to the ear.

Her gaze shifted, and she watched the thick veil of smoke spiraling from the smoke hole of the ceremonial lodge. The smell of sweet grass burning met her approach. She was now only a few footsteps from the entrance to the lodge where she would join her beloved.

Suddenly realizing the quiet of the stronghold, compared to the thunderous beats of the drums and rattles which wafted from the ceremonial lodge, Alicia looked over her shoulder. No one was outside the ceremonial lodge. Not even children or dogs. Only the loose tongues of the tepees licked lightly in the breeze.

This had to mean that everyone had crowded into the ceremonial lodge to witness their chief taking a wife.

And the fact that they were there, to see Cloud Eagle marry a white woman, made Alicia think that she was now openly, fully, accepted by them all.

She stepped up to the larger lodge with a happy heart. As Pure Sky led her inside, her knees grew weak with anticipation. Her pulse raced when she felt the eyes of the people upon her. The crowded faces in this larger lodge were like shining points of light in the semi-darkness; the central fire and the smoke hole overhead were the only source of light.

She quickly noticed that the women had put on what they had of beads and fringed leather ornamental clothing. Babies were swathed and sewed into their upright cradles. The warriors and young braves wore only their breechclouts. The young girls wore long and flowing buckskin dresses.

Then Alicia was aware of only one set of eyes when she found Cloud Eagle sitting on a high platform, autumn flowers spread in front of and around it.

Cloud Eagle's eyes drew her to him, and Alicia felt as though she were floating on wings toward him. The love she felt for him at that moment was so intense that it made her insides glow with a sweet warmth.

She gazed at him and smiled, her eyes finding him clothed in only a breechclout. He had not even put on his moccasins. It was as though his partial nudity was conveying to her that he was offering himself to her as though he were newborn in his love for her.

She swallowed hard and brushed a tear from her eyes as she took one last step to reach him.

When he stood over her, she expected him to offer her a hand to help her up beside him.

Pure Sky did not let go of her hand. Instead, she drew Alicia away from Cloud Eagle again.

Around a big fire, many women gathered in a circle. Alicia was guided to the center of the circle and left there.

She eyed Cloud Eagle warily.

When he nodded to her, giving his approval of what was happening, she sighed heavily.

Suddenly the women closed upon Alicia with a weird sing-song chant; the drumbeats were now low and scarcely discernible, the rattles quiet.

The women drew back from her then and shaded their eyes with their hands and looked slowly around the lodge, as though searching for lovers of their own.

They closed in upon her again, singing with

their lips close to her body, until she was folded within the circle of women.

Again they departed from her.

An elderly woman, dressed in a long, colorfully decorated buckskin gown, began to sing alone. At the height of her song, she went to the fire and plucked a burning twig from it.

Alicia's eyes were wide and she sucked in a fearful breath when the elderly woman came toward her with the fiery twig. She looked past the woman at Cloud Eagle. Again he nodded his approval.

Alicia waited stiffly, then gasped with pain when the elderly lady thrust the burning twig onto the palm of her hand. Alicia bore the pain in silence, for she knew that to cry out, or to drop the twig, would be to fail Cloud Eagle, and perhaps the test of his people who were watching with guarded anticipation of what she might do.

The fire on the small twig began fluttering. It burned only a little while longer, scorching her flesh as the flames moved down the full length of the stick.

Then it flickered and went dark.

Pure Sky blew the ashes from Alicia's hand, gently took the cane from her, then moved away, back into the circle of her people.

All heads nodded, and a murmur was heard above the crackling of the large central fire.

Then everyone shouted and praised her, saying that she had proved to be brave enough to marry their chief. Also, her life would be long. If the twig had burned only halfway, then gone out, her life would have been brief.

But since the twig had burned clear to the end,

it had proved that her life-line was long and that she would remain beside their chief into their shared old age.

Alicia smiled from one to the other, even as she wanted to blow on the flesh of her hand, which still felt as though it were aflame.

Cloud Eagle was suddenly beside her. She smiled up at him, then her smile faded when Moon Shadow came and began sprinkling *hoddentin* in the air around her and Cloud Eagle.

But to her relief, he was soon gone. She did not want him speaking over her and Cloud Eagle. And she wondered if she could ever learn to accept the Apache's holy man. She knew that she must. He was second in line of importance to the Apache, next to their chief.

Cloud Eagle turned to Alicia and took her hands. "My *Ish-kay-nay*," he said. "This day has been long in coming, but it is here now and you are my wife. Man is the planter, like seed in Mother Earth. I will plant many seeds inside you. They will sprout into children which will bless our union."

She was stunned to realize that somehow they were now married. No actual words had been said to make it so. She had to believe that the ceremony with the women had been a big part of sealing the relationship between her and the man she loved.

As had the burning twig.

"Cloud Eagle, my handsome husband, I will be wife to you and mother to our children, with a singing heart," she murmured. "I love my life with you. I would have been an empty shell had I not met you."

Cloud Eagle enfolded her within his arms. He

lowered his mouth to her lips and kissed her passionately.

Moon Shadow appeared again as if by magic and sprinkled cattail pollen in the air, signifying fertility. After Moon Shadow left, Cloud Eagle carried Alicia outside.

She glanced her brother's way as a horse was brought for him. They had already said their good-byes, for Cloud Eagle had told her that after the brief ceremony, he would take her away to a private place.

She clung around Cloud Eagle's neck with one arm and waved with the other to Charlie as he mounted the horse, his eyes never leaving her.

He gave her a wink, then rode away, flanked on each side by several warriors.

Tears splashed from Alicia's eyes as she watched Charlie ride from the village, and then she was transported to a world that included only herself and Cloud Eagle as he broke into a soft trot and carried her in the opposite direction.

Pure Sky caught up with them and handed Cloud Eagle two buffalo robes, which he slipped over his arm.

Alicia rested against them as he carried her beyond the perimeters of the stronghold.

He ran with her until they came to a canyon.

There he set Alicia to her feet, and together they climbed the canyon wall.

On a mesa high above, they spread the buffalo robes beneath piñon trees. Here, away from the noise of their people, in the sweet smell of the piñon, they found love again within each other's arms.

Meditatingly, with devotion and love, Cloud Eagle disrobed Alicia. On her knees, she reached her hands to the waist of Cloud Eagle's breech-clout and slipped it slowly over his hips.

When it was tossed aside, he knelt down before her and placed his hands at her ivory-pale breasts and cupped them within his palms. When he touched her nipples, they grew hard at once. He smoothed his thumbs over them, then leaned toward her and took one between his teeth.

She twined her fingers through his thick black hair and drew his mouth closer. She closed her eyes and threw her head back in ecstasy, already feeling the pulsing of the blood through her body. She was coming alive again with a kind of slow fire that licked its way through her veins. The heat flowed through her body.

Cloud Eagle slipped his hands downward and clasped them gently to her waist, then guided her down onto the buffalo robe. He knelt over her and kissed her with his quavering lips, then moved to her side and began kissing his way down her body, where her belly was just showing signs of her pregnancy, the ribs above it brushed with the softness of light and shade.

As his lips and tongue ventured lower, he paused where the hair at the juncture of her thighs made a sudden cloud of shadow.

When Cloud Eagle separated the hair, and delved into the rose-red slippery heat of her body with his tongue, the feelings of ecstasy came to her at once, startling her anew.

Sighing, she tossed her head from side to side, sweat pearling her brow. She escaped into a world of passion, burning and throbbing. She fought going over the edge into total rapture and was glad when he positioned himself over her and filled her where the curling heat was spreading, threatening to burst into flame.

She reached for him and placed her hands at his cheeks and drew his lips to hers. As he magnificently filled her and pushed into her, filling her deeper, she kissed him. She threw her legs around him and drew him even more deeply into her, her throbbing center feeling as though it might explode from the searing sensations flooding her senses.

Cloud Eagle placed his hands at her buttocks and lifted her against him. Over and over again, he thrust into her. His mouth seared into hers. He crushed her breasts against his chest, wanting to feel all of her tonight as they found paradise again within each other's arms. His breath caught against her lips when he felt the magical web of bliss enwrap them together, as though they were one breath, one heartbeat, one soul.

He plunged more vigorously into her. He slipped his mouth to the hollow of her throat and spoke her name as he felt his body burst into flame and he spread his seed deeply within her.

Alicia clung to him. She joined him and traveled the same road of ecstasy with him. She rained kisses across his face as she came down from her cloud of pleasure. She stroked his back.

Cloud Eagle held her as he rolled to his side beside her. He drew her close, his passion rising again against her thigh. He moved to his back and lifted her above him. Their eyes locked in a silent understanding. They smiled, a smile that reached clear to the stars that had begun to appear overhead, gleaming and twinkling like diamonds against the black sky.

Alicia placed her hands against his thighs and closed her eyes as he shoved his renewed hardness deeply within her.

She rode him, again and again.

Chapter Thirty-Six

It was the month of June. During this month, the mescal bloomed. A large plant with thick, fleshy leaves that spiked murderously outward and massive red flower stalks, it was easy to spot. The mescal was a staple of the Apache diet. The large crowns yielded food that lasted many months.

On the mountain slopes not far from Cloud Eagle's stronghold, the bulbs of the mescal had been gathered and placed upon heated stones in a ditch four feet deep and twelve inches long. Then they were covered with grass, followed by a thick layer of soil.

The mescal had cooked for several hours in this efficient pressure cooker.

A good number of Cloud Eagle's people, and even those of Thunder Roars' stronghold, had gathered to enjoy the mescal.

It was a joyous time for Alicia as she sat on a blanket and watched Dreaming Wolf, her two-year-old son, playing with Thunder Roars' children.

Her gaze shifted proudly to Snow Flower, her precious eight-month-old daughter. She was swinging in a *tshoch* that had been hung between two live oaks and playing with a canopy of beads and protective charms that were strung high above her.

Alicia's hand slipped to her abdomen, where another child was growing. She smiled to herself when she thought of how fertile she had proved to be. Cloud Eagle never ceased praising her for her ability to become with child so easily. He told her over and over again how he enjoyed the laughter of many children in a tepee.

She was surprised at herself over how much she adored having children. While she was growing up, that was the last thing on her mind.

Her priorities had changed when she met Cloud Eagle. Being a woman, and behaving like one, became of prime importance, for she had never desired anything in her life as she desired Cloud Eagle. And now their children had made their lives, their marriage, complete.

Wickedly happy, she inhaled a deep breath, enjoying the sweet fragrance of early summer. The red fruit of the strawberry cactus dimpled the desert floor, and the deep pink flowers of the devil's head were brilliant and eye-catching. Yellow flowers bloomed in the mesquite.

Alicia's garden had been planted. Wielding a pointed stick, she had loosened the warming earth and punched shallow holes into which she had dropped corn, bean, and squash seeds.

Corn sprouts were already shooting through the rich earth.

She was pleased with all of her labors of love. She wanted no other life than this. The Apache were a gentle people, faithful in their friendships.

Often she thought of her brother. She enjoyed the wires that he sent to her. He had praised her for taking the time from her busy family life to make sure he received letters from her. Of course, when he received the letters, the news was somewhat old.

She smiled into the wind, thinking that he should be receiving the news just about now of the new child that she was carrying within her womb. She could envision in her mind's eye the twinkling in his eyes as he thought of being an uncle three times when he had teased her as a child that she would never give him that opportunity.

But tomboys could change into beautiful women, he would then tease.

"Charlie," she whispered. "My sweet brother Charlie with the flaming red beard and dancing dark eyes."

"Did you say something?" Cloud Eagle asked, as he came and sat down beside her.

"I was thinking of my brother, that's all," Alicia said, turning her eyes to Cloud Eagle. She placed a gentle hand to his cheek. "Are you through talking with Thunder Roars? I thought you'd never come back to enjoy this beautiful day with me and Snow Flower." She looked past her shoulder at Dreaming Wolf, who romped and played with Thunder Roars' children. "He's all boy, darling. Our son is going to be a great leader one day."

Her gaze shifted and her smile faded when she caught sight of Lost Wind's daughter, Pale Susan, who stood timidly away from the other children, her head down. It made Alicia's heart ache to see the child behave so bashfully.

Yet she could not find it in herself to go to the child and urge her to play with the other children. This daughter of Lost Wind's was also Cloud Eagle's child. Both she and Cloud Eagle had agreed to leave the child to the guidance of Lost Wind and Thunder Roars. It was best for the child's sake not to be pulled between two sets of parents. In her heart, Thunder Roars was her father.

Thunder Roars went and knelt down before Pale Susan. He lifted her into his arms and carried her over to Lost Wind. Alicia watched as they played with Pale Susan together, soon making her laugh.

The look on Lost Wind's face as she gazed up at Thunder Roars was one of absolute adoration. And it was the same as he gazed down at her. It was apparent that he had tamed her spiteful tongue. Even when Lost Wind looked toward Alicia, the bitter jealousy was no longer there in her expression. Lost Wind seemed at peace with herself and her past.

When Dreaming Wolf came laughing to Cloud Eagle and bounced against him, knocking his father to the blanket, Alicia's attention was drawn to them. Tears sprang to her eyes as she watched father and son pretend they were wrestling. Cloud Eagle's throaty laughter as he grabbed Dreaming Wolf by the waist and playfully threw him into the air, then caught him, made Alicia's heart swell with pride.

Cloud Eagle sat down and placed Dreaming Wolf on his knee. "My son, remember well my teachings," he said. "Your arms and your legs are your friends. Run and fight if necessary so that your soul will not became a slave to them."

"I want to be just like you, Father," Dreaming Wolf said, his words spoken eloquently for a two-year-old.

"I was taught by my father that the whole ambition of a growing boy is to be a brave warrior," Cloud Eagle said. "The highest admiration among our people is reserved for the very ablest warriors and chieftains."

"I will hunt with bow and arrow one day, Father?"

"Yes, you will hunt with the *pesh-e-gar*. It is straight and carries true. Your father is proud to say that he can send an arrow more truly than most warriors."

His gaze took in his son's features, so unlike his mother's. He was Apache in every way, from the color of his skin to his proud black eyes to his thick black hair.

His gaze moved to his daughter, and he smiled. She was her mother through and through, even to her shock of red hair. And her eyes. They would steal many a man's heart when she came of age!

Dreaming Wolf jumped from his father's knee when several boys came for him. His little legs took him quickly away again, into the center of their games.

Cloud Eagle spread out on his back and pulled Alicia down beside him. He cradled her close as they both looked heavenward at the turquoise sky. "My *Ish-kay-nay*, are you *parah-dee-ah-tran*?" he asked.

Alicia turned on her side and leaned up on one elbow, which took her close to his face. "I have learned many Apache words and phrases, but I have not yet heard that one," she said. "Tell me, Cloud Eagle. What did you just ask me in Apache?"

He ran his fingers through her red hair, the silkiness of it against his flesh pleasuring him. "I just asked you if you were one without cares in this world?" he said, smiling into her eyes. "If you are one of contented disposition?"

"Need you truly ask?" she said, brushing a kiss across his lips. "Of course, darling, I could never be happier than I am now."

The sound of horses arriving in the distance drew Alicia and Cloud Eagle apart. They moved to their feet and went to stand with the others as they watched the horsemen come into view.

"General Powell," Cloud Eagle said, curiously. "He did not send word to ask for council. Why then is he here today with a full battalion of soldiers?"

Fear gripping her heart, Alicia placed her arm through Cloud Eagle's and clung to him. Deep within her heart she had feared the day that something might happen to destroy the peace between Cloud Eagle and the United States Government. Since Cloud Eagle's peace council with General Powell when she was with child with Dreaming Wolf, a smoke had been shared betwcen them often. But the meetings were always pre-arranged by a soldier who came and asked for the council.

Today did it take a whole battalion, and even the presence of General Powell himself, to seek council with Cloud Eagle?

No, Alicia thought. This was not the way it was done. There was something wrong. As General Powell came closer, she could see the solemn expression on his face, and she knew that the news was not good.

Everyone but General Powell drew rein beyond the gathering place of the Apache, where the pleasant aroma of the mescal plants proved that their steaming process was now over. Yet no one ventured to uncover the smoking pit. Everyone stood numbly by, waiting for General Powell to dismount from his horse, to tell them the reason for his arrival today.

A young brave took the reins from General Powell.

"Welcome," Cloud Eagle said, greeting the general with an outstretched hand. As Cloud Eagle clasped the general's hand, Alicia stood stiffly beside Cloud Eagle, refusing to give up her hold on him.

"I have brought word of a war," General Powell said solemnly. He eased his hand from Cloud Eagle's. "It is a war being fought between white men. The Confederate Army attacked Fort Sumner off the shores of Charleston, South Carolina, in April."

"White men are fighting white?" Cloud Eagle said, raising an eyebrow.

"Yes, white men," General Powell said, his voice drawn. "It is a sad time in the history of the United States. Brothers are actually fighting brothers."

"And the cause of this strange war?" Cloud Eagle said warily, fearing any news of war.

"There are many reasons," General Powell said, clasping his hands tightly behind him. "But you do not need to worry yourself over them. As far as I know, the war will not be fought on the soil of your forefathers. But I felt it my duty as your friend to let you know that a war is being fought."

"And I appreciate the warning," Cloud Eagle said somberly. "The white brothers who go against one another buy peace for their bodies with the most violent of war—the murder of their souls."

"I fear that is so, Cloud Eagle," General Powell said, nodding.

"Do you wish to have a smoke with Cloud Eagle before you return to your duties at the fort?" Cloud Eagle offered.

"No, not this time, Cloud Eagle," General Powell said. He turned and returned to his horse, taking his reins and swinging himself into his saddle. "I'll return soon with more news of the war, and where it is being fought. I will explain then the terms of the war as I learn them."

Cloud Eagle nodded and held his palm in the air. "Peace," he said.

"Peace," General Powell returned, then wheeled his horse around and rode away.

Alicia gazed up at Cloud Eagle. "It truly seems that we won't be affected by the war," she murmured, yet fearing silently for her brother's welfare, although she doubted that he would be enlisted to fight in the war. A one-armed man would not be able to defend himself, much less those around him.

Cloud Eagle turned to Alicia. He took her hands in his. "My *Ish-kay-nay*," he said thickly. "Any war being fought anywhere is bad. I fear that this war may in the end become a threat that the Apache will have to deal with. Brothers who would murder brothers are capable of anything, especially violence against an innocent Apache people."

"Darling, please don't think about it," Alicia said, flinging herself into his arms. "We are far from the fighting."

And then her attention was diverted when Dreaming Wolf came and tugged on her skirt.

"Mama, is syrup ready yet?" he asked as he looked up at her with his trusting dark eyes.

"The mescal," Alicia said, looking quickly up at Cloud Eagle. "It should be time to uncover it. Let's fill our hearts and minds with festivity, darling, instead of wars."

Cloud Eagle lifted Dreaming Wolf onto his shoulder. Alicia smiled up at him trustingly as they went to the deep pit where the soil and grass was being removed. Soon everyone ate and laughed and sang.

Alicia clapped her hands in time with the drum's beat as Dreaming Wolf and the other children began dancing the colorful Apache dances. As her son's little feet thumped out the rhythm of the drum, Alicia gazed up at Cloud Eagle.

"Everything is too perfect to allow talk of a white man's war to interfere with our happiness," she said, glad when he nodded and smiled warmly down at her.

He whirled her around and into his arms. "My *Ish-kay-nay*, the white men have much to learn," he said. "If they asked this Apache chief, I would tell them that a man's heart should always hold a place for courage and wisdom, and should respect what he can never conquer. It is sad that they must learn by losing loved ones. I hope never to don war paint again against any man." He cast his son a sidewise glance. "Nor do I ever want to see our son's face striped with war paint."

"Please say no more about warring," Alicia said, shivers running up and down her spine. "Just hold me. Just kiss me."

Cloud Eagle placed his hands at her waist and swept her close. They started to kiss, but a stirring in the brush behind them drew them apart. Everyone else was too involved in the fun of the moment to notice that another intruder had arrived. Cloud Eagle grabbed his knife from its sheath and moved stealthily toward the shadowy cluster of bushes.

Just as he reached them, Gray leapt out, his fur matted with mud and cockle burrs. Snow soon followed, limping from the loss of her right front paw.

Alicia and Cloud Eagle were at a loss for words at the sight of their missing coyote pets. It had been more than two years since they had seen them!

Alicia squealed with joy and started to go to them, but Cloud Eagle extended an arm out in front of her to stop her.

"It's Gray and Snow," Alicia said, questioning Cloud Eagle with her eyes. "Surely you recognize them."

"I would never forget them," Cloud Eagle said. "But they may not remember *us*. They have lived in the wild for too long."

Alicia jumped when a third coyote came slinking from the bushes, its tail between its legs.

"Is that Snow's mate, or . . . or offspring?" Alicia asked, quickly noting that the coyote was a male.

She sighed and fell in love immediately with

two snow-white coyote pups that wandered out into the open next. Snow flopped over to her side to allow them to nurse.

"The coyote that is not familiar to us is Snow's mate," Cloud Eagle said, chuckling. He slipped his knife back inside its sheath. "And they seem to see us as friends. Snow would not so openly nurse her pups in the presence of strangers."

Gray went to Alicia and rubbed against her legs knowingly. Alicia fell to her knees and hugged him to her. "Thanks for coming home and bringing Snow and her pups with you," she murmured. "We are truly a complete family now."

The other male coyote crept closer, its eyes wary.

Alicia slowly offered it a hand. He sniffed it, then licked it.

"Even *you* are welcome," Alicia said, smiling over at Cloud Eagle. "Darling, if our coyotes have survived the hardships of life these past two years, it gives me hope for all *our* tomorrows."

Cloud Eagle gave her a slow, beckoning smile.

Alicia gave Gray another hug, then moved into Cloud Eagle's arms and reached her lips to his. When they kissed, they were swept away again by the tempest of their love, their savage spirits united for all time.

Dear Reader:

I hope you have enjoyed reading *Savage Spirit*. To continue my *Savage Series*, in which it is my endeavor to write about every major Indian tribe in America, my next book will be *Savage Pride*, about the Choctaw Indians. This book will be filled with much excitement, adventure, romance, and suspense! I hope you will buy *Savage Pride* and enjoy it!

I love to hear from my readers. I respond personally to every letter. For my newsletter and information about The Cassie Edwards Fan Club, please send a legal-sized, self-addressed stamped envelope.

Warmly,
CASSIE EDWARDS
R#3 Box 60
Mattoon, IL 61938

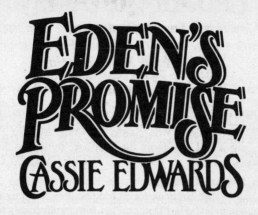

CASSIE EDWARDS

*Enjoy torrid passion and stirring romance
from the bestselling author of more than
seven million books in print!*

Secrets of My Heart. Rescused from death on the Western
plains by handsome James Calloway, young Lenora
Adamson gives herself to him body and soul. But James is
a footloose wanderer who claims the whole frontier as his
home, and it will take more than her love to tie him down.
_3445-X $4.99 US/$5.99 CAN

When Passion Calls. Lovely Melanie Stanton has been
promised to Josh Brennan for as long as she can remember.
But marriage is the last thing on her mind until Josh's long-
lost brother returns to his family's vast spread to claim her.
_3265-1 $4.99 US/$5.99 CAN

Roses After Rain. Rugged Ian Lavery thinks he can survive
all the dangers that vast and untamed Australia has to offer—
until he meets Thalia. Wild and sweet, their passion goes
beyond the bounds of propriety.
_2982-0 $4.50 US/$4.95 CAN

Author Of More Than 4 Million Books In Print!

**"Powerful, passionate, and action packed,
Madeline Baker's historical romances will
keep readers on the edge of their seats!"**
—Romantic Times

Callie has the face of an angel and the body of a temptress.
Her innocent kisses say she is still untouched, but her
reputation says she is available to any man who has the price
of a night's entertainment.

Callie's sweetness touches Caleb's heart, but he and the
whole town of Cheyenne know she is no better than the
woman who raised her—his own father's mistress. Torn by
conflicting desires, the handsome half-breed doesn't know
whether he wants her walking down the aisle in white satin,
or warm and willing in his bed, clothed in nothing by ivory
flesh.

_3581-2 $4.99 US/$5.99 CAN